Even in the darkest night . . .

Behind the first one, more and more of the animated trees followed, flowing out of the darkness like a swarm of ants—a seemingly endless supply appearing as if from nowhere. Their branches creaked and tangled together as they converged on Strongroot, filling the swampy space with a new, moving forest.

Joram felt stuck in place. His heart pounded. His mind raced, but he couldn't move. So full of fear, all he could feel was the vibrating soil beneath him, shaken by the movement of the army of trees headed right for him.

"Joram, run!"

. . . a flame of hope might burn.

Ascaeus strained to see into the gray-blue mists swirling before him. There. Movement. Was it them? No, only the fog coiling around an errant breeze. Listening was no use. The muffled scratchings, flutterings, and creaks of the forest to his left revealed nothing, and the hills to his right kept silent. He reached out with his mind, trying to sense their approach, but the chill twilight clung to its secrets.

Still, Ascaeus knew they would come. How could any cinder who received his or her summons resist the call? Beneath the despair his kind wore like a shroud there remained a faint glimmer of hope—a desperate, fading dream of a time when their curse of the Extinguishing might be lifted, when they might be purified in the ultimate Fire.

But the SHADOWMOOR night is darkest of all.

Veteran MAGIC: THE GATHERING® authors Scott McGough, Cory Herndon, Will McDermott, and Jess Lebow join newcomers Jenna Helland, John Delaney, and Denise R. Graham; and MAGIC insiders Doug Beyer, Matt Cavotta, and Ken Troop for a collection of all new stories set in the endless night of the SHADOWMOOR world.

TWO WORLDS, ONE SERIES

Lorwyn

LORWYN CYCLE
BOOK I
Cory J. Herndon and Scott McGough

Morningtide

LORWYN CYCLE
BOOK II
Cory J. Herndon and Scott McGough

Shadowmoor

SHADOWMOOR CYCLE
ANTHOLOGY
Edited by Philip Athans and Susan J. Morris

SHADOWMOOR CYCLE
NOVEL
Scott McGough and Cory J. Herndon
June 2008

MAGIC
The Gathering®

Shadowmoor Cycle • Anthology

Edited by
Philip Athans & Susan J. Morris

Shadowmoor

©2008 Wizards of the Coast, Inc.

Cover art by Adam Rex
First Printing: April 2008

9 8 7 6 5 4 3 2 1

ISBN: 978-0-7869-4840-6
620-21857740-001-EN

U.S., CANADA,
ASIA, PACIFIC, & LATIN AMERICA
Wizards of the Coast, Inc.
P.O. Box 707
Renton, WA 98057-0707
+1-800-324-6496

EUROPEAN HEADQUARTERS
Hasbro UK Ltd
Caswell Way
Newport, Gwent NP9 0YH
GREAT BRITAIN
Save this address for your records.

Visit our web site at www.wizards.com

CONTENTS

Ode to Mistmeadow Jack
Scott McGough & Cory J. Herndon.....................1

Five Brothers
Ken Troop 89

Paths
Denise R. Graham.........................107

Mark of the Raven
Jess Lebow 137

Meme's Tale
Will McDermott.........................171

Pawn of the Banshee
Doug Beyer.........................197

Expedition
Matt Cavotta.........................225

Sootstoke
John Delaney.........................249

The Cloudbreaker
Jenna Helland.........................277

About the Authors 309

ODE TO MISTMEADOW JACK

Scott McGough & Cory J. Herndon

Jack Chierdagh crept through the fog outside the kithkin doun of Mistmeadow, moving with the confidence of one who knew well the ground beneath his feet. The secluded little village's namesake was a perpetual cloud of thick, stagnant, cheerless smoke and haze that never burned off and never broke up. The permanent fog bank covered the village and the surrounding wilds for a day's walk in every direction, miring the doun in damp, dismal gray. Jack's featureless eyes glittered, reflecting the rare moonbeam or odd bit of starshine that filtered through the fog. His eyes were sharp, but he barely needed them this close to home.

The kithkin's stocky body floated along with the mist, matching its speed and direction so well Jack might as well have been smoke himself. A night bird's haunting call stopped the kithkin short. He held his breath until the bird repeated its call two more times, then closed his eyes and counted to five in the silence. Everyone knew it was bad luck to move while a night bird was singing, and everyone knew exhaling before the song ended was a sure way to get your shadow stolen and woven into a bird's nest.

Once Jack was sure the night bird had moved on, he resumed his ghostly progress through the woods. He was the youngest and newest member of the Mistmeadow militia's patrol detail, but Jack was already a good scout well on his way to becoming a great scout . . . at least, that's what everyone said. Jack knew these opinions to be genuine and heartfelt, but he also knew that everyone who so praised him also quietly gave thanks or expressed relief while doing so. They hailed him as brave, noble, and talented all the more fervently because it was he and not they who volunteered to crawl around in the gloom.

Not that Jack blamed his fellow kithkin. Everyone knew what terrible dangers lurked in the fog, and no one in his right mind sought such danger lightly. Feral packs of boggart raiders marauded in from the west. Diseased and vicious ash treefolk lurked in the south. Wretched, half-dead cinders shambled down from the crags to the north. The only safe transit to and from Mistmeadow was via the Big River to the east. And then one still had to reach the river safely and retain enough thread to buy off the brutal merrows who ran the docks.

The folly of Mistmeadow's founders had been in choosing its site specifically for its natural defenses—*because* of the remote hills and fog rather than in spite of them. Those intrepid and harried kithkin pioneers soon found that the fog and terrain that concealed them also hid their enemies, and now those many threats—figuratively, and often literally—pounded on the village walls. Over the years, Mistmeadow had been attacked by everything from a ravenous boggart horde to a dueling pair of hundred-foot-tall treefolk to the determined but ultimately unsuccessful Emerethne faerie clique.

Jack was unaccompanied, but he was not alone, no kithkin ever was. He smiled as his thoughts triggered a cascade of memories rippling from one end of the mindweft to the other. The kithkin of Mistmeadow had bested each and every danger that came out of the fog, endured every boggart siege and outlasted every violent cinder.

Life in Mistmeadow was little more than a series of

evolving threats and sustained responses, and everyone knew it. But it was life. Each new generation of kithkin warriors, merchants, scouts, and clerics stood as validation of the founders' folly—and as one in the eye for the filthy armies out there foaming, snarling, and howling in the fog. Another year and they were still there.

Jack drifted to a halt when he spotted an indistinct figure ahead. He checked his location and nodded to himself. He had constructed a simple scarecrow several days ago to mark the outer limit of his patrol, and the figure he saw now was much like the one he remembered. Its torso was an old shirt stuffed with twigs and dead leaves. A single stout branch formed two outstretched arms, with another tied crosswise for a spine to anchor the figure upright in the soil. Its head was a rough woven sack stuffed with grass that Jack had crowned with an old felt hat. It was a rushed, crude effort, misshapen and lopsided, and even now it dropped bits of dusty flax and dried moss in the gentle breeze.

Jack crouched close to the ground and edged forward. The forlorn shape was almost as he remembered it . . . but not exactly. He stopped breathing and fixed his blank white eyes on the scarecrow. It was definitely much larger than Jack remembered, now fully three times his own height. The scarecrow's spine may have been there, but a thick, unruly column of reeds and twigs that stretched from the figure's torso to the ground below obscured it. The rough fabric of a featureless face surrounded something far harder and more substantial than a few handfuls of dry grass.

In the back of his mind Jack felt the other residents of Mistmeadow responding to his concern as ripples in the mindweft. They took in his anxiety, curiosity, and involuntary exhilaration at this peculiar discovery, and mulled it over.

The wave returned to Jack as a tide of controlled but full-blown fear. Everyone recognized a potential, paradoxically familiar threat in this unfamiliar figure, but only Jack could personally evaluate that threat. Without complete information or unreserved confidence from Jack himself, the kithkin of Mistmeadow quickly prepared for the worst.

Jack exhaled then deliberately sipped in a fresh lungful of air. With a single thought and a bit of effort, he quieted Mistmeadow's concerns before they became strong enough to distract him. The scarecrow was different from what Jack expected, yes, and inexplicably so. Yes, there had been tales of other strange things in other villages, but those were just tales and one could only trust one's own village when all was said and done. So far this scarecrow, Jack's scarecrow, had not moved and did not seem dangerous.

Jack edged closer. Everyone knew the doun had not survived this long by ignoring strange things just because they did not seem dangerous. Jack nodded and drew his long knife. He also drew a small wooden skull, a totem he carved himself and had blessed by the most exalted cleric in the doun. The skull was enchanted to protect Jack from poison and fire, and it comforted him even though it did not seem especially useful against this particular opponent, if it turned out to be an opponent at all. The scarecrow was unlikely to use poison and could not use fire, not without igniting itself. Jack ruefully wished he had fire of his own just to see how quickly an enemy made of dry tinder would burn.

A stale breeze cleared some of the fog away, giving Jack a clear line of sight to the scarecrow. He squeezed the wooden skull totem tight and extended his knife a fraction of an inch.

The scarecrow's head twisted down toward Jack with

a sharp rasp. He froze and fought to keep his hammering heartbeat from spreading to the rest of the village. Eyeless and faceless, the scarecrow stared at the concealed kithkin through the mist. The column of reeds and twigs supporting it shuddered as if a small family of rats had awoken inside it.

In one smooth motion, Jack sprang to his feet and hurled his knife. The blade sliced into the scarecrow's chest, but he had packed the creature's torso so loosely the knife plowed straight through and burst out the opposite side. Cursing himself for wasting the dagger, Jack drew a solid wooden baton from his belt and backed away from the scarecrow. If the foul thing got loose and charged him, one solid swing through its neck would surely decapitate it . . . and one into its chest could burst it wide open, perhaps even disintegrate it completely if his aim was true.

Yet the scarecrow did not attack—it merely shuddered with more vigor than ever. It bent its outstretched arms at the elbows it didn't have and the bundle of sticks below its waist dug into the dirt like spindly legs with dozens of sturdy toes.

The scarecrow heaved free of the pole that had until so recently served as the thing's spine. The ramshackle figure then settled down onto the ends of its twig-feet and let its gangly, awkward arms swing freely.

"You're in Mistmeadow, stick-man," Jack said. He raised his baton. "And whatever you are, you're not welcome here."

The faceless, shambling thing did not reply.

"I am your master and creator," said the kithkin, as much to his own surprise as the scarecrow's—assuming the scarecrow could be surprised. "You must do as I command. Leave this place."

For a long time, the scarecrow's visage stared remorse-lessly into his, and Jack stared right back, determined not to lose his nerve unless all of Mistmeadow did. Yet even with the extra effort, he jumped when the scarecrow whirled in place on its twin columns of reeds, sticks, and temptingly flammable tinder. But before Jack could even think of striking a spark, the scarecrow scuttled off into the fog, crackling, clattering, and thumping into temporary oblivion with the most awkward gait Jack could imagine.

The kithkin waited until the unsettling sounds faded away before he allowed himself to exhale. He was at the very edge of Mistmeadow's territory already, and the direction the scarecrow headed would take it even farther from the doun.

"Oh, and don't even think about . . ." Jack began, but gave up with a half-hearted sigh. He should have remembered that little detail, if only to reassure the dounsfolk. Jack decided there was no benefit to pursuing the ramshackle thing now, a judgment quickly affirmed by the mindweft.

The subtle joy of discovery rolled from Jack to his fellow kithkin. There had been numerous reports lately of strange things moving herky-jerky through the mist, but no one had been able to say exactly what they were. Until this encounter no one had seen one of the interlopers clearly. Jack could still hardly believe the things were animated scarecrows—let alone that one built by Jack's own incorruptibly honest hands had been animated—but as what he'd seen moved from kithkin to kithkin and the idea became belief in Mistmeadow, the scout found himself forced to accept it. After all, he'd seen it with his own eyes.

One mystery solved, then, but the solution now posed

several new and significantly more troubling questions. Who or what had brought the makeshift things to life? How? For what purpose? And most importantly, how much of a threat were they to Mistmeadow?

Jack didn't try to formulate any answers on his own, but calmed his thoughts and allowed the matter to disperse into the mindweft. All he volunteered was what he'd seen and the memory of assembling the scarecrow in the first place. He knew he hadn't performed any charms or incantations and that the scarecrow had been perfectly mundane when he left it. Let hundreds of kithkin minds work on the problem simultaneously, Jack reckoned, and eventually one or more of his kin would add a flash of inspiration or a little-known fact to what was already known and what Jack had just seen. The dounsfolk would eventually assemble each element into an answer the Mistmeadow kithkin could understand and ultimately, a policy to pursue.

Jack tried to withdraw from the depths of the mindweft but it drew him back in like the tide. Rather than fight the gentle but insistent pull, Jack abandoned himself to it. He kept one ear turned toward the retreating scarecrow and one eye open to his surroundings, but otherwise Jack forgot himself and submerged into the thoughts and feelings of his fellow villagers.

Someone's coming, they all thought. Jack didn't know who, not at first, or why the arrival was important . . . but the common mind of Mistmeadow provided partial answers to his questions before he even finished formulating them.

Someone new was coming, someone unlike them. The arrival of someone not of Mistmeadow brought urgent tidings: a new crisis to confront and new options to consider. Those in Mistmeadow with better first-hand information were both excited and alarmed by these prospects, though the mindweft itself was too confused to provide any useful detail.

Intrigued, Jack sheathed his baton, retrieved his knife, and pocketed his skull totem. He sacrificed stealth for speed as he worked his way back through the fog, the mindweft confirming his patrol was over.

* * * * *

Jack joined the hushed crowd of Mistmeadow dounsfolk huddled together in the town's broad central square. Two hundred or more of his fellow kithkin had effortlessly arranged themselves as close to one another as possible without actually touching. A line of overhead torches cast a sickly yellow glow over the area to create an irregular chamber of diffuse light amid the otherwise endless and perpetual dark. Hundreds of unblinking eyes stared, wide open and waiting, into the infinite night.

The assembly didn't wait long. Not long after Jack arrived, Mistmeadow's leader, Cenn Molla Welk, strode to the center of the square. She was an older woman, gray and wizened, but her voice was sharp and her mind was even sharper.

Cenn Molla positioned a three-legged stool on the cobblestones and stepped up onto it. It was a small stool and she was a small woman, but she towered over the diminutive residents of Mistmeadow. Molla tossed her head to clear a lock of silver-white hair from her eyes and raised her hands over her broad, round head.

"My friends," she said. Initially, almost everyone was startled by Molla's voice, as almost everyone was more accustomed to hearing her thoughts than her words. "Thank you for coming to listen in person. Mistmeadow has a decision to make. It was presented to me as your leader, but I am a cenn, not a queen." This brought more than the expected amount of laughter from the villagers, belying their tangible anxiety. "I do not make decisions for you, but with you," she said, quieting the laughter with her trust and confidence.

Jack nodded, his approval of Molla's words joining the ripple of support that slowly rolled across the square. Everyone liked Molla because Molla had done a good job of keeping them all alive—and she had an undeniable way with words.

"Kithkin of Mistmeadow," Molla said. She extended her hand to the cottage on her left, and the crowd silently parted between Molla and the cottage's front door. "I present Maralen, who speaks for the Wilt-Leaf elves."

The mindweft seethed in shock and horror as a tall, willow-limbed figure emerged from the cottage. Everyone was expecting a fellow kithkin from a distant doun, a long-lost cousin who had traveled far to bring them important news. No one was expecting an elf, let alone one so lanky and predatory.

"Listen to what she has to say," Molla said. "Hear what she has to offer. Then let us decide on it together."

The tough woven material of the elf's drawn hood stretched over the elegantly sweeping horns below. The lithe woman's legs were freakishly long and her body appallingly slender, as if some dread mystical force had taken a properly proportioned kithkin maid and stretched her out into some kind of two-legged stick insect shape. She was taller than any Wilt-Leaf the doun had ever seen.

Jack felt more than simple mistrust or tribal revulsion

churning among his fellow kithkin. The assembly's collective reaction was decidedly suspicious, hostile, and growing malevolent. The mood became ugly when Molla climbed down from her stool and the elf climbed up. Mistmeadow's leader yielding to an alien, an elf? If the cenn herself hadn't called them here and presented the hooded maiden as an honored guest, the crowd could have easily become a mob and painted the doun's gates with this Maralen's blood.

Jack shared the crowd's hostility, though his was slightly tempered by curiosity. Surely the elf maiden knew the risk she was taking, as did Molla. What had the stranger said to the cenn to arrange this sudden audience? What could Maralen say now to overcome Mistmeadow's palpable fear and distrust of her?

The elf pulled back her hood to expose her fine, curving horns and her heart-shaped face. Her hair was black and luxurious, her eyes dark and wide. She stood silently for a moment, craning her face as she scanned the crowd. Maralen bowed deeply at the waist, perfectly balanced atop the tiny stool.

As she straightened once more, the elf inhaled deeply. Raising her hands and stretching them wide, Maralen began to speak. "Mistmeadow," she said. "I will be brief, as I am an unexpected guest."

An unwelcome guest, Jack thought, though he could not be sure if the snide correction originated in his brain or filtered in from the majority of those listening.

"Your doun is in danger . . ." Maralen went on.

Our doun is always in danger, the crowd thought.

"Beyond the normal dangers it contends with every day. Far beyond, and far worse. Worse, and bigger."

The crowd's reaction grew louder, more insistent, and

for a moment it lost its perfect unity. Worse than boggarts? Bigger than treefolk?

Oblivious to the silent debate, Maralen kept talking. "A giant has been roused southeast of here."

A kithkin at the far end of the square shouted aloud, her voice shrill and mocking. "You brought us together for that?"

"You're wasting our time, elf. And yours."

Maralen waited for the heckling to subside then said, "A giant has been roused, and is on her way here. A very large and very dangerous giant."

"Bollocks!"

"Yeah! Haven't you ever seen a century oak treefolk?"

"Bigger than any giant. Much bigger."

"And we fight them off three, maybe four times a year."

"This giant is unique," Maralen said, still unperturbed by the catcalls. "I would not have troubled you otherwise. Her name is Rosheen Meanderer."

Jack recognized the name, as did many others. A cold feeling of concern took hold of the assembly. Rosheen Meanderer was a name that commanded respect, even awe. Oldest and largest of the giants, she was blessed with the gift of prophecy and madder than a rabid weasel. For the first time since Maralen started speaking, everyone gave the elf their full and undivided attention.

"Rosheen is coming through this region. The swathe of destruction she has cut so far is more than wide enough to encompass Mistmeadow and everything around it. Her progress is rapid and steady, and it obliges every living thing to get out of her way. Citizens of Mistmeadow, I fear your doun is in her way. You must go or Mistmeadow will be trampled flat, along with any kithkin who remain inside."

The elf paused to allow her audience to fully digest her words. Jack's reaction was perhaps the most dismal of all. He knew better than anyone else in the courtyard how unlikely it was to find safe refuge in the wilds outside Mistmeadow's walls.

"All is not lost." Molla's steady voice cut through the mounting panic in the square. "Hear her out."

An old man beside Jack shouted, "But what can we do?"

Maralen's smile was both sad and hopeful. "Reach out to your neighbors," she said. The crowd murmured but Maralen raised her voice over them. "The Wilt-Leaf tribe is just on the other side of the river. Vigilant . . ." Maralen wavered slightly and a strange flicker of sadness crossed her dark eyes, but she continued forcefully. "The elves are dedicated to preserving that which is good, healthy, and beautiful. Their mission is to protect things . . . things like Mistmeadow." Jack felt a tiny ripple of pride roll through the attentive minds of the doun.

"With their help," continued Maralen, "you can avoid Rosheen's frenzy. When Rosheen moves on, the vigilant will help you rebuild—for Mistmeadow can be rebuilt so long as her clever and industrious residents survive."

"Mistmeadow can do far more than merely survive." The kithkin who interrupted the elf stood at the back of the assembly, but his voice was loud, strong, and even. A moment of concern flickered across the mindweft, the speaker was not of the doun. The anxious moment passed when the crowd realized that even though the stranger was not from Mistmeadow, he was one of them, a kithkin.

The citizens of Mistmeadow stepped aside to let the robust figure through. Jack's skull buzzed with excitement as the crowd recognized Donal Alloway, warrior-cenn of Kinscaer, the formidable leader of the largest and most prosperous kithkin community in the world.

Alloway was of average height, but extremely lean and wiry for a kithkin. A black leather cloak with a stiff, high collar hung across his broad shoulders. The collar framed a face both stern and handsome set beneath slicked-back black hair, and he wore a huge sword on his hip that was nearly as long as he was. The blade hung at an angle just off the horizontal—woe betide anyone foolish enough to stand behind the warrior-cenn should he turn quickly—yet Donal Alloway's footing remained balanced and assured. His polished boots clicked against the cobblestones as he approached Maralen's speaking perch.

"You all know me," Donal Alloway said, and he was right, everyone did, "what I've accomplished, and what I'm capable of." His eyes darted back and forth across the crowd and his gaze was sharp and accusing. "I thought I knew the brave kithkin of Mistmeadow. But in listening to you scrape and grovel before this . . . elf . . . seeing how quickly you turn to them without once consulting us, your own kin . . . after all this, I wonder if I ever knew Mistmeadow at all." The unexpected scolding stunned and silenced the dounsfolk in an instant.

"I am amazed," Alloway continued, "truly amazed, my cousins, and disappointed. Did you believe a threat to Mistmeadow would escape my notice? Or that having identified the threat I would simply abandon you to it? I too have heard of this giant, Rosheen Meanderer, and her rampage. I too recognized the danger she poses to Mistmeadow. I came to offer my help and my protection. All of your brothers and sisters in Kinscaer will stand with you against those who would destroy you, no matter how large or how numerous. But I must warn you, I will burn Mistmeadow to the ground and make war on Vigilant Eidren himself before I allow your noble kithkin doun to form an alliance with Wilt-Leaf."

Maralen stepped nimbly down from the stool. She faced Donal Alloway across ten feet of empty space. "This isn't a debate, Cenn."

"No, it is not," Alloway laughed harshly. "It's an insult. Why would good, honest kithkin throw in with elves from the perilous east when their own flesh and blood calls to them from Kinscaer in the warm, safe south?"

"The elves are just across the river," Maralen said. "Kinscaer is three days away at least. Can this flesh and blood arrive in time to do Mistmeadow any good?"

"I came here from Kinscaer in less than a day," Alloway said. "No one knew I was here." He raised his hand over his head and shouted, "Who is to say I don't have a hundred archers with me already, standing by and waiting for my signal?"

"I am," Maralen said. "If you came that fast you came alone. Rosheen only turned this way a few days ago. But it'll be days more before you can assemble any kind of meaningful fighting force. The giant will have come and gone by then."

"Oh? And why is that?"

The elf woman frowned. "What?"

"Why is the giant coming at all? What 'roused' her and sent her this way in the first place?"

Maralen's eyes narrowed. A thin, sharp smile curled the corners of her mouth and she cocked her head to one side. "You do cast quite a long shadow, don't you, Cenn?" she asked. "But you are misinformed. No matter how numerous and skilled your spies and scouts"—the elf's voice dropped into a terse whisper—"they are inferior and unreliable compared to the ones I employ."

"Perhaps," Alloway said. "But if so, that is not the only unreliable thing present at this gathering." The black-clad cenn drew his giant sword and pointed the blade at Maralen, its tip steady and unwavering. "My reach extends even into the Wilt-Leaf Forest, milady. I have the confidence of Vigilant Eidren himself. And I'm reliably told that the Wilt-Leaf sent no envoy to Mistmeadow."

A soft, audible gasp floated up from a hundred kithkin throats. Maralen's hard, sharp eyes did not blink.

"No offer of aid from Wilt-Leaf," Alloway continued. "No promise of protection. No foundation for a long and lasting alliance. And no Wilt-Leaf maiden named Maralen." He slashed the air with his sword. "Who are you, stranger? Who are you really? Did you come here to exploit the giant's rampage? Or are you just the bad omen that precedes misfortune? Molla Welk did this doun no favors when she received you. Leave Mistmeadow before your presence brings us even worse luck."

Maralen glanced past Alloway. The crowd was quickly growing hostile and aggressive behind him. "You will regret this, Donal Alloway," she said. Then she turned to the throng and said, "As will Mistmeadow. The cenn of Kinscaer doesn't want to protect you from me, my suspicious friends—he wants to enslave you. Your tribe has a name for this, I'm told. A word to describe a relationship where one party has all the power and the other does all the work: *lanamnas*. That is what Donal Alloway offers Mistmeadow. Permanent lanamnas."

Alloway blinked in both astonishment and amusement. "You don't know anything, do you?" he said, and everyone who heard him had to agree.

Chuckling, Alloway lowered his sword. "Lanamnas is natural. Lanamnas is how we get things done." He spat at her feet. "No outsider could ever understand."

Maralen's expression grew dark. "Accept his aid," she said to the dounsfolk, "and you will have his agents and spies on every street corner inside of a month."

"Would elves on every corner be any better?" Alloway sheathed his sword. "Take my advice, false envoy, and get out of Mistmeadow while you can still walk. The giant is a kithkin problem, and we will deal with it."

The elf straightened to her full height and sadly shook her head. "Forgive me, Mistmeadow," she said. "I should have been more persuasive. I will do my best to remember you when you are gone." Maralen drew her hood back over her horns. She walked toward the far end of the square, toward the doun's main gates.

Several dozen kithkin refused to move out of her way, and many more moved forward to block her path.

"Let her through." Molla Welk had climbed back up on the stool and she shouted over the square through cupped hands. "She entered Mistmeadow on my invitation and spoke as my guest. She is not to be harmed or hindered until she leaves."

The angry kithkin stepped aside. No one wanted to bring the curse of a faithless host down on Molla as the cenn, for it would surely spread to the rest of them.

Without another word or a glance backward, Maralen strode out of the town square. She continued down the cobblestone street until she passed through the doun gates and disappeared into the fog.

Scores of kithkin voices all spoke at once as soon as Maralen was out of sight. Jack felt a nauseous rush as audible words and inaudible thoughts competed for his attention.

After the initial surge of excitement dwindled, the crowd's reaction became organized, coherent, and whole. *What do we do now?*

Molla hesitated and Donal Alloway's voice filled the gap. "I have a plan to save you," he said.

Someone voiced the crowd's first and most immediate hope. "Are your archers standing by, like you said?"

"No," Alloway admitted. "But only because they wouldn't be much help. No, this is a problem to be avoided, not confronted. Your lives are paramount, but I know a way to save your homes and businesses as well. It will be dangerous," Alloway said. "But if you will put yourselves in my hands and follow my stratagem precisely . . . a single one of you can save the whole doun. One brave kithkin will fend off this giant."

"How?" Jack said, and his voice was joined by a hundred others.

"By the same method that has kept your village safe for generations: misdirection. We can't allow the giant to come through here, or even near here. To keep her away, we just have to find the right lure. Once we have something she wants more than she wants to keep blundering in this direction, we can lead her somewhere else, somewhere she won't cause any harm."

A warm flush of hope swept through Jack. Donal Alloway was onto something. This was precisely the sort of magic at which Mistmeadow's adepts excelled. The doun knew at least a dozen spells to irresistibly draw an enemy's attention.

"What's the right lure?"

"How do we find it?"

"We need a personal item from the giant. Something . . . intimate." Alloway warmed to the crowd, his voice charming, engaging. "A swatch of her clothing, a token she regularly employs, or a charm she wears. Best of all would be a lock of hair or a droplet of freshly shed tears."

"I'll do it," Jack said.

"How do we make a giant cry?"

"I'll do it," Jack said again. The thoughts and voices fell silent. The kithkin around him quietly edged away, leaving Jack in a space by himself, but all eyes were upon him.

"I'll do it," Jack said once more. "Just show me how to find her and teach me the spells I need."

Donal Alloway smiled triumphantly at Jack. "Who is this fellow? Is he as capable as he is confident?"

"He is," Molla said. "Jack Chierdagh is one of our best long-range scouts, if not our most experienced." She chuckled, and nervous laughter erupted from the crowd. They all expected great things from Jack, and Jack had never been so sure of that as he was now.

"Come forward, Jack." Jack obligingly stepped closer to Alloway. "You understand what I'm asking you to do? Rosheen won't come to Mistmeadow but she will come after you. You'll have to find her, rob her, enchant her, and then stay ahead of her for some time. Can you do all that?"

For a moment Jack felt nothing from the mindweft. Then the full support and gratitude of the entire doun washed over him, surrounded him, and buoyed him up. It had been far too long since Mistmeadow had a proper hero, a fabled favorite son or daughter who adventured on behalf of the doun, served as its champion, its chief defender, and its standard-bearer. Be our hero, the mindweft told him, so that we'll be here to sing of your exploits for years to come.

Donal Alloway must have felt the surge of support swirling around Jack. The cenn of Kinscaer threw his arms over his head dramatically and shouted again, "Can you do it, Jack?"

"I can," Jack said. "I will." He choked back a small knot of humility that was struggling up his throat. "If everyone else helps."

The roar of approval answered Jack's question even faster than the mindweft. Of course everyone would help. Everyone needed a hero.

* * * * *

It didn't take long for Jack to prepare, with advice from Donal Alloway—who was quickly becoming a trusted member of the Mistmeadow community—and Jack's own experience. He decided to wait until moonrise to depart, for Alloway agreed the giant Rosheen Meanderer, while an imminent threat, was still some ways off. Even kithkin eyes would have trouble navigating the mists during the moonless hours.

Besides, Mistmeadow told him as one, it was only right. The hero should have a last night of preparation, celebration, and good rest. A worn-out hero was defeated before he'd even faced his first challenge.

Jack first noticed Molla's daughter watching him during a rousing dance inside the warm confines of the Welk Lodge. Keely Welk was playing the role of hostess and seeing to everyone who hadn't a full mug or a full plate. Her furtive glances sent Jack's way were not accusatory or stern, but merely her eyes seeking his.

Strange how Jack never noticed before how much like tiny twin moons those eyes were. He'd known Keely since they were both kithlings, and in those days Jack had done his best to avoid Keely's attention at all. He'd been much more interested in chasing blue moon-lizards, hunting hootfowl, and learning to be a scout.

These days Keely taught kithlings how to perform their first simple auguries, such as how to predict when the moon would fall behind the hills, when the Big River would rise and flood its banks, or—for very young kithlings—when dinner might arrive.

Though they'd grown up together and lived in the same village, in the last ten years Keely hadn't greeted Jack with much more than a nod. Therefore, when he left his memories behind and returned to the present he was somewhat surprised to see Molla's daughter had abandoned her post near the kitchen. Keely moved across the chamber with an easy grace, smiling at him sweetly beneath those dazzling moonlike eyes.

"Jack," Keely said. Her tongue seemed to catch on her lips and whatever was to have followed caught there too. The beautiful eyes narrowed in momentary frustration.

"Keely." Jack cursed himself for failing to come up with something more interesting than that, but this individual feeling was not shared by the larger group, for the mindweft egged him on.

Keely cast a glance around the lodge. Like most kithkin gatherings, there was music and singing—or more accurately, drumming and singing. It was enough to dance by, especially when the dancers could think as one and everyone was free to sing or not sing as they pleased, but never out of key. At the moment a dozen or more singing dancers moved in unison like colored bits of glass in a kaleidoscope.

"So," Keely continued, "it has to be you, does it?"

"Everyone agreed," Jack said. "I'm eager to do it." He found his own pale eyes drawn to the sandy floor as he said it.

"*I* didn't agree," Keely said calmly. More and more kithkin left their dancing and dining to observe the bold would-be hero and the captivating daughter of their most important leader.

"You don't think I can do it," Jack said. He looked around and noticed the two of them had the full attention of the gathered celebrants. Molla looked on with an inscrutable expression of expectation. Alloway, the stranger who was strange to them no more, also watched from Molla's right.

"I don't think you'll fail," Keely said quietly, unembarrassed. "But I don't think anyone can succeed."

"You're wrong," Jack said. The mindweft's eyes were upon them and hadn't come to a consensus as to which of them actually was right or wrong. When they failed to do so, Jack realized the Mistmeadow kithkin were not, as a mind, considering the possibility of anything but Jack's success. Heroes didn't fail. No, they were all watching because affairs of the heart did not usually make it through the 'weft with any real success. Some things were personal, even for a kithkin.

So the mindweft rippled with expectation much the same as Jack had seen on Molla's face, but he still didn't quite understand what was being expected.

"If anyone can do it, Jack Chierdagh," Keely said, reaching out to pull Jack's chin up from his chest and look him in the eyes, "you can."

He took a step toward her and slipped an arm around her waist. She took his opposite hand and held it out and up, automatically slipping into the simplest of dance forms. Keely looked up at him—they were nearly the same height—and at last their eyes met once more. Jack's heart pounded, something it rarely did on the trail even when facing the fog's most dangerous threats.

This was right, everyone could see that, and so Jack and Keely began to dance. The rest of the kithkin watched for a while, then one by one they paired off and did the same. For an hour, maybe two, Mistmeadow was under no threat and nearly every kithkin in Welk Lodge was absolutely certain Jack Chierdagh would succeed, and none more so than Keely Welk.

The community needed a hero, and a hero needed someone to return to. To an outside observer with no understanding of kithkin ways, it might appear sudden or false, but that observer's opinion mattered little. All that mattered was Keely's fervent belief in the courage, heart, and love of a kithkin she'd barely spoken to in ten years. She would keep him strong, as strong as the spirit and will of the Mistmeadow kithkin who had called him to serve.

Yes, Jack could tell without asking she would be waiting for him when he returned, but to his dismay, Jack was one of the few kithkin present who wasn't so sure about their prospective hero's chances.

* * * * *

Jack set forth with his hooded lantern held before him like a trophy. He had everything he needed for his journey packed and ready to go an hour before moonrise. His service as a scout had already provided Jack with a tough leather jerkin, which fit snugly over his new set of traveling clothes; a short kithkin sword, which hung from his left hip; and a sturdy crossbow with twenty-odd bolts which he strapped to the side of his pack.

He marched into the dark woodlands surrounding Mistmeadow and up the lonely road leading north. The road would cross the giant's destructive path at some point, and then he could follow the wreckage to Rosheen. Everyone knew how to track a giant.

He examined the map by lanternlight. Roads outside Mistmeadow were unreliable at best. Not that the roads themselves collapsed or washed away—not usually—but they tended to wander a bit, as if they grew bored of heading east and so turned north for few months, and then turned back to the east when they tired of north. Alloway's map provided the current arrangement, only a couple of roads still existed beyond the fringes of the area the scouts patrolled. One was the road Alloway had traveled to reach Jack's doun, the other—leading off in the opposite direction—was the path Alloway recommended to intercept the giant.

Jack had left behind the only possessions he didn't need or couldn't use: his springjack; the peculiar elven sculpture his grandmother had left him; and a four-foot string of icy, faintly magical river-glass beads. Others within the community would have a use for the springjack. The sculpture and beads were gifts—keepsakes he'd left to Keely.

"Jack!" It was dizzying, having Keely's voice in his ears overlapping her name in his thoughts. He turned as Keely came running through the mists. She wore traveling garb similar to his, but rumpled and somewhat too large—clearly she'd borrowed clothing from one of Jack's fellow scouts. She wore a smaller pack similar to his, had a short bow slung over her shoulder, and carried a long dagger tucked into her belt.

"You shouldn't—" Jack began, but Keely was already in his arms, her face pressed against the rough leather on his chest, and he could feel she was shaking. Not out of breath, no. She was sobbing.

"I have to go," Jack said, and even as he felt his heart

beating in fierce opposition, even as the dazzling moonlight in Keely's eyes filled with stunned disbelief and unwilling tears, he felt the woven minds of Mistmeadow confirm he was making the right choice.

Without another word, Jack placed a steadying hand on Keely's cheek and kissed her. She returned the kiss in kind, and for a few glorious moments there was no giant, no doun, no enemies at the gates, and no mists clinging to the hills. There was only Jack and Keely. Then he pushed her away.

Tears still rimmed Keely's eyes, but her sobs had subsided. "Take this," said Keely as she pulled the dagger from her belt. "The souls of many a Welk keep it sharp."

"Thank you," Jack said, and placed her hands—still clutching the dagger—between his own. "You'll get it back, safe and sound."

She nodded, knowing that even if it wasn't true, she had to believe it. The hero walked alone, but carried the doun with him like a shield.

Keely kissed him again for luck, turned, and let out a short, stuttering whistle. A well-trained springjack from the Welk stables emerged from the mist. Keely slid into the saddle of the tame beast, squeezed her knees against its side, and bolted back to the doun through mists only a kithkin or a springjack could hope to navigate.

Jack watched her go until he could no longer see the distant, dark shape through the mist and then tucked Keely's silver dagger into his belt. He didn't know the weapon, but it was nicely balanced and would throw as easily as it would cut or stab.

More importantly, the dagger reminded him of her faith in him. The dagger would be the talisman that reminded the burgeoning hero what he was fighting for. Jack wondered that he could carry the thing, so loaded down with hopes and prayers. If he were a rampaging giant and someone came to take something personal and important of his, the dagger would be their primary target.

With a determined sigh, he turned from the mists and stepped into the world outside Mistmeadow.

The untried hero thought he was prepared for any danger the road might pose, but he hadn't anticipated the road itself would simply stop a mile or so from the edge of the mists. Alloway's map showed it clearly, but in reality, it wasn't much of a road at all—more like a seldom-used 'jack-run.

And it was dark. If the lack of any real visibility hadn't made him spark the lantern ten minutes before, he might well have walked straight into the rough, unforgiving surface of the biggest tree Jack had ever seen. That record was to be short-lived—inside of thirty paces he saw two more that were even bigger.

Jack didn't recognize the exact type of tree, as they were unrelated to the ash that comprised most of the Wilt-Leaf forest. These trees weren't as tall, for one thing, but their trunks were enormous. Thick, broad roots gripped the soil and supported boughs wide enough to shelter every kithkin in Mistmeadow if a sudden rain blew in. As if in answer to his thoughts, a leaf fluttered down atop his head. Jack snatched the leaf and examined it closely.

They were oak leaves . . . but according to everything Jack knew and had been able to glean from the map, oak trees shouldn't be there. When a tree that big was where it wasn't supposed to be, either dark conjuring magic had moved it or the tree had walked there. These oaks weren't trees at all, but treefolk.

Jack prepared to make his way around. Confronting

treefolk that would otherwise remain rooted was not only bad luck, but also a good way to get pulled into thirteen pieces before one walked a mile.

Jack held the lantern close to his chest, turned, and plunged into the deadfall that bordered the path. He hacked at the dry, reedy wall with his sword, his other hand clutching the hilt of Keely's dagger. Jack slashed at the vines and pushed himself through bramble thickets that zealously tried to keep him in place. It was awkward, and took him almost another hour to work his way around the treefolk stand and return to the road on the far side.

He slipped over a mossy root and ducked under another that had grown into an archway adorned by a collection of wiry spiderwebs. The view through the arch made Jack freeze—quite dramatically and certainly heroically—with his mouth in the act of pronouncing the first syllable of a word he immediately forgot. It was understandable, he reasoned, to forget what you were about to say when the world tosses you into the sky.

All at once, the thicket surrounding Jack left the ground and ascended rapidly into the moonlight. He flailed his arms and found a pair of sturdy branches against which he steadied himself as the forest rose ever higher into the sky. The branches were connected to other branches that in turn branched from branches that in turn branched some more, all of them carrying along a most unwilling passenger.

The monstrous, three-legged oak treefolk stopped suddenly, sending a jolt through both Jack's arms. He'd hooked a foot under a thick vine which, in turn, slowly enveloped a branch in much worse shape than the other two. Jack spared a glance at them and his heart sunk. Still he clung desperately to his handholds and forced himself to think. He hadn't expected to be up a tree, but it wasn't as if he'd never climbed one before. Everyone knew how to climb a tree, and climbing a treefolk was not all that different in principle. The main difference was the movement.

"Don't look down, Jack," he told himself moments before the same warning came back through the mind-weft. Both warnings were too late and Jack was seized by vertigo. His knuckles went white and his hands and face reddened as he struggled to steady his breathing and pull his pale eyes away from the road below.

Four hundred feet below, by his estimation. He wasn't just in the boughs of the treefolk colossus. Jack's face snapped up and he saw that he was still at least a hundred feet from the *real* top of this gargantuan tree.

Yet he was looking up—exactly the right thing to do. The dizziness and nausea went by the wayside and Jack began to climb. He could probably see the entire region from the top of the treefolk, and as a fall from his current height would surely kill him there was no reason not to go higher. He'd never get a better chance for a bird's-eye view of Rosheen's approach.

Going up wasn't bad, as the oak's boughs offered plenty of handholds and panic roosts. And he needed the latter more than he thought he would. Once the oak really caught its stride, the upper boughs waved wildly and erratically in the cloudy, moonlit sky. Any pretense of climbing ended since one misstep could fling Jack half a mile, so instead he did his best to sight Rosheen.

The first landmark he spotted was impossible to miss. The Wanderbrine snaked through the forest just under half a mile away, and Jack was getting closer to the Big River by the second as the oak monster followed its mysterious whims. Or, Jack, thought with a start, its orders. Was this treefolk working for enemies of Mistmeadow, under the control of some wicked elf or bloodthirsty cinder?

A wave of encouragement, more distant now—the oak moved quickly when it wanted to—brought him back to his search. Rosheen Meanderer didn't appear to be on this side of the river, but Jack spotted her on the far rise as the bough in which he rode swung backward.

As far away as Jack was, she almost looked like a kithkin matron reclining in a meadow. Not that kithkin matrons ever did any such thing, and even if they did, Jack had never met any matron as hideous as that.

He'd never have seen it from the forest floor even if every tree in the Wilt-Leaf has decided to lie down and allow him a look. He could only guess how far away she must be, though as a scout he had a lot of experience making such guesses. He sighed. Even if he did get across the river without merrow trouble, he had a long walk ahead.

"What I wouldn't give for a springjack," the kithkin said aloud. "No, a *flying* springjack."

At that moment a stunned Jack thought he saw just that very thing. Something did pass in front of the moon, didn't it? Something with four legs, horns, and . . . wings? Before the kithkin could even begin to figure out what that something was or where it had gone he heard a distant but still shocking roar emerge from the giant. With alarming speed she rose from her crouch to her full height and shouted at the moon in what sounded like incomprehensible frustration. And then, with no more warning than that, Rosheen Meanderer came rolling down the crags like an avalanche. She disappeared in a cloud of dust that billowed into the sky and briefly obscured the moon.

"Give for a springjack," said something overhead that sounded curiously like Jack. This puzzled and unsettled the actual Jack, who thought for a moment he was speaking to himself without realizing it.

"Springjack," the voice repeated, "for a springjack."

He forced himself to look away from Rosheen long enough to scan the branches overhead. The boughs were filled with movement, which was to be expected when the tree itself was ambling along at a steady clip. But something wasn't moving like the rest. No, not something. Some *things*.

"*Flying* springjack," one of the things said.

"What I wouldn't give," squeaked another.

No two of the shapes were alike, though it was hard to make out exactly what they *were* like against the clouded sky. The shapes themselves were black as night, none bigger than a rabbit, but possessed of far too many limbs, eyes, and teeth for Jack's taste. Although they were still a good twenty feet up, they were climbing down. He felt a pulse of fear that wasn't his own—Keely, sensing what he was seeing, even at this great distance.

"It's all right," Jack said aloud.

"It's all right," one of the tiny mimics repeated.

On the word "right" a sharp, stinging pain jabbed him in the ribs and he looked down, horrified to see one of the creatures had approached from below. It had sunk a single, flat fang in gap in the side of his jerkin. He dare not let go of the branches while the boughs were still waving, so he instead let his feet leave the lower vine and twisted his body violently enough to fling the little monster back into the branches of the walking oak.

As if on cue, the rest of the creatures exploded from all around him. They dropped onto his back, his legs, and his shoulders. One sunk a fang into his left big toe and was rewarded with a kick that sent it flying into the darkness.

He could no longer contain a scream as the things swarmed over him, biting, and Jack felt one of the monster's clawed hands reaching for his belt, closing around the dagger. He roared in fury, batting the beast away with one hand and drawing the blade with the other.

A moment too late, he realized what he'd done. And worse, he'd done it at the bottom of the bough's forward swing, when his momentum was the strongest. Without a hold on the oak's branches and still covered by the most determined of the foul little mimics, Jack was launched into the night sky. He closed his eyes, determined that Keely would not see what was coming until it was too late. Jack used every ounce of willpower within himself to close his mind off from the doun, from Keely, from everyone.

Just before he struck, he could have sworn he heard his own voice calling from roughly four hundred and fifty feet above him, "Don't look down, Jack."

* * * * *

Jack expected death to feel cold, and this was certainly cold. But for a kithkin afterlife, it certainly seemed . . . wet.

He lay face down against what felt like smooth, worn gravel to his bruised face and arms. Except for his shoulders, arms, and face, in fact, the rest of his body was under cold running water that coursed angrily around the disruption he'd created in the steady currents.

"Where?" he tried to ask, but instead spat out a mouthful of sand. At the same time he felt the stings of a thousand tiny cuts all over his body and involuntarily wriggled like a snake dropped on an anthill.

The mimics were gone, or they'd let go of Jack and been carried away by the tide. He blinked sand from his eyes and wearily pushed himself to his knees. The moonlight was enough to make out dozens of deformed and devilish black shapes upon the sandy riverbank. One of them twitched a batlike wing, causing Jack to start, but it appeared to only be a death spasm. Upon closer inspection, the hideous things had not died from the fall—a cursory inspection showed no sign of injuries. Either the mimics were allergic to water, moonlight, or. . . .

He turned to gaze at the towering shape on the far side of the Big River—for it could only be the Wanderbrine—and saw the monstrous oak impassively standing there. Had it simply reached the edge of the river and stopped? Was it watching him?

The parasitic creatures must live within the treefolk's branches, he reasoned, and at the same time he saw tiny shapes scampering behind the oak leaves. Could those little monsters survive outside of their host's boughs? Struggling to his feet and walking to the sandy shore, he crushed one of them under his boot. It popped with a satisfying squish. It would seem not.

Let the oak watch. He had a giant to find. A giant who, judging from the sounds of her impossibly heavy footsteps, was headed in his direction.

"Well," he said to no one in particular. "I suppose the first step is to find my way back to the path."

The expected surge of agreement and relief at his unexpected survival didn't come, and he was momentarily puzzled. Then he remembered—during the fall he'd done everything he could to keep Keely from experiencing his death. He'd done his best to tear away the connection. Best if they thought he just vanished rather than knowing he was dashed to death upon the rocks by a tree. To say nothing of what it would do to poor Keely to experience his death.

Jack closed his eyes. "Keely," he said.

"Who's that, then?" growled a voice from over Jack's shoulder, dripping with menace and what sounded like a great deal of saliva. He whirled on the speaker in time to catch the flat side of a black axe blade in the temple. As the riverbanks spun wildly around the moon, Jack felt his knees fold beneath him and he flopped back onto the rocky sand.

Before blackness took Jack he heard another voice. "Go get the boss and make sure he brings his pet landwalker. They'll never believe what the nets dragged in."

* * * * *

Something cold and smooth was pressed against Jack's face, along with the now-familiar grit and sand of the riverbank. His right hand still gripped the handle of Keely's dagger, but his left was folded uncomfortably under his chest. At least this time I'm already armed, Jack thought. And there's no water running into my trousers, either.

Jack heard more of the growling voices he'd heard before he lost consciousness, and a sound like leather drawn against a rock—merrows, at least partway out of the water, for they were slithering to stay upright as they argued.

"Why can't we just drown him?" one of the merrows said. "Take his stuff and drown him. That kithkin rabbit-meat can be tasty. And he might have some thread on him." Keeping his eyes closed—they could be watching for the merest blink—Jack guessed the speaker was directly in front of him, four or five feet away.

"The boss gets to make that call," another said. "Especially if there's thread involved. I might take that dagger, though. Fine piece, for landcraft." Jack placed this second speaker a few feet west of the first.

The boss? Jack had no idea who ran this stretch of the river. So long as whoever it was remained on, in, or near the river, it hadn't really been Mistmeadow's concern.

"The boss ... well, maybe this time'll be different," said a third speaker, and with that Jack accounted for the three distinct voices he'd heard. This one was behind the other two but a bit higher in elevation. Looking over their scaly shoulders, no doubt. "We haven't caught one o' this ilk since—"

"Since when?" asked a sharp, clear, voice—a *kithkin* voice—that emerged from a spot some twenty feet north of the trio of merrow brigands. "How long has it been since you caught one of my 'ilk,' Wrybert?"

"Landwa—er, Brigid!" said one of the merrows—not the one called Wrybert, but the over-the-shoulder speaker. "We didn't see you."

"Or hear me," the newcomer spoke with barely concealed contempt and a merrowlike burr that made it difficult to tell the speaker's gender. As the voice drew nearer, Jack's ears followed the confident footsteps as they left the grassy riverside and dropped onto the sand, closer with every stride. "You people couldn't hear a giant dancing. Now, what is this? Land raids have to go through me, boys, you know that. If you've been picking off scouts from the douns and planning not to cut Sygg and me in on the take, you're even bigger fools than you look."

Jack desperately wanted to open his eyes, if only to confirm this was truly a kithkin. A female, by his best guess. Because if the newcomer was a kithkin, something was terribly wrong with him ... or her. He couldn't sense her mind at all, not a flicker of recognition in any mindweft he recognized, though she now stood perhaps two feet away, between Jack and his merrow assailants. Then again, he couldn't feel any more sign of Keely or Mistmeadow either. This might just be a rogue . . . it did happen from time to time, a kithkin cast out by the mindweft forced to find a way to survive among the others.

But had he cut himself off from *all* kithkin? Even among strangers of different douns, there was mindweft, however weak or fleeting. This stranger had no presence, but an absence—an emptiness. Either that or this creature was no kithkin at all. An imposter of some kind, perhaps.

Jack realized that as he'd been working all this out, the voices had fallen into silence. Even the newcomer's footsteps had stopped. And then, for a split second, he felt the soft breath of the stranger fall upon his brow.

"Heard enough?" the newcomer asked with a bit less contempt than she'd shown Wrybert. Jack blinked involuntarily and saw the stranger's face mere inches from his own. She—he could see the newcomer was definitely a "she" now, though her voice was still rough—was crouched over his head. Her thin-lipped mouth widened into a bitter smile. "How long have you been awake? These dolts don't know to look for breathing. I do. You should work on control if you're going to spy on me or mine."

For a moment Jack simply opened his mouth, uncertain what he should say. With no meeting of minds, it was like speaking with a scarecrow. The newcomer's eyes were hooded beneath a leather cowl. The rest of her clothing was an odd approximation of scout's traveling gear, but patched together in places with scaly hides and coils of silvery merrow lines. The curved wood of a fine bow emerged from behind her left shoulder, and the feathered ends of several arrows emerged from behind the other. Around her neck was a thick black scarf that hid her chin and seemed to glitter in the moonlight.

Who was this kithkin? *What* was she? No rogue he'd ever heard of had led a gang of merrow brigands. Most fell to begging or boggarts before long. He pushed himself into a seated position, careful to keep the dagger pressed against the sand. The stranger rocked back onto her heels. "Well?" she asked. "What are you doing here, Mistmeadow?"

"How do you know where I'm from?" was the first question that sprang to Jack's mind, and his dry mouth didn't stop it from escaping.

"Have to earn my keep somehow," Brigid said with a wicked sneer, and was met with appreciative guttural laughter from the merrows standing behind her. The fishmen were all the same shade of purplish gray, as if their entire scaly bodies were made of bruises. Each wore a belt slung with a variety of lines, hooks, tightly wrapped nets, and curved knives made from the teeth of monstrous amphibians. Their spiny skull-crests pulsed in time with their flexing gills, and huge, limpid eyes reflected six moons back at him. If not for the pale, almost white tattoos adorning their arms and torsos Jack probably wouldn't have been able to tell one from the other.

"You—you're a blank," Jack said. "Why can't I—?"

The blow came faster than he'd have thought possible—a fist wrapped in hard black leather slammed into his jaw and knocked him flat on his back. He blinked and spat out blood, thankful he still had all his teeth, and tried to focus on the stranger who stood astride his prone form like a conqueror.

"You talk too much," Brigid said. "Listen to me. If the boys didn't bring you back from some bloody raid, you came here on your own. Exactly what kind of fool are you?"

"Jack," Jack said. "My name is Jack. I just want to cross the river. There's a . . ." Did he dare warn them a giant was coming? Would they even care, or would this gang of thugs simply laugh and spitefully make him watch as Rosheen Meanderer crushed everything he held dear?

"There's a what, Mistmeadow Jack?" asked Brigid. "Spit it out."

She certainly didn't speak like any kithkin he'd ever met. He wondered how long this stranger had lived among the merrows.

"A giant," Jack said at last. "Headed this way. She's going to crush my doun. I need to get a token of hers so we can ward her off."

"That's a subtle plan for dealing with a giant, isn't it?" Brigid smiled and shook her head. "Bloody dangerous for the poor soul who has to collect the token. What makes you so sure Rosheen is going to crush your village, hero?"

"Because she's crushing everything. She'll probably even crush the lot of you."

"Threats, Jack?" asked Brigid.

"Facts," Jack snapped. Brigid took a cautious step back as he rolled forward onto his feet and stood, clutching the dagger before him in what he hoped was a defensive and mildly threatening manner. "Rosheen Meanderer is chasing something through the sky, and she doesn't care what gets in her way. Everyone knows giants don't ask before they cross rivers," he added, "and when they do, the river's rarely the same."

"The river's always the same," growled another newcomer, a merrow who looked nothing like the trio of slithering bruises opposite Jack. "It's the land around it that changes."

"Boss!" Wrybert exclaimed, his gruff growl now a simpering whine. "We didn't know you'd get here so quick!"

"What you don't know would fill an epic, Wrybert," Brigid murmured loud enough for Jack to hear.

"Who's this, Brigid?" the boss asked, ignoring the sycophantic trio. Even if Wrybert hadn't identified him as the leader of the river brigands, Jack would have known this was he. The boss's scales were a silvery blue, his eyes shimmering and fierce beneath spiny, venomous-looking brow-fins that moved with every involuntary flex of the boss's wide, fanlike gills. His mouth was adorned with barbels like a catfish sage. He wore a typical merrow kit but without nearly as much in the way of equipment—the boss clearly had henchmen for that. The leg-fins that supported his powerful trunk as he rose from the Wanderbrine and slithered toward them kept him strong and steady, nothing like the others who wobbled like drunkards. The boss was a merrow who didn't let little things like air and land slow him down.

"Says his name's Jack," Brigid said, confidently turning her back on Jack to face the boss. Jack looked down at the dagger still firmly gripped in his hand and felt a bit insulted. "Just wants to pass through." The kithkin chuckled wickedly and a flash of moonlight reflected from her hidden eyes as she shot a look over her shoulder at Jack. "Doesn't look like he's worth much to me."

"I'm . . ." he started in protest, and then what Brigid had said sunk in. Was she trying to let him go? Or arrange for his quick murder and disposal? "I'm crossing the river," said Jack, determined to give away as little as possible. "That's all."

"Oh, that's not all," the boss snarled. "No one crosses without paying a toll. You earn your passage or pay it."

"You'd better have some thread on you," Brigid told Jack with quiet menace. Since the boss paid her no heed, Jack assumed this was a routine the two had performed before. "Or you're going to have to fight those three for his entertainment. It's been a slow evening. If I had my way, we'd just strip you, knock you on the head, and leave you for the next caravan to pick up. Simplest thing, really."

This Brigid, whoever she was, was not necessarily looking out for her boss's best interests. The giant was a threat he could hear even now in the distance. Rosheen's pace had slowed, but it was steady and growing closer. How could the merrows miss it? Or were they so confident in the safety of their home that they simply didn't care? No river need ever fear the stone, as the saying went. He suspected the bruisers were too stupid to get it, but Brigid had clearly caught the import of what Jack had said even if her boss had not.

"Well, that's just fine, then," the boss said as warmly as a water-dweller could. "Brigid is right. Been getting a bit tired of watching these three knock each other around. Especially seeing as how they're so damned reluctant to do any permanent harm to their idiot kin." With a flash of movement Jack could barely follow the boss pulled a bone knife from his rig and sunk it into Wrybert's chest, some fifteen feet away. The merrow gawked in surprise, and blood surged from his gills and mouth. With something between a *flop* and a *thud* Wrybert hit the sandy bank, dead.

The remaining two brothers were too busy gaping in shock to do anything, and Brigid merely stood there with her arms crossed, expectantly. Jack didn't need to read her mind to know what she was thinking: Now it's up to you, Jack. I did all I could, but I've got a job to keep.

"I see you've got a fine piece of cutlery there, Jack," the boss said. "We'll be keeping the rest, but I'll leave you your clothing. No use for that landwrap. Now here's what's going to happen. You're going to kill those two before Brigid here can return to the bank with a bottle of my finest brinewater. If you do, you'll share it with me and you'll be on your way. If you don't, Brigid will give me the whole bottle, kill you, and then maybe kill those fools if she feels like it. That's how Brigid is."

Jack couldn't be certain, but he thought he saw a grimace briefly settle onto the other kithkin's features. It was hard enough to tell without the mindweft, let alone without a look into her eyes.

"But boss," the shorter of the remaining two bruisers said. "Let's just kill him and—"

Another knife was in the boss's hand in the blink of an eye, but he did not let fly. "Wryllick."

"Right," said Wryllick. The merrow turned to Jack, and the look of pure hatred surprised the kithkin hero until he remembered this fish-man had just watched a brother die.

"Right," Jack said. He dropped into a crouch and moved instinctively opposite the two merrows so he could watch them both. The bruisers were slow to act, but the twin black axes made Keely's dagger look like a letter opener and his short sword was somewhere on the long path to Mistmeadow. Further, there could be even more merrows just under the surface of the water, and even if there weren't, the brothers had a lot more room to maneuver if the fight was confined to this small bit of sand. He did spare a glance at Brigid, who watched impassively. The hidden eyes focused upon Jack, but it was impossible to say what Brigid was really looking at, or what she was thinking.

Thinking. Mistmeadow . . . Keely.

Nothing. Not a whiff of their thoughts, hopes, or prayers. Just him, Jack alone, against two merrows twice his size and with vengeful murder in their hearts. Everyone knew—no, *Jack* knew—that this was when a hero would face his fear and win the day.

Jack had wrestled enough at the occasional tournaments between douns to know that in this sort of duel the first combatant to lose his cool would either quickly win or quickly die. None of the three seemed ready to be either killer or killed, especially the two merrows. In fact, Jack saw, they weren't expecting this. *They have no plan and neither wants to be the first. It's up to me. I might be able to hit one with a dagger, but then I'd be without a weapon. . . .*

Weapons. The bone throwing knife still stuck from Wrybert's lifeless chest, and with the maneuvering that had been going on—kithkin hopping and sidling, merrows sidewinding and shifting their stumpy legfins—the corpse was actually closer to Jack than the dead merrow's brothers.

Jack lunged at Wrybert's corpse and jerked the throwing knife from his chest. The two brothers both leaped in foolish alarm—disturbed from their bloody, simmering thoughts by his sudden action—and before either could raise a hand Jack hurled the boss's weapon overhand with all his might, clumsily, but close enough that clumsy got the job done. The blade drove into Wryllick, sending the merrow flopping onto the sand in agony and clutching at the knife embedded in his ribs.

"Wryget," the stricken merrow croaked. "Help."

Jack was taken aback for a moment and skidded to a halt a few feet away from Wryget, who had dropped to his brother's side.

"Poison," Wryget said as Wryllick's flopping settled into twitching spasms.

"Yes." The boss chuckled.

"But—I didn't mean to," Jack said before he could stop himself. Ah, yes, Jack, the apologetic hero. Perhaps he could politely apologize to Rosheen Meanderer when the rooftops of Mistmeadow lodged painfully between her toes.

"I know," the boss said. "I decided to offer you at least one kill on the house, as Brigid would say."

"He's dead," Wryget said in awe. Clearly the biggest of the bruisers hadn't been the brains of the trio. He turned on Jack and roared. "He's dead! You killed him—why? We would've gone easy on you."

"That's why," the boss said. "You three have been getting on my nerves. Brigid and I have already discussed it, and we're ready for some new hirelings. "

Wryget gently set Wryllick's body on the sand and pulled himself to his full height, almost twice as tall as Jack. Without taking his eyes off the kithkin, he picked up his dead brother's axe in his empty hand, and with a low, murderous growl that emerged from his croaking gills, lunged forward.

The merrow bruiser was enraged to the point of madness, but was still slow compared to an alert kithkin with a sound sense of balance. Jack sidestepped the first axe blow easily, and ducked out of the way of the second with only a bit more effort. As Wryget continued past him toward the water, Jack swiveled in the loose sand and gravel on one foot and drove the other into the middle of the merrow's back. Wryget tripped over his own legfins and flopped into the water with a splash.

Jack didn't waste any time, but he wasn't going to become the boss's hired murderer, either. Instead of moving in for the kill as the stunned merrow slowly turned around in the shallow water, Jack reached down and picked up a smooth river rock about the size of his fist.

"Ha!" he heard Brigid exclaim, followed by a murmured curse from the boss. With accuracy born of a lifetime spent bringing in small game to feed the kithkin of Mistmeadow, Jack hit Wryget squarely between the eyes. The merrow flopped back into the water, arms splayed, and lay there looking up into the sky as the slow currents of the Wanderbrine's shallows pulled him slowly downstream.

"He's going to live," the boss said as Jack turned to face the grizzled, one-eyed merrow. The kithkin hero couldn't contain his grin.

"I know," Jack said.

"But he's also soon going to be out of your reach. You won't be able to kill him." The boss growled. "Weren't you listening to the rules?"

"Sygg," Brigid said, addressing the boss by name and sending a chill down Jack's spine. "He's had enough. Wryget won't be back. What's the point?"

So the boss was Captain Sygg—one of the most notorious killers in the Big River. Sygg hadn't hunted the waters near Mistmeadow for years, but even Jack had heard of his bloody reputation. And here he was, in the flesh, replying to Brigid, "The point is a merrow's only as good as his word. I'm not going to let anyone walk away doubting my word. Not now. I haven't seen these waters for some time, and people need to be reminded I do what I say."

"But Captain," Jack said, hoping to buy time as he sidled toward the landward side of the sandspit, "I believe you, I just don't want to work for you. I'm nobody, and my job is only important to—important to me."

"I wasn't talking to you!" Sygg roared, and Jack dodged

just in time to avoid another poisoned knife. It soared past his ear and plunged into the center of the river with a splash. Sygg spat on the sand. "Coward. Kill him, Brigid. He's no good to us."

"Brigid," Jack said, regaining his feet, "you don't have to fight me."

"No, I'm afraid I do," Brigid said. "There's really no alternative."

With that, the strange kithkin pushed her hood back from her eyes and looked into Jack's own pale orbs. But Brigid's eyes were not like his, not like any kithkin's. The stranger's eyes were smaller, and black as the moonless sky.

Then one of the eyes winked and Brigid gave him a nod.

"No," Jack said, "I guess there's no alternative." He held the dagger in an easy grip and took a defensive stance, facing Brigid as he'd faced the merrows.

"Good," Sygg said. "If you want something done right, Brigid, you've got to do it yourself."

"I know, Boss," said Brigid. "If there's one thing you've taught me in my time with you, it's that." And she drove a black-gloved fist into Sygg's soft, vulnerable underbelly.

Where the same blow might've made a kithkin double over in pain and expel all the air in his lungs, in the merrow killer's case a blue-white flash sparked from the kithkin's fist and Jack heard a sizzling sound. Sygg's eyes spat sparks and he spewed a vile, brackish stream of river water from his mouth and gills. Brigid followed the first blow with a second to the temple that was not as flashy as the first but even more effective—Jack felt a bit of sympathy as the captain flopped out down unconscious on the spit.

Jack moved forward, dagger drawn, uncertain if Brigid meant to turn on him next.

"Wait," the strange woman said, raising a hand. "He's out cold. He'll die if he doesn't get back into the water." With a surprisingly gentle shove, Brigid pushed the murderous merrow into the shallows, where soon he was floating after Wryget. Jack hoped for the latter's sake they wound up in different places.

"Why did you do that?" Jack asked, sudden anger flaring in his chest. "Who are you? What are you?"

"I'm the one who's going to talk you out of chasing after that," Brigid said, pointing at a somewhat familiar four-legged shape in the distant sky. It dawned on him that the giant's footsteps had stopped for the moment, and as he watched, the bizarre creature in the sky wheeled and turned back, now galloping improbably back in the direction the giant had been coming from. Soon the four-legged . . . goat? Yes, it was a goat, and the goat would pass directly over their heads.

"I'm after a giant, not a giant goat," Jack said.

"Yet following that goat is the quickest way to find Rosheen Meanderer," Brigid replied. Jack looked at her skeptically, and she added, "You're chasing Rosheen and you don't know about her goat?" She snorted. "In my day, heroes were better informed. But I know that determined look . . . at least, I used to. You won't let me talk you out of this, will you?"

"No."

"Not without a potential skull fracture for you and a guilty conscience for me." Brigid sighed. "So be it. Well, if you're going to die, hero, you should die heroically." The stranger hooked a thumb up at the huge goat capering among the clouds. "The merrows keep close tabs on what we landwalkers are up to. I was there when Sygg got the news that Rosheen was running amok. He laughed. Said he wondered if she'd get her goat back before she trampled everyone else to death. The goat's hers. She wants it back. If you follow it, you'll find her."

Jack's mind raced as he stared at the strange cloud beast. "If that's true," he said. "I will be in your debt."

"I'm not through. You say you need a talisman? Something of hers? I may have just the thing. Sygg's people say the faeries are interested in Rosheen lately. They're keeping a close eye on her. We hear things about a journal, a journal the Fae want to see. Rosheen's an oracle, you know. Could be all kinds of interesting stuff on that scroll." Brigid locked her dark eyes on Jack's. "Or that long roll of parchment, or maybe a writing slate. Whatever it is, Jack, it's important to her. Maybe you can use it."

"I think I can," Jack said. "But before I did I'd want to know what you get out of it."

"Nothing," Brigid said. "Not yet, anyway. But if you make this happen, well, maybe that would make it possible for me to make something else happen. Make it possible for me to do something else for somebody I owe. If I were out to hurt you I'd have left you to the merrows. You have to learn who to trust, Jack, or you won't last two days as a hero."

Jack nodded. "Thank you, Brigid. For everything." He glanced past her to the river. "I'd feel safer if we could've killed Sygg," he said grimly.

"No," Brigid replied, her dark eyes narrowing and her strange complexion turning sour. "That's not going to happen now."

"Aren't you out of a job, too?" Jack asked.

"My job is looking after Brigid," she said. "But I'll find other employment if I can't convince Sygg he still needs me." Brigid unhooked her bow and quiver, nodding to a spot up the sandspit where Jack saw his pack and equipment had been dropped. "If you ask me, you don't need all that, it's just going to slow you down. From here on out, things'll be moving faster than you expect. But this," she said, holding out the bow by its grip, "will help you keep up."

"Why are you doing this?" Jack asked. "Why won't you tell me who you—"

"I'm like you," Brigid interrupted. "Least, I used to be. I wanted to be the hero of . . . of another doun, far way from here. But that was a long time ago." Without waiting for that to sink in, she asked, "Who did you leave behind?"

"A girl," Jack said automatically. "Keely."

"Maybe that was my problem," said Brigid distantly. "I never had anyone to come home to." She snapped back to the present as the galloping of the goat in the sky grew louder. She held up the bow again. "Do you know what this is?" she asked him.

"It's a . . . well, it's a bow, isn't it?" Jack replied.

"At times," she said. "And if you don't know a wingbow when you see one. . . ."

He considered her, the black eyes, the curious accent, the odd equipment, but could not fathom what the stranger was talking about. "I know wingbows," he said. "That's not a wingbow. They're smaller, like crossbows."

"This one isn't," said Brigid. "But I'm glad you've got at least some experience. You're going to need it. Now watch closely, Jack." With a flick of her wrist, she twisted the grip of the bow. Immediately a set of twin batlike wings snapped out of the stock and the entire contraption shimmered with the faintest bit of magic.

"You hold it up like this, and—whoa, steady there—it catches the wind to get you aloft. Once in the air, a combination of magic and steering carries you on the currents of wind the way a merrow floats on the river. All you have to do is steer and hold on."

"All right," Jack said. This wingbow didn't look anything like the kind he was familiar with. It didn't even have any shoulder straps. "More like a suicide stick," he muttered.

"Yes," Brigid replied. "You have a keen eye. But it's all you've got. Now, take it. Hold it out straight. Wait for the wind, and then step with it. After that, just use your weight to steer."

"How do I get down?" Jack asked, taking the curious device from the stranger and flicking the grip around, snapping the wings back into place.

"Not like that," said Brigid. "Lock in the wings and you'll die. Just ride the currents and hit the ground running."

"How do you know all these strange things?"

"I don't know much of anything, really. But I do know that a hero can't just rely on the thought—on the *mind*weft of his village. He relies on himself, and the occasional mysterious benefactor."

"That's really all you're going to tell me, isn't it?"

"Yes," Brigid said, "and if you don't get a move on, you're going to miss your goat. I won't be going anywhere near Mistmeadow, so you'll just have to report back yourself after you've taken care of everything. Follow the goat to the giant. Take the giant's scroll." Brigid offered her hand and Jack took it firmly. "Good luck, Jack."

It took another roar from the giant, who had obviously seen the goat gallop past, to remind Jack of his purpose. With a last glance at Brigid, who was already disappearing into the Wilt-Leaf, he slung the wingbow across his back and set off after Rosheen Meanderer's lost livestock.

* * * * *

Brigid worked her way through the hills northeast of Mistmeadow. The kithkin woman was no scout, but she knew a thing or two about woodcraft and a great deal more about being a hero. In her day she had both composed and inspired rousing songs of high adventure. Mistmeadow and its fledgling hero needed far more than a song, however. The deeper she went into the wilds, the more certain Brigid was that even the gift of the wingbow wouldn't be enough to keep Jack or his village alive.

She stopped beside a Canker-ridden ash and checked her bearings. Maralen the elf was easy to find these days. All one really had to do was look for her. If one didn't meet with some lethal and seemingly random mishap as soon as one set out, Maralen herself would appear and politely inquire regarding one's interest.

Brigid hiked down into a marshy basin. Finding Maralen was one thing, talking to her was another, but pinning the slippery elf down on particulars was a truly daunting and fruitless endeavor. Fortunately, Brigid had spent most of her time recently in the company of Sygg's merrow cut-throats, and between what she learned from Sygg and what she knew herself there was bound to be something of use to Maralen.

"Hello, Brigid." The elf maiden materialized in the shadows at the edge of Brigid's peripheral vision. She greeted Brigid with her green hood lowered. She smiled wearily and her dark eyes glittered. "What do you want?"

"I know you're busy," Brigid said. "Believe me, I know."

"How do you know, exactly?"

"Oh, I've got my sources. Even you'd be surprised how little escapes Sygg's notice."

"I see. Unfortunately, Brigid the Brigand, I'm not interested in banter today."

"Too bad. Banter's always part of striking a deal."

"Oh? And are we striking a deal now?"

"Not yet. But I know about something you don't. Something you want, something you don't want anyone else to have. And I'd like to bargain with it."

Maralen's smile faded. She tossed back her horns. "You've learned something from Sygg."

"I have. And to open our negotiations in good faith, here it is: The faeries are interested in Rosheen's journal. Dozens of them, maybe even hundreds."

"And what is that to me?" Maralen's mask of disinterest was almost perfect. In fact, it probably would have fooled anyone other than Brigid, who was an expert bluffer.

"Nothing," the kithkin said. "Though I'd say that to someone like you, who doesn't have hundreds of faeries at her beck and call, the notion of hundreds of faeries acting in concert ought to raise a few questions. Maybe even a few concerns. Because if they're not *your* faeries . . ."

"Point taken," Maralen said crisply. "But surely you realize I've had Rosheen under close watch for some time now. You're not telling me anything I didn't know."

"Oh, I'm sure you knew about the journal, but I bet you had no idea about the interest of others, did you?" Brigid smiled confidently. "Tell me I'm wrong."

Maralen's jaw clenched for a moment. "What do you want?"

"I want the hero of Mistmeadow to succeed," Brigid said. "So should you."

"Me? Why is that, exactly? I don't see how your altruism overlaps with my—"

"Self-interest," Brigid finished for her. "But that's only

because you're thinking about too many other things at once. Focus, now. Isn't it better for you to have Mistmeadow intact and out from under Donal Alloway's thumb?"

"Mistmeadow already made that choice," Maralen said. "They chose unwisely."

"No, Mistmeadow chose a fellow kithkin over a strange elf. Your relative merits had nothing to do with it."

"Bad luck for Mistmeadow."

"And for you. If Jack gets the journal, Rosheen goes away, Mistmeadow endures, and everybody wins. Everybody except Alloway, of course. And those other faeries who want the journal." Brigid smiled again, flashing her white teeth. "Doesn't that suit you?"

"It does. But then again, I don't need Jack or Mistmeadow to get the journal," Maralen said.

Brigid's expression faltered a bit. "How about if I sweeten the deal? I'm out of a job and you seem to be lining up all the warm bodies you can muster. What do you say to taking me on as your agent?"

Maralen's stern eyes softened with amusement. "Agent?"

"Agent, retainer, henchman. Whatever you want to call it. Freelance muscle. Hired goon. What do you say?"

The elf maiden coolly crossed her arms. "I say I don't need you any more than I need Jack or Mistmeadow."

"See, now that's another argument, not a refusal." Brigid clapped her hand and rubbed her palms together. "That means we have a deal, right? All that's left is to settle on a price."

"You are stubborn, kithkin, I'll give you that. But so am I. I like you, Brigid. I've always liked you. But that doesn't mean I'll help you."

"Does it mean you won't?"

Maralen cocked her head to one side and stared at Brigid through narrow eyes. In return, Brigid continued to smile a wide, forced, frozen smile, one hand fully extended for Maralen to take and the other clenched tight against the kithkin's hip to keep it from trembling as she waited for her answer.

* * * * *

Jack easily kept Rosheen's goat in sight, but catching up to the giant beast was another matter. As the hours blurred by, Jack saw the cloud goat as he did the sky, or the moon, or the horizon itself, impossibly high, impossibly distant, and impossible to reach. Worse, he was beginning to hit the limits of his own physical endurance. He'd already been knocked on the head, punched in the face, and bitten a hundred times in a hundred places, and now he faced sheer exhaustion—the one enemy that would always win in the end.

He never lagged and never wavered, however, because kithkin heroes persevered. Now that he was the bearer of a hero's weapon as well as a hero's purpose, Jack had a much truer understanding of what that meant. He no longer felt his doun, but he held Mistmeadow and everyone in it with him nonetheless. From that he could draw the will and the strength to keep going.

The wingbow rattled between Jack's shoulder blades with each step, but the contact strengthened Jack instead of paining him. Each sharp tap was a reminder of the honor and responsibility with which Brigid had entrusted him, just as the slap of the dagger against his thigh was a reminder of why he'd set out to find the giant in the first place.

Jack straightened his back, checked the position of

Rosheen's goat overhead, and picked up his pace. His quarry had led him a long way in a short time and he was well outside of any territory he recognized. As he jogged after the giant, the army of twisted, skeletal trees surrounding him thinned out. The sound of the river was faint and the ground underfoot was sodden and mushy. The world around him grew wetter, more marshlike, and Jack's progress slowed as he had to work to pull his feet out of the sucking mire without losing his boots.

Jack adapted his thinking to the shifting terrain. Marshland like this presented a unique blend of familiar foes mixed with new and unknown dangers. The air was so foul and stifling Jack had to force his lungs to accept it. There was a host of poisonous creatures and toxic plants here that were completely foreign to the forests of Mistmeadow. All around Jack sinkholes, tar pits, and quicksand made the land itself seem hungry and hostile.

Of the predators that hunted here as well as in Mistmeadow, merrow cutthroats were probably the most serious threat. So far none of the stagnant pools Jack had seen were big enough to conceal the aquatic creatures, and that was just fine by Jack. After meeting Sygg and his crew, Jack wasn't eager to meet any more.

The kithkin was also thankful not to see any indication that boggarts had been by recently. Everyone knew the boggart raiding parties bound for Mistmeadow originated in these swamps. Before the gluttonous little fiends attacked, they used these dark, secluded bogs to cast their vile spells and work themselves into frenzies of bloodlust.

In all, Jack's close and ongoing survey of his surroundings left him surprisingly optimistic. There were many things in this region that could kill him and were eager to do so, but none close by. He formed a circle with his thumb and forefinger and spat through it so his good luck would hold.

He checked the cloud goat's position in the sky, shifted his pack, and adjusted the wingbow across his shoulders. He still wasn't ready to take to the sky again, but he saw now simply keeping up with the goat wasn't enough. At his current pace Jack would never find the giant and return to Mistmeadow in time, not even if the predatory monsters he expected to find never showed up. He needed to use the tool he had been given, to summon more of its power and make it work for him.

Jack approached a long, narrow clearing between two gently rising hills. The tree-lined path inclined upward and as Jack drew close the ground below his feet firmed up. A somewhat cooler and less noxious breeze wafted out from the clearing's far side. It enveloped Jack and he inhaled deeply, simultaneously clearing his chest and his head.

Things are looking better, he thought. Yes, indeed. Jack nodded, rechecked the position of the cloud goat, and looked out over the promising new path before him. He nocked an arrow onto his wingbow, crouched, and carefully scanned the shadows between the trees that bordered the lane on each side.

For Jack was no fool, and only a fool would take the easiest, most inviting route through a bog. Everyone knew the old kithkin saying, "You can't be too suspicious when everyone wants you dead." If unknown persons hadn't planted and tended this impromptu boulevard to lure in the desperate and the unwary, then some rank and mindless horror had no doubt claimed this welcoming patch as its hunting ground precisely because it did *not* seem ominous.

Jack's eyes raked through the gloom as he slowly advanced. Less than a quarter of the way down the length of the lane, he saw something move. It was a ragged, irregular shape, its outline a tangle of gnarled sticks and broken timber. It might have been a camouflaged boggart or a treefolk that hadn't yet achieved its full size, but whatever it was it was trying very hard not to be noticed.

Once he'd spotted the initial figure, Jack was able to pick out half a dozen more among the trees. The darkness concealed their colors and the specific details of their appearances, but each was much taller and wider than Jack. Though their individual shapes varied wildly, each stood more or less upright. Their silhouettes betrayed a series of broken, unkempt, irregular things.

Jack locked his eyes and his arrow on the closest of the shadowy figures. He did not draw and would not loose until he had a better idea of where its vitals were, but for now he trained the arrowhead on what he presumed was the creature's upper torso. Assuming it had internal organs that breathed or pumped blood or digested food, Jack's arrow would find them there.

The closest figure muddled forward into the lane. Once it had detached itself from the surrounding shadows, Jack saw the creature more clearly. It was vaguely person-shaped with a head, torso, two arms, and two legs, but its body was horribly misshapen. Its limbs were fleshless and bare, and both pairs of twisted arms stretched all the way down to the ground. Instead of hands and feet with fingers and toes, the hunched creature dug into the loose soil with four splayed clusters of rootlike tendrils. Its waist was no wider than its legs, but its chest was broad and swollen like a mound of rain-soaked leaves. Its long, rectangular face bent forward at the center and its rough-textured flesh bristled like a tightly wound ball of twine. Slowly, deliberately, it shifted its arms and legs until its blank face was pointed at Jack. It let out a dull, airless groan.

It was a scarecrow, Jack realized, another inexplicably animate collection of debris like the one outside Mistmeadow. That scarecrow had been his, but Jack could not imagine a fellow kithkin assembling the horror that shambled toward him now, nor fathom its purpose. The wild scarecrow seemed more like a thing that spontaneously wove itself a body from marsh trash rather than one deliberately constructed and brought to life.

Fresh questions about these monsters raced through Jack's head, but he pushed them aside once more. The Mistmeadow mindweft was far away, well beyond his current reach. He'd have to wait until he returned home to nudge the collective toward this new and increasingly common entity. In the meantime, he had to decide how to handle this lot right now, and on his own.

More of the scarecrows ambled forward to stand beside the hunched, loping thing still staring blankly at Jack. He had noticed half a dozen initially, but soon there were almost a score of the misshapen creatures on the path. Jack kept his arrow trained on the first one he'd seen, the one with the bent rectangle face. He held his bowstring taut until the last of the scarecrows had oriented on him. His mind raced and he weighed his dwindling options, but the decision was taken from him when the scarecrows all reached some sort of silent consensus and simultaneously shuffled toward him.

Jack let his arrow fly. Below its crooked head, the hunched scarecrow's upper body burst into a cloud of dust and buzzing gnats, but the creature itself barely flinched. It kept coming, slowly, and Jack said a silent prayer of thanks for their careless, unhurried pace.

He loosed his second arrow at the next closest scarecrow, a mishmash of wood, fabric, and stone topped by a bulbous wasp's nest. Jack's arrow lodged in the thick brambles that supported its papery skull, but like its fellow this scarecrow didn't seem troubled by a bolt through its vitals.

Arrows were not evening the odds at all, but Jack continued to sink them into the scarecrows' ramshackle bodies. The wingbow felt right in his hands, and it was embarrassingly easy to put shaft after shaft into the field of targets shuffling toward him. Brigid had presented the weapon to him as a means of fast travel, but it was also swift and sure and deadly accurate.

When he had hit every last scarecrow on the path and each had an arrow stuck in its body (or a ragged arrow wound torn clear through), Jack stood up and lowered his weapon. He paused to confirm the cloud goat was still visible overhead, for once glad that the giant beast seemed a permanent fixture in the northern sky. The giant's distant footsteps were erratic, as if Rosheen had not decided on the best way to approach the creature, and Jack couldn't tell if that heavy tread was drawing closer or moving way.

The ghastly things moved with a disturbing chorus of groans, creaks, moans, and squeaks, their movements slow and confused, whereas he was an experienced woodsman and an expert scout. If Jack were willing to brave the darker, thicker paths through the marsh, he could easily circle around the scarecrows and press on without losing sight of his quarry overhead.

But Jack's thoughts went back to Brigid's words upon giving him the wingbow, and then further back to the drills and lectures that he'd never thought he'd use. He bore a hero's weapon. He ought to take advantage of it.

Jack extended the wingbow at arm's length and held it parallel to the ground. He concentrated on the bow in his fist, feeling the weight and texture of the hard, polished wood. There was magic in it, power as well as purpose that sang out to him, begging him to employ it. There was magic in him, too, both in his own mind and in the larger shared Mistmeadow collective.

Jack lifted the empty wingbow in one hand. His grip and his stance were firm and steady, the muscles in his arm as tight as if he held an arrow at full draw. He moved his eyes away from the scarecrows and focused only on the bow. Its smooth surface shone in the darkness. Jack felt his arm and spine stretching, snaking upward toward the night sky as his feet rose out of the wet dirt. Jack flicked his wrist, twisting the wingbow around in a quarter turn.

Something inside the solid piece of wood clicked. That single sharp snap vibrated down Jack's forearm, which replied with a click of its own. Sheer, batlike wings dropped down out of the bow.

A sudden gust of wind blew in from behind him. The breeze took hold of the membranous wings and filled them. The kithkin's stomach dropped, his head spun, and then suddenly he was high in the air over the heads of the approaching scarecrows. He gasped, as much from surprise as from the momentary inability to breathe. I'm flying, he thought giddily. Flying on a wingbow like a proper kithkin hero.

At the apex of Jack's arc the gusting wind failed. Weight returned to his limbs and his body. The outward-bulging bat wings fluttered and then fell slack.

"Damn and damn again," Jack said. He struggled to renew the spell and regain his lost momentum. He held his body rigid and ground his teeth. He stared at the wingbow so hard that everything else blurred. Up, he commanded it. Higher. Up. Up, damn you.

The bow in his outstretched arm drifted down until it and Jack both pointed at the ground. Jack felt his heart beating, and each booming pulse echoed in his temples. *Fly,* Jack thought. *Go up. Up, I say. Fly, fly now.*

Instead, Jack plummeted down as the last of the wingbow's magic failed ... or perhaps he had failed, it was difficult to say. In either case, the device's wings retracted out of sight before his eyes. Beyond the outstretched bow, Jack watched the pitiless black expanse of marsh and skeletal trees rushing up to meet him. Getting off the ground had been easier than he expected ... too easy, in fact ... and now his first wingbow flight would end with a good deal more blood and sorrow.

"Damn, damn, double-damn it all," he whispered. Jack saw a black-barked tree limb hurtling toward him and curled his body into a tight ball just in time to smash knees-first through the branch. Jack hissed in pain. Icy, stinging agony shot down the front of his legs from his kneecaps to the tips of his toes. The wingbow popped out of his grasp.

The impact stole a great deal of his downward momentum and sent the kithkin spinning end over end. Blindly clutching for the wingbow and half-hoping to latch on to another branch, Jack threw his arms out. It was agony, but grabbing the tree forced the rest of his body to straighten out. The more of him that stayed in contact with the trunk, the slower he'd fall. Jack was sure he felt individual layers of flesh scraping away from his arms, legs, and face, but he hugged onto the tree trunk as hard as he could.

The muddy ground slammed into the soles of Jack's feet

and drove his knees between the tree and his torso. The air exploded from Jack's body in a throaty, guttural grunt. His knees throbbed, seemingly several times their normal size and his lower back was full of icy needles . . . but he was alive.

He had landed well clear of the scarecrow mob, more than halfway down the tree-lined lane. Jack forced himself to roll onto his stomach, and with all of his arms and legs working together he was able to push himself up into something between a squat and being down on all fours. In the distance, the scarecrows all shuffled and shambled through their jerky marionette dance. Soon they would all be facing Jack once more, though thankfully they had grown no speedier during his abbreviated flight.

Jack was bleeding and raw, but nothing was broken. He felt a few chipped or cracked teeth that would make it hard to enjoy very hot or very cold tea for the next few weeks, but if that was the extent of his lasting injuries he vowed he would never complain about them. The kithkin slowly stood up, grimacing. The muscles in his legs felt like they were tearing away from his bones as he rose, but soon he was upright. He scanned the ground around him until he spotted the wingbow, fully intact and none the worse for wear but for a light covering of mud along its upper half. Jack slipped the wingbow back over his shoulder and climbed up onto the raised path between the trees.

The scarecrows were persistent, but they were in no hurry and would never reach him before he exited the lane . . . provided his legs didn't cramp up and drop him helplessly to the ground between here and there. Jack realized that was in fact a likely notion, and so he turned and limped away as quickly as his hobbled gait allowed.

Moving somehow quieted his sore muscles and aching

bones, and so the farther from the scarecrows Jack got, the faster he went. His pace was far from impressive, slower than his duties as a scout demanded . . . but in these circumstances it was outstanding. He was moving at least as quickly as the average Mistmeadow civilian, and while that would not help him catch Rosheen's goat, it would get him out of this desperate place in one piece.

Jack's hopeful mood soured even as his pace continued to improve. He was whole, but he was definitely injured. He no longer had the speed or the endurance to maintain pursuit. The wingbow—or at least his poor handling of it—was the cause of his current predicament, so now he had to make it the solution as well. He had to master its flight, and quickly, if he wanted to be there when Rosheen found the cloud goat.

Gingerly, without breaking stride, Jack slipped the wingbow into his hands. He had made it work once, albeit clumsily. Perhaps if he didn't go so high . . . perhaps if he concentrated on forward rather than up, he could sort out the mechanics of descending without injury. Once he knew how to take off and land safely, he could work on sustaining the stretches in between.

Jack slowed slightly. He extended the wingbow out in front of him and stiffened his arm. His mind, so used to sharing and sparring amid hundreds of others in the Mistmeadow mindweft, reached out to the wingbow as if it were alive and conscious, and more, as if it were an old and respected friend.

Forward, he told it. He made a game of it, coaxing the wingbow along. *Fast. Flight. Forward. Fast forward flight.*

The bat wings appeared on either side of Jack's hand. He smiled and kept coaxing. The wind kicked up behind him and he rose up in his boots until he was walking on the balls of his feet.

Fast, forward flight, he told the wingbow. *Fast forward flight.*

The wind gusted behind Jack, pressing against his back and shoving him forward. His feet left the ground for six paces, and then Jack hit the ground running.

That's it, he thought. *Again.*

He concentrated on his clenched fist and a stronger gust of wind blew by. It scooped Jack up and carried him a hundred feet or more forward, but only a few feet off the ground. Jack's boots kicked up gray mud and his legs complained, but he maintained his balance and continued to surge forward.

With a shout, Jack sprang forward and the wind lifted him off the ground once more. He went a good deal higher than he'd intended, half the height of the nearby trees, but he soared cleanly over a very long stretch before descending. The wind was strong behind him as he touched down and bounded farther down the trail.

Jack felt light and exhilarated, the aches in his back and legs fading away. I really can do this, he realized. I *am* doing it. Now I really am flying, the wingbow isn't flying me.

When Jack next landed, the scent of charred wood and sulfur ended his reverie and he stopped. The pungent odor stung Jack's nostrils and set his cracked teeth on edge . . . which in turn sent a dizzying jolt of pain up through his upper and lower jaws. A headwind rose to resist the gusts urging him forward, and Jack turned his face from it.

Jack's attention was drawn to a strange, stony hill up ahead to his right. It was well over twenty feet tall, easily fifty feet around, and so massive that it pressed deeply into the marshy soil. Jack took a careful step forward and saw the mound's surface was covered in thick, square stones that had been uniformly shaped and polished by expert masons.

Jack came forward, carefully approaching the stone mound without noise or sudden movement. Such cairns were not common near his home, but Jack had seen them before. They were either cinder burial mounds, boggart hideouts, or both. Jack had never seen a live creature on or near one of the cairns, but there was always evidence of who had been there. Patches of glazed rock and sooty smears told tales of the cinders' ghoulish custom of self immolation. Boggart filth and bloody bones betrayed those feral bandits' wake.

He moved closer to the cairn until he felt heat radiating from it. His worst fears confirmed, Jack quickly stepped back and readied an arrow. He had never encountered a hot cairn before, but everyone knew the mounds gradually cooled once the dying cinder had completely burned away. Heat from this cairn at twenty paces meant the funereal ritual must have happened recently.

Jack prepared to skirt wide around the cairn but a charred, crumbling figure scrabbled up on top of the mound before he could move. Jack remained where he was, eyeing the first live cinder he had seen in quite some time. The funeral rite for which this cairn had been built had indeed been performed recently . . . in fact, Jack realized, he may have interrupted it before it was complete.

The cinder on top of the cairn stared blankly at Jack, not quite registering or reacting to his presence. From the waist down it seemed no different from an elf—long, powerful legs clad in tough, weathered britches, though the figure's feet were more like a kithkin's than an elf's. Also, instead of hooves or shoes, the cinder's feet were shod in tarnish-black boots made from overlapping strips of metal. Its forearms bulged grotesquely at the wrist as if it wore a pair of thick charcoal gauntlets.

From the waist up, the figure was a blackened, crumbling half-skeleton of brittle coal and ash. There was no flesh at all on its frame, nor were there soft internal organs for its half-complete rib cage to protect. Its face and jaw jutted forward from the top of its spine, a rigid, black, death mask with nothing but stale air and coal dust glittering behind it. Jack could see clear through those dreadful hollow sockets to the marsh trees behind the cairn, and he shuddered.

Cinders unnerved him like none of Mistmeadow's more frequent enemies could. Boggarts were cunning vermin. Treefolk were malicious brutes and, he thought ruefully, occasionally gigantic, silent monsters. And the merrows were greedy, avaricious scum.

The cinders were all that and worse. They raided and killed like the rest, but cinders had no interest in plunder for profit. They did not attack to take things of value for themselves, but to ruin and destroy those things so that no one else could have them. Where a boggart horde would gleefully slaughter a kithkin family, tear down their farmhouse, eat their livestock, and steal all their valuables, cinders would simply set fire to everything—the barn, the fields, the farmhouse, and everyone in it—just to watch it all burn.

If cinders were alive at all—and the subject was much debated back in Mistmeadow—then they were little more than the living embodiments of malice and woe. Whatever kept them going was not life, nor the joy of living, but a grim determination to spread the misery and desolation of their own wretched half-life.

The cinder atop the cairn must have seen Jack by now, though the crumbling black figure had not yet acknowledged him. Slowly, Jack relaxed the bowstring. He tightened his grip on the wingbow and stretched his arm out straight.

The cinder responded. It drew a flaking black sword from its belt, releasing a shower of coal dust and grit across the surface of the cairn stones. It crouched slightly and turned its empty face fully toward Jack. A ghastly hiss rolled out from the cinder's permanently snarling mouth, and then it sprang.

The awful thing covered half the distance between the cairn and Jack in its first leap, and then smoothly sprinted on toward its prey. Unlike the scarecrows, cinders were terrifyingly fast . . . but Jack was ready.

His arm shot up and he twisted his wrist a quarter turn. The wingbow clicked and the bat wings descended. The wind gusted behind Jack just as the charging cinder raised its blade.

Jack held his ground until the cinder started its downswing, and then he shot forward and up, narrowly missing his enemy's falling blade. Jack sailed forward and descended into the mud. Triumphant, he turned back to face his pursuer even as he readied the wingbow for another jump.

He heard a soft whistling sound and caught a whiff of sulfur before a corroded metal blade came slashing down toward his bow arm. Jack barely managed to twist the wingbow back and block the blow before the strike cut through his arm at the elbow.

A metallic clang rolled past him and then echoed back from the nearby trees. Jack felt the shock of the blow across his entire body, but whoever had carved the wingbow used stronger stuff than whoever had forged the second cinder's sword. Jack's weapon was barely nicked, but the sword's edge cracked and crumbled. He considered drawing Keely's dagger, but then he wouldn't have a free hand. For now the bow had better hold, he told himself.

The second cinder spun its sword as it advanced so that the unbroken edge was facing Jack. This creature was taller and broader than the first but less substantial. It had only one arm, no ribs, and its jaw hung far below the rest of its face, completely detached and hovering in front of its chest.

The second cinder eyed Jack's wingbow. "Look," it rasped, the word drawn out like a dying man's last breath. "A tiny hero." Both cinders began to laugh, a slow, throaty, stentorian chuckle that chilled Jack so deeply it became hard for him to think.

Though larger and less intact, the second cinder was as fast as the first, so fast that Jack had to throw himself backward to avoid being decapitated by his enemy's follow-up stroke. He tumbled and rolled to put more distance between himself and his assailant.

The second cinder charged after him, but Jack extended the wingbow and activated it. The wind blew him away from this attacker and back toward the mound. As Jack descended he saw the first cinder rushing to intercept him.

This won't work, he realized. He could fly fast enough to avoid the cinders, but not far enough to escape them entirely. Eventually they would corner him or he would make a mistake, and then they would burn him with their foul hands or cut him to pieces with their filthy crumbling blades.

Jack summoned another gust of wind that plucked him off the top of the cairn before his full weight settled onto it. Good thing, too. The first cinder's swing would have cut both Jack's legs off at the knee had he lingered a fraction of a second more. Jack came down roughly where he had first spotted the cinder cairn. He steadied his stance and turned to eye his opponents. At least now they were both in front of him.

Just as the appearance of an inviting path had done before, this welcome turn of events made Jack suspicious. He heard no strange sounds, saw no unexpected flashes of motion, but he nonetheless snapped his arm straight up and commanded the wingbow to carry him away. Jack rocketed upward to the tops of the trees before his momentum failed. As he fell, Jack saw a third cinder lurking just behind where he himself had just stood, and this one bore a long-handled battle-axe that had just been robbed of its target.

That is it then, Jack thought. Endlessly dodging three cinders was even less promising than endlessly dodging two. They would wear him down in short order—all they had to do was space themselves out properly and he'd never have more than a second or two to land and relaunch.

Jack struggled for a solution, for some way of surviving long enough to devise a means of defense or escape. His eyes turned back along the way he'd come, toward the tree-lined lane and the shambling mob of scarecrows. What would a hero do?

Jack smiled even as the cinders positioned themselves before the cairn to greet him no matter where he landed. He knew perfectly well what a hero would do, and he also knew it would work.

As he approached the ground Jack pointed the wingbow back toward the scarecrows and called upon the wind. A crosswise gust yanked him sideways and away, well clear of the waiting cinder's axe, and deposited Jack back at the edge of the cairn's clearing.

Jack's feet were moving before they touched the dirt. His knees were still stiff and sore, but he didn't need them for long. Besides, he didn't believe he could outrun a cinder on his best day.

Jack whistled up another gust of wind and disappeared into the dense woods. Maybe he couldn't outrun a cinder, but with the wingbow he could outdistance one . . . or three, for that matter. He heard the trio of grim killers pursuing him, silent but for the thump of metal shoes on wet soil and the grate of stone against crumbling stone in their joints.

Jack landed and bounded forward again, buoyed by the wind. He was gaining a stride or two with every jump, but the cinders were not slowing down. If anything their pace grew faster and more fervid with each step.

When he spotted the scarecrow's clearing, Jack put all his strength into his next leap and covered the entire distance in one fell swoop. This gave him an extra second or two to catch his breath and assess both the situation in front of him and behind him. In front, a score of scarecrows still milled around in the tree-lined lane. Behind, the cinder trio bore down on his position with their dull red eyes glowing in the gloom.

Jack retracted his weapon's wings and nocked an arrow. He sighted on the first available scarecrow target, a slow-moving heap of twigs and toadstools with a dull metal pot for a head. He loosed the arrow and it struck the pot cleanly off the crude figure's mounded shoulders.

One by one the other scarecrows all turned toward Jack. He resisted the urge to fire a few more arrows into the crowd. Instead, Jack spun in place and snapped his arm up and over the approaching cinders. What would a hero say? Jack asked himself.

"Cinders, meet scarecrows," he called. Without turning, he added, "Scarecrows . . . cinders."

The wind rose, hurling Jack up and over the cinders. This time the gust did not die once he achieved his apex. Jack soared on the wind, higher and faster until he could see both the cairn ahead and the scarecrow clearing behind with a simple twist of his neck.

Robbed of their target, the cinder trio plunged headlong into the crowd of scarecrows. A confused melee began, black blades striking sparks and wood chips from ramshackle bodies. One of the cinders became tangled in the formerly pot-headed scarecrow's body and both figures fell into a single thrashing heap.

Jack experienced a fresh flicker of disappointment that these cinders weren't alive enough to have actual flames burning in their carbonized bodies. He still wanted to see what happened when fire combined with creatures made out of kindling, but that was clearly something that had to wait for another day.

Jack stared back at the clumsy battle until he was certain the combatants had completely forgotten about him, and he breathed a sigh of relief. Not only had he escaped, but he was flying again, and with better control than ever before. He was no longer taking prodigious leaps by clinging to the wingbow as if he were the tail of a kite, this was sustained flight. He wasn't a true kithkin hero yet . . . the cinder's mocking laughter was a bit premature on that score . . . but he was more a hero now than he ever had been.

Jack searched the sky until he spotted Rosheen's goat. He knew it was far away, very far away—perhaps farther away than it had ever been since he started tracking it. From his current lofty position, however, it seemed well within reach.

"You can stop any time now," he whispered to the goat. "Find Rosheen, or let her find you. I can hear her out there, so you must, too. The sooner you reach her, goat, the better it will be for everyone."

The giant cloud goat paid Jack no mind as it snorted and stamped its way across the sky. Unperturbed, and in fact exultant in the joy of his newfound skill, Jack followed.

* * * * *

Much later, when the tedium of the endless chase began to weigh on him afresh, Jack decided something. If he ever mentored the next generation of Mistmeadow heroes—and he fully intended to, with Keely at his side—he would be sure to tell them to never follow a cloud goat at anything less than extremely long range.

It wasn't the perilous updrafts or the aching in his shoulders and arms that prompted this decision. Nor was it the danger of being so close to such a creature or the near-certainty that Rosheen Meanderer would spot him before he managed to get close enough to swipe the giant's precious trophy. No, what prompted Jack to caution future heroes was the smell. Cloud or not, a goat was still a goat, and the goatly aroma in this creature's wake was enough to make a boggart choke.

Even through the smell, Jack maintained his focus. The goat was a means to an end, a stepping stone to Rosheen. He was still unable to spot the giant, though he could hear her endless, babbling roar echo off the distant hills and back again. The sounds had bounced back and forth over so many crags and cliffs before reaching Jack's ears that there was no way to trace them back to their source. He had to rely on the goat's instincts—a goat, he reminded himself, that didn't really seem to want a reunion with its master.

"Well, look at you," a sharp, tiny voice said from behind Jack's ear.

"Gyah!" Jack yelped and very nearly let go of the wingbow.

"I truly never expected to see one of you ground slugs this high up." The sound brought a tinkling laugh from the faerie on his shoulder, and it zipped into the space before him, effortlessly keeping pace as she flew backward so that she appeared to be carelessly hovering.

The faerie was a typical example of her kind . . . except for the fact that she appeared to be alone, and in Jack's experience, faeries were never alone. He'd met a few as a scout and he found them to be irritating little pranksters who, on occasion, displayed a bloody-minded sensibility that frankly unsettled him.

"What's the matter, little hero?" the faerie, a female, tittered. "You've been muttering to yourself for quite a while now. I thought you'd appreciate someone real to talk to . . . but if you prefer we can leave you alone with this imaginary 'Keely' you keep whispering to."

Another faerie, a bit smaller but otherwise identical to the first, rose into his field of vision. This time he didn't even start. "There are two of us here for the ground slug to talk to," the second faerie said. "You're not alone here, Iliona."

"Shut up, Veesa," the larger first faerie replied. "I'm offering our magical aid to the bold kithkin hero."

"Oh, I love those," said Veesa. "But only the tragic kind."

"Hush or you'll give the whole game away. He wants what we want and so we're all going after it together." Iliona smiled sweetly and batted her eyes. "Right, Jack?"

"What are you talking about?" Jack growled, trying to keep the cloud goat in sight. "How do you know my name?"

Veesa sniffed, slightly offended. "We know everything. We're faeries."

Iliona nodded. "That's right. We know you. We know what you're doing. We know you're seeking a trophy."

"A talisman," Veesa said.

"A magical something or other from that giant. One you can use to keep her from walking all over your stup—your quaint and charming little homey village."

"I don't know if I'd call it 'quaint,' " Jack said with a nod, "But otherwise, yes. That is what I'm planning to do. How did you know that?"

"We're faeries!" Veesa squealed, now visibly irate. "We know all!"

"All right," Jack said. "You're faeries. You know all." He nodded toward the cloud goat. "So tell me this: How do I find the giant and get the scroll away from her?"

"You have to know where to look," Iliona said.

"And how to be sneaky. We're the best at that, the best *ever.*"

"But can you tell me where to look?" Jack said.

"We can," Iliona said.

"But we won't."

"We'll do even better. We'll take you there."

"You know who Rosheen is? What she looks like?"

"Oh, we've seen her," Veesa said.

"We've seen her a lot," Iliona agreed. "Up close, too. You think the *goat* smells bad. . . ."

"He doesn't care about that," the second faerie said. "He's a hero. A *kithkin* hero. And he's on a mission to get what we want."

"Right. And so we're going to help him. Because some-one asked nicely."

"Hmph." Veesa sulked. "Help him help us."

"Um, right," Jack said. "Listen, if you have some advice, please tell me. If not . . ." He paused. Everyone knew if you told a faerie what you wanted, they'd invariably do the opposite. "If not," he finished, "I'll know that faeries are no smarter than cinders."

"We hate cinders!" Veesa exclaimed. "Faeries rule the skies, and cinders make the sky stink worse than a hundred cloud goats."

"I've been told," Jack said, encouraged, "never to trust a faerie."

"Bah!" Iliona said. "Trust me when I tell you, we'll show *you* whom not to trust!"

"Go ahead, then," Jack said, hiding a mad grin, "Prove me wrong. How do I find Rosheen? How do I get the scroll?"

"To find her, just follow us," the faerie called Iliona said. "As for the scroll, that's a longer —*oof!*"

A third faerie had slammed into Iliona's narrow midsec-tion, knocking both tackler and victim from Jack's field of vision. Veesa remained, hovering stunned and wide-eyed before him.

"Hey!" Veesa managed, just before a fourth faerie tack-led her from the sky and out of Jack's sight.

Jack shook his head in frustration. Faeries playing games. What else had he expected? He kicked himself for even speaking to the little devils. Frivolous gadflies that couldn't hold a thought in their heads long enough to share it with him, and even if they could there was no guarantee it would help him. The whole quartet was probably related and the whole clique was obviously toying with him for their own amusement.

With a shift of his hips he veered slightly to the east. The goat was slowing down. Perhaps it was drawing close to Rosheen . . . yes! As the unlikely creature galloped low over the endless forest, the giant herself burst from the foliage with a roar.

Even at this distance, Rosheen Meanderer looked every bit the enormous monster of legend: well over fifty feet tall, covered in dirt and debris, with a thick mane of black hair that lay like a knotted cape across her broad back. Words poured out of the giant's mouth, a steady deluge of incomprehensible babble. Jack recognized perhaps one word in ten as Rosheen's endless roar vibrated against his spine.

Rosheen's eyes were wide-open and mad, empty black pits in a face like rocky crags. Those enraged eyes glared at the sky and her huge, oversized arms swatted through empty air as the cloud goat swooped down, taunting Rosheen in an ancient game whose origin had long ago been lost.

"Scary, isn't it?" an unmistakably Fae voice said from behind his left ear.

"No," Jack said, refusing to be baited. The voice sounded different this time, and as the speaker launched from his shoulder and took a position in front of him, he saw that indeed this was neither Veesa nor Iliona, but one of the others who had tackled the first pair. "I'm not scared a bit of that giant. But faeries, now," Jack warned, "faeries are starting to annoy me."

"Typical," said a second faerie—the one who had tackled Veesa—as it rose into his field of view. "We do him the good and useful service of beating up those two turncoats and he won't even have a proper conversation with us."

"He at least ought to thank us, Gilly."

"I quite agree, Fioni. What ever happened to the famous kithkin conviviality?"

"It still exists," Jack said. "But it's in short supply these days. Now would you mind getting out of my way? I'm very busy tracking that goat."

"Oh, yes," Fioni snapped, "it's all about *you,* isn't it? You and your precious goat. We're just faeries, we flit all over the place carrying messages, poisoning messengers, doing all the *hard* work, and then you 'heroes' come and take all the credit. I tell you, Mr. Kithkin, I've about—"

"Fioni," Gilly said, "shouldn't we be getting to the, you know, the offer?"

"Offer?" Jack said, shifting his weight again to take advantage of a new updraft that would keep him on a course for Rosheen. "What offer?"

"We're going to help make you the hero you always wanted to be," Fioni replied, and when she continued, her high-pitched voice took on the tone of an officious diplomat. "The Great Mother Oona, Queen of All Fae, offers her assistance."

Jack failed to hold back a smirk. "Oona does, does she? Now I know you're playing games with me. Tell me, is this the kind and soothing Oona from 'Glen Elendra Lullaby' or the stern and angry Oona from 'How the Faeries Got Their Blessed Wings (and the Boggarts Got So Damned Ugly)'?"

"Oona is Oona," Fioni and Gilly said together. Their eyes were stern and sharp. "There is only one Great Mother."

"Of course," Jack said. He thought for a moment and then added, "What about those other two? You said something about turncoats."

"Those"—Fioni sniffed—"were not true faeries. They have been cast out for serving a false, fake, and phony pretender."

"They're nothing!" Gilly squealed angrily. "And we fixed 'em good, so don't give those two turncoats another thought. Go on, Fioni. I love it when you talk all grand like that."

"Yes," Fioni said, her officious tone unchanging, "quite."

If he hadn't been preoccupied tracking a giant goat— and a giant giant—Jack might have found the entire thing comical. As it was, his patience was growing thin. "Look, ladies . . ." he began.

"As I said, the Great Mother wishes to help you," Fioni said.

"Why?" Jack asked. The goat wheeled again and was coming in for another low pass, like a moth that couldn't stop fluttering past an open flame. The giant, calmer now but no quieter, had stopped running. Rosheen crouched low, waiting for her chance with surprising cunning and patience even as she continued to bellow random words.

Jack was glad no kithkin ever had so much trouble with a springjack as this giant seemed to be having with her goat.

"You seek the giant's scroll," Fioni said rhetorically, and for a moment Jack thought he felt the tendrils of another mind within his own.

"And if I do," Jack said at last. "You're here to help me?"

"We are," Fioni said.

"When did you plan to get started?"

"Oh, you are bold," Gilly said. "And cheeky."

"Quite the hero," Fioni agreed. "You're headed for greatness, aren't you Mr. Kithkin?"

"Jack. Jack of Mistmeadow."

"Mr. Jack," Fioni said amiably. "Mr. Mistmeadow Jack.

All right, here's what you do. Wait until the giant catches her goat, yes? While she's preoccupied, you swoop in and grab the scroll. It's tucked into her—*oof!*"

Jack blinked in alarm as again, the faerie speaking to him was caught in a flying tackle by another of her kind—one of the original two, from the look of it. If they were all from the same clique, they certainly played rough with each other. Gilly was quickly swept away in precisely the same manner, and Jack found himself flying half-blind and barely prepared toward a charging cloud goat.

"Wait until Rosheen catches the goat," Jack repeated. That, at least, was good advice. But Rosheen had better catch the damned thing on this pass, or—

"Or you're doomed! *Doomed,* Mr. Mistmeadow Jack, the hero!" said Iliona, fluttering back into view with a bit of a swagger.

"Hello again," Jack said. "What happened to the others?"

"Though all faeries rule the skies, we Vendilion rule the skies the most!" Veesa said, rejoining her sister. Both looked a bit more haggard than before. "Not those stupid slaves!"

"Most of the Vendilion rule the skies," Iliona said bitterly.

"Most of the Vendilion!" Veesa cheered, then added, "Stupid Endry."

"What's an Endry?" Jack asked.

"Never mind," Iliona said. "All right, Jack, we've gotten rid of those fancy-pants lickspittles for a while, but they're persistent. You're going to have to work fast if you're going to—if we're going to help you."

"Let me guess," Jack said dryly. "Wait for the giant to catch the goat?"

"Yes!" Iliona said. "And then you need to get to her belt."

"The scroll is in her belt?" Jack asked. Finally, some real information.

"Yes," Veesa said. "Her belt contains the talisman you need. That giant . . ."

"She's a bit of an oracle, you could say," Iliona explained. "She collects stories about the world and then writes down her visions in the same big scroll, like a journal. It's always on her, like stink on a kith—like flies on a springjack. Now here's what *we'll* do to help you that those others wouldn't have done."

"We're going to create a *diversion!*" Veesa squealed. "Isn't that magnificent? A *diversion!* So adventurous."

"We'll make sure that between the goat and us, that giant isn't paying attention to her belt. The scroll," Iliona said, "is in a big pouch on the left side. A scroll-shaped pouch. Just grab it and get away."

"Wouldn't a giant's scroll be, well, *giant?*" Jack asked.

"That's the best part," Iliona said. "This is how you help us help you."

"To help us to help you help us," Veesa added.

"It's magic," Iliona said, fixing her sister with a sharp-eyed glare. "The scroll, that is. Just fold it up and keep folding. It will keep getting smaller and smaller until it fits in your pocket."

"I can do that," he said, and though he saw no major flaws in the plan other than the faeries themselves, he decided to try.

"Splendid," Iliona said. "Then follow us, and be careful. We're about to run headlong into a charging goat."

"So look sharp, hero." Veesa crinkled her nose. "The smell alone is potentially lethal."

* * * * *

The three of them—two Vendilion faeries and Jack—made less than a beeline for Rosheen Meanderer, who now made her appeal to the goat from atop a small hillock. The farmhouse that had occupied the hillock only a few moments before was now a pile of wreckage at the giant's feet. Thankfully, it seemed no one had been home when Rosheen came calling, but Jack shuddered to see the wreckage. He couldn't help but imagine all of Mistmeadow in a similar state.

"I'm not going to be able to do this," he whispered to himself, and started abruptly when the smaller of the two Vendilions shouted back to him as if he'd spoken in her ear.

"Yes you can, Jack! We were told we'd find a hero here, so you're our hero!"

"You're Mistmeadow's hero, too!"

"You're everyone's hero!"

Jack sighed. He didn't feel like anyone's hero at the moment. With the goal Alloway set for him in sight, Jack now realized he didn't trust Alloway. Kinscaer's cenn hadn't warned Jack of any of the dangers he would face, dangers the Kinscaer leader must have known of before coming to Mistmeadow. The map Alloway provided—long since abandoned with the rest of his pack on the banks of the Wanderbrine—had been worse than useless. To Jack, it suddenly seemed obvious that Alloway wanted him to fail.

Perhaps, he thought with a sickened feeling, the elf woman had been right. Maybe all Alloway wanted was to add to Kinscaer's power within the Wilt-Leaf. It was a troubling thought, almost paralyzingly so, and without the mindweft to guide him. . . .

"Jack, look out!" Veesa yelped. Her tiny fist bopped him on the end of the nose and Jack blinked. Then he ducked, just in time to avoid the hooves of Rosheen's goat as they thundered by his head.

Had Alloway lied to him? Of course he had. Jack had just seen a giant goat gallop across the sky and within yards of his own head and lived to tell the tale. *Anything* was possible. Which meant success was possible, provided he didn't get trampled by said goat.

"Veesa, *you* look out!" Iliona shouted to her sister, and each flitted out of the way of Gilly and Fioni, who clearly were not ready to abandon the tried and true midair tackle tactic. Iliona and Veesa were ready this time, and each Vendilion sister managed to twist out of the attacking faeries' path.

"I hate them *so much*," Veesa snarled. To his surprise, she turned to Jack and barked an order like the commander of a scout detachment. "Go get that map. Iliona and I have *work* to do." The little faerie somehow made "work" sound synonymous with bloody murder. Veesa and Iliona broke off, swooping out of Jack's view, and he heard the distant sounds of tiny but fierce midair combat.

The goat's thundering hooves came in shorter, sharper bursts. It was tiring. Soon Rosheen would succeed in laying her hands on the straying creature. Jack let his altitude fall away slowly, and when the goat passed overhead he ducked and dived after it. Veesa had given him an idea.

There was no telling when the faeries would be back or which pair of faeries it would be. He would secure the scroll first and worry about who wanted it from him later on. And to do that, Jack had what he realized was quite a clever idea—more importantly, it was the only idea he had.

Jack bid the wingbow to lift him up, over the goat, down toward the monstrous beast's neck, and slowly drew the dagger. Clutching it to his chest, Jack reached inward for the impossible joy he'd felt in Keely's presence, the blazing pride of the doun's belief in him, and the courage required of the mosquito to sting the thing that could crush it without a second thought.

"Mistmeadow! Keely! For the doun!" And with that, Jack drove the dagger into the base of the cloud goat's skull. The blade pierced the thick hide with surprising ease and Jack used his momentum to shove the point into the thick, wiry fur up to the hilt, beyond, up to his elbow, his shoulder . . .

There! He'd finally struck a nerve. Moments before they reached Rosheen, Jack wrenched his arm free and kicked off the goat's back. The beast veered to the right so that Rosheen, instead of catching the goat in her arms, took a thick, horned skull squarely in the sternum. The impact knocked Rosheen from her feet, and the giant's landing stirred up a tremor that probably knocked the plates off of the shelves as far back as Welk Lodge. The goat landed atop Rosheen and the giant, moving with alarming speed for something so huge, immediately wrapped the creature in a bear hug. The goat let out a deafening bleat, and Rosheen roared triumphantly in response.

Neither of them paid Jack any notice as the wingbow spiraled down like a tumbling maple seed to alight on the giant's belt. Without snapping the wings back into shape, he flipped open the clasp on the cylindrical pouch on the giant's belt and hauled with all his might on the thick roll of sturdy, hidelike paper within. Still hugging the goat, Rosheen rolled over onto her back, but by then Jack had the journal free and was already folding it.

He took back to the air as he folded the journal again, and again, and again, trapping it between his free hand and his rib cage. He marveled at the way it lost weight and substance with each crease, but it was still a thick, stiff papyrus no matter now small it got.

When it was small enough, Jack placed the journal inside his own belt pouch. The dagger was gone, still lodged in the goat's neck, but Keely would understand. At least Jack had put the gift to good use.

Rosheen's roar came hot and fast, tinged with a foul odor and blind rage, and it nearly knocked Jack out of the sky. The giant had lost her grip on the goat once more, and now the fickle beast was again galloping away through the sky. As Jack let out a chuckle of victory, he saw Rosheen's flat black eyes find him. The giant then slowly glanced down at her belt and the open pouch still hanging there. With another furious roar, Rosheen charged at Jack, and the kithkin scout desperately willed his wingbow to rise higher into the sky.

"Stay back!" Veesa cried, and a tiny pinprick of blue light shot from the faerie's hands as she zipped past. It struck Rosheen on the nose, stopping the giant momentarily but adding to her fury. When Veesa's sister did the same, it only drove Rosheen into a more pronounced murderous frenzy.

They're crazy, Jack said to himself. This is all crazy. But he had what he came for. All he needed to do now was to get back home.

"Have at you, giant!" Iliona cried, ducking a mighty swat from the snarling monster. There was an entire swarm of faeries now—not just the Vendilions and the other two, but trios, quartets, pairs and loners fluttering around Rosheen Meanderer's head like a cloud of gnats. Dozens of the diminutive creatures were stinging Rosheen's eyes and face, slowing the giant's pursuit of Jack and allowing the kithkin to put more and more distance between them.

Jack peered closely and saw Veesa and Iliona heading toward him, zigging and zagging to avoid the giant's waving hands. Following close behind the Vendilion sisters were Fioni and Gilly.

"Have you got it?" Iliona asked.

"Yes," Jack said.

"Give it here," Veesa said.

"No chance. I need it." Jack clutched Rosheen's scroll tightly to his chest.

Fioni screeched and rose up behind the Vendilion. With Gilly shouting encouragement, Fioni drew back her arm and hurled something glittering toward Jack.

But Veesa struck before Fioni's arm completed its arc. Jack saw a blur of sharp metal and a long, horizontal slash opened up across Fioni's throat just before the wide-eyed faerie dropped from the sky with a sickening gurgle.

Fioni's last blow had been struck, however. Small and sharp as a shard of glass, the dead faerie's dagger punched through the skin on the back of Jack's hand. Cold numbness spread outward from the wound and Jack realized Fioni's weapon was envenomed. His throat half-closed and his grip on the wingbow grew slack. The wind that held him aloft withered, and Jack began to fall.

Something was tugging at the scroll in his hands. Jack looked down to see Gilly straining to pry his treasure loose . . . until Iliona flashed by, leaving a long, ragged tear in all of Gilly's wings. The stricken faerie held on to the scroll for a dizzying moment, but Iliona's second pass tore Gilly loose and sent her hurtling toward the ground below.

Jack quickly followed. There was some residual lift left in the wingbow, but he was descending quickly and picking up speed all the time. Nearby, Rosheen was alternately swatting at the cloud of stinging faeries around her head, stomping the ground like an angry bull, and lunging for her goat. Between her size and her vast reach, the giant seemed to be everywhere at once.

Veesa floated down beside Jack, matching his downward momentum. Her voice was calm, disinterested. "Have you still got it?"

Numbly, Jack nodded.

Veesa motioned impatiently. "Hand it over."

Jack closed his eyes and squeezed the scroll even more tightly against his torso. He shook his head as the coldness inside him continued to spread and intensify.

Veesa scowled. She zipped in close to Jack's face and kicked him lightly across the nose. When he didn't react, she shrugged. Then the smaller Vendilion dropped down to Jack's waist and pried the scroll from his grip with barely any sign of visible effort. Jack moaned helplessly as the tiny figure buzzed up and away from him.

Veesa brandished the scroll. "Got it," she called.

"That's that, then." Iliona flew down to her sister and they both cast one last look at Jack. "Wait," Iliona said. "Aren't we forgetting something?"

"Who knows?" Veesa said. "Miss High-and-Mighty Maralen keeps changing the job on us. First it's the scroll, then it's the hero, then it's both. I lost track of what we're supposed to take care of a long time ago, and by now I'm way past caring. I have more important things on my mind."

Jack tried to speak, but his tongue was thick and frozen. The ground was coming up very, very quickly. If he could have spoken, it would have been to speak Keely's name one last time.

"No, no, no," Iliona said. "We're supposed to get the hero and the scroll, remember? That's it, I'm certain.

Because someone asked nicely on this one's behalf."

"You carry him, then." Veesa tossed her head and veered away. "I've already got something."

"It'd be much easier if you'd help," Iliona said.

"Good point," Veesa replied. She flew out of Jack's sight without another word or backward glance.

"Miserable little thing," Iliona muttered. "Still, what can you do? Family is family." She was now alongside Jack's ear and he could hear her clearly. "Brace yourself, hero. This is probably going to hurt."

A thin blue cloud formed around Jack. His downward momentum stopped short and he doubled over, suspended at the waist as if Iliona had tied a cord around his middle. It felt as if Jack's insides were being forced out of every available exit, and his vision went white. For a long time, all Jack heard was the sound of the wind rushing past his ears.

At least he still heard something. Fioni's dagger was apparently unable to deliver more than a drop or so of poison, which didn't seem to be enough to kill a kithkin outright. Obviously the little devil had been counting on the fall to finish the job for her.

Sensation slowly returned to his aching body and Jack realized he was safely on the ground. He could feel the tremors from Rosheen's tantrum vibrating up through the soil below him, but the giant herself was nowhere in sight.

"The scroll," Jack groaned. His cold fingers grasped at the air between him and Iliona.

"Never mind that," Iliona said. She hovered over Jack's supine form, directly over his upturned face but well out of arm's reach. "Rosheen won't be going any closer to Mistmeadow. She's got her hands full with those other faeries and the goat. By the time she sorts all that out, we'll be long gone and she'll be ready to rampage in a different direction. With a little encouragement from us, of course."

"Keely," he said.

"There you go again. Who is this person? What is she to you, anyway?"

Jack let his leaden arm fall across his chest. "Everything."

Iliona rolled her eyes. "If you say so. I'm going to put you to sleep now, Hero of Mistmeadow. You'll wake up well clear of here, right outside your home village. You may dream of Keely, if you wish." Iliona smiled cruelly. "Though it'll do you more good to dream about what you're going to do next. You barely have a home to save any more. Oh, and I have a message for you from Brigid . . . remember her?"

Jack didn't reply, but Iliona went on. "She says Mistmeadow needs a hero." The faerie floated down and stood lightly on the tip of Jack's nose. Iliona crossed her arms and said, "I say it needs a hero who knows how to keep himself alive better than this. Veesa and I won't be here for you all the time, you know. Do you think you can manage on your own from now on?"

Jack closed his eyes. He tried to answer Iliona, but all that came out was a slow, ragged wheeze.

"I'll take that as a yes," the faerie said.

* * * * *

Jack woke with the smell of Mistmeadow in his nostrils. He opened his eyes and confirmed that he was in fact right outside the doun. He still had his wingbow, so he knew the past day or so had actually happened . . . but he did not have the scroll.

Stiffly, Jack got to his feet. His entire body was sore and

his head ached mightily. He had failed in his quest, but all the same he was oddly exhilarated. He followed the trail through the fogbound woods until the gates of the doun stood before him.

The gates were open wide. Jack saw a crowd of his fellow villagers milling around in the square. Most wore hiking packs stuffed fat with gear. There was a long line of carts all laden with wares and ready to move out.

"Jack?" Keely's voice was even sweeter than Jack remembered. "You're alive!"

He turned as the kithkin maid rushed toward him from inside the gates. Keely ran into his open arms, and her embrace sent him staggering back a few steps.

"You did it," she said, squeezing him hard. "All by your-self. Rosheen is already moving on."

"I didn't do anything," Jack whispered. "Except nearly get killed."

"Well, Rosheen changed course. Whatever you did, it worked. You saved the doun."

"Maybe." Jack pulled back and looked deep into Keely's eyes. "But if I did, what's happening here?" he said. He jerked his chin toward the line of kithkin who were clearly preparing to leave. "Where's everybody going?"

"Many have already agreed to take Alloway's offer," Keely said. "They're going to Kinscaer. They say Alloway can protect them better than Molla." She glowered, dark anger flooding her features, but to Jack she was no less beautiful. "Almost a quarter of the village started getting ready to leave right after you did. A lot more are in the square now, getting ready to follow."

"But Rosheen changed course,"

"That she almost came here at all convinced some that Mistmeadow wasn't safe anymore—that it never was."

Jack made a show of glancing at the ground around them. "I don't see your bags packed."

"I'm not going anywhere," Keely said angrily. "Molla isn't just my mother, she's the best cenn a doun could ever have. Alloway is a viper and I don't trust him."

"Nor do I. And I bet Molla is staying, too?" Keely nodded. "Good. That makes three of us, then."

Keely's eyes sparkled. "Three?"

"You, Molla, and me," Jack said. "As long as there's a doun, it'll need a cenn." He remembered Brigid's words, passed to him by Iliona. "And a hero."

"It's Jack," someone yelled. "Jack's come home!"

Excitement rippled through the mindweft and Jack allowed himself to bask in its familiar tingle for a moment. Soon everyone would know that the Hero of Mistmeadow had returned. And if the first honest reactions from the collective were widely held, they also knew he hadn't done what he set out to do. And they didn't care. It didn't matter how inadvertently he had saved them, it didn't matter that he'd needed saving himself—only that they were all saved.

"You see?" Keely shouted. "Who needs Donal Alloway when we have a hero of our own? Huzzah for Jack Chierdagh! Huzzah for Molla Welk!" She raised her voice even louder and many of the assembled villagers stopped what they were doing to join her. "Huzzah for Mistmeadow!"

With one arm linked in Keely's and the other bearing the wingbow high over his head, Jack moved through the gates. Cries of "Mistmeadow! Mistmeadow!" echoed across the square and the mindweft alike.

Jack held back, keeping his more somber thoughts to himself. The world around them was a terrible, dangerous place, and their home was constantly beset by the direst of threats.

But Mistmeadow had both a cenn and a hero once more. And it was a hero who knew how to keep himself alive . . . or at least, one that was better at keeping himself alive than he had been. Not all threats were external, he thought, picturing Donal Alloway. Threats and salvation are often both not what they seem.

The adulation of his fellow villagers drew Jack in, lifted him up, and carried him along. He let his private worries evaporate in the warmth of Keely's smile. For the first time since he'd left Mistmeadow Jack felt the mindweft. The doun was still afraid, but now there was more hope than fear as his friends, family, and neighbors abandoned their parcels and carts in order to rush out and welcome their hero home.

KEN TROOP

Wander's Journey

Once upon a time, there was a young kithkin named Wander. One evening Wander looked around his doun and saw the same fields of sharp nettlewheat, the same herds of springjacks, and the same kithkin scything the nettlewheat and tending to the springjacks he had seen a hundred times before. That night, Wander resolved to see something new.

Before twilight the next day, without breathing a word of it to anyone, Wander took his pack, his sword, and a few tricks every kithkin should have, and set off on his journey. He saw many wonderful things that day. He saw a perfect circle of smooth, rainbow-colored rocks that stank of the Fae, which he avoided; a waterfall where the water fell toward the sky instead of the ground; and a small procession of traveling elves, beautiful with their fine horns and garments, who paid him no notice as they passed by, thanks to a touch of see-me-not powder.

At the end of the day, as he sat in his camp near the edge of the forest munching on the biscuits he packed for dinner, he reflected on all he had seen. Though he didn't know where he was going or where he'd end up, the day had been absent of nettlewheat, springjacks, scythes, and kithkin. And that made the day worthwhile. With a smile of contentment on his face, he had just resolved to sleep when a twinkling light from the forest caught his eye.

Knowing he could scarcely sleep without knowing if the light was a threat, he crouched low and slowly approached it. The moon was high and full overhead, and it shone strongly enough to aid him in avoiding the thick, gnarled roots that threatened to trip him. The twinkling light continued to blink in the distance, and Wander noticed what a pretty light it was, changing color from purple to blue to red to gold, always blinking and changing, always just a little bit farther away.

Then the light blinked out and did not return. Startled, Wander looked around and realized he had no idea how long he had pursued the light. Further, and more troubling, he was deep in the forest and had no idea of how to get back to his camp. He was a kithkin, full of tricks both innate and manufactured, but those were tricks for the grasses and douns, not for the middle of some deep, dark, forest he had never before seen. Just before despair set in, a few new lights twinkled around his head.

"Hi there, big-eyes!"

"Greetings!"

"Welcome!"

Three tiny voices flitted by, calling in his ear. The bodies the voices belonged to were also tiny, their forms almost impossible to discern in the shadow of their gossamer wings. Wander had heard of the Fae, but had never met a faerie until now.

"Hello," he started, hesitantly. "I am Wander."

"Merry!"

"Berry!"

"Cherry!"

The three faeries looked at each other and giggled. "Nice to meet you, Wander!" they said in unison.

"Are you lost?"

"Hungry?"

"Tired?"

Wander just nodded. The cenn of his doun had always warned him to not trust the faeries, but they seemed welcoming enough, and Wander needed whatever help he could get.

"Then follow Berry!"

"Then follow Che—I mean Berry!"

"Yes, follow!"

And then, again, in unison, "We know how to get you out of this forest!" They flitted off, and Wander hurried after them.

He followed the faeries for a long time—what seemed like hours, though the moon was still high in the sky. He would have worried that they were lost, but the forest did seem to be getting less dense around him. There were fewer trees, and the ground was getting much softer, even damp in places. The three faeries never wavered, engaging in continual conversation with him, though they had trouble keeping their names straight. Odd creatures, these faeries. They kept giggling throughout the entire journey.

At last they emerged from the forest into something much bleaker—a marsh. A few blackened, dead trees defiantly poked their spiky wood fingers into the air, and the smell of moss and decay was everywhere. This place was far worse than the forest they had come from—something Wander had not thought possible. He turned to the faeries and noticed they had not stopped to look around as he had, but rather had gone on ahead.

He started running after them, "Merry! Cherry! Wait!"

Their tiny voices carried easily in the crisp night air.

"Oh no!"

"Can't stay!"

"Time to leave!"

"This place is much too dangerous to stay, Wander."

"Glad we could get you out of the forest!" Their giggles faded to silence as they easily outdistanced Wander.

Now Wander was truly lost. Still, he was a kithkin. He had gotten himself into this situation, and he would get himself out of it. He looked in his pack for a biscuit to take the edge off his hunger, but all that was left in his pack were a few crumbs. He did not see how the faeries could have taken all his food, or why, but he also was sure he remembered packing plenty of food and drink. He still had some see-me-not powder, and a few other odds and ends, but that was hardly of use to a hungry kithkin in a swamp. Wander set his priorities. First, he had to get out of the swamp. Then, he had to find some food.

Wander wandered until the moon had set and risen twice, and still he found himself stuck in the swamp. The see-me-not powder was gone—spent in avoiding all manner of strange creatures who seemed to bear him ill will. He was ravenous and thirsty but there was no food or water to be found.

Then the twinkling light he first followed into the forest appeared right in front of Wander's eyes. Desperate, he followed the bobbing light until it finally hovered over some pale green mushrooms nestled in the base of a dead tree. Then the light disappeared again. Wander was so hungry that when he saw the mushrooms, he grabbed them, uprooted them, and gobbled them up without a second thought.

Feeling hopeful and energetic for the first time since his nightmare began, he went trundling off, certain he would find the way out. Then wave after wave of stomach cramps hit him, and he collapsed into the mud. Chills and cramps racked his body, and spikes of intense pain kept him doubled over, twitching, on the ground.

Before the moon set again, he was still. When the moon started to rise again, the worms of the swamp had burrowed into Wander's skull and devoured first his glazed, luminous eyes, then his flesh. Eventually, Wander's body was reduced to bones, and those bones sank into the mud, never to be seen again.

Might's Journey

Wander had a brother, Might. Might was a famous kithkin, renowned for his strength and prowess in combat. It was Might who fought off the cinder invasion almost single-handedly, and it was Might who won the bolo-tossing contest year after year.

When Might heard that Wander was missing, he immediately set off in search of him. Wander often went on little trips and journeys, but before, he had always come back by the end of the day. This time he had been missing for almost a week. Might had no idea what direction or destination Wander had in mind, but he was resolved to find Wander and bring him back home safe and sound.

When Might neared the end of the plains, he saw a rocky crag poking up over the horizon. It was exactly the kind of thing Wander would have explored. It was certainly the first such landmark Might had seen. How could Wander not be drawn to it?

As he drew near the crag, it became clear that what he had assumed was just a big rock was actually a large number of smaller rocks—large being relative, as each one was still half again as big as Might himself. But climbing the rocks posed no problem for one of Might's strength, and he bounded up the crag, calling Wander's name and hoping they could both be home before nightfall.

As he leaped to the top of the crag, he heard movement behind him and turned. The expectant smile on his lips died as there approached six of the ugliest creatures he had ever seen. Much bigger than a kithkin, with misshapen, animalistic faces, and each one having a different set of protruding horns. Boggarts. He had heard of boggarts, but never seen one. What few stories he knew about them suggested that the only thing their feral race understood was violence. Well, that was a subject Might understood as well.

They growled at him menacingly and slowly approached him. They had no weapons as far as he could see, so he put down his sword and balled up his fists.

"Who's your leader, then!" he snarled at them. The boggarts stopped and looked at each other. They seemed hesitant. Then one of them, the biggest and ugliest of the bunch, stepped forward and rushed Might.

Now here was a fight! After a day of anxiety about Wander and about being separated from the rest of the kithkin, a good knockdown brawl was just what he needed. Might didn't even bother tripping the boggart leader as he rushed into him, desiring the exchange of body blows as a good warm-up. The boggart was strong and ferocious, but Might was stronger, and had received many a better blow from an uppity springjack in his time. Soon the boggart was bleeding heavily, and Might had broken off one of boggart's horns in his hand. A few more blows to the boggart's stomach, and the boggart reeled away. Seizing the opportunity, Might came in close and thrust the broken-off horn through the boggart's stomach and all the way out his back. The boggart fell over and lay still, bleeding on the ground.

"All right, then. That was your leader—the biggest and the toughest of you. Now he's dead and I'm barely scratched! Unless you lot want more of the same, you'll take me to my brother." Once more, the boggarts looked at each other and made no movement. While Might was busy cowing the five boggarts in front of him, he failed to notice the large number of boggarts who had crept up behind him until he heard one of them grunt.

Might turned just in time to see the rock that caved in his skull. Might's body collapsed to the ground, motionless. The boggarts were now in more familiar territory. They scrambled up the crag, fighting amongst each other to get the choicest bits of meat from the two bodies in front of them. During their fight, more boggart bodies were added to the feast, and the few victors left enjoyed a meal they would never forget.

Kind's Journey

The third brother of Wander and Might was named Kind. Kind was the doun's healer, and he was renowned amongst the kithkin for his powerful magic and tinctures. He could heal a kithkin near death, and mend both warrior and springjack. During his time as the doun's healer, no kithkin or beast had been lost to an untimely death.

When Kind heard that both Wander and Might were missing, he set out in search. He packed a large bag full of his most potent potions and dusts, not wanting to miss anything that might be of use to his two missing brothers. Kind traveled until the moon set and he came to a small rivulet in the nettlewheat field. The rivulet opened up into a stream, the stream opened up into a small river that divided the plains from the forest.

Kind knew that the river might have drawn Wander's attention, so he resolved to follow the river and see where it led. Kind was aware of the dangers outside the fields, and so he stayed in the plains rather than crossing over into the forest, while he traveled.

He had only gone a short distance when he came across a strange body on top of a rocky outcrop in the river. He looked around and, seeing no one else around, he stopped and took one of the powders from his bag. He blew a little of the powder in the direction of the body, but there was no shimmer in the air. No fakery here. The being was still alive, but not for much longer.

Kind jumped over the span of water between him and the rock and examined the body. It had a fishlike face, with a humanoid torso and arms, and a large blue fish-tail. A merrow. Kind had never seen the fish-people in person—only in a few illustrations he had of the world's various fauna and how to treat them. The merrow had a deep, gaping wound on its side, from which blue, viscous blood would pulse out, each beat slower than the last. The cut was clean and long, an elf's blade perhaps.

The merrow lifted his head and looked at Kind. It made a piteous but barely discernible cry, then its head fell back to the ground. Kind looked through his bag and brought out two potions, one powder, and a small sewing kit. He lifted up the merrow's head and poured one of the potions down its throat. The merrow started to thrash but almost immediately calmed down and became still. The other potion he poured directly into the merrow's wound, and his bleeding stopped. He took a needle and thread from his sewing kit and went to work.

Some time later, he mixed the powder with what was left of one of the potions, and spread the mixture into the now tightly sewn up wound. The merrow would live. Kind was busy preparing a new mixture for the pain when the merrow lifted its head again. It made the same piteous sound as before, followed by a long, slow hiss. The merrow looked afraid and in agony. Kind finished his mixture and leaned close to apply the pain unguent. He reflexively whispered the words he would whisper to any kithkin, "It's all right, it's all right, it's all right, it's all right . . ." when suddenly he found he couldn't talk anymore.

He looked down to see a glistening red dagger in the merrow's hand and blood, *so much blood*, pouring from somewhere, down to the ground below. Only as Kind collapsed to the ground did he realize his throat had been sliced. The last thing he saw was the merrow opening up his bag and rummaging through it, and then his vision and cares both ceased.

Kind didn't see the merrow discover all the treasures in his bag, nor did he see the excitement and avarice in the merrow's eye as it sought to bring all the treasures back to its lair. Unfortunately for the merrow, its undue exertion tore open Kind's meticulous stitches and soon the merrow bled out to death a little ways down the river. Were Kind alive, he would have been greatly saddened by the death of his patient.

Clever's Journey

The fourth brother of this family was named Clever. The smartest of all the kithkin in the doun, Clever planned the battle strategies when the cinders invaded, Clever planned the new buildings, and Clever planned the layout of the doun. With Clever's leadership, the doun prospered and grew as it never had before.

When Clever heard that three of his brothers had gone missing, each one going off alone after the other, he looked for his last brother to help him go in search of the two missing siblings, for no kithkin had any business going outside of the doun alone. But his other brother was busy defending the doun from the cinder who had grown bold in Might's absence, and Clever knew he had to find his brothers by himself.

Clever pondered the situation and came to a few conclusions. Wander had probably gotten bored and decided to go off exploring. When Might saw that his brother was missing, he probably went off in search for him without thinking about the futility of the search—acting without thinking was one of Might's specialties. Once Might and Wander were both missing, Kind set off after them knowing the futility but feeling such pain at the thought of his brothers being hurt that his empathy overwhelmed his common sense.

Clever thought his conclusions were likely accurate, but that still did not help him discover the fates of his three missing brothers. And should the worst have befallen them, Clever did not want to share that fate. His brother might be able to figure it out, but taking him away from his battle with the cinders would be disastrous. Clever had to figure it out himself.

Clever had heard of an elf sage who lived deep in the nearby forest. If a quarter of the rumors were true—and Clever had once calculated that, on average, a quarter of rumors are more or less true—then the elf sage could discover the current whereabouts of his brothers, whether they were at land, river, or grave.

Clever read the one treatise he could find about the elf

sage and the location of his abode. Then he wrote a long note to the fifth brother, detailing all his thoughts and conclusions about the other three, pinned it to his brother's door, and set off on his journey. After about half a day of traveling, he came to the forest's edge. The forest looked vast, dense, and forbidding—though Clever told himself that was because he had only ever known the plains. The forest would seem a comfortable home should he have been raised in it. It was all a matter of perspective.

He stood there for a few moments, allowed himself a small shudder, then entered the forest. As he walked, Clever dropped small grains of dust—dust invisible to any eyes but those of a kithkin—so as to mark his path home. He had to stop many times to avoid the denizens of the forest, but he slowly made headway toward the sage's abode. Until he came to the ravine.

In front of him spanned a large gap of empty air. A lone bridge, flanked by two withered trees, was the sole means of travel across the ravine. The bridge seemed sturdy enough, however, made with good wood, rope, and fine craftsmanship. Clever believed the sage to be not far beyond, but as he approached the bridge, one of the trees moved.

It was decaying, its wooden limbs besot with mold and cankers, but alive, and the length of stick it carried in one hand was more than enough to bring Clever's calculations to an untimely end. Clever had never seen a treefolk before, only read about them, but facing this one, he felt reading about them was the appropriate way to get to know them. Clever still had a few tricks on him though, and so he waited.

The treefolk gave Clever a sickly smile. "I am the guardian of the bridge. If you wish to pass, you must defeat me."

"Defeat you? But I am small and harmless. I am merely searching for knowledge of my lost brothers. Surely you have no need to defeat me."

"Nonetheless, little one, if you wish to cross this bridge, then you must deal with me."

"And must it be combat? What type of sport would that make for such a powerful and mighty creature as yourself? Surely there must be some other form of challenge we can engage in?"

"So you wish to match wits with me, little fleshling?" And here the treefolk laughed. "I've seen the merrows in their shoals and the boggarts in their caves. I've seen a dragon in the sky and the queen in her glen. I've seen more moonrises than you've seen blades of grass. Your entire life is but an eye-blink to me, and you will have been dead for time unimaginable before I take my last breath. Yes, let us match wits."

"A riddling, then?"

"Yes, that sounds fine."

"And if I win, I get to pass, unharmed by you and yours?"

"You win? That will not happen, bloodsack. But yes, if you win, you can pass by, unharmed by me and mine. And if I win. . . ." The smile on the treefolk's face grew wider.

Clever reached into his bag and drew out a small stone. "You'll swear it on this truthstone, then?" The treefolk hissed and drew back a step, and for a moment Clever thought it would come to fighting afterall. But the treefolk just stood there, all amusement gone.

"Yes, fleshling, yes. I swear it on your precious rock! If you win the riddling, you will receive no harm from me or mine. I swear! Get it out of my sight, now!"

Clever looked at the truthstone, and it glowed a strong

blue. Satisfied, he put the stone back into his pocket. "You may go first, O Wise Elder." No one, not even Clever, knew who created the rules of the riddling, but almost everyone knew the rules. Riddle posed, riddle answered. The first missed riddle determined the loser. Clever pulled out two small vials of fine sand, each riddler had his own timer. If a riddler ran out of time, he lost.

Many neophyte riddlers started with their toughest riddle in order to gain an easy victory. But for experienced riddlers who played the game often, the better strategy was to start with a number of easy riddles in order to waste some of their opponent's time and perhaps lull them into a false sense of superiority. But you could only succeed if you knew you could answer their riddles quickly. Whether the tree's first riddle was easy or hard would tell Clever much about the shape of the conflict to come.

"No bigger than an acorn nut, yet its close covers the whole world."

Clever smiled. "An eyeball."

Clever's turn. "I burble. I meander. Always wet, never dry. What insignificant offshoot am I?"

The treefolk sneered. "A baby."

And so it went. Despite his anxiety over the fate of his brothers and his doun, Clever felt a savage joy—a true riddling, and with the stakes so high! Clever and the treefolk went back and forth with their riddles. The treefolk was quite good. He posed more than a few that Clever had never heard before. But Clever was able to live up to his name and found the right answer each time, though Clever had precious little sand left in his timer. Now was the time for his hardest riddle.

"I'm stronger than any foe, yet I have never won. I always promise and always betray. I am here tomorrow and gone today. To live without me is cruel, and with me crueler still. What am I?"

The treefolk's smile and banter disappeared. While he had more sand left than Clever, it was not by much. As each grain of sand fell to the earth, the treefolk grew angrier. The final bit of sand in the treefolk's timer passed through, and still he had no answer.

"What was it, bloodsack? You must have a real answer or else your life is mine! What was the answer?"

"Hope," said Clever.

The treefolk screeched and collapsed to the ground, though whether because he had lost to Clever or some other reason, Clever never knew. Either way, the treefolk had been beaten, and Clever could cross safely. Clever knew the riddling had taken a lot of time, and he hurried across to find the elf sage as quickly as he could, but first he fell.

Clever's last thought was, "Ahh, the bridge was an illusion," before his body, obeying laws greater than Clever's desperate wishes, met forcefully with the hard ground deep below. Eventually the night gaunts gathered to eat the remains, with the ravens enjoying what few scraps were left after that.

And the treefolk guardian, who should have enjoyed this trick, found no pleasure in much of anything for awhile as he went back to guarding the bridge. He never did a riddling again for the rest of his life.

Hero's Revenge

The fifth and last brother of the family was named Hero. Hero was the most famous kithkin not just in his doun but in all the douns of the land. He was stronger than Might, a better wizard than Kind, and smarter than Clever. He was the close confidant and principal agent of the cenn of their family's doun, and the cenn often sent him on missions and tasks to keep the doun safe that could only be handled by Hero. Recently, Hero had been busy fighting off an aggressive cinder invasion, a task usually handled by Might, but with Might nowhere to be found, it had fallen to Hero. He wiped out the invading force using a combination of magic and martial prowess.

Afterward, Hero came back to his cottage to discover the note Clever had left for him. It was dated a few days ago, and Hero immediately set about discovering the whereabouts of his brothers. He descended to his workshop and prepared a mighty divination spell, using the better part of the day.

When he finished the spell, and saw the visions of his brothers' fates, Hero sat in his workshop and cried. He had been close to all of his brothers, even Wander, who typically did the least work and got into the most trouble. He grieved not only for his personal loss, but also for the doun's loss. All the brothers had worked together to making the doun safe and prosperous in what were, back then as now, dangerous and difficult times. Losing four of those brothers, even if the one left was the most powerful, was a grievous blow to the doun.

Hero knew the right course of action was to mourn his brothers and then go back to caring for and protecting the doun. But the grief was so strong in his heart that he could only think of avenging his brothers. Yes, the merrow and most of the boggarts were already dead, but he could still find the treefolk, the faeries, and the few remaining boggarts, and wreak his vengeance. Besides, he had just destroyed most of the cinder army, and it would take them a long time to regroup. If any time was appropriate to handle this matter, it was now.

In the dead of night, Hero set off for the forest. He knew, both from his own missions and his divination spell, exactly where the treefolk dwelled. As he walked, he would occasionally see kithkin grains on the ground, and he would sadly remember Clever's trick of finding his way home. But the time for grief was past. It was time for revenge.

As he approached the bridge, the treefolk lumbered to life, a grimace on his face as he said, "I am the guardian of the bridge. If you wish to pass, you must defeat me." Hero said nothing but started running at the treefolk, drawing a rune inscribed dagger. The treefolk swung his club at Hero, but Hero easily dodged and leaped up the back of the treefolk, climbing up and stabbing his dagger through bark and wood in the treefolk's back. The treefolk screamed in agony and tried to shake the invader off, but found he could not move his limbs or trunk.

Hero climbed up to the back of the treefolk's head, and whispered in his ear, "You are already dead. There is no outcome from here that ends with you alive. The only uncertainty in your future is how drawn out and painful a death yours will be. It could be very long. Very painful. You have lived a long time, yes? Yes, I think you have. You know how painful this can be, then."

"What . . . who are you?" The treefolk had not felt this kind of agony or fear in a very, very long time.

"The bridge. Who created the illusion of the bridge? Who set you as guardian? Answer me truthfully, and your death will be as quick as a breath, and as painless. Lie or fail to answer and there will not be a single being in this land, no matter how horrible his lot, who would wish to trade places with you."

The treefolk shuddered. "The faeries! The illusion is from the faeries. They created the bridge, and they installed me as its guardian. It was a spell, it was not my doing. It was . . ."

Hero recognized the truth of his words, and true to his word he twisted the dagger once, spoke a word of power, and the treefolk, with a sense of relief that had eluded him since he'd riddled with Clever, died.

Next it was time to punish the faeries of the forest. Hero spent a while looking for the right flowers, and then spent time amongst the flowers with some ingredients he had brought. The moon rose high in the sky before a small group of faeries entered the glen Hero had prepared and saw the beautiful flowers—a bright purple variety that had never before been seen in these parts. All of the faeries in the glen clustered around to see the exotic flowers and inhale their delicate aroma.

A short time later, Hero checked in on the glen to make sure that there had been no survivors. Tiny little faerie bodies littered the glen. Hero smiled and left.

His next destination was the hills far from his doun, to see if any of the offending boggarts still lived. He was striding through the familiar grasses of his doun's meadows when his focus on revenge made him unaware of the increasing deep *thooms* and tremors until a gigantic foot flattened him into the ground.

Having all of his bones, muscles, and blood occupy the same horizontal plane in the space of half a second was a fatal outcome, even for a kithkin of Hero's powers. The giant who had trod upon Hero had, in truth, not seen nor felt the kithkin either before or after the accident. Doomstomper was his name, and he was sleepwalking, and could be sleepwalking still, dreaming the same mad dream, even unto this day.

As for Hero, there was almost nothing left of him save some bright reddish goo on the plains, and after the blood seeped into the ground, there was nothing left at all.

With all five of the doun's most powerful and feared guardians gone, the cinders eventually did regroup and attack the doun. This time they were able to scour the doun clean, killing all of the doun's kithkin and burning the doun down to the ground, leaving nothing behind but ash. To this day the doun goes nameless, and it, and the kithkin who lived there, only live on in stories like this one.

* * * * *

Now, little kithkin, why have I shared this sad story with you? If you learn nothing else, learn this—if, for any reason, you must leave the doun, never leave the doun by yourself. For no matter how strong or brave or clever you might be, the land out there is ever your match and more, and only through our numbers can we survive.

Better still is never leaving the doun at all. Unless, that is, you're willing to see all that you've ever loved and cherished wiped from life by the malicious outsiders who constantly seek our deaths.

Good night, children, sleep well.

DENISE R. GRAHAM

They were coming.

Ascaeus strained to see into the gray-blue mists swirling before him. There. Movement. Was it them? No, only the fog coiling around an errant breeze. Listening was no use. The muffled scratchings, flutterings, and creaks of the forest to his left revealed nothing, and the hills to his right kept silent. He reached out with his mind, trying to sense their approach, but the chill twilight clung to its secrets.

Still, Ascaeus knew they would come. How could any cinder who received his or her summons resist the call? Beneath the despair his kind wore like a shroud there remained a faint glimmer of hope—a desperate, fading dream of a time when their curse of the Extinguishing might be lifted, when they might be purified in the ultimate Fire.

How long had he and the other sootstokes searched this wretched world for clues to the Rekindling? How much ridicule and even loathing had they endured from their own kind for clinging to their belief that some day they would rise from the ashes of their lives to emerge as children of fire?

Too long. But no longer.

Ascaeus laughed. It was a hoarse, rasping sound, like the hiss of the mists against the embers that formed his body. Most cinders had lost the inclination to laugh, perhaps even the ability. Ascaeus saw laughter as a vanishing art form, and also as a weapon in the ceaseless struggle against the living doom of his kind. He practiced laughing as a battle cry. He practiced it for the brazen optimism of it. But most of all, he practiced it so he wouldn't forget how. Concentrating on creating a brighter sound, he laughed again.

"Fool!" a voice sizzled from the fog.

Ascaeus spun toward it. Dark forms emerged from the mists, some casting a pale, flickering glow against the smothering clouds. As they drew closer, Ascaeus recognized his fellow sootstokes, Irassu and Galleris, leading a handful of cinders from the settlement in the nearby swamp.

"Do you want to bring all the treefolk and boggarts in this forsaken place down upon us?" the voice continued. The voice belonged to a smoking cinder who shed ash from his brittle form with every step.

The cinders glanced around nervously at the mention of treefolk. A gathering of cinders so close to the woodlands would surely be perceived as aggression and draw immediate attack.

A tense moment passed before Irassu waved a spindly limb at the one who had spoken. "This is Caldera. And these are Saria, Javonis, Heladus, and Rissian."

Ascaeus eyed the meager band. He'd told Galleris and Irassu to bring all the cinders they could find between here and the settlement. Either the cinders in this corner of the world had further diminished, or they were too frail to make the short trip, or they had abandoned hope and refused to come. Sad scenarios all. He tried to keep his tone light. "Thank you all for coming," he said. "I would have come to you, but my mission is urgent, as I'm sure Irassu and Galleris have told you."

"They said you have new information that could help us," replied the one called Heladus, patches of flame flitting over her jagged, blackened limbs.

"Not just help us," said Ascaeus. "Save us. I believe I have discovered the key to the Rekindling."

Astonished gasps and hisses went up from the cinders. "What is it?" rasped Javonis. "Tell us!"

"On my travels I overheard some elves. They spoke of a river of burning stone deep within a maze of caves not far from this very spot."

The cinders exchanged glances. "You mean the Serpent's Maw?" said Caldera.

Ascaeus hesitated, confused. "You've heard of it?"

"Of course!" Caldera snapped. "A foul place, full of drafts and water. Even merrows. No one goes there."

"But the elves said—"

"Elves!" said Saria. "What would they know of dangers to our kind?"

"I heard the place is haunted by sluagh that steal the souls of any who venture there," said Rissian. "And if the sluagh don't get you, something else will."

"But the river of burning stone," said Ascaeus, "if we can find it, it will save us all."

"There's no way to know that without going," said Heladus.

"But we do know the way is too dangerous," Rissian added.

Caldera shook his head, and more ash fell around him. "We should have known it was another false alarm."

"The Fire Crystal wasn't a false alarm," said Ascaeus. "All the tales surrounding those plains told of it. It must have been taken."

"You've wasted our time," said Javonis. To the others he added, "Let's go." The cinders looked at one another. As one, they turned and started walking.

"Wait!" Ascaeus called after them. "If we all go together,

we have a better chance of finding it!"

Saria glanced over her shoulder. "Your fool's quest would sooner kill us than save us. Better to resign yourself to the path of sorrow like the rest of us, sootstoke."

With that, the cinders disappeared into the fog.

In silence the sootstokes watched the shifting mists, as if expecting the cinders to reappear. They did not.

"Well," Ascaeus said at last, "I guess that leaves it to us three then."

Galleris gave a start, but said nothing. His gaze darted everywhere except toward Ascaeus.

Irassu shuffled his feet. "I'll go with you as far as the mouth of the cave." His voice was thin as smoke. "If the place is half as dangerous as everyone believes, we can't all go down there. If you don't make it back, someone has to continue our search. And warn others not to attempt the caves again."

"But that's why I need your help," said Ascaeus. "I have no doubt dangers await, but with three of us—"

"With three of us, we'll draw more attention and attract danger to us. Besides, we don't all have your reckless enthusiasm. I'll wait at the cave's entrance as long as I can. If you make it out alive, whether you find what you're searching for or not, I'll help you get word to the others."

"What about you?" Ascaeus asked Galleris.

Sparks skittered across his limbs. "Don't look at me! I wasn't even planning to go as far as the cave."

"But you will," said Irassu. It wasn't a question.

Galleris sighed. "Yes. All right. But only to the mouth of the cave."

After an awkward silence, Ascaeus coughed. "I guess we should be on our way then."

Irassu and Galleris followed Ascaeus, skirting the woods

and the hills. The heavy fog made progress slow. The three companions had to pick their way over jagged boulders and fallen trees, a blasted land claimed by none and safe for no one.

Now that Ascaeus knew reaching the river of burning stone fell solely on his shoulders, he was even more eager to be on his way. The sooner he began, the sooner this undertaking would end. And when it did, he would deliver the key to the Rekindling to his kind. The end of his journey would mark the end of the path of sorrow and the beginning of a new world for the cinders.

"Slow down, Ascaeus," Irassu rasped. "You'll run us headlong into a boggart gang at this pace."

Without meaning to, Ascaeus had been moving faster and faster. Too fast through these dangerous lands in this blinding fog.

"Sorry," he said. "I just keep thinking how glorious it will be."

"It will never happen if you get yourself killed. You need to keep your wits about you. Focus on staying alive to succeed."

Ascaeus didn't reply. Irassu was old, very old by cinder reckoning. Though he was a sootstoke, his outlook often resembled the fatalistic bent of most of their kind.

"Maybe the others are right," said Galleris. "Maybe those caves are too dangerous. There are so many other places to search, safer places. Maybe you shouldn't go down there."

"Stop," said Irassu.

"I was only trying to—"

"Stop!"

Ascaeus turned at the sharpness in Irassu's voice. He never spoke in such a tone, especially not to the easily rattled Galleris.

Irassu had halted in his tracks. He held up a hand to quiet the others and paced in a small circle, staring hard into the mists. Then his stance relaxed. "Thought I heard something."

His companions peered into the fog, listening.

"I don't hear anything," said Galleris.

Irassu nodded, and Ascaeus started to move on. "Wait," said Irassu.

Galleris crouched slightly, ready to defend or run. "I think I heard something that time, too."

"No," said Irassu. "I didn't hear anything this time. But now it's too quiet."

Ascaeus strained his ears. No faint rustlings. No scraping of tree limbs in the breeze. As if the world itself had paused to listen. The mists muffled sounds, but they didn't silence them entirely. Perhaps this was no ordinary fog.

And yet it seemed to be lifting a bit. The change had been gradual, and so Ascaeus hadn't noticed. But now he could see glimpses of the crags and ridges rising to their left, and dark flashes of the bent and barren trees off to their right.

A dull rattling came from somewhere within the woods, though Ascaeus couldn't tell exactly what direction the sound came from. He glanced at the others, and their stiff postures told him they'd heard it too. But it had stopped, and it didn't come again. It was probably just the clacking of dead branches in the breeze.

A few tense moments passed. Then the three companions continued on their way, though slowly now and without speaking.

Then a new sound drifted through the mists. At first Ascaeus thought it had the ring of water trickling over stones, but soon he realized it was a voice. Someone was out there.

Ascaeus stopped and held up a hand, but Galleris and Irassu had already stopped. They'd heard it too. Soft, sharp muttering filtered through the fog, too muffled for Ascaeus to make out any words. He strained to hear other voices, trying to figure out how many creatures prowled in the gloom, but he could only make out the one.

He glanced at Irassu, who shook his head, then at Galleris, who shrugged. With small, cautious steps, Ascaeus continued forward, the voice growing louder and more distinct with each step.

Ascaeus paused then motioned toward the hills. The others nodded. Better to avoid a confrontation if possible. As one, they sidestepped up the uneven ground.

A stone broke loose under Galleris's foot with a soft *snap*.

"What?" said the voice, clear now and much too close. "Someone is trying to sneak up on Aerawn? Who is it?"

Galleris went into a crouch again. This time it was clear he intended to bolt. Ascaeus grabbed his arm, a twinge of jealousy rising as the heat from his friend's limb warmed his hand. Tiny flames danced around his grasp.

Irassu ventured farther into the hills, and Ascaeus pulled Galleris after him.

"They cannot hide from Aerawn," said the voice. Though it was strong, it had a sighing, almost moaning quality to it. "We will sniff them out."

More noises followed—creaking, rattling, and scraping. The three travelers crept deeper into the hills, their gazes locked in the direction of the voice. A dark form lurched from the mists, looming over the sootstokes, its gnarled limbs jutting from a trunk that seemed misshapen beyond all possibility of life. Yet alive it was. And coming for them.

The cinders stood as if frozen.

The treefolk took a few more steps then paused. He was a black poplar, even more twisted than most of his kind. The smell of rotting vegetation rolled from him in waves. Sprawling black patches on his bark marked the progress of the Canker, and fungi clung among his moldering roots. Though the cinders stood right in his path, he turned from side to side, millipedes scuttling across his eyes.

Ascaeus raised a hand to cast a spell, but Irassu caught his shoulder. *He's blind.* The older sootstoke mouthed the words. He signaled for Ascaeus and Galleris to keep still.

The treefolk sniffed. His mumblings came in rapid fire, his jittering, twisted branches keeping time.

"Who comes this time? What do they want? Aerawn will find them. We will fix them like all the rest. No one hides from us." He sniffed again and shuffled toward the sootstokes.

Irassu bent to pick up a rock and tossed it into the woods.

Aerawn turned toward the sound, muttering again. "There they are! Have more kithkin come to feed the tree-folk with their little bodies? They think they come to hack and burn, but we teach them. We teach them." Raising his voice, he added, "Come, little kithkin! Aerawn will not harm you."

Irassu crept higher into the hills, one slow step at a time. Ascaeus and Galleris kept right behind him. They paused to look over their shoulders at the black poplar stalking toward the forest.

Aerawn sniffed as he went. His voice rose and fell as he talked first to his unseen enemies, then to himself. "We smell your tiny torches, naughty folk. We teach—what? Not torches? Not kithkin? Not here? What then? Something sneaky. Sneaky, sneaky somethings trying to trick Aerawn."

The sootstokes exchanged uneasy glances, but soon Ascaeus saw where his friend was headed. A boulder the size of two cinders hung over the edge of a low ridge.

"Sneaky somethings. Must be faeries! Always sneaking and pestering, flitting and spying, whispering and tricking." Aerawn turned, homing in on the sootstokes' scent. He began the awkward climb into the hills. It was hard to believe a creature so mangled could move so quickly. "Come out, tiny faeries! We will teach you a new game."

The trio of cinders reached the top of the ridge, but the boulder would do them no good if Aerawn kept to his current path. Ascaeus gestured for Irassu and Galleris to wait where they were. He headed down the hillside, angling away from the others and from Aerawn to draw the treefolk over that way. After a few steps, he started running, knowing the treefolk would hear him.

The black poplar paused, listening. "Sneaky Fae think they can fool Aerawn with the same trick twice. Stupid faeries!" He took another step up the hill then paused again. "What? No flutterings? No gigglings? Not the Fae! What then? What!" His branches rattled in frustration as he resumed his ascent toward the cinders.

Sparks sizzled across Galleris's body. Ascaeus feared his terrified friend would make a break for it and doom them all.

"No trick," called Ascaeus. "I will burn your woods, and you cannot stop me!"

The black poplar jumped, straightening as much as his diseased body would allow. "What! It threatens us!" Snarling, he took a few steps, angling down the hill toward Ascaeus.

Now he was where they wanted him. Irassu and Galleris pushed against the boulder.

Nothing happened. The jagged rock that looked so unstable wouldn't budge.

Aerawn paused again. "Wait. It wants us to chase it. That means. . . ." He turned back toward the other soot-stokes and sniffed the air. A hideous grin split his face. "Yes! More somethings. Closer somethings." Back up the hill he went.

Drawing on the magic of the swamp, Ascaeus focused a spell on one of Aerawn's roots. A black spot formed and spread. In an instant, the root withered and went limp.

Aerawn stumbled to a halt. "Cold!" he said, grasping at his decaying extremity. "And pain! What trick is this? Aerawn will crush the sneaky somethings."

While the treefolk was distracted, Irassu stretched a hand to the edge of the ridge just under the boulder. A section of solid rock the size of his fist blasted away.

Aerawn startled at the sound. "What now? A weapon? A trap?" Continuing toward them, the black poplar called, "Come out, little somethings!"

Again Irassu and Galleris put their backs against the boulder and pushed. This time it shifted. Not much, but enough. They rocked it back and forth a few times. Then the two sootstokes gave a final heave. The boulder toppled over and thudded downhill.

Galleris lost his balance and tumbled after it. He scrambled for purchase, but the cascade of rubble falling in the stone's wake carried him with it.

Aerawn bellowed as the boulder landed on his roots, lodged against his trunk, and stopped rolling, pinning the treefolk to the ground. "Evil somethings! We'll get you!" He lunged at the sootstokes, and his trapped roots tripped him. As he flailed, one of his branches struck Galleris and coiled itself around his leg.

Galleris screamed as the treefolk dragged him closer, twining his limbs around him. The guttering flames scattered over Galleris's body flared and leaped to the branches. They blackened and began to smoke.

Aerawn let out a roar of pain. He released Galleris and recoiled. "Cinders!" he snarled. "Sneaky cinders! We know what to do with cinders." He began fumbling at the boulder, painfully wriggling his roots out from under it.

Ascaeus ran to pull Galleris out of the treefolk's reach. Together they hurried back to Irassu's side, and Ascaeus let out a laugh. "We did it. Let's go!"

"Not me," said Galleris, keeping an eye on the treefolk while moving farther away. "I'm going back to the swamp."

Ascaeus glanced at the struggling Aerawn. "But—"

Irassu laid a hand on Ascaeus's shoulder. "Go on then," he said to Galleris. "Continue your own search."

Galleris hesitated. Then he nodded and hurried back the way he'd come.

"We will teach them regret," Aerawn muttered. He had nearly worked himself free.

Ascaeus and Irassu didn't waste another moment. They turned their backs on Galleris and ran. The mists had withdrawn to wisps and tendrils that laced the land like cobwebs, making their flight easier. The blasted hills fell away under their feet. When the two sootstokes could no longer hear the curses of the black poplar, they slowed to a walk.

"Why did you let Galleris go?" Ascaeus asked at last. "His flame is stronger than both of ours combined. We may not make it without him."

"His power might save us, but his cowardice would more likely get us killed," Irassu replied.

Denise R. Graham

Ascaeus considered his friend's words then nodded. The constant distraction of Galleris trying to bolt would put them in danger. And two travelers would draw fewer foes than three.

They walked on, stopping only for brief rests or at sounds that might signal danger. After they'd gone a few miles, the forest on their right gave way to the tall, dry grasses of the plains. The hills continued as far as the eye could see.

"There should be a dry streambed not far from here," Ascaeus said. "We'll follow it to a ravine. That's where we'll find the entrance to the caves. The elves gave clear directions for reaching the river of burning stone."

"The elves you overheard were generous with their information," the older cinder remarked. "Are you sure they didn't know you were listening? It could be a trap."

"No," said Ascaeus. "Two were reporting to a third after returning from the caves. There's something down there they feel should be hallowheld, but they had to return for help. They said they lost a companion and barely made it out alive."

Irassu grunted. "And this is where you want go?"

"Not just want to. Have to. I believe this will save our kind. We're making history here, Irassu. The cinders' path of sorrow will become a path of flame, and we get to make it happen." Ascaeus pointed. "You see? There's the streambed up ahead."

They followed the dry trail until it led to a ravine. A few times during the climb down the steep sides of the narrow ravine, rocks slipped away under the sootstokes' feet, forcing them to grab for handholds. But the gulch was not very deep, and soon they were able to walk along the floor to the mouth of the cave. Twin pillars of stone flanked the opening, tapering at the bottom to resemble fangs: the Serpent's Maw.

"Are you sure you don't want to come with me?" Ascaeus asked Irassu one last time. "I'm sure history will make room for one more hero."

"I'm too old for heroics," said Irassu. "Besides, someone has to stay on the surface to let the others know whether you succeed or fail."

Ascaeus nodded. "Well, I guess this is it then. Next time you see me, I'll have the key to saving our race."

"I hope you're right," said Irassu.

There were a lot of things Ascaeus wanted to say to that, but his journey called, so he simply said, "There's only one way to find out." With that, he ducked between the stony fangs. The temperature dropped immediately. Lacking even the meager light of the surface world, a deep and permanent chill suffused the cave. The walls were made of a dark, glassy stone broken into facets that reflected the faint glow of his own embers. He rounded a curve in the tunnel that cut off the last bit of light from the entrance. The air smelled thin and dank. The smooth floor sloped away, leaving room to walk upright. After a few more turns, the path widened, becoming less oppressive.

Ascaeus squared his shoulders and lengthened his stride. The sooner he got to the river of burning stone, the sooner he could leave this place of sinister tales and bring about the Rekindling of his kind. He knew the other cinders saw him as nothing but a delusional fool, even more so than the other sootstokes. They all thought he was reckless. Many believed he was truly mad. They scoffed at him, calling him "cheerful," even "enthusiastic." Because it had no place in their world, most of them no longer remembered the word that best described Ascaeus, optimistic. Whatever the others thought of him now, he would redeem them all—himself included. He would return a hero.

The way led ever downward, twisting and coiling back on itself like the serpent it was named for. When at last it opened into a large chamber, Ascaeus pulled up, surprised at the size of it. Dark pockets along the walls revealed several paths. The sootstoke took a deep breath.

The elves had said the river of burning stone was at the bottom of the caves, which could be found by always choosing the steepest path downward. All he had to do was check all the paths and figure out which one would take him farther from the surface.

He found a loose stone and with it scratched an arrow on the wall pointing back the way he'd come. Then he circled the chamber, checking each path as he went.

Something moved in the shadows overhead, and he froze. The warnings of the elves and the cinders came rushing back to him. Could it be the sluagh, come to steal his soul? He had to hold his breath to hear over his own nervous gulping for air. Straining to listen, he peered into the darkness.

A whisper of sound came from all directions, and he fought the urge to crouch in terror like Galleris. Then he heard a faint squeaking.

He shook his head. Bats! The sootstoke let out a short bark of laughter, and the winged shadows stirred, flying in worried zigzags near the ceiling.

Ascaeus resumed his search. Most of the paths were fairly level, a couple rose from the chamber floor, and a few led downward. He found the one with the steepest slope and set off down it.

The way wound onward, sometimes intersecting with other paths, sometimes leading to wide spaces with more paths to choose from. Now and then he heard trickling water through the walls. Here and there he saw the slow drip of a stalactite. In one chamber he found a small waterfall emptying into a shallow pool. Some of the passages were draped with spiderwebs. Fungi hugged the floors. Claw marks and rubble were scattered throughout the caves. Ascaeus pressed on.

As he approached another wide chamber, a new sound reached him. It seemed familiar, but he couldn't place it. He thought it was a voice, but it didn't have the steady pace of speech. Then he recognized it. It was singing!

The creatures of Shadowmoor didn't often indulge in song. What manner of being would find cause to sing in this forsaken place?

The sootstoke stepped cautiously from the tunnel into the space beyond. It was smaller than most of the chambers he'd seen so far, but it still had three paths leading from it. It also had something none of the others had, light. Growing around a stalagmite near the wall was a circle of mushrooms with a faint green glow. Marking the path behind him, he started toward the formation, just out of curiosity. The singing came again, closer this time. The voice sounded like a child's, but it had an unnatural quality to it. It echoed hollowly, distorting slightly.

Ascaeus turned in every direction but saw no one. Though the singing seemed to come from just above him, he saw no movement among the ridges and crevices of the ceiling. He started for one of the openings.

Giggles like the ringing of glass bells brought him up short. He looked around again. Nothing. Silence. Was he imagining things? Again he headed for the next passageway.

The giggles came again, this time from right behind him. Ascaeus whirled, but all he saw was the empty chamber and the circle of glowing mushrooms. He eyed them suspiciously. Madness. Mushrooms didn't sing and giggle. He turned once more to go.

"Boo!" a child's voice called out, echoing through the chamber.

Ascaeus jumped and spun around. "Who's there?" he demanded. "Show yourself!"

"I can't," said the little voice.

A girl's voice, Ascaeus guessed. "Why not?"

"Because I'm only a spirit now," she replied with a note of sorrow. "I was a physical being once, but that was a long time ago. Now my spirit has no home."

Ascaeus wasn't sure what to make of that. "Do you have a name, spirit?"

"I'm called Fireschild. Who are you?"

"Fireschild?"

"Your name is Fireschild too?" she asked.

"No, no. I'm Ascaeus. But you . . . you were a cinder too?"

"Not a cinder. A child of the flame. I came from the burning river."

Ascaeus gaped. "That's why I came here! To find the burning river."

"Oh, it's not far from here. Do you want me to take you there?"

"You would be doing me a very great service," said Ascaeus. "But tell me . . . why are you now a spirit? What happened to you?"

"I don't want to talk about that."

"I just meant. . . . It wasn't because of the burning river, was it?"

A chorus of giggles erupted at that.

"Are there other spirits with you?" Ascaeus asked,

scanning the chamber and finding it as empty as before.

"Of course not. I don't like your silly questions. I'm going to leave."

"No! Wait! I'm sorry," said Ascaeus. "Please stay. We can go to the burning river together."

There was a pause. "All right," Fireschild said at last. "But I get to ask the questions. Agreed?"

"Agreed."

"Fine. Then take the path to your right."

Ascaeus crossed the chamber. At the opening on the right, he paused. "This one slopes up," he said. "I heard the way to the burning river always leads downward."

"That's just the easiest path to find," said Fireschild. "It's not the best way. This way takes a little longer, but it's safer."

"Longer? How much longer?"

"Not much. A day, two if you're slow."

"I want to get there as fast as possible," said Ascaeus. "Let's take the shorter way."

"Not me," Fireschild replied. "That way is too scary. Bad things lurk there."

The sootstoke hesitated. "But they can't hurt you, can they? And if we get separated—"

"The shorter way is full of hobgoblins and merrows," she said, "and a nasty elemental has been hanging around those tunnels, too. I can take you that way, but you probably won't get very far. And I like having company. So few travelers venture here these days."

"Oh." Neither the elves nor the cinders had even mentioned hobgoblins. Ascaeus shuddered to think what might have become of him and his quest if he hadn't stumbled upon Fireschild to guide him. He set off up the path she'd indicated.

As he walked, she asked him questions. She was curious

about everything: his life, the sootstokes, the relationships of the cinders, and the settlement in the nearby swamp. Ascaeus told her everything, relieved to have someone to talk to on the otherwise dismal journey. They passed through count-less chambers and tunnels, some leading up, some down, some level. At times it seemed they were going in circles. Yet they encountered no living things, and Ascaeus knew he'd made the right decision in following Fireschild.

Ascaeus's steps started to drag. He'd had no idea caves could be so vast. "I think I'll rest here a while," he told her. "Just a short rest, then we'll go on. All right?"

"All right," said Fireschild. "Shall I sing you to sleep?"

"That would be wonderful." Ascaeus stretched out on the tunnel floor, weary in every part of his being. Fireschild's voice rose above him, beautiful yet eerie with its hollow echoes. A smile tugged at his mouth as he drifted off to sleep.

His dreams brought him little rest, though. Images of Galleris struggling to escape the black poplar warred with memories of the scorn of the cinders. Visions of his tri-umphant return to save his kind scattered before mobs of hobgoblins and merrows. At one point he dreamed a swarm of sluagh were trying to steal his soul. They tugged at him, bickering with each other over their prize.

"It's mine!"

"It is not! Give me that!"

"Hey! Quit shoving!"

He thrashed in his sleep, flailing his arms to fend them off. His hand struck something in the air, and he sat bolt upright in the dim cave. Angry hisses echoed around him.

"You had to wake him up, didn't you?" a small voice complained.

"Well, if you hadn't been trying to take it all for yourself—"

"If you'd all just shut up he might fall back asleep!"

"You can't take my soul!" Ascaeus cried. "I'm not dead!"

This brought on a gale of laughter like the ringing of glass bells.

Ascaeus jumped to his feet and looked around. At last he spotted them. A clique of faeries flitted nearby, fighting over something he couldn't see clearly. "Where's Fireschild?"

"Look. Now he's up," said one faerie in a voice that sounded just like Fireschild's, except this voice didn't echo itself. "We could've harvested plenty for everyone if you'd all kept quiet."

"And he didn't even have any good secrets," said another faerie. "Great plan, Xaana."

"There was nothing wrong with my plan," the one with Fireschild's voice replied, "except for the fools who were supposed to execute it."

"You mean there is no Fireschild?" Ascaeus demanded, irritated at being ignored. Cold dread ran through him as he began to understand. "You tricked me! This isn't the path at all."

"Figured that out all by yourself, did you?" said a dark-eyed faerie, somersaulting backward as a clump of stuff pulled free in his hands. A smaller faerie flitted after him, grasping at the stuff.

"You!" Ascaeus pointed at the one called Xaana. "You have to take me back to where you found me."

She laughed. "Find your own way. You can't give us enough dreamstuff to make it worth the trouble." To the others she added, "Let's go. We can split it up later."

After a last bit of squabbling, they started to fly away.

"Wait!" Ascaeus had no idea where he was, how to

reach the burning river, or even how to get back to the surface to start over. He ran after the faeries, but they were too quick. He couldn't let them get away! Panicking, he drew upon his own meager embers and set a flicker of fire on Xaana.

She cried out and spiraled to the ground. The others stopped and hovered over her. A wisp of smoke curled from one wing jutting from her still form. She groaned and sat up, holding her head. "What happened?" she asked.

"The cinder smoked you," said the dark-eyed one, pointing at Ascaeus.

Xaana's nose crinkled, and she looked over her shoulder. At the sight of her smoldering wing, she gasped. She glared at Ascaeus. "Get him!"

"Uh-oh," he said. He scrambled back down the passageway. The Fae chased him, stabbing him with tiny barbs that pierced even his tough skin. He yelped and swatted at them as he ran.

"That's far enough!" called Xaana. "Let's go!"

The faeries zipped back up the path. Before Ascaeus could follow, Xaana gestured with her hand. The opening to the path disappeared. In its place stood solid stone, exactly like the rest of the chamber walls.

"No!" Ascaeus rushed to the place where the tunnel should be and threw himself against the wall. "It's just an illusion! Just an illusion!"

But the illusion held. Ascaeus slumped to the floor. He took a deep breath. The faerie's spell couldn't last forever. He marked the place where the opening should be, hoping the illusion would dissipate by the time he was ready to return to the surface. In the meantime, he'd have to search for another way to the burning river.

Ascaeus paused, listening hard for any clues that might

tell him which way to go. But all he could hear was a vast silence and, somewhere far in the distance, trickling water.

He turned and continued down the tunnel. He'd just have to search the caves until he found either the burning river or the markings he'd left to show the way out. The elves said the river was at the bottom of the caves, so he returned to his original strategy of always choosing the paths that led downward. As he walked, he heard a noise, faint at first, then growing louder. A slow knocking or thumping. It seemed to be coming from deep within the walls of the caves.

Ascaeus's steps faltered. He'd heard tales of hammering sounds coming from caves just before they collapsed. He imagined the tunnel falling in on him, crushing him, forever burying not just him but all hope for the cinders.

He shook off the horrible vision and forced his breathing to steady. He hurried onward, willing himself to walk. If he panicked, he was bound to run into merrows or hobgoblins. Irassu was right. He had to keep his wits about him. As he rushed along, the knocking grew fainter until he could no longer hear it at all. What if the caves collapsed behind him? Nothing he could do would change that. Even if there was a collapse in one area of the tunnels, he might still find another escape route. All he could do was press on and hope.

Here, far below the surface, time lost all meaning. There were long stretches when he was certain he was wandering in circles. He had no idea how many hours passed before he stumbled upon the small chamber with the glowing mushrooms.

Ascaeus let out a laugh, and it echoed back at him from all around. He'd stumbled upon the very place where the Fae had first led him astray! A quick search revealed the mark he'd made showing the way out. He laughed again. All was not lost.

But now he had a decision to make. Should he go back to the surface and forget this forsaken place? Should he give up, return to the swamp, admit the others had been right and he never should have made the attempt? Or should he continue his search, find the key to the Rekindling that waited below, and save his kind?

To quit now would mean he'd gone through all his struggles for nothing. The Fae had simply delayed him. Nothing had changed. He'd wandered endless paths and come to no harm. Of course he'd go on. He laughed again. Taking the lowest path, he set off with a fresh spring in his step.

It didn't take long for the realities of the caves to reassert themselves. Strange noises followed him. Was that wind or water? Or had the Fae returned to torment him some more? Perhaps it was a merrow or some other creature lurking in the shadows. Was it afraid of him, or just biding its time?

Ascaeus pushed these thoughts away, but they kept creeping back. To distract himself, he tried to imagine what the burning river would look like. Would the flames be red and orange, or perhaps blue and green? Would it be wide and slow, or narrow with a fast current? The suspense kept him going when his fear told him to turn back. Visions of the burning river filled his mind and made him overlook the flicker of light up ahead.

But only for a moment. At first, he thought his eyes were playing tricks on him. The light winked into darkness, but soon it flared up again farther away.

Had he found it? Was this his first glimpse of the river of burning stone? He rushed forward for a better look.

The tunnel opened into a large cavern with stalagmites

jutting up all across the floor. The meager light from Ascaeus's embers didn't reach the far side, and the only other light was the pale glow of mushrooms scattered among the stalagmites. The place smelled dank, and the sound of dripping water echoed dully. There was no sign of the flickering light.

Then Ascaeus saw it again, off to his left. He moved toward it, weaving between the jagged stones that hid and revealed the light by turns. No matter which way he went, he couldn't seem to get any closer to it. It appeared and vanished and reappeared, each time just a bit too far away for him to get a clear view of it. Yet his eyes couldn't stop looking for it. There was something beautiful and hypnotic about it. There it went again. It must be the river of burning stone. Now if he could just get to it. The glimmering flames beckoned to him, more wondrous than he'd imagined. In his mind, he saw all the cinders wrapped in the dancing fires. Gone was the path of sorrow, replaced by the path of flame. And for the first time in Ascaeus's knowledge, the cinders were truly alive. Rekindling. Redemption. The vision filled him with a feeling he'd never known. What was it?

A piercing cold bit into Ascaeus's very being, jerking him from his reverie. The glow from his embers was much weaker than usual, far too dim to light his surroundings. He glanced down, and water filled his mouth and nose. He sputtered and coughed, fighting to get his head above water. His feet barely reached the ground. Where had all the water come from? The icy chill threatened to wash the life from him. Frantic, he looked around in the darkness and spotted the flickering light. Only now there were several lights, floating above the water, drifting away from him. At last he saw them for what they really were, torches. Their flames cast an eerie glow down on the creatures bearing them, twisted things like nightmarish faeries.

Ascaeus had never seen the like before, but he realized they must be duergars, an enigmatic race that lured travelers into bogs and such. The duergars paddled along on shallow boats, and Ascaeus averted his eyes to avoid the snare of their torchlight. He managed to turn and flounder in the opposite direction. The ground rose steadily under his feet, and soon he emerged from the water. He was relieved to find his embers hadn't been doused. The black waters had only hidden their light. Now he could see what seemed to be an underground lake stretching away into the darkness.

When he reached the shore, he fell to his knees, shivering. Whether from the cold or his near-fatal encounter, he couldn't say. He'd always hated water. It terrified him. He had a vague memory of nearly drowning as a very young cinder, no clear details, just an icy panic that dragged at his soul. Yet it plagued him all his days.

He pushed these thoughts away to focus on his more immediate problems. How long had he wandered under the duergars' spell? How far had they taken him from his path?

A splash from the lake brought him quickly back to his feet. He peered into the murky cavern, fearing the duergars might return for him. But their torches were already fading in the distance. Still he shielded his eyes from them, in case their spell could reach him even now.

The splash came again, and Ascaeus felt certain he was not alone. Surely merrows lurked in these waters. He had to get away from here, but he didn't know which way to go. Though the lake had nearly done him in, it was also a sign of hope. Water always sought lower levels, so perhaps the path to the burning river lay nearby. He chose the nearest tunnel and headed away from the lake.

Everywhere he went, he found more water. The cold and damp filled the caves here. Surely he'd feel the heat from the burning river if he were close. That must mean he wasn't close after all. He kept going, marking the path behind him at every intersection to keep from wandering in circles. Yet he couldn't shake the feeling of being followed, watched, hunted. He could sense something out there in the darkness, always just out of sight, observing him. Waiting. Doubts and dark imaginings haunted his every step. Perhaps he'd never find the right path again. He could wander, lost and alone, all the rest of his days. What would he do if the duergars returned? Or the Fae? And what new predators waited in the next chamber? And why did the thing lurking in the blackness not just kill him and get it over with? The constant dangers and uncertainties were wearing away at his hope, but he clung to it like a lifeline. Giving up was not in him, and so he pushed on.

He walked until he was almost walking in his sleep, placing one foot in front of the other more by habit than intention. His mind became numb from fear and the endless plodding. When he noticed the change in temperature, at first he thought his mind was playing tricks on him. But soon he rounded a bend and saw reflections on the walls of a pale glow from a chamber up ahead. Fear and fatigue dropped away. Ascaeus ran.

The tunnel opened onto the largest chamber he'd seen yet. Warmth washed over him as he rushed into the clearing. Before him lay another lake, as dark as the last one and stretching from one side of the cavern to the other. Behind the lake, flowing into the chamber through one wall and disappearing somewhere behind a cluster of stalagmites, was the river of burning stone, its white flames a beacon in the darkness. A narrow path bridged the lake, leading to the ledge beside the burning river.

How long Ascaeus stood gazing at the blazing white river, he could not say. Basking in its light and warmth filled him with a serenity he'd never thought possible. This was it! He knew it. This liquid fire would rekindle the cinders and turn their path of sorrow to a path of pure flame.

He let out a laugh, and it echoes rang through the cavern like the clamor of warring boggarts. Something about the place amplified and multiplied the small sound to a roar. He covered his ears and waited for the noise to subside. When it did, he started toward the stone bridge that would take him to his destination.

As he drew closer to the bridge, he saw fissures in the stone and gaps where chunks of it had crumbled away. It was barely wide enough to allow him to cross. If any more of it fell away, it wouldn't hold him. He eyed the water warily, remembering the biting cold of the other lake. It was difficult to tell, but this one appeared deeper. He took a hesitant step onto the bridge.

It didn't give way under his foot, and he heaved a sigh of relief. He knew he was being foolish. No doubt the bridge had stood the test of ages. But after his recent ordeal, water terrified Ascaeus more than ever.

But he couldn't stop now, not with the salvation of his entire race so near. With his arms out for balance, he began the long walk across the bridge. Though his steps started out small and cautious, they fell faster and faster until he was nearly running.

A splash in the lake stopped him dead in the middle of the bridge. The sound repeated and expanded to fill the cavern. Had part of the path fallen into the water? Keeping his body completely still, he peered around, searching for gaps in the stone and finding none. Had the thing from the other lake followed him here? He shuddered at the thought and willed his legs into motion, slower this time. His breathing came in shallow gulps. When the ledge was just a few steps away, he threw himself forward, his legs buckling under him as soon as he cleared the bridge. He sank to the solid ground, relief flooding over him. Before him lay the river of burning stone.

Joy overwhelmed him. He threw his head back and laughed. The clear, bright tones echoed throughout the cavern, growing and rising until it seemed the entire cinder race was laughing with him. He had to cover his ears, but he couldn't stop laughing. He laughed until his sides ached, until his face hurt, until he was exhausted.

As his laughter drained away and the echoes of it began to fade, he heard a new sound. Low at first, then building. A deep rumbling, like thunder, joined by dull thuds from far away. Loud cracking and rasping sounds arose. Ascaeus scrambled to his feet to scan the chamber, but the ledge beneath him shook, knocking him to the ground again.

Soon the whole cavern was shaking, and a series of deafening crashes filled the air. Ascaeus threw his arms over his head and curled into a tight ball as chunks of rock and then whole stalactites broke loose from the ceiling and rained down around him. A section of the ceiling opened up, and water poured onto the bridge. The narrow path gave way under the force, tumbling into the lake. The water level began to rise. Huge cracks opened in the cave walls on either side and the flood rushed through them. Little by little the shaking subsided, and the cavern shuddered into stillness except for the sound of rushing water.

Ascaeus climbed cautiously to his feet and turned in a slow circle. The newly formed waterfall that rushed from the ceiling into the lake showed no sign of stopping. It appeared an underground stream had found a new course. The burning river flowed as before. Now he could see where it plunged into the cavern floor to continue its course beyond the depths of the caves.

Ascaeus was trapped on the barren ledge. There would be no rekindling of the cinders. With his laugh, he'd doomed them all. His mind reeled, unwilling to face the choice before him. Should he try to use the burning stone to bring about his own rekindling? It could prolong his life, only to leave him sealed in this cavern, staring into the abyss of his personal eternity. Or should he forget the Rekindling and grant himself a quick death in the cold, black lake?

Had the others been right about him all along? Had he been mad to ever believe, even to hope? Was hope nothing but madness masquerading as a reason to live?

He searched his soul and found no answer. All he had was a choice. There was no point in waiting. No rescue would come. Deep in their withered hearts, the others would feel only vindication at being proved right. His failed quest could not bring them disappointment or regret, for they never expected it to succeed. Oh, what he would give to prove them wrong, to see the looks on their faces when the mad sootstoke delivered the key to the Rekindling to all the cinders.

What he would give. . . . There was his answer. If the burning stone could bring about his rekindling, his hope of bringing salvation to the others would live on with him. Yes, he'd face an eternity alone, searching for an escape or waiting for a new way out to form, but someday, some distant day, he would emerge from this place. And when he did, his success would be all the sweeter. He would redeem them all, and he would prove that they'd been wrong and he'd been right all along. The years of mockery would end, and they would be forced to admit they'd been the fools.

He tried to laugh again, but all that came out was a hollow coughing sound. No matter. He'd have an eternity to work on it. Ascaeus closed his eyes and took a deep breath, letting it out slowly.

With a leap, he let the river of burning stone embrace him.

JESS LEBOW

Look for the Mark—shaped with wings
This is the Raven
The one who shall deliver the forest
And relieve us of our burden
　　　　　　　　—Partial inscription from the Oaken Tablet

A cold wind swept in from the east, shaking the bare branches and whistling through the walls of Strongroot safehold. The storms just before the Aurora had always been unpleasant, but they had never been this bad.

The sky seemed to break open, brilliant flashes of red, orange, blue, and purple sailing overhead. It was as if the heavens were coming apart, and what little daylight illuminated Shadowmoor was trying to escape through the cracks. Every few moments, the world lit up, then was once again plunged into its perpetual twilight. The flashes made long, freakish shadows on the floor of Ravens' Run forest, turning an already terrifying place into something born of nightmare.

A strange crackling noise accompanied the light and wind. It rose in pitch and grew faster and more frequent. At its worst, it sounded like gravel falling from the sky, impacting the dead branches and magical walls of the safehold. Then, suddenly, it would drop down low, slowing to an almost imperceptible murmur, as if it were threatening to stop. The cycle had continued on and on, lasting for more than a day.

High atop Strongroot, elf sentries kept a watchful eye on the surrounding forest, and an even closer one on the changing sky above. Though the Aurora came every year, it always brought with it a feeling of unease. The light storms and whipping wind created a tremendous sense of foreboding, as if the potential for danger lurked somewhere not far behind the crackling flashes.

Through it all, the cry of a baby floated on the wind. It was soft and terrified, just like every baby. The sound, if made by an adult, would have struck fear and panic in the hearts of the sentries. But coming from a newborn, it just made them smile—a cause for hope amidst the despair and desolation of Ravens' Run forest.

Deep inside the protective walls and wards, Tekla Ironleaf had just been handed a baby elf, wrapped in a soft, tattered blanket—her firstborn son. She stared at him as he cried, tears of joy in her eyes. The skin on his face, cheeks, and forehead was all wrinkled, further bunching up with his wailing.

The chamber glowed dim blue, lit by four magical braziers, one in each corner of the room. The floor, built from real wood, was completely filled, every last bit of space covered with elves. After all, it wasn't every day a new baby was brought into the world. It had long been considered good luck to witness a birth, and these days good luck was hard to come by.

Beside Tekla, the two lifewards who had assisted with the birth looked at the pair. Such an occasion called for smiles and warm wishes for better days ahead. But both seemed nervous, even worried.

"Do not fret," soothed Tekla, noticing their unusual demeanor, "he will stop crying soon. There is nothing to worry about."

The lifewards looked at each other, one wringing his hands. "That is not what disturbs us."

Tekla Ironleaf was a vigilant—one of the five chosen and proven leaders of Strongroot. Daily it had been part of her duty to calm the fears of those who looked to her for guidance. But on the day she gave birth, it seemed somehow out of place.

"Well," she said with a smile, "perhaps we could talk about this another time." She looked down at her newborn, nestled in his blanket on her belly. "Right now, I must get acquainted with my son, Joram."

She cooed at the baby, and ran a finger across his cheek. "Let's get a better look at you."

Her eyes grew wide as she pushed back the tattered cloth. In the dim light of the room, she had revealed a dark black mark on her son's cheek. She rubbed at it with her fingers, thinking perhaps it was simply detritus from the birth, but she knew that wasn't the case. She had seen the lifewards clean and dress him. The mark did not come away, no matter how hard she scrubbed.

"What . . . why didn't you tell me?" she stammered, not taking her eyes off her son.

Unlike other birthmarks Tekla had seen, this one had shape—a picture, clear and simple. Right there on Joram's face was the undeniable form of a dark raven, standing sideways, looking up at the baby's forehead.

"It's the raven. I . . . I always believed in the legend, but never thought it would be . . . be *my* child," she said, her smile growing wider. "He's been born with the mark." Tekla turned to the lifewards. "The time has arrived. There is hope after all."

The lifewards grew even more agitated. One turned away, walking to the other side of the room. His spot was immediately filled by some of the other onlookers, eager to get a first glimpse of Tekla Ironleaf's new son—the one with the mark of the raven.

A chill ran down Tekla's spine. Something wasn't right. She gripped Joram to her chest. "What is it you aren't telling me?"

The lifeward took a deep breath, and let it out slowly. "I am sorry Tekla," he said. Then he took hold of the tattered blanket and pulled it away from the baby's head.

Terrified whispers filled the room.

Tekla's entire body went numb. She stared at the smooth, clean head of her new baby boy. It looked somehow grotesque, unfinished, or mutated. It wasn't, of course. In fact, it was shaped exactly as every other elf baby's head, round and smooth. But where there should have been two fuzzy little nubs—the beginnings of the strong curving horns that would jut out of his forehead and back across his skull—there were none.

"But . . . but how could this happen?" Tekla shook her head, disbelieving. "He has the mark?"

Horns were the measure of majesty and worth for every elf. The more tines an elf had on his horns, the more good he would bring into the world—the more blessing had been granted to him. It was rare when an elf was born without horns. Indeed, there were none in the safehold who had grown up without them.

There was a reason for this. The law of the council was very clear on the matter. Elves born without horns were to be exiled, separated from the rest of the safehold for the remainder of their days.

A murmur filled the room as the news spread through the onlookers. They gossiped and pointed, not sure what to make of it. Their voices grew in volume as more of the elves began to speak, each trying to talk over the next. Then a heavy, somber voice rang out over them all, and silence descended once again.

"Let us pass," commanded a gray-haired elf from the back of the room. Mullenix the Elder, the longest lived of the elves in Strongroot pressed his way through the crowd. He was the leader of the vigilant's council, the five elves who collectively made all the pertinent decisions regarding the safety and well-being of the safehold—and the only one who carried more political might than Tekla.

Lithe and wiry, Mullenix moved with the grace of an elf half his age. He carried himself with the confidence and stature of someone who had seen the worst the world had to offer, and still lived to tell the tale. Indeed, his chest, shoulders, and face were crisscrossed with tales of their own—battle scars from years of fighting the treefolk in Ravens' Run forest. It was rumored that many of the wounds were so old that Mullenix himself did not even remember how he got them.

The crowd parted as best they could, allowing Mullenix and the three other vigilants to work their way to the delivery table.

Wrapped in his mother's arms, Joram's wailing had quieted to a soft murmur. He hadn't yet opened his eyes, but the initial shock of being born seemed to have passed. The newborn began to coo as the four other vigilants approached.

Not one for long speeches, Mullenix held out his long, slender hands.

"Give me the child."

Tekla squeezed Joram closer to her chest. "What are you going to do, Mullenix?"

The older elf sighed. "I will not harm him. I simply want to see him."

The other vigilants nodded their agreement. As part of the vigilant council, Tekla had known each of these elves for a long time. She didn't need to hear them speak to know this was an argument she just couldn't win. Reluctantly, she handed her newborn son over to the leader of the vigilant council.

Lifting Joram out of the tattered blanket, Mullenix held him up out of the shadow of the crowd, where the light from the braziers gave him a better view of the child. The baby opened his eyes, looking around the room and kicking his legs. But if he was disturbed by being taken from his mother and held up for all to see, he didn't show it. Not a sound came out of the newborn.

Everyone in the room gasped, all of them clearly able to see the black raven-shaped mark on the baby's cheek. The rest of him was exactly as it should be, all the parts in the right place—hooves, hands, legs—except the obvious.

Turning him one way then the other, Mullenix examined the baby as if he were a newly found artifact. When he was finished, he handed Joram back to his mother. Then he ran the long, thin fingers of his right hand over the sharp, angular bones of his chin.

The other elves in the room waited in silent anticipation, watching their eldest ponder the fate of their youngest.

Finally, Mullenix straightened, nodding to himself. "I have a proposal for the council," he said, talking to Tekla and the other vigilants, but saying the words loud enough for everyone in the room to hear. "This baby has the mark. The inscription on the Oaken Tablet is very clear about the significance of this."

" 'The one with the mark will end our twilight,' " chanted the crowd in unison, reciting from memory the words inscribed on one of the oldest and most treasured artifacts held in the vaults of Strongroot.

"My proposal is this," continued Mullenix. "We delay our judgment upon this boy until he reaches adulthood—his fourteenth year. If, at that time, he has not grown horns, we shall know that this is not the real mark, and he shall be exiled from these halls, as the law of the council states."

Mullenix looked at each of the vigilants in turn, then cast his eyes upon Tekla. "What say you?"

Tekla kissed Joram's cheek, thankful for the mark and the uncharacteristic mercy bestowed upon her and her son on this day. "I say yea."

"Yea," replied the other vigilants, each in turn, unanimously agreeing to the proposal.

"So it has been spoken. So it shall be done."

* * * * *

Joram walked to his mother's chambers. He'd been summoned from his bed before he'd even woken. The knock at the door roused him from the few moments of restfulness he'd had during a mostly restless night.

As he walked, he passed his friends and companions. The safehold was not a large place. Everyone knew everyone else. Almost everyone here had been on hand when he had been born, or so his mother had told him. But today, Joram felt like a stranger—an outsider in his own home.

The other elves' conversations silenced as he passed. They stared as he came near, averting their gazes when his eyes met theirs.

Yesterday had been like any other day. Joram had laughed and smiled, played games and done work with all of his friends. Today however was different.

Today was Joram's birthday—his fourteenth birthday.

Most young elves looked forward to their fourteenth year. It was a rite of passage. The year in which a child became recognized as a full-grown adult. At fourteen, elves could participate in the communal meetings. They could take part in the actual day to day activities of the safehold. Best of all, they could join the scouts that left the safety of Strongroot to search for things of beauty, items that had been lost or discarded among the rotting trees of Ravens' Run and were in need of the elves' protection.

It was a great honor to discover something hallowheld— lost beauty deemed worthy of being ensconced in the vaults deep below the safehold. Many a young elf dreamed of the day he would return to Strongroot with something brilliant and beautiful tucked under his arm. Joram and his friends had spent countless hours making up stories of how every elf in the stronghold would be waiting for them when they arrived after such a find.

There was very little to do inside the safehold, and until the age of fourteen, no one was allowed to leave the safety of the magical wards protecting the vaults. Ravens' Run was a foul and dangerous place. Even those who were allowed to travel through the inhospitable world that surrounded the isolated elves' home did not do so often or for long stretches of time.

So the young elves entertained themselves by adding details to their stories. The tales grew longer and more involved with each passing year. Recounting your fantastical visions of heroism and conquest was just part of being young in Strongroot.

Most young elves looked forward to their fourteenth birthday as the day their stories could finally come true. But not Joram. Today was the day he learned his fate.

Today, instead of joining a scouting party, he would be judged by the vigilant's council.

As he drew closer to his mother's chamber, Joram scratched at the dark mark on his cheek. It felt strange, even after having lived with it his entire life. The skin was thicker and coarser than that on the rest of his face. His other cheek was soft and smooth, but the mark was rough, like a callous.

He had wondered often what his life would have been like without the mark. His mother said it saved his life. Joram figured it must be his lucky charm. As he made his way to the end of the hall to stop in front of his mother's chamber, he wondered if it had enough luck left in it to save him from what was sure to be his exile.

Stopping in front of the heavy, polished wood, he straightened himself up and took a deep breath. There was nothing he could do at this point. His fate was entirely in the hands of the council of vigilants—the council his mother now headed.

Taking one last look around, he steeled himself and knocked on the door.

"Enter," came the muffled voice of his mother.

Joram pushed open the door and stepped through. His mother, Tekla Ironleaf, stood beside the other vigilants. She wore her formal robes—layers and layers of heavy, ornate fabric that cascaded off her thin shoulders to the floor. The tailing edge of the gown spread out on the ground like a pool of water. Three of the other vigilants stood beside her, just outside the reach of her robes.

Mullenix the Elder, the fifth and last member of the council, sat on a stool, looking feeble. He had been wounded several years before in a treefolk attack on the safehold. Though he recovered from his injuries, they left him physically unable to carryout his duties as the head of the vigilants council, and so that honor had passed to Tekla.

"Good morning, Joram," said his mother. She looked less than happy.

"Good morning," he replied, noticing that she did not mention his birthday.

"You know why you have been summoned here, child?" interjected Mullenix, not bothering to get to his feet.

Joram nodded.

"Then it is time for us to begin," announced Tekla, her voice and body language marking her transformation from mother to head of the vigilants' council. "This boy's life is in our hands. What arguments are there for us to hear?"

One of the other vigilants cleared his throat then proceeded. "Mark or no, this boy has put us all at risk. His presence here has caused us to be more of a target. The treefolk can sense him, and his lack of horns. He is bad luck. Plain and simple."

"These recent attacks are clearly a sign. Joram is a blight on our safehold," said another. "How much longer can we be expected to accept the burden of his misfortune?"

"He is a member of our clan, and is entitled to the same safety as the rest of us," argued Tekla.

Mullenix stood up from his seat, struggling to his feet with the aid of a cane. "We could argue this for ages, but you know the law of the council," said the elder, clearly agitated. "Whether or not you choose to see that the safety of Strongroot is at stake, Tekla, the simple fact remains that today is Joram's fourteenth birthday. He has not grown horns. According to the proclamation that all of us accepted, today he must be put out."

Joram lowered his head, looking at his feet. He had

known this would be the verdict of the council, but hearing it said out loud made it somehow more real.

"That was the agreement," echoed the other vigilants.

Hobbling as he walked, Mullenix moved to take Tekla by the hand, gripping it in his own. "I am sorry," he said a small amount of sympathy creeping into his voice, "but we have been as lenient as possible."

Tekla lowered her head. "Yes, I know." She looked up at Joram. "May I tell them?"

Joram stood up as straight as he could, trying to be brave. Then he nodded.

The leader of the vigilants smiled at her son, her pride in him showing through the sadness.

"We are aware of the treefolk attacks on the safehold," she said, speaking to the other vigilants on behalf of herself and Joram. "And we will not argue against the will of the council. Instead, Joram has volunteered to leave the safehold, of his own power and will, as a gesture of good faith. He is an upstanding member of this community, and he only wishes to leave in good standing—not as a banished citizen." Tekla looked at Joram then to each of the other vigilants in turn. "What say you?"

The rest of the council looked to Mullenix, who appeared to be thinking it over. After a long moment of silence, he spoke.

"This seems rational and fair. I accept this proposal."

The other vigilants nodded their agreement.

"Then it is the law of the council, and it shall be done." There were tears in her eyes as she spoke the next words. "Joram. It is time for you to leave."

* * * * *

The portal slammed shut behind Joram, and suddenly, for the first time in his life, he was all alone. Turning around, he took in the dank, black forest that surrounded the safehold. For fourteen years he had wanted to leave the confining walls of Strongroot. But not like this.

The weak, pale morning light tried to reach into the forest through the bare branches of the trees. Feeble shadows flickered here and there, but it was clear that darkness reigned in the bowels of Ravens' Run.

Everything was damp, the forest floor spattered with puddles. Where the roots of the trees lifted out of the water, moss and fungus took hold. What solid ground there was seemed to creep and crawl, as if the soil itself were alive. Toads and snakes frolicked in the mud, their slithers and hops adding to the sense that the entire place was moving.

And everything was permeated with a terrible stench. Joram had been to the top of the safehold and had looked down on the forest floor before. He knew of the "rot" as many of the older elves had called it. The swampy water and the dying vegetation had a particularly foul odor. He'd smelled it before, but here it was nearly unbearable. The stench stung his eyes and assaulted his nostrils. Trying his best to not breathe it in, Joram covered his nose with his hand, and began breathing through his mouth.

Turning around, he placed his hand on the outer wall of what had been his home. The smooth, hard wood hummed with magical power. From here, Joram could tell that Strongroot did not really fit in with the rest of the surroundings. It had been created here as a place to store and protect beauty. It had been constructed entirely out of magic—the collective efforts of maybe a hundred elf mages.

Its warm, clean surface seemed so inviting, so hopeful

and promising. But right now, that just made Joram sad. He would never see the interior again. He would never see his friends or his mother. Somehow all of this didn't seem real. As if at any moment someone would come out and let him back in—a practical joke played on all young elves when they turned fourteen.

Perhaps if he just waited right beside the safehold wall, they would take pity on him and let him back inside. He might as well. He had nowhere else to go.

Trying to pick out the driest spot he could find, Joram squatted down with his back against the Strongroot wall. Placing his hand on his head, he rubbed his smooth, horn-less scalp, and he waited.

* * * * *

Morning turned to afternoon, then to evening. Joram nodded off several times, his chin drooping to his chest before he woke up and tried to shake himself awake. Eventually, he gave up and lay down, resting his head on his hands and curling up on the soft moss at the base of the wall.

* * * * *

Joram awoke with a start. It was the next morning. An entire day had passed, and no one had come to let him back in. Lifting himself up from the ground, he brushed away the dirt and twigs that stuck to his face and arms. Then he knocked on the smooth wood of Strongroot.

"Hello," he said, his voice sounding very small to his own ears. "Hello. I'm still here."

But if anyone heard his plea, they didn't respond. The

realization that the other elves just didn't want him around was beginning to set in, and with it, a deep sadness.

Just then the forest floor began to shake. Water in the puddles rippled and sloshed. Higher up, in the dead branches, creatures of some sort scampered frantically, their claws clicking on the hollow wood. The sound of trees being pushed aside, their roots torn from the ground, echoed through the forest.

Something was coming this way—several somethings.

High up above, a sentry on the top of the safehold called out. "Treefolk!"

The soil beneath Joram's feet pounded up and down. Turning around, he lifted his fist to once again knock on the wall, to plead for them to let him in.

But he stopped short.

Even if someone did answer this time, he wouldn't be safe. His entire life, the elves of Strongroot had blamed him, the one without horns, for their misfortunes. No doubt this too would be laid at his feet.

Behind him a huge creature burst through the stationary trees—a treefolk. The late-morning light, what little there was, cast narrow shadows on the angry beast's hide—long thin creases of wavy bark, chipped, cut, and gouged from axes and claws no doubt.

It moved quickly—quicker than its size would suggest. Spindly roots spread out from its base, effortlessly carrying the weight of the massive creature. They picked their way over the soil and through the puddles as if they were the legs of a hundred giant spiders. Up above its branches swayed menacingly as it shifted its weight, balancing against the twisted terrain below.

Behind the first one, more and more of the animated trees followed, flowing out of the darkness like a swarm of ants—a seemingly endless supply appearing as if from nowhere. Their branches creaked and tangled together as they converged on Strongroot, filling the swampy space with a new, moving forest.

Joram felt stuck in place. His heart pounded. His mind raced, but he couldn't move. So full of fear, all he could feel was the vibrating soil beneath him, shaken by the movement of the army of trees headed right for him.

"Joram, run!"

Joram looked up, way up, to see his mother looking down from the very top of the stronghold.

"Go now," she pleaded.

His mother's words brought him back from the brink. Stuck between the wall and the oncoming treefolk, Joram had little choice but to run.

Bolting down the length of the wall, Joram took off as fast as he could. His hooves sank into the soggy ground, the mud reluctant to release him from its grasp. Water splashed in his face, and he stumbled forward as he ran, just barely able to keep his balance.

The treefolk continued to come. More and more of them pouring out of the darkness into the pale late-morning light. Joram looked back over his shoulder, a shudder running down his spine. The tall silhouette, thick roots, and Y-shaped branches on top—these weren't just any treefolk. These were black poplar, the worse kind. With thick trunks, and powerful boughs, they could do a lot of damage in a big hurry. Worse was their temperament—mean and meaner, known to attack first and never ask questions.

Over the past few years, the black poplar had been disappearing from Ravens' Run forest. Joram had heard the other elves talking about how the once common treefolk were becoming scarce. Some of the returning scouting parties had even recounted tales of kithkin hunters surrounding the mighty trees with torches and hatchets— cutting them to shreds and burning them alive.

Their inability to get along with other creatures, or at times even with other treefolk, had made them no allies. Slowly the black poplar had been hunted down by those seeking revenge. Now they were in danger of becoming extinct.

By the looks of things, this obviously made them none too happy.

The first of the treefolk came crashing against the safehold. It leaned forward, gaining speed, and rammed what looked like its forehead right into the smooth outer wall. Its heavy branches followed, one after the other, making Strongroot sound like a giant wooden drum.

Then another smashed into the wall, and another. The entire safehold began to rumble, as if it were being shaken by an earthquake. Each of the black poplar in turn added their branches to the pounding. There was a rhythm to their beating, and they fell into synch with each other. The regular intervals of pounding sent shockwaves rippling through the magically grown walls of Strongroot.

The wall undulated under the assault, visibly moving. To Joram, it looked like the waves on the puddles. It warbled and shifted, huge creases sailing down its smooth surface, one after the other. More treefolk came to join the attack. They filled every empty space, pounding on anything they could touch.

Still skirting down the edge of the wall, Joram felt the pit of his stomach leap. All around the trees moved. It seemed the entire forest was coming for Strongroot—and for him. Black poplar closed in. Their roots churned up the mud and soil, sending tiny creatures scattering in every direction. Swarms of insects clouded up around Joram, disturbed from their slumber by the lumbering treefolk. Wart-covered toads and black, slithering snakes fled before the marauding horde. They too crashed into the wall, hopping and sliding up against its smooth surface, unable to go any farther.

Joram stopped running. Ahead of him the black poplar had already reached the wall. He was trapped—treefolk ahead and behind, and more closing in from the forest. They would be upon him any second. He would be crushed under a thousand crawling roots, or worse, slowly, methodically torn apart by stout, leafless branches.

His back up against the safehold, Joram watched the gap between him and the charging trees quickly close. Absently, he swatted at the insects fluttering around his face. There were so many. He could hardly see through them, and he felt a slight pinch. He'd been bit on the cheek—the one with the mark.

Suddenly, something appeared out of thin air. No, it had been there all along, it was just . . . getting bigger, much, much bigger. In the blink of an eye, a mosquito grew to gargantuan proportions, and it fluttered its enormous wings at a furious pace. The water in the puddles splashed up on Joram, thrown by the churning wind from the giant insect.

The black poplar drew within a branch length of the wall, swinging their mighty limbs as they came. The mosquito dodged one way then another, narrowly avoiding the blows. Then, as if just realizing that it could fly, the creature ascended into the sky. Its wings whipping the air into a frenzy.

Without thinking, Joram leaped for the insect's legs,

wrapping his arms around all six of them and holding on for dear life. Up and up they went, branches sailing past, barely missing as the mosquito dodged expertly out of the way. Joram too shifted side to side, avoiding the tangled wood as it grabbed at his feet and legs.

Dangling below the mosquito's thin, frail-looking body, Joram was lifted high into the air. Off the ground, past the treefolk, over the top of the safehold, and into the sky they went. More branches came down on the unlikely duo as they reached the canopy.

Then finally they were free.

Sailing into the open air, Joram felt a wave of relief followed quickly by a sense of awe. Up until yesterday morning, he had never seen anything but the inside of the safehold. His whole life, there had always been something overhead. Even on the top of the safehold, there were branches hanging high above. But here, way up in the air over Ravens' Run, there was nothing but wide-open space. Here above the trees, the sky was not much brighter than it seemed from the forest floor, the same dirty gray as always.

Looking down through the empty branches, he could just make out the outline of Strongroot far below. It was now surrounded on all sides by the angry treefolk. But from up here, they looked much smaller—didn't seem as threatening as they had on the ground.

Joram looked up and out, over the rest of the world. At that very moment, he was seeing more than most elves would see in a lifetime. To the north, south, and west, the Ravens' Run forest stretched on and on, seemingly forever. But to the east, there was an end. Just over the edge of the trees, Joram could make out a long, open field, covered in what looked like tall, brown grass.

It was hard to tell, but it looked like there were several creatures just standing around in the middle of the field. They vaguely resembled the elves, tall, upright, two arms and two legs. But their skin was similar in color to the dry grass of the field, and they were clearly fatter than elves.

That was all Joram was able to make out, because the next moment, he fell.

The giant mosquito he had been clinging to suddenly shrank—transforming back to its normal size. Without its huge, powerful wings, it could no longer support the weight of an elf, and Joram came crashing back through the branches. He tumbled head over heels, completely out of control. Something hit him in the shoulder, and he spun sideways. Then he was knocked on the other side, and he spun back. The world began to blur. Joram's heart pounded in his chest, his muscles clenched against the impending impact.

There was a splash, and everything went dark.

* * * * *

"You are awake?" said a voice from the darkness.

Joram pressed his forehead to the soft, cool ground. He remembered falling and seeing the running river. Then he remembered hitting the water, and that was it.

Joram blinked. His head hurt, so did his shoulder. Rolling to his side, he felt his stomach lurch, and then its contents came up all at once. Joram hadn't eaten in over two days, so there was very little but the water he had swallowed. It spilled all over the muddy ground, as Joram heaved several times.

"Oh, I see . . . not so well after all. Not so well indeed."

Eventually his stomach stopped contracting, and Joram was able to look up. He was on the muddy shore of the river, at the edge of a forest clearing. A sloping hill led away from the embankment, lined at the top and on the sides with dead or dying trees. In the middle of the clearing were several piles of branches and a few large rocks, but no elf or creature that Joram could make out.

Joram lifted himself up onto his elbows and wiped the water out of his eyes. Still he did not see the owner of the voice.

Until one of the trees moved.

Smaller than the black poplar that had attacked Strongroot, this treefolk was missing most of its branches. The bark on its trunk was dark, and it had sloughed off in several places. Huge patches of orange fungus grew in lumps between the creature's limbs and trunk. It dripped down the treefolk's sides, slopping onto the ground in goopy piles as it moved.

Its face was twisted and gnarled, one side of its mouth decayed and collapsed. The orangey goop dripped into its eyes and trailed down the dark bark, leaving a silvery trail as it slowly made its way to the forest floor.

Joram scrambled away, slipping off the embankment back into the river. He knew exactly what that orange fungus was—every elf knew. It was called the Canker, and it could infect anything it touched. Much of Ravens' Run was being slowly devoured by it.

"There is no need to be alarmed," said the treefolk, "I will not hurt you."

Joram stood in the swiftly moving water, his hand on the steep shore to keep his balance. "You . . . you're a canker witch," said the young elf.

The decrepit treefolk lowered its branches. "That's very

observant of you. My name is Amur Brokenlimb, and this is my home."

Joram didn't know what to make of the sloppy treefolk, so he stood his ground, not moving.

"You must be getting very cold in that water, very cold indeed," said Amur. "You should get out before you get sick."

Joram hadn't noticed it before, as his attention was focused on the canker witch, but he was in fact shivering.

"I give you my word," coaxed the treefolk. "You will not be harmed while you are in my home." Amur's face curled up into what Joram could only assume was a smile. "I will make a fire, so you can get warm."

His skin covered in goose pimples and his fingers slowly losing their feeling, Joram nodded his agreement, and sloshed his way out of the water.

The canker witch clapped his branches together in excitement. "Come. Come," he said. "My home is up here." The tree druid turned around and began to shamble along, its root-feet struggling to pull its bulk up the hill.

Joram followed, keeping a considerable distance.

It took a long time, but Amur eventually reached the top of the hill. Coming over the crest, Joram looked out over what must have once been a beautiful palace, but had become little more than a pile of ruins. Alabaster-colored bricks, now covered in black decay, lay strewn across a wide, mostly open space. The remnants of walls—built both out of these same bricks and the trunks of huge, magically crafted trees—traced long, connected lines across the ground. None of them retained more than a few feet in height, but it looked as though at one time they had reached toward the sky.

A shiver ran up Joram's spine as he and Amur picked

their way through the maze of fallen walls. This would be what Strongroot would look like if it were torn to the ground. In his mind, he pieced together what this structure had once been, and the elves or creatures who had lived here. This was the sort of place the scouting parties would be searching for, to find pieces of the past and bring them back to be held safe until the darkness had passed.

"This is a shee knoll," explained the tree druid, obviously noticing Joram's wonderment. "It's the ruins of something once great, something from long, long ago."

"How did it get like this?" asked Joram, climbing over a huge brick.

"No one knows. No one knows." Amur threw his branches in the air. "But perhaps one day we will find out. Yes, one day indeed."

Reaching a spot where the crumbled walls described a large open space, Amur bent over and began gathering dead branches from the ground.

"Please, sit. Sit. I shall make you a fire. And then you will be warm." The canker witch began piling the branches against each other.

Joram wandered to one of the fallen walls and sat down on the crumbled bricks. They were like nothing he had ever seen. The material was so white, almost pure. It seemed so out of place in the middle of the decrepit forest.

Finishing his pile, Amur cast a small spell upon the damp wood. A flash shot from his hand, and the branches caught fire—the flames burning black. Then he motioned Joram over.

"Come. Come. It's much warmer here."

Joram hopped down and walked over to the fire. As he got closer, he could feel the heat radiating off of the broken branches. It felt nice on his face, and it made the rest of him feel that much colder.

Amur ambled over to the opposite side of the fire, looking down at Joram through the rising heat and thin column of smoke.

"So how did an elf like you get out here? And all by his self. Strongroot is quite far. Shouldn't you be inside your home, safely tucked away from the rest of the forest?"

Joram stopped rubbing his hands and looked up at the canker witch. "How did you know I was from Strongroot?"

The tree druid chuckled. "There is only one safehold in Ravens' Run. You elves are all from the same place."

"Oh," replied Joram. He suddenly felt very lonely.

"So then, why are you not there? Instead you are out here."

Joram shrugged his shoulders, trying to focus on the warmth of the fire. "I don't live there anymore."

"I see," said Amur, studying Joram. "Does it have to do with that mark on your face?"

Joram instinctively covered the mark with his palm. "No," he said, feeling rather self conscious.

"Oh no?"

"No," replied Joram, lowering his hand.

"Then why is it then? Surely you are not lost in Ravens' Run, wet and cold, simply because you want to be."

Joram took a deep breath and looked up at Amur. "It's because I don't have any horns." He touched his bald head.

"They made you leave?"

Joram nodded. "They said I was bad luck. Said it was my fault that the black poplar kept attacking the safehold."

Amur laughed, a strange sound somewhere between a cackle and a yodel. "They really believe that?"

Joram nodded.

"Well I can tell you it has nothing to do with you or your horns," admitted Amur. "The black poplar are just angry—at everybody. And your home happens to be very large and right in their way, which makes them doubly angry."

"In their way? Of what?"

"There are two small tribes of black poplar in Ravens' Run. Strongroot sits on the path between them."

"Oh," said Joram, suddenly feeling a little better. "So . . . it's not my fault?"

Amur laughed again. "I'm quite certain the black poplar have no idea you even exist. Horns or not."

Joram scooted along the side of the fire, getting a little closer to the tree druid. "Do you think you could tell that to my mother? Maybe she would let me back in if you did?"

"I do not think your mother, or any of the elves, would listen to *me*," said Amur.

"Oh," said Joram, his hope turning to disappointment.

"But perhaps I have something else that might help you."

The canker witch shambled over to the edge of the shee knoll. Pushing aside a tangle of dead braches, piled twigs, and broken bricks, he revealed a large copper sphere. Covered in thick patches of verdigris, the artifact looked ancient.

Joram immediately perked up. "What's that?"

"I do not know its name," said the tree druid, returning to the fire with the artifact. "But I believe it can give you what you most desire." Amur placed the artifact on the ground and took several steps back. "Go on," he urged.

Twice the size of Joram's head, the sphere had two large indentations—one on each side—that looked like handprints, and it appeared to be split down the middle, a seam running the entire circumference between the two handholds.

"You would give this to me?" asked Joram, overwhelmed by the generosity of the treefolk. This was the sort of thing every young elf dreamed about—finding a thing of such beauty in the dying remnants of the forest. He hesitated. "But I have nothing to offer you in return."

Amur waved a branch. "I'm sure you will find a way to repay me, when the time comes. You do want to repay me, don't you?"

"Yes, yes of course," said Joram, his eyes glued to the beautiful sphere.

"Then for now, consider this a gift," said Amur. "You can find a way to repay me later."

Overcome with excitement, Joram picked up the artifact. It was heavy, and felt very solid. Unlike many of the hallowheld items he had seen placed in the vaults, this one was still in good shape—no dents or scratches, just some tarnish.

"Do you like it?"

Joram nodded.

"I think the other elves will too."

Joram placed both hands inside the globe. As he did, it started to vibrate, the whole thing humming and shaking his arms.

"Just twist it," said Amur, "and you shall have what you need."

Joram paused for a moment, thinking about what it was that he most desired. More than anything, he wanted to return home, to see his mother again, and to be accepted back into the safehold. He thought for sure just showing up with a thing of such beauty would be enough for them to let him back inside. What more luck could he ask for?

Taking a deep breath, he twisted the artifact.

The two halves of the sphere glided easily over each other then locked into place. The humming grew in intensity, and the verdigris began to shake loose, falling away. Underneath was a brilliant copper shell that shone brightly in the pale light.

Joram's hands grew warm, then his forearms and shoulders too. It felt as though something were creeping up his body, slowly washing over him bit by bit, filling him with a new energy and spirit. His grumbling stomach was quieted, and his hunger pangs went away. His cold flesh became warm, his goose pimples disappearing as he relaxed.

The energy swept up his neck to the top of his head, and his scalp began to tingle. It felt as if a hundred tiny little creatures were crawling all over his smooth skin. Joram closed his eyes. It felt so nice, so powerful.

Then the vibrating stopped, taking the surge of energy along with it. Joram opened his eyes, startled by the abrupt change, and he looked down at the orb in his hands. Already the edges were beginning to tarnish again. Faint bits of green creeping up from the sides of the handholds.

"Well?" asked Amur, his decaying mouth open in a wide grin. "What do you think?"

"About what?" replied Joram. "It didn't do anything. Just hummed a little."

"Oh no? Then what are those on your head?"

Joram put the orb on the ground at his feet, and reached up to touch his head. His heart leaped in his chest.

"I . . . I have horns! Two of them," shouted Joram. He ran his hands over the new growth. "And . . . and they have tines!"

"Yes," said Amur, admiring the elf's new horns. "I

would think that you could get back inside your home now, if you wanted."

"Yes, I think I could," replied Joram, so overjoyed at his new luck. "Do you know which way it is? I don't mean to be rude, but I would very much like to show my mother my new horns."

The tree druid smiled. "Of course," he said. "I understand. But before I tell you how to get home you must first tell me your name."

"Oh," said Joram, feeling rather guilty for not having even told his new friend his name. "My name is Joram." He smiled. "Now Joram Twohorns."

"Well, Joram Twohorns, take good care of that orb. Don't ever let it get too far from you—"

"I won't. I'll put it in the vault and watch over it forever," interrupted the young elf, still overly excited.

"Good. See that you do." Amur bent over and began tracing something in the dirt beside the fire. "Now, in order for you to get home, you must first follow the river all the way to the lake, then head to the east from there. It will take you at least two days, but a young elf such as yourself should have no problem. . . ."

* * * * *

Arriving back at the wall to Strongroot, Joram couldn't help but smile. He was returning home from a successful artifact hunt—with a tremendous prize. It was a dream come true.

The ground around the wall was mucky, churned over no doubt by the black poplar's attack. The wall itself was heavily damaged. Huge cracks and crushed-in dents were scattered across its surface.

As he approached the base of Strongroot, a scouting party of nearly twenty elves stepped past the wards and into view, appearing as if out of nowhere. Safewrights, most of them, they were the guardians of the safehold, charged with keeping safe not only the objects of beauty in the vaults, but also the elves inside the walls.

"Stop right there," shouted a safewright guardian, lowering a chevalblade as he approached.

The others followed suit, spreading out to surround Joram.

"Do you not recognize me?" asked Joram, stopping where he stood. "I have not been gone that long."

There was commotion in the back of the scouting party as someone pushed through.

"Joram?" said Tekla Ironleaf, surprise in her voice. "Is that you?"

Joram smiled. "Yes mother." His smile grew even wider as he touched his head. "And I've grown horns."

Tekla Ironleaf pressed through the safewrights, pushing their blades toward the ground as she passed. Rushing to Joram, she grabbed hold of her son with both arms, squeezing him against her with all of her might. "It's a miracle."

Smothered by his mother's embrace, he held the orb under one arm, squeezing it to his body as tight as he could. He didn't want it to come popping out.

When his mother finished crushing him, Joram took a step back and lifted his prize into the air, holding it up for the entire scouting party to see.

"And look what I found."

The verdigris had all but completely covered the outer shell of the orb, but some of the brilliant copper still shone through.

Placing his hands inside the handholds, Joram activated

the sphere, twisting it again, as Amur had shone him in the shee knoll. The orb hummed, and once again power surged up his arms, filling him with energy.

This time, however, Joram wished for his home to be repaired.

He could feel the energy surge through his stomach and down through his legs. Slowly it spread out, touching the muddy ground and turning it into a patch of lush, green grass. The other elves stepped back, awed by the show of power.

But the orb wasn't finished. The energy swiftly overtook the scouting party, moving past them to reach up into the side of the safehold. The sections of the outer wall that had been smashed in by the black poplar lit up with a bright white light, the damage knitting itself back together until it was whole and pristine again.

"He has brought us the end of our burden," whispered Tekla.

A familiar voice bellowed from out of the safehold.

"What is going on here?" Mullenix the Elder stepped from the wall, limping as he and the other vigilants closed in on Joram and the scouting party.

Joram held up the copper orb, now shiny and beautiful. "I have returned, and with an artifact for the vaults."

Mullenix snatched the sphere and examined it, a scowl on his face. "And where did you find this?"

"In a shee knoll, just along the river," replied Joram.

The old elf took a long time in examining the artifact, checking over every seam and glimmer.

"It is up to the council to decide what goes into the vault—and what does not." Placing his hands in the handholds, Mullenix twisted the two halves, just as Joram had.

But instead of humming and filling the old elf with

power, a black light emanated from the sphere. Tendrils grew from the artifact, reaching out toward each of the elves. The safewrights pulled back, but they weren't fast enough. The strange light accelerated, closing the gap and taking hold.

Where it touched, the elves' skin began to fray and decay. Huge pustules grew, burst, and withered as the entire scouting party was stricken.

"The Canker!" shouted Tekla Ironleaf as she dropped to her knees, her left arm falling from her body as the disease took hold.

The other elves screamed in pain, their bodies being quickly devoured and twisted by the orange plague.

Then the black light reached the wall of the safehold. Where it had before knit together the crushed sections of wood, now it took them apart, rotting the magical wood from the inside out. Huge holes began to appear in the structure, exposing the inner halls, rooms, and walkways of Strongroot.

Joram couldn't believe his eyes. "What . . . what's going on? This isn't . . . the orb gives you wishes. It grew back my horns."

A heavy rumbling echoed through the forest. Branches and trees snapped and crunched as something huge and heavy marched toward the elves. Then an army of treefolk appeared, more black poplar. This time, however, they were being led—by Amur Brokenlimb, the canker witch.

Mullenix the Elder fell to the ground, dropping the orb as his body was eaten by the Canker. He pointed at Joram.

"You did this to us," gurgled the old elf, his voice almost a whisper. "You have destroyed us all."

The other vigilants were slowly dying from the Canker as well. The denizens of Strongroot fled their swiftly disintegrating home. It was madness. Screams of terror and pain filled the forest. Meanwhile all Joram could do was watch his friends and his mother come apart at the seams.

"Amur, what are you doing?" shouted Joram. "Stop them. This is my home."

The black poplar spread out, chasing the hobbled elves and crushing them, one by one under their powerful roots. Others charged toward the safehold, pounding even bigger holes in its decaying outer wall.

The canker witch ignored the young elf's plea. Instead, he moved right toward Joram, bellowing as he drew nearer. "Joram Twohorns, I have come to receive my payment."

"Payment?" asked Joram, backing away from the slow tree druid. "But look at what the orb has done. Your gift has ruined everything."

"Everything has a price. And you said you wanted to repay me," replied the canker witch. "I heard you with my own ears."

Several of the other black poplar moved toward Joram, all of them much faster than the canker witch, and they closed on the young elf.

Taking one last look at the crumbling ruins of Strongroot, Joram turned and ran, bounding into the darkness ahead. The screams of dying elves echoing in his ears, overtopped only by the tromping and smashing of the black poplar as they pursued him.

Leaping over roots, puddles, and huge lily pads, Joram headed east—for the edge of the woods. Anywhere he could go in the forest, the treefolk could find him. But if he left the forest, perhaps he had a chance to get away. He'd seen a field of some kind, not too far from Strongroot. He would head there. See if the trees could catch him in the open.

But the farther he got from his ruined home and the

sphere, the weaker he became. His legs began to grow tired, his breath labored, and his stomach grew uneasy. His pace slowed, but he forced himself on.

Finally, he caught a glimpse of a faint light at the edge of the woods—a place where the open sky could be seen through the thick branches and heavy trees. Every step brought with it more pain and withering fatigue.

Stumbling out of Ravens' Run, the sky opened up above him, just as it had a few days before while he had clung to the legs of the giant mosquito. No longer surrounded by decaying trees and grasping roots, Joram found himself chest high in dry brown grass. It tore at his skin as he pressed on, the tops grabbing at him like millions of little fingers but letting him pass all the same.

Up ahead he could see the creatures standing in the middle of the field. It looked as if they hadn't moved a single inch since the day he had first noticed them. They were tall and brown, almost the same color as the dry grass that seemed to spread out forever.

Joram's legs finally gave out, his body completely drained, and he collapsed to the ground, crashing into a pile at the feet of one of the strange creatures. His stomach cramped, and he wrapped his arms around his belly trying to contain the ache.

Rolling onto his back, Joram looked up at the sky—and the bound pile of grass he had mistaken for a creature. Suddenly it all became clear. They hadn't moved because they weren't alive. They were scarecrows.

A heavy rustling filled Joram's ears, and the weak light was suddenly blocked out by the huge grinning visage of Amur Brokenlimb.

"I told you not to let the orb get too far from you," said the canker witch.

Joram could hardly speak, his entire body felt as if it were being crushed under a tremendous weight. "What . . . what do you . . . want from me?"

Amur touched Joram's face with a branch, the orange canker dripping onto his skin. "Only to be repaid for my gift."

"But . . . but the orb has destroyed my home," said Joram. "I have nothing to give you."

Joram could feel the weight lift from his body as his energy and will to struggle flowed out of him. His eyelids grew heavy, and he could no longer keep them open. He rested his head on the ground, and submitted to the tree druid's spell.

* * * * *

Sometime later Joram opened his eyes again. The pain and cramping, the fatigue and heaviness were all gone. He felt alive, awake, and healthy.

Looking around, he realized he was back inside the forest, the grass field nowhere to be seen. Amur Brokenlimb stood before him, the orb resting beside his roots.

"Where am I?" asked Joram.

"At home," said Amur.

Joram lifted himself to his elbows. Where there were once tall, smooth walls, there were now none. Where there had been hallways and classrooms, and . . . and the vault protecting all the beautiful things the elves had gathered to protect, now there was nothing but the ruined remains of Strongroot safehold. It looked just like the shee knoll—traces of a once-beautiful place.

"Now for the rest of the payment," said the tree druid.

"The rest of the payment?" said Joram, lifting himself

to his feet. "You have taken everything. My home is destroyed, and everyone is dead."

"That was the first part of your payment," explained the canker witch. Reaching to the ground, he lifted the copper orb and handed it back to Joram. "This is the rest."

Joram took the artifact. "I don't understand."

"Now it is your burden. Keep it close. You saw what happened when you ran too far away." The decrepit treefolk walked into the forest, leaving Joram standing by himself where he had been only four days before.

Just before he disappeared from view, Amur turned and shook a canker-covered limb at the young elf. "How you choose to use it from here is up to you."

WILL MCDERMOTT

Meme slept.

And while she slept, Meme dreamed.

Horrible creatures towered over her, pointing at Meme with long, pale, almost translucent fingers. Strange sounds, like the shrieks of a kelpie, escaped their thin lips as bright eyes stared right through her. Meme felt herself falling into the large, black pools in the centers of those frightening eyes.

She tried to escape, tried to make her small legs move, but her body wouldn't, or couldn't, obey the commands of her mind. It was as if she had been buried. She couldn't feel her limbs. She couldn't feel anything at all, except terror. Her heart beat loudly in her head, sounding like the wing beats of a great raptor, pounding out a staccato tempo in her ears.

Meme opened her mouth to scream, but only gurgles issued forth. This seemed to amuse the horrible creatures. They tossed their heads back, and wild, braided hair waved like serpents above them as they opened their mouths and cackled like gwyllion hags.

Frightened, and now infuriated by the derision of her bizarre captors, Meme's heart began to beat ever louder, ever faster, drowning out the cackling laughter and the shrieking voices. It no longer sounded like wings so much as the pounding of drums.

The beat increased and yet she began to hear voices

again, above the incessant din. But these voices were different, familiar. The voices cried out in pain, cried out for help. Meme heard her name on the wind. It called to her to awaken. "Meme!" the voice called. "Meme. Run, Meme. Run!"

"Mama?"

* * * * *

Meme awoke to the sounds of battle. All around her, boggarts scrabbled at one another, kicking up dirt and crashing through the scrub brush growing around the warrens. One tall, hairless beast she knew to be named Dren charged at the much smaller boggart standing over Meme—her mother. Dren lowered his head as he charged, his widely-spaced horns bearing down, but Meme's mother stayed resolute and barked out an order for Dren to stop. She looked down at Meme.

"Run, Meme. You cannot stay. Not now. Not anymore."

Dren's thick skull impacted Meme's mother in the chest, knocking her back against the hard edge of the warren. Before her mother could roll out of the way, Dren wrapped his long arms around her. His momentum bore them both to the ground, where he began swinging his head back and forth, trying to impale her on his horns.

Meme's mother rolled around under Dren's weight in an effort to squirm free. Meme didn't know what to do. She felt as transfixed by fear now as she had been in her dream.

Other boggarts advanced up the warren-lined hill toward the fight. Large and small, covered in thick fur or hairless like Dren, with horns of all shapes and sizes, they came as Dren and her mother struggled on the ground at her feet. Some brandished clubs or jagged-edged daggers, others just bared their long claws, but all the eyes of the incoming mob blazed red with mindless hatred, staring not through Meme, like the creatures in her dream, but directly at her.

They came for her. The boggarts were coming for Meme.

But why? They were her family . . . her friends. Weren't they?

"Run Meme," cried her mother. "Run now, baby. Please!"

A few moments later, Meme found herself above the warrens, running through the foothills into the perpetual twilight, away from the only home she'd ever known. She dared not look back. She tried to shut out the screams that rang through the still air. Tears streamed down her cheeks, but she kept running.

* * * * *

Auntie Geg sat on his throne—the hollow of a gnarled, vine-covered tree blackened by soot, dirt, and bodily excretions—and gazed out on his domain with tired eyes. The world seemed so drab. Cloaked in shadows, the trees loomed over his warrens like scarecrows, inert and lifeless. Dank air filled with the myriad scents of decay hung like a blanket of fog around the old shaman, invading his throat and nostrils, further deadening his senses.

Geg sighed, his fat lips twitching with the passing of air. The old boggart longed for the sensual pleasure of something new, something vibrant and alive in this gray, stagnant world. In this, he was unique in the warren hills. Most boggarts were content with whatever meat they could snatch in their claws or cut down with their swords, often falling upon a bloody carcass and devouring it whole in a rage of gluttony.

Geg, though, fed on spirits, on life itself—and his tastes tended toward the bizarre. The more varied and interesting the life, the better. He drank in the very essence of the beings he "ate," reliving their experiences, existing vicariously through the life-force of others. His diet of late had been bland. He hungered for something new. He hungered for life.

Geg sighed again and shifted his great bulk on the stump as he eyed his offspring arrayed before him. They were his army, his gatherers. They were also his emergency rations. Geg cast a simple shamanic spell to summon his eldest son, who shambled over, a vacant look in his eyes as he stared straight ahead at a knothole on the twisted tree above Geg's head.

He nodded at the boy towering over him and motioned for him to kneel, the slightest tinge of magic attached to the gesture. Geg's feeding habits had increased his magical abilities over the years. Unlike most boggart shamans who specialized in flames or flowers, Geg commanded much more primal and personal powers, having ingested the experiences of many strange and amazing sorcerers. It actually took little effort to command his children, though. Their spirits had long ago been broken by force of will and long, hard days of mental and physical torture.

The boy—Geg could not even remember the lad's name—dropped to his knees, his overlarge ears flopping against his twisted horns as he bowed at his father's feet.

Geg reached out with his wide, fleshy hand, laying it between the horns atop his son's head. For a moment, he caressed his eldest's matted hair, curling his thick claws down to encircle the lad's ears and tap lightly on his neck and cheeks.

He grasped more firmly and exerted slight pressure to turn the boy's bowed face upward. He looked into his son's eyes, staring right through the orbs down deep into his soul, allowing his magic to take hold of the boy's mind, his memory, and his essence. As Geg drank it all in, a fine, pink-tinged mist escaped from his son's mouth, nose, eyes, and ears. It swirled in the air and drifted up toward Geg, who breathed it in with deep gulps.

The boy twitched, his head quivering for a moment, perhaps attempting to pull away from his father, but Geg's control was too complete, too eternal, and the slight head shake ended at the same time the mist stopped billowing forth from his orifices. Geg released his grip on his son's head and let the lifeless husk fall to the ground at his feet.

Without a word, two of the boy's siblings came forward, their eyes as vacant as still pools, and dragged the corpse of their brother down into the warrens.

* * * * *

Meme collapsed in a heap. She couldn't run another step. If the other boggarts came for her now, they would find her easy prey. She lay in a tight ball on the ground, breathing in irregular gasps, her hands wrapped tightly around her body as if they were the only things holding her heaving stomach inside her body.

When she could think and breathe normally, Meme asked herself the question that had plagued her since she began her headlong flight into the twilight, "Why?"

Why had her family and the friends of her mother

turned on them? The memory of her mother pinned beneath Dren, fighting for her life—fighting for both of their lives—caused tears to well up in her eyes. "Why, Mama?" she said as the tears flowed. "Why?"

Meme had never really fit in. She had no real friends. The other boggart children called her "softie" and enjoyed poking her until she cried. So, Meme had learned to keep mostly to herself in the warren. She had her mother and that had been enough. Now she didn't even have that. No warren, no home, no family, and no mother. Meme was alone.

The tears came again, in force this time. The young girl sobbed into balled-up fists, tears streaming down her lithe fingers to drip onto the hard ground, making tiny divots in the dust. She shuddered as each wave of emotion wracked her little body.

After a time the tears stopped. Not because she had fallen asleep, not because the emotions had faded into the eternal twilight. Meme simply had no tears left to cry. Her eyes had run dry.

She uncurled her body and pushed herself off the ground. Standing on her own two feet again, Meme found that beyond the tears and her fear, beyond the raw emotion of the bloody morning, an odd state of calm had awoken inside her. She cocked her head to listen for sounds of pursuit. She heard none.

She truly was alone now, for the first time in her short life. But this time that thought didn't send her into a catatonic fit of tears and screams. She simply brushed the dust from her ragged clothes and looked around at her surroundings, searching for a new home.

Behind her a great series of crags towered over rocky foothills. Lined with warrens and topped by twisted and blackened trees, these hills stretched out almost as far as she could see. Something inside Meme told her she would not be safe here in the warren hills—not now, not ever again. Ahead, at the distant edge of the foot hills, she could see a line of deeper shadow rising out of the twilight-cloaked hills. The forest.

Meme's mother had told her as a child of the terrible creatures called elves, enemies of the boggarts, who lived in the dark shadows of the forest. She had explained that the forest had so many trees you couldn't see the dim sky above, couldn't see your enemy until you blundered upon them in the dark. The tribe would sometimes venture into the forest to hunt, but she was never to go there alone. It was too dangerous.

She looked closer at the shadow of the forest looming in the distance. The boggarts were no longer her family, and the warrens no longer her home. Perhaps she could find a new home in the land of her enemies. Meme set out for the forest, her ears straining to hear the guttural barking and growling sounds of boggarts as she picked her way through the warren-laden hills.

* * * * *

The life experience of Geg's eldest did not sate the shaman for long. It was always the same. His children sought out new entities, new sensations for Geg to feed upon, for Geg to enjoy. But the world of the boggarts held little left of interest to Geg. His thirst grew ever stronger, his appetite for stimuli ever greater with each life he drained. He longed for something new, something fresh to experience, something that would satiate his burning desires for more than a few hours.

He sometimes sent his children out into other lands to look for fabled creatures such as scarecrows, cinders, and elves, but though they served him well in the warrens—for all boggarts had learned to fear and respect Geg and his children—their minds were too clouded with commands, too dulled by control, to operate independently in unfamiliar territory.

However, Geg had felt a stirring in the land earlier this morning. Something had come alive within the warrens—a fresh soul had blossomed in the middle of his kingdom. Geg had no idea how such an event could have occurred with such suddenness, how he could have missed such a vibrant entity in the heart of his own domain.

Perhaps his own senses had become as dull as the souls he consumed—perhaps this was an aberration of the sensual explosion that he often experienced after ingesting the fullness of a life. He had saved his eldest for just such a boost, had needed that lift after what seemed like months of drab, lifeless souls.

Whatever the case, Geg's senses had extended a thousand-fold upon the consumption of his eldest's life experiences, and in that moment he had felt the life of a vibrant being explode into existence out in the warrens. Immediately, Geg had dispatched all his children, sent them out to scour the land for this new being, this dynamic, alive, and yet somehow alien creature that had infiltrated his realm. Tonight Geg would sup well. He would imbibe the sweet nectar of the beautiful flower that had blossomed in the twilight. Tonight Geg would experience the richness of life once again.

* * * * *

Meme's legs ached. Her feet throbbed with every step. The boggarts moved throughout the warren hills, finding new feeding grounds and new holes to inhabit, but her mother had often carried her during those trips. All Meme had to do was look up, eyes opened wide, a slight quiver on her lips, perhaps a tear hanging precariously at her cheek or chin, and her mother would spread her arms wide and lift Meme into the air, carrying her the rest of the day.

Quivering lips and tears would do her no good now. There was no one to hold her, no one to carry her. She looked across the foothills to the horizon and was disheartened to see the bulging shadow that marked the edge of the forest hadn't grown much larger.

"This will take forever," she lamented. Hearing only her echo in response, Meme realized there was no one to console her either. She sighed and wiped dried tears from her face, smearing dust into her nostrils and lips.

Spitting and sneezing as the dirt tried to invade her body, she trudged on. Every once in a while, a small whimper escaped her lips, but her resolve strengthened with each painful step. She would be strong like her mother. She would survive. It was all she could do. It was all her mother had ever wanted for her. Of that Meme was certain.

Meme had no idea how long she had walked. The twilight world of the warrens changed little from meal to meal, day to day. The sky was a constant turmoil of reds, oranges, and purples vying for dominance over the barren hills. She had often wondered how her mother and the other adults knew when it was time to get up or go to bed or eat the noonday meal.

Now she realized that she hadn't eaten at all this day. Her stomach gurgled in response to the thought. Boggarts ate voraciously, spending most of their days either hunting or eating. Meme had no idea how to hunt and had no weapon. She doubted she could even catch a bloated toad like the ones the other boggart children sometimes put in her bedding, but she had to try.

She needed to find water. Animals always congregated at the water. It was the only hunting lesson she remembered from her early attempts to learn the ways of the boggart tribe, and thus fit in with the other children.

Where had she seen water? Her tribe's warrens had been near a crag-fed spring. Out here in the middle of these barren hills, though, she might not find any water at all. Her mother said that the cinders had burned all the water away, which Meme had always thought was just another story to scare her into staying close to home. How could cinders burn water, anyway?

Just then, Meme heard a sound, a sizzling and crackling sound like a rat might make as it twisted slowly on a spit over the fire. That thought probably came from her stomach, she realized, but before she knew what she was doing, Meme's stomach guided her feet toward the sound, which seemed to come from somewhere over the next hillock.

Huffing and puffing, her stomach now growling so loudly she was sure it would scare off any small animals she was likely to find, Meme climbed to the top of the hill. The sizzling grew louder with every step. As she neared the crest, it began to sound like a bubbling pot of moss and lizard stew. She rubbed her gurgling stomach as she reached the top and looked down into the small valley on the other side.

Meme gasped and her hands clamped over her mouth to suppress the scream that would have surely followed. For there at the base of the hill, standing at the edge of a small pond that popped and sizzled as if on fire, towered a seven-foot-tall cinder.

Black soot covered its skeletal body and small wisps of smoke drifted into the air from the pitted bones of the cinder's arms, chest, and shoulders as it stuck the ragged-edged blade of an ebony sword into the water over and over again. Each time the blade sliced the surface, the water roiled and steamed. A seething mist spread out from the tip of the blade, threatening to engulf the small pond.

Meme didn't move a muscle, dared not even take a step back down the hill for fear of making enough noise to alert the cinder. But it seemed intent on boiling away all the water in the small pond, and after a while Meme steeled her nerves and slowly backed away.

She might have made it but for a small rat, oblivious to its danger, that scurried out from a hole, drawing the furious attention of the cinder. It reeled around at the noise and skewered the rodent on the tip of its sword. The acrid, but familiar smell of burning fur filled the air for a moment as the rat ignited from the heat of the sword.

Meme squeaked at the sight. Not a loud squeak, not much more than the sound a rodent might make upon bursting into flames. But it was enough. The cinder's head snapped up at the sound and stared at Meme, its fire red eyes burning into hers. Raising its sword, the smoking rat still impaled upon the end, the cinder opened its mouth and screamed.

* * * * *

Dren had already told them everything he knew. Why did they continue to claw at his flesh? Geg's children had arrived shortly after his midday meal. Dren had been sucking the last bit of gristle from his claws when they stormed into the middle of the warrens. He had backed into his own hovel, hoping they had not come for him—or at least would find someone else to haul away before noticing him.

Dren was not the actual leader of the tribe, but all boggarts in these warrens followed his lead because he was the fiercest fighter . . . as his father had been before Geg's boys had hauled him off to the shaman. Everyone knew that you did not return from a trip to Geg. No one knew what Geg did to those who were summoned, but all were sure it had to be worse than death.

Some tribes had fought back against the children of Geg, and some even killed the shaman's offspring. Those tribes had suffered the full wrath of Geg, who had left his thorny throne and descended upon them with the full force of his magic, chasing the last of them through the warren hills until they all lay dead and rotting, left to feed the carrion eaters as a warning to others.

And so Dren hid in his hole, his eyelids mere slits as he watched Geg's children roam unmolested through the camp. They stopped at every hole, dragged out the boggarts skulking within, and pinned them to the ground as they sniffed at them. Dren had never seen the children of Geg do this before. It was curious and terrifying.

They eventually pulled the beaten and broken body of Dina out of the warren where he had tossed it earlier, after the abomination she'd been protecting had run off into the hills. Geg's children sniffed at Dina's corpse for a long time, jabbering at one another every few minutes. They then searched the rest of her warren, bringing a tattered blanket out into the middle of the camp.

The one holding the blanket pointed at Geru, the supposed

leader of the tribe. Geru was an old boggart, barely fit to hunt, let alone lead, but Dren had never challenged the old fool, for it was often better to lead from the side than from the top. This seemed like just one of those times. But then, Geru did something unexpected. After just a few claw swipes across his ugly face, the weak boggart leader pointed at Dren's hole and screamed at Geg's children.

"Dren is who you want. Over there. Over there!"

Dren could only smile. He had obviously underestimated Geru all this time. The old boggart was not quite the fool he had thought. But Dren would not go so easily into the twilight. Before they reached his warren, he exploded from the hole, spearing the first of Geg's children in the stomach with his right horn. He bore the large boggart to the ground, whipping his head to the side upon impact. Blood sprayed out of the gash followed by bits of pink, fleshy organs.

Dren stood and grabbed the next child of Geg by the throat, intending to slice through the soft skin and leave it to bleed to death as he turned his attention to the last two. But before he had the chance, Geru slammed into him below the knees while several other members of the tribe grabbed Dren by the shoulders and dragged him to the ground.

"You would doom us all?" screamed Geru, as he dropped the weight of his entire body on Dren's thighs.

"To save myself?" said Dren as he tried to kick the leader's bulk off his legs. "Yes." This last word came out as little more than a grunt, for the two tribe mates who had grabbed his shoulders landed on his stomach and chest at that moment, pinning him to the ground.

The one holding the tattered blanket loomed over him then and began questioning Dren about the creature Dina had been protecting. Dren quickly told Geg's children everything he knew about the abomination: how they had awoke to find the strange creature in their midst that morning, how he had gone after the beast, only to be attacked by Dina, who protected it so fiercely it seemed as if she thought the abomination were her own child, and how the creature had run off in the middle of the battle.

But all of that had done little to assuage the anger of the children of Geg. The one with the blanket continued to rip bits of flesh from his face and chest as his own tribe mates, those who had stood beside him against Dina and the creature, held him to the ground.

As Dren's life drained away with every drop of blood that spilled from his many wounds, he could only think that perhaps there might still be some way to get free and wreak vengeance upon the children of Geg as well as Geru and the rest of the tribe. In his mind, at least, he fought to the very end, just as his father had before him, unrepentant and unforgiving.

* * * * *

Smoke billowed from the cinder's mouth as it screamed at Meme. Before she could react, the ash black creature sprinted up the hill, its joints crackling and snapping as it ran, like logs burning in a fire. The scream echoed back at Meme from the hills behind her, making her jump thinking another cinder had somehow come up behind her.

In that moment of confusion, Meme ran down the hill toward the cinder. Realizing her mistake, she tried to stop, but her feet skid on some loose rocks and, as she tried to catch her balance, she pitched forward into a tumbling roll. Head over heels, she tumbled down the hill as the cinder sprinted up toward her. Unable to change direction in time, they collided.

The sharp edges of the cinder's legs tore through Meme's ragged top and sliced into the skin on her back, which immediately began to blister from the heat. Meme screamed from the pain, but a moment later the heat subsided as she barreled on past the blackened monster.

She caught a glimpse of the cinder in a heap on the ground behind her as she rolled on down the hill. Smoke wafted up from the ground around its bony feet, knees, and hands as it clambered upright after the impact. The fire in the cinder's eyes seemed to burn even brighter as it ran back down the hill.

All Meme could do was continue rolling and hope she could stay ahead of the smoking skeleton. That hope was quickly dashed as she splashed into the steaming pond at the bottom of the hill. Meme came to a rest, sitting in the hot water like a chunk of meat in thin broth. Behind her, she could hear the crackling of the cinder's body as it descended upon her again.

Without even thinking about what she was doing, Meme crawled out deeper into the water. She glanced back to see the cinder stop for a moment at the edge of the pond. It glared at her from the shore and then stuck the rat-impaled tip of its sword into the water. Bubbles rose and popped on the surface as the water began to boil around the sword.

The water around Meme began to warm up, but did not boil. She stood and ran, splashing through the steaming pond to the other side. Perhaps the cinder sensed its prey getting away. Perhaps it merely grew impatient. Meme couldn't tell, but it gave up trying to cook her in the pond and entered the water behind her.

Steam erupted from behind Meme, the hissing of the

pond almost completely masking the crackling sound of the creature's joints. Meme looked over her shoulder, but couldn't see the cinder any longer. A fog of steam covered half of the pond already. She ran on, but her short legs could only move so fast in the deepening pool.

Suddenly, Meme was underwater. She had blundered into a deep spot in the middle of the pond. She flailed her arms and legs in a panic, churning up the water as she sank toward the bottom. Her chest began to ache, but she fought back the impulse to gasp for air. Above her, the churning water bubbled as it grew intensely hot. The cinder had found her! She tried to swim away, but her thrashing movements did little but turn her around.

Just as she thought the boiling water would cook her alive, the intense heat began to fade. A moment later, Meme screamed, releasing a barrage of bubbles and much of her remaining air as the cinder floated into view. But the smoldering beast had been extinguished, the glow in its molten eyes spent. The lifeless, black skeleton sunk past Meme, coming to rest on the bottom of the pond.

Meme's head and chest throbbed from lack of air. Pushing her fear and pain down as she had done earlier, Meme reached out and grabbed hold of the skeleton and began climbing toward the surface, eventually standing on top of its skull to get her own head above water.

She gulped air into her lungs. The charred rat floated nearby. Meme grabbed it before pushing off the cinder's head with her feet to propel her back toward the shallows. Dripping wet, gasping and choking to expel water from her lungs, Meme stumbled back to shore and dropped to the ground.

Her chest ached. Her head throbbed. And her back felt

as if it were still on fire. But Meme had survived. And in her new world, that was all that truly mattered. She bit into the blackened rat and ate as she stared at the pond that had saved her after almost taking her life away.

After a while, the fog dissipated and the muddy water cleared. Meme gazed at the reflections of the surrounding landscape, intrigued even though she could see no more than a few scraggly trees and the dusky sky mirrored there.

She had rarely seen reflections. Her mother always brought her water from the spring, saying the watering hole was too dangerous for her. Marveling at this new sight, Meme crawled over to the edge to get a better look. What she saw next, though, frightened her even more than the cinder. Staring back at her from out of the water was the image of one of the horrible creatures from her dream.

* * * * *

Meme immediately looked up and behind her to locate the strange being she saw reflected in the water. It wasn't until she turned back to the reflection itself, raising her hand to strike at it, that the full realization of what she was looking at dawned on her.

The image in the water with its wild hair, long ears, narrow eyes, and thin lips—the same features as those awful creatures from her nightmare—that image, with its hand poised to strike, was her own reflection.

"But how?" she asked out loud. She was a boggart, wasn't she? Mother was a boggart. She lived with a boggart tribe, ate with them and migrated throughout the warren hills with them.

But then other memories flooded her mind. Boggart

children jeering at her, poking her whenever she tried to play with them, calling her names and putting warty toads in her bed clothes. She also remembered the adults pointing and whispering to one another whenever they thought she and her mother weren't looking.

All of that had long been overshadowed by the love in her mother's eyes, the compassion in her warm embrace, and the full measure of devotion Meme felt from her mother's every gesture, touch, and word. She had been loved and that had been enough . . . at least until this morning.

Meme still had no idea what had changed, why the rest of the boggarts had turned on her and her mother. She felt no different. Her mother's actions as she protected Meme proved her feelings were no different than they had been when the tribe bed down the night before.

Earlier in the day, Meme would have simply blamed herself—had, in fact, felt it had been all her fault. Now, she wasn't so certain. But if it was not something she had done, then what? If only she could figure it out, perhaps she could go home again.

But as soon as that thought entered Meme's head, she rejected it. The warrens were not her home, and she definitely had nothing left back there to return to. No, she had to find her own people. As much as it scared her, Meme had to find the creatures from her dream.

And with that insight came another even more profound epiphany. It all seemed so obvious to her now. The entirety of her life came down to four little words. "I am an elf," she said.

The forest wasn't the home of her enemies as her mother had warned her. It was home of her true family. How she had been raised by her boggart mother in the warren hills might forever be a mystery—just as the boggarts' sudden animosity this morning—but for now, she had a goal, an end to her journey in sight.

Meme leaned down toward the water, touched her lips to the reflected mouth of her mirror image and drank deeply from the pond. Then, tossing the rest of the charred rat to the ground beside her,-she stood and climbed the hill. Facing the looming shadow of the forest on the horizon, she set off to find her people. She set off for home.

* * * * *

Sned, the new eldest son of Geg, a particularly large, broad-chested boggart with small horns and long, pointed ears, led the main group searching for the fleeing child. Upon hearing the description Dren had given shortly before his death, Geg had informed them all that the girl was an elf and would most likely head for the forest.

Father had chastised Sned for killing Dren, and a sharp stabbing pain behind his eyes constantly reminded the eldest of that lashing. But the beastly boggart had killed his brother. He could not be allowed to live. Father would soon realize that, and then the pain would cease.

For now, Sned simply plodded on toward the forest. He wore the girl's blanket around his neck. From time to time, he brought its tattered edges up to his mouth and nose to inhale the sickly sweet odor and refresh the scent that he followed.

Sned lived for the hunt, reveled in it. Of all the children of Geg, Sned was perhaps the best tracker, and among the fiercest fighters. He had often brought in choice morsels for his father, and this had brought the large boggart a measure of autonomy within Geg's constant control. Sometimes that extra freedom allowed for impulsive actions, like killing

Dren, but Sned knew that as long as he continued to feed his father's unusual appetite, he would not become the next entrée, as his brother had earlier that day.

Bringing this elf to his father, alive and ready for consumption, would provide for many more dusk-filled days of relative freedom. Sned slapped one of his brothers in the back with the flat of his axe and growled at the rest when they turned to look at him, spurring them all on in their quest.

After a time, Sned stopped them to sniff at the ground. He took another whiff of the pungent blanket and then buried his nose in the dirt at the base of the hill where they had stopped.

He held up one hand, his long claws splayed wide, motioning for his brothers to wait. The relief in their eyes as they dropped to the ground for a brief rest almost made the eldest son of Geg smile. He was half-tempted to order them to stand while they waited, but knew that a rest now would mean more speed later, so he let them sit while he clambered to the top of the barren hillock.

When he reached the top, Sned felt disappointed. He was certain the girl had been here—might be here still—but he could see nothing at the bottom of the hill save a small pond. It was odd, though. An oasis like this in the warren hills should be full of life. Why had no boggart tribe set up warrens here? Where were the rodents and lizards, and those predators that lived on such small creatures?

Sned sniffed the air again. He definitely smelled the elf girl on the wind. Her disgustingly sweet scent almost made him retch. But there was something else as well. A tinge of ash and charcoal hung in the air, covering this small valley like a blanket of fog.

A cinder dwelled here. Had it killed the girl? If so, his

father would be very displeased, and after his impulsive act earlier, Sned feared father might blame him for losing their quarry.

He loped down the hill to look for any signs of the cinder or the girl. The pond was cool to the touch. Ripples spread out from his hand in perfect half-circles. There had been a cinder here recently, but it had obviously left some time ago. But what of the elf?

As Sned was about to stand, he spied the remains of a dead rat. He snatched it up, skewering its little body on one long claw and raising it to his face. But instead of eating the leftover snack, he inhaled deeply. The sweet nectary odor of the girl mixed with the sooty smell of the cinder on its charred body.

Had the cinder found the girl as she ate, burning both of them with its smoldering touch? If so, where was her blackened body? He examined the dead rat closely. Its fur was completely gone and the skin black and cracked from the intense heat, but the area around where the head had been chewed off was pink and moist with fresh blood. The girl, it would seem, had eaten the rat after the cinder burned its flesh.

Sned popped the half-eaten rat into his mouth and proceeded to sniff around the edge of the pond until he found her scent trailing away up the hill. He followed it to the top and smiled. Ahead of him, in the distance, the edge of the forest rose up over the warren hills.

* * * * *

The forest loomed in front of Meme like a giant, dark mouth ready to engulf her. She felt as determined as ever to enter and search for her real family, but some of her old fears held her back. What if she got lost? What if the elves weren't her people? What if they turned on her as the boggarts had? What if they didn't want her?

Meme took a deep breath as her mother had taught her to do when the world got too big and started pressing in. She blew the air out slowly through pursed lips then filled her lungs again. She began to calm down.

As she blew out the second gulp of air, Meme heard something that made her shake all over. She'd been careful all day to listen for the sounds of pursuit. Several times she had turned away from the forest as guttural growls and barks on the wind warned her of warrens ahead. She'd avoided detection by boggarts her entire journey—until now.

Meme glanced behind her. Standing atop a hillock a little ways off, she could see a small group of boggarts, all brandishing weapons. One raised its arm and pointed directly at her. The boggarts broke into a run, rushing headlong out of sight down the hill.

Why had she stopped at the top of the hill? She had left herself exposed and now would pay the price for that mistake. Meme could hear the voice of her boggart mother in her head: "One mistake is all it takes, Meme." This memory was almost immediately replaced by another, more recent one. "Run, Meme! Run!"

No tears flowed as the emotional image of her mother fighting Dren stuck in her mind's eye. Meme simply obeyed the order and sprinted down the side of her own hill. The boggarts were only two rises behind her and the forest was still several hills off. Meme knew her short legs would not keep her in the lead for long, especially when climbing back to the top of each mound.

At the bottom of the hill, she devised a plan. Instead of

running up and down each hill, she would run around the base of the mounds. It was a longer route, but just as her pursuers had disappeared from sight when they ran down the hill, she must now be out of sight for them. If she could just stay one hill ahead of her pursuers, they might not find her again before she reached the trees.

It almost worked. After a few agonizingly long minutes, the forest rose up in front of Meme. The only problem was a short stretch of open plain between the hills and the trees. Out in the open, her pursuers pounding the ground and growling behind her, Meme sprinted with every last bit of energy she had to the forest's edge.

They caught up with her just as she reached the trees. Meme expected to feel the slice of a sword or axe at any moment as the growling boggarts rushed up behind her. Instead, the lead boggart grabbed at her as they ran, his claws raking across her blistered back and grasping at her hair.

Meme dodged back and forth, using the trees to block her larger pursuers. Perhaps giving up on taking her on the run, the boggart jumped on Meme and drove her to the ground. They tumbled forward, their combined momentum crashing them into the base of a large tree.

The boggart found his feet first and grabbed Meme roughly by the arm, lifting her off the ground until her face came even with his. He exhaled a dank, musky breath on her and smiled. Meme glanced down at the boggart's neck, recognizing her blanket tied there like a necklace or a trophy. Now she had become the trophy.

The boggart's smile of triumph, however, quickly turned to a look of utter disbelief and horror a moment later when, from out of nowhere, a dagger sliced through the air and imbedded up to the hilt in his neck.

Meme dropped to the ground as the strength left the large boggart's arms. She rolled to the side to avoid the bulk of his dead body when he collapsed next to her. Blood spread throughout her blanket and spilled onto the ground beside the boggart.

Meme looked up just in time to see the elves standing in the trees before they disappeared, just as silently as they had arrived. A lone elf, a female, lingered and locked eyes with Meme. Unlike the visions of horrible creatures in her dream, this elf was beautiful. Her soft, white skin practically glowed in the darkness. Her eyes sparkled as a smile curled her thin lips up at the corners.

The elf woman tilted her head as she gazed at Meme, perhaps pondering what to do with her or trying to determine what exactly she was. Meme looked down at herself. Though their features were similar, any elf beauty she possessed was buried beneath layers of dirt and blood and the ever-present taint of the feral boggarts she had once called family.

Was this her mother? Were the elves the family she sought? Those questions, like so many others, would remain unanswered. A moment later, the elf woman shrugged, as if to say she did not have the answers either—that Meme would have to seek out those answers for herself—and then she too slipped away into the trees.

* * * * *

Meme stood and looked at the rest of her boggart pursuers. Their bodies lay strewn around her, silently bleeding out anything that remained of their life-force. She then stared deep into the foliage of the trees where the elves had disappeared. She understood now. She did not belong in either world—not in the brutal, ugly world of the boggarts out in the foothills, nor in the beautiful but mysterious forest world of the elves.

Perhaps one day she might fit in with her people in the forest, but that day was not today. For now, more than anything, she needed sleep. Tomorrow she could find some hole or tree to call home . . . at least for a time. But for tonight, the ground looked terribly inviting.

Meme began to move deeper into the forest to find a soft patch of ground away from the carnage of the battle, but then turned and walked back to the body of the large boggart who had snatched her up. Stepping onto his wide chest, she leaned over and ripped her bloodied blanket from his neck, leaving a long red streak on his pallid skin.

Then, placing one foot on the dead boggart's face, she grasped the hilt of the dagger and yanked it from his neck. She hopped down and headed off into her brave new world, wrapping the blade in her blanket as she walked. She just might need that in the days ahead. You never knew what the twilight would bring.

DOUG BEYER

Raiding-time on elf lands was Yasgo's favorite part of the night. After the weapons were properly sharpened, and the shamans' dances under the moon were complete, it was time to slink and stamp through the clawed briars to the groves of the elves. Yasgo liked the sensation of nettle-wheat scratching at his fur. It scraped away clinging spiders and toughened his skin. He liked to scythe through the stalks of nettlewheat with his sword. If they folded under his sword edge, it told him the blade needed sharpening. But tonight they hewed neatly in two and fell over in a pile. Sharp. Ready.

Elf lands smelled good, like hope and hot cooking. Yasgo couldn't see the glow of the elf tower-light yet, but the smells told him they were near. Yasgo gave a signal whistle, to tell his raidmates that the elf lands were near, and let the smells wash over him. Roasted tubers and meat. Dried herb bouquets. Cervin flesh. All were faint still, but his nose knew them immediately.

Yasgo licked his chops.

No answering whistle came. That was odd—usually Furto and Joffin were quick with their return signal. Furto had grown fat on the elves' tasty cervin mounts since they discovered the tower standing among the nettlewheat, and Joffin was mad for that foamy elven cauldron-tea. Yasgo suspected there was something deeply wrong with a bog-gart who loved a beverage brewed by elves, but he didn't complain to the raidmother. Each boggart had a passion, an obsessive favorite thing in the world. And each night they would raid wherever those things could be found.

He heard a noise—a scream. But not a scream of a boggart or an elf—something Yasgo had never heard before. He instantly wished he had never heard it at all. It was a sound that made him writhe with revulsion, go cold and perspire all at once. It began at the far end of the nettle-wheat field, and swept past him like a shockwave. The wheat didn't move, but Yasgo felt as if his insides were trying desperately to come out. He imagined the skin being flayed from his body, and his innards unrolling out behind him. The scream was swallowing everything, devouring the world at the periphery of his vision, irising down into a cluster of dull stars in the sky.

Then the scream passed. Yasgo wobbled, and realized he was still standing. He checked the skin on his arms—not a scratch. A cricket whirred. Yasgo was entirely unhurt.

The others, he thought. He didn't stop to think any farther than that. "Furto! Joffin!" he called, dashing through the nettlewheat in their direction.

The stalks were jagged and clutched at his arms and legs. Yasgo knew there would be lacerations for moving through the wheat at this pace—but why was it tearing at him so viciously? It was as if the meadow itself was trying to prevent him from getting to his warren mates.

"Oey!" he called, and he stamped his feet. "Joffin!" Answer me, he thought. Why won't they answer? "Furto!"

Yasgo spied a glint of metal and headed toward it. It was Furto's dirk, lying against Furto's limp claw.

"No. . . ." He shook his head.

Ribbons of flesh had separated from Furto's body like

hairy strips of paper. Furto lay in a mangled clump, his revealed organs shriveled and black. His eyes bugged out as if they were still seeing something horrible, and his tongue lolled out.

Yasgo staggered back and fell over the remains of Joffin.

Yasgo shrieked. And he didn't stop shrieking until he realized he was running and felt his speed in the bowing of the wheat stalks.

Slow down, boggart. Slow. The nettles are ripping into you. Slow. Stop. Breathe.

He stopped and bent over with his hands on his knees. Their bodies had shown no sign of physical attack— no sword slashes, no broken bones. They looked like crabapples rotten from the inside, fruit whose skin opens to reveal only hollow decay.

Yasgo felt the world spinning around him. He shut his eyes against the spinning, but then the images of his two mates, hollowed out like gourds, flashed against his eyelids. He tried to press his palms into his eye sockets to blot them out, but there they were, again and again.

"Oey, Yasgo!" said Furto's dead face. "It take us! We just night raid, like any night, and lady take us!"

"Not fair," agreed Yasgo to the vision.

"Yasgo, lady must pay," said Joffin's death-sneer. "She take us. Not time. Not right."

Yasgo gritted his teeth and did what always made him feel better—he grabbed the worn leather of his sword hilt. He drew and slashed, stepped and slashed again. He lunged and disemboweled a nearby crabapple tree. He grunted and hacked around him, spelling out childish justice in the air.

This would not solve anything. Furto and Joffin were not

coming back. He roared—but the roar was stifled in a gasp. He saw movement, some dark figure pausing to regard him from a field away. It seemed to notice his gaze and turned away quickly, melting into shadow.

The lady. The beast that killed his mates. Yasgo ran after it.

"Get back here! You'll pay! You took them! Give them back!"

He leaped through the wheat, his pace accelerated by rage. As he ran, he found purchase on the large rocks that punctuated the field and bounded over the sea of nettles one stepping-stone at a time. By the time he reached the place where he had seen the figure dart away, he was standing on a ledge of masonry. He peered around and saw no sign of movement. But he saw that he had entered elf lands.

The rocks were not natural boulders in the field, but a broken stone wall. The wall, crumbled in some places from thousands of years of neglect—and several consecutive nights of boggart raiding—separated the wild corridors of Shadowmoor from an ancient safehold of elves.

The elves were worshipers of nature, Yasgo knew. Nature was, of course, an entirely stupid thing to worship. In this withered world, worshiping nature was like worshiping the process of growing old, or the course of adder's venom spreading through a victim. Nature was a series of sightless cycles designed to destroy life over time. Yasgo knew it. Furto and Joffin knew it. Elves seemed to think it was otherwise. Yasgo stepped down from the low wall into elf territory.

The safehold was a stone tower surrounded by a radius of impassable bramble. The tower was oddly tapered, thin at the bottom and wide at the top, like the conical breath of some subterranean dragon angry at the sky. As Yasgo looked up at it, it appeared to sway in the wind—probably an illusion of the vertiginous height. Sickly light shone from the top.

"Halt," said a female voice. Yasgo turned and saw only the point of a long blade.

* * * * *

"I don't understand, *Druai*. This spell is designed to . . . give what back?"

"All of it. The nightmares. The screams. The darkness."

"What makes you think it was . . . given to us? Darkness suffuses the world, and fills the dreams we faeries traffic in. What makes you think it isn't as much a part of Shadowmoor's identity as you or I, or the queen?"

"Oh, it's part of our world now, no question. I don't expect the spell will succeed. No, I just want to do my part to throw off what our world doesn't deserve. I know in my heart that the darkness is a cuckoo's egg."

"I think I follow . . . An intruder in the nest?"

"Lain by an external intruder. Which means our nest, our world, was particularly well suited to absorbing darkness. And what absorbs darkness, Scion?"

"Light, I suppose you mean me to say. But *Druai*, I don't believe this was a world of light. You have no evidence, just a feeling."

"It's an educated feeling. Think of this: What purpose do the elves serve?"

"Ha. Sustenance for all other creatures, if I recall the old joke."

"They do more than that. They struggle, and they change this world. They are the only elements in this world that protrude out of the uniform darkness. They're Shadowmoor's catalyst. Without them, darkness would dominate. Where they roam, it recedes, if only a tiny bit."

"So they can change the world? Purge the darkness forever?"

"No. There's no hope for their kind—not while the banshee still roams. Death is all we can all look forward to. But their ability to change the darkness—it supports my thesis. Shadowmoor has more than its fair share of darkness."

"Fair share! You speak as if there could be more to have."

"There are other . . . places. Other sources of darkness. Sources that have contributed to our own."

"You are the gloomiest, most strange-minded faerie ever born from the pollen of Oona, even for a learned *druai*. The idea that this world contains only a portion of all the possible evil out there . . . preposterous. What purpose would it serve for another world to contribute its darkness to ours?"

"To reduce that world's supply. To brighten other worlds."

"So Shadowmoor is a filter?"

"Shadowmoor is a receptacle. Of evil."

* * * * *

The elf who stood before Yasgo was beautiful, flawless and ghostly like a kithkin child's skin. She had put herself between him and the safehold tower, as if she guarded it, yet she was dressed for travel. Yasgo must have run into her as she was about to take a journey.

"You're far from home, boggart," she said. Her accent was strongly Elvish, melodic, almost singsong.

As she stood scowling at him in a battle stance, Yasgo thought he saw a spark in her eyes, like a lantern burning from within. It was like the glow that sometimes lit the east on the clearest of nights, but never quite reached out to brighten the sky. Or like the glow of the raidmother's eyes when she was about to cuff a misbehaving brat.

"I'm . . . not raiding," he said. It was true, now.

Her blade was steady, held with the flat exactly perpendicular to the ground like a sheer cliff, and pointing straight at the boggart's eye. If she lunged, he wouldn't be able to see it for a fraction of a second, he would miss his chance to defend, and he would die. He was in her control.

"You lie," she said. "I, Valya of the Lochran Safehold, must destroy you."

Yasgo's usual answer to an elf's challenge would be to chop at her lithe kneecap as hard as he could with his blade, but he didn't. Her sword point was out of focus, too close to his eyeball to discern. He found himself staring at her wrist, the taut tendons that maintained her grip on the laces of bent flax, and at the angle of her elbow next to her bracer. He gasped at himself. He was about to be slain by an elf, and he was . . . admiring her?

* * * * *

As the banshee drifted, her toes hung just far enough into the bog water to drag two Vs of algae and rotting debris along behind her. Her body was weightless, bowed back gently at the waist as if propelled by some unseen force at the small of her back, and her hair floated like underwater snakes. Yet everything felt heavy to her. She let her head loll to one side.

The swamp below her feet stank of the final arc in every

natural cycle. Pale fungus grew on the slime of decaying life. Flies drifted in little clouds from one unrecognizable heap of rot to another, nestling special seeds inside each host that would soon bloom into more flies.

Under her wispy veil, the banshee began to mouth words, and tilted her head to and fro with the meaning of those words. If anyone could have seen her eyes, they would have communicated the song's deep sorrow. But she produced no sound, not even a dry wheeze. She dared not.

As the banshee drifted past a stump, her hand grazed the head of a frog. The creature stopped crooning, and in the banshee's wake, flies dropped to the ground.

* * * * *

Yasgo regarded the elf Valya, tall in her defender's armor. He had tasted the meat of many elves, but he had never been so taken aback by one's bold, resolute glow.

She reminded Yasgo of a particular rowan treefolk from his youth—one that he and his raid party had worked for three nights to finally fell. The rowan had dug its roots deep in the hillside and spread its branches wide and proud under the night sky. Even as Yasgo and his warren mates rocked it free of the compressed earth, it reached high. Yasgo's cousin had made wooden clubs from it, and poking-sticks to wipe the mud from boggart feet.

Valya's blade quivered near Yasgo's eyeball, but she drew it back. She seemed to have decided something.

"You're not part of a warren, are you?" the elf asked.

Yasgo felt strange, conversing with an elf. Like having a conversation with a swamp quail. Or an apple. "Not anymore. Mates got killed. Before their time. Now, move! I have to chase the beast, bring it back for the fire."

The elf glanced toward the horizon, and adjusted a strap on her traveling pack. "You seek what I seek, I suspect. But I'm afraid I can't allow you to hunt it. I think you'll still spoil my tracking, even in your . . . state. Go on back to your warren, or wherever you belong now. I'll take care of the killer for you, be assured."

Yasgo's temper boiled. Insolent elf! But again he couldn't bring himself to chop at her legs. Instead he said, "No. I'm coming with you."

* * * * *

The night that Mother and Father left her, Valya was still a child. Full of the pride of duty, and eager for their praise, she assured them that she would take care of the garden until they returned.

Briarberry clung to the stones of the safehold's tower, its vines blanched and dry but elf-sturdy. Climbing gourd, of both the spined and blackseed varieties, twined around stakes in the battlement soil and reached for the glow of the moonstone that studded the underside of the eaves above. Valya's favorite was the sickle beans, curved pods of gold hanging from a network of gravity-defying, spiral stems. She always suspected the sprouts grew magically, perhaps infused with drops of invigorating dawnglove or just awed into success by the attentions of Mother and Father.

Valya's promise to tend their garden was based on the assumption of their eventual return. When they left to answer the call of Trendan's Safehold in faraway Wilt-Leaf Forest, it was reasonable to assume they would be gone a while—a matter of several nights, certainly, and more than a week would not have been surprising. The fact that they had taken with them the trappings of war—sheaves of defender's leather, chain jerkins, their favorite blades, and the greatbow that was Grandfather's—wasn't unusual. Such a long journey across Shadowmoor demanded such precaution, and besides, Mother and Father had returned from many such calls bearing meager wounds and dripping with tales of glory, compassion, and honor.

In hindsight, Valya decided that it was Mother's gift that should have warned her of their failure to return. On this particular occasion, Mother, her hands sheathed in warrior's leather, placed upon Valya's head the ring of herbs that Father had given her when they were young lovers in faraway Wilt-Leaf. The dry braid of stems had retained both its shape and its fragrance, and made Valya think of the feasts elves held under the stars every year, full of hope and laughter.

This gift, so dear to Mother and so precious to Valya, must have been the signal, she thought. When Mother gave the herb crown to me, I should have understood it as the message that our time together was at its end.

It was Grandmother who informed Valya that Mother and Father were slain at Trendan's Safehold, along with the other elves who were called to defend it. A boggart raid had become a massacre.

"But Grandmother, how could boggarts overcome an elf safehold?"

"Hush, child. Your kin fought bravely. That is all we could have asked of them."

"But—mere boggarts? Why did the safehold fall? Why now?"

"Death finds everyone in this world, child. It takes us all in the end. Your mother and father met it with eyes clear and swords drawn, which is all anyone could ask. You'll understand that soon enough."

"But—"

Grandmother bundled her into bed that night, and laid the crown of herbs on the pillow by her cheek. After she left, Valya tucked the crown into her nightshirt, against her heart. It was dry and its edges scratched her skin. But she left it there, hoping the gesture counted somehow, that in some small way it made up for her weakness and insignificance.

* * * * *

Yasgo and the elf walked in silence. Yasgo felt a strange sense of lightness, as a moth or a spider's web must feel. Then a flash of Joffin's face brought back a pang of rage. He stepped up his pace.

The field of nettlewheat had fallen away, revealing a steep, narrow valley. A creek crawled along the bottom of the vale, winding its way between patches of bulbous toadstools and hunched, leafless trees. From the trail they had followed, it was clear that the creature they sought had come this way. But the trail was slighter here in the thin underbrush of the valley.

Yasgo sniffed. "Check there. Down by the creek."

Then he and Valya froze. Noises.

From across the valley they heard gibbering in snorts, whines, and grunts, like the conversation of a mongrel pack. A raiding party of boggarts appeared over the hill, armed with jagged spears and maces, jabbering to each other in the excitement before the hunt. Without warning, two muscular boggarts locked horns in a sparring contest. They twisted savagely at the neck, swatting at each other with their spears, until the weaker one yelped and yielded. On impulse, a shaman clubbed the winner with a large mace, from the end of which dangled a person's skull as decoration, possibly an elf's.

"Get down," whispered Valya. "They may not have seen us yet."

Yasgo was delighted. "Tattermunges! I talk to them. They help us find the beast."

"No—Yasgo, they'll kill us. They'll kill me. We have to hide now."

Yasgo wasn't so sure. But the way that Valya crouched behind the tree trunk reminded him that he and his warren mates were on a raid for elf flesh earlier that very night. So he couldn't blame Valya for her caution. Still, Furto and Joffin had lost their lives to a horrible creature of the shadows, and the Tattermunge boggarts would want to know about it. They could be a great ally against the monster when the time came. He had to tell them.

"You stay here," he said. "I bring them with us. I explain."

"They won't listen, Yasgo. They'll tear me apart as soon as they see me."

"We do see you," grunted a voice behind them.

The companions jumped and turned around. There stood two Tattermunge scouts holding serrated daggers. They must have traveled ahead of their raiding party, hiding when Yasgo and Valya appeared, and then emerging from their hiding spots after the elf and boggart passed right by them—a classic ambush.

"Time to eat," grinned one of the scouts.

"You'll die before you take one step—" Valya began.

Yasgo screamed and lunged at the speaker with his sword. The scout fell back defensively.

The other Tattermunge scout grabbed a wooden whistle from around his neck, and blew on it, hard. The shrill sound shot across the valley to the rest of the raiding party. The sound was cut short in an awkward gasp, as Valya ran the boggart through the chest with her sword, but it was too late. The Tattermunge boggarts looked directly at them, and began running down the valley wall toward them.

Yasgo's attacks had not landed, but the first scout hadn't touched him, either. The Tattermunge scout pounced on Yasgo, his dagger raised in both fists and his eyes wild, when Valya's sword came down across the boggart's arms. They fell clean away, did a slow flip in the air, and dropped to the ground. The dagger stabbed into the earth harmlessly. The scout fell on his face, made a choking sound of unexpected shock and blood, and stopped moving.

"All right," said Valya, turning to face Yasgo. "If you can divert these raiders just right, I might be able to take them one at a time. We need to drive them into a line, so let's move between these two trees, so that they come at us in just the perfect—"

A missile of fire roared across the valley and exploded against a tree just behind them. The tree burst into flames, and a shockwave of splintery heat whooshed past. Yasgo could see that someone new had thrown the fire spell, an enormous figure that had appeared behind the Tattermunge. It was a tower of muscle and scraggly moss, like a mountain that had decided to awaken into the form of a man. The giant's back still dragged a century's worth of loam and overgrowth behind it, the cape of a woodland hibernator. Giants sometimes adopted bands of boggarts as their servants, as boggarts could be cowed by any display of ferocity more resounding than their own, and they were good at finding food.

The giant brought his mitts together in a spell-casting gesture. Fiery light began to glow between his fingers, and the Tattermunge boggarts streaked across the valley toward them in a chaotic mob, jabbering as they came.

"New plan," said Valya. "Run!"

*   *   *   *   *

"How goes the spell, *Druai?*"

"Not well, Scion. Darkness . . . clings to this world. I'm not sure I can move much of it, to send it back whence it came. In fact, I don't see that any of it has been forced away by the ritual."

"Well, it's probably for the best. It's probably not a faerie's place to attempt such . . . unusual things. Come, we'll find a giant to steal dreams from, and make a night of it."

"I think I was close. I attempted to create a sort of geyser, a stream that would lead this world's darkness up into the sky, out of Shadowmoor. The stream did appear, foul and full of death, and when it streaked into the sky I thought my dream might come true. But it peaked, and fell back to earth again, somewhere far away. For all my effort I merely *moved* some of the darkness, redistributed it. And . . . I may have caused some deaths."

"Oh! What died?"

"A boggart, maybe more than one. But more importantly, I think I aroused the banshee. The ribbon of darkness drew the banshee like a moth to flame. It followed my spell to its landing point, to the warren of boggarts."

"That doesn't necessarily mean any of them died."

"I'm afraid it does. Where the banshee walks, death follows. It's the law of the world."

* * * * *

Valya's legs felt like rubber, and her lungs burned. She had been running along the creek from the valley, with the boggart bounding next to her like a miniature cervin. She had heard no more echoes of fiery missiles booming behind them for over an hour now. The giant and his Tattermunge underlings must have given up on them for slower prey. So she stopped and heaved for breath. The boggart followed suit.

No more giant, but now they, and the trail of their quarry, were thoroughly lost.

Yasgo's ears and nostrils widened, and his eyes almost bugged out as he searched the gloom. For a simpleton, he was determined and resourceful, Valya thought. It almost made up for the savagery of his kind. How did his strange state befall him? He didn't seem to notice his predicament, and his senses were still keen, so she didn't bring it up.

"What's next?" she asked.

"Not sure," said the boggart. "Can't smell it. Can't see far."

So much for keen senses, thought Valya. The icy cold creek they had followed had joined a larger brook, one of the clawed fingers of the Withervine River. Valya put two fingers in the water and tasted them, but got no sense of the trail. On either side of the creek, treefolk slumbered, their roots dipping into the edges of the water. Blind trout wriggled around their roots.

One treefolk, an old crabapple crone, had its eyes open, and looked the boggart and elf up and down.

"Strange you're in such a hurry to chase it," said the crabapple.

Yasgo blinked. "It killed my warren mates."

"So? What do you think you'll get from it? It already took what it needed from you."

"Need to find it. Get mates back." He patted the hilt of his sword. "Kill it." Again he peered off into the darkness.

The crabapple harrumphed and shook the branches high on her crown. "You'll not find it from down there. Climb my branches—you'll be able to get a better view." The crabapple was definitely climbable—her three trunks provided good handholds as they spiraled upward.

"Don't do it," said Valya. She had no time to rescue a boggart from a tricky, probably hungry old crone.

But Yasgo was already climbing. Valya sighed.

The crabapple grinned at her. "You're after it too, eh? What's an elf doing with"—she shook the thick branch Yasgo was climbing on—"a *tacharan?*"

"I seek the same creature," said Valya. "It is the force that took my parents from me. This boggart is helping me find it."

The crabapple grinned horribly. "Oh, I believe you'll find exactly what your parents found."

"I see it!" said Yasgo. "The bog is that way. We aren't far."

* * * * *

The muck had a will and malice of its own. Valya clambered as best she could from one wobbly rock to another, trying to keep her legs free of its surface. But anytime she slipped—or worse, when she ran out of firm ground, and she had to jump purposefully back into the swamp—the muck welcomed her back with algal fingers. When she pulled against it, it pulled back on her boots and thighs twice as strong. She found that maintaining a high, marching step was impossible. Instead, she dropped her chest into the brackish water and alternately waded and swam, pushing her body mostly horizontally over the surface. She was reasonably sure her feet were touching the bloated organs of rotting creatures on the bottom, or something equally unpleasant. The stench was unholy.

The boggart didn't seem to notice the stink—in fact, it was his sense of smell that they were relying on to track their prey. Back in the dry nettle fields, the banshee had bent the wheat stalks enough for Valya's tracking instincts to identify. It had left no footprints. Mother and Father had told her once that some spirits had no feet at all, only wisps of mist where their legs should be, or bloody stumps where their feet should be, or clouds of flies where their lower bodies should be. Valya didn't ponder which of those options might currently be the case.

Not that footprints mattered much in the swamp. There was no wheat to bend, so only traces of scent connected them to their quarry. The creature's cloak and veil bore a sour, rotting odor, which Yasgo could apparently detect even through the nauseating miasma of the marsh. The little boggart leaped through the muck like a toad, nimble enough to balance on most swaths of algae, and buoyant enough not to sink like a stone when he couldn't.

Yasgo scrambled onto a mossy plane of rock. He frowned into the gloom and took a slow, wary sniff. "Up ahead. Smells stronger," he said.

Valya's feet touched down onto an incline. The waist-deep muck gave way to a mound of peat that spread up into mist before them, the top of its hump invisible. Dead trees clung to the edges of the mound like the last hairs of a balding kithkin. Somewhere in the mist, Valya heard a crow caw twice. She crawled up the slippery peat island behind her companion, her sword sheath clapping against her thigh.

* * * * *

As Valya and Yasgo crested the mound, the apparition they sought turned to face them. This was the banshee, the legendary reaper of Shadowmoor, whose touch was pain and whose wail was death. It appeared as a young girl wrapped in a soiled, rotting, wet gown, with a thin veil made of a misty material. She hung in the air just above the ground, her toes barely touching the peat of the island and her veil floated around her. Her eyes were blank white.

When the banshee spoke, it was as if her voice crawled out of her throat like a centipede. "Return to your home, Valya of the Lochran Safehold."

"How do you know me?" Valya spat.

"I knew your parents."

"No. You *slew* my parents."

Her stare registered nothing. "What I know, I slay," the banshee said.

"This ends now. Before this night is over, I will extinguish you."

"Then this night will never end."

Valya unlaced her scabbard from her waist and let gravity unsheathe her sword as the wooden sheath fell to the ground. With a swift jab of her boot, her eyes still locked on the banshee's white orbs, she cracked the scabbard in two.

The banshee raised her arms, her fingers limp. Her skin looked sodden and translucent like a drown victim's, barely clinging to her bones. Her veil and hair floated in slow motion.

Valya lunged. The sword bit into empty space where the banshee had been a moment before, the metal carving a slow arc through weirdly thick air. The banshee was suddenly next to her, against her, her hollow eyes wide against the dirty mesh of the veil. Valya saw the banshee's fingertips grasping toward her bare arm. She somersaulted out of the way, then turned and recovered her stance.

"You'll not get your hands on this elf, death-bringer," she said.

"But don't you see? I don't need to touch you to kill you. This is useless. If I haven't been sent to you, then this isn't your time. Go back to your safehold, remember your parents fondly, and find contentment in what time you have."

"You may know my name, but it's clear you don't know me. My mother and father were defenders of life. They had hope for this world—that one day, Shadowmoor would sing with joy and beauty, and that creatures like you would shrivel and die. You're a blight on this world, death-bringer, and I'll cut you out of it or die trying."

"That last part is accurate," said the banshee. Her voice was like a rasp inside Valya's head. It scraped against her mind with dry menace. "But you don't understand. We are not enemies—our role in this world is the same. You and I are like sisters."

Light glowed through Valya's fingers, clutching the sword hilt. Her finger bones showed through the skin. "I have no sister," the elf said, and she leaped into the air. As she sailed over the banshee and aimed one palm at the creature, the air felt thick again, and her arc slowed. Still, she completed her spell. As she slashed down at the banshee with the sword, shafts of light tore through the air from her other hand, aimed directly at the veil.

Again the banshee jumped positions in the blink of an eye, moving clear of the attack. Her expectations off, Valya fell awkwardly through the viscous air. It held her aloft a moment longer, and her lunging miss rotated her farther than she had anticipated. When she landed, her ankle bent and snapped under her weight, and she collapsed.

* * * * *

Yasgo looked on in horror. The banshee's veil spread out around her, enveloping both her and the elf in a billowing mist. As he saw it, inside the mist, Valya was moving and fighting unnaturally slowly, as if battling underwater. Her face was all determination and her features glowed with intensity. But she looked like a sodden leaf rolling helplessly in a vicious river current.

Meanwhile the banshee was moving normally. She easily sidestepped the elf's thrusts and bolts of light. Yasgo thought it looked as if she were leeching existence from Valya, consuming several moments for every one that Valya was permitted. It was draining her of vigor and animation, causing her to move slower and slower until she would stop being entirely.

"I must stop this," he thought.

Yasgo took up his sword and charged at the unnatural cloud of the banshee's veil. His momentum died as he approached it, however. He felt pressure pushing back on his chest, growing stronger as he tried to push his way in, until he couldn't take another step into the haze. He swung his sword partway into the cloud, trying to slice at the banshee, but it hit nothing. Either he was too far away to hit the creature, or his sword was made of smoke. He howled in frustration. Neither the banshee nor the elf seemed to notice, as if they were miles away.

The banshee and the elf looked as if they were attempting to speak to each other, in weird, clipped bursts. The sounds they were making were nonsensical to Yasgo's ear, just an aural muck of garbled jabbering. He wondered what words they thought they were saying to each other, but clearly, he thought, no conversation could be taking place.

They must be going mad. Even if he could somehow save Valya from the leeching banshee, her mind would be broken, unrepairable.

Valya was making a slow attack on the banshee. The banshee moved clear of the elf effortlessly, and she fell, clutching her ankle. Her sword tumbled away.

Through the cloud, Yasgo could see the banshee rotate her head toward him. She inclined her head to him slightly, as if in a gesture of gratitude. Then she turned back to the prone elf.

* * * * *

The ankle was going to require a more powerful mending than Valya could muster under the circumstances, that much was immediately clear. Her sword had left her hand at some point in her fall, and against such a swift foe it was useless to waste a moment trying to locate and recover it. She willed herself to look up at the banshee, and it took her head and even her eyes too long to roll into position.

The banshee's mouth was open, and widening. She stepped toward her, moving in birdlike jerks. The banshee's jaw stretched horribly, cracking and popping suddenly as it unhinged, revealing a cavernous black hole of a mouth in the depths of which Valya thought she could perceive infinity. Valya heard a dry, scraping wheeze from deep down in the banshee's throat, the long inhale of a horror known for its scream.

No time left, she realized. This was it—this was her final moment. Suddenly her thoughts turned to her childhood and the doting days of her mother and her father. She thought of Father's strong hand guiding her through the fencer's stances, his booted feet shuffling along next to her own. She thought of Mother's lilting voice, her easy rhythm in speech, her polished words of wisdom and hope, and the childish songs that Valya would compose for Mother to sing. She thought of how beetles crawled on their plants, climbing the spirals of the sickle beans, and how they dropped to the loam of the tower garden after they had nestled their eggs among the plants. Having fulfilled their purpose, she thought, most living things she had known simply gave up their lives. They neither sought death nor avoided it—it came to them, and they accepted it. Meanwhile, the husks of their parents sank into the dirt to nourish the world that fed their young.

She thought of the crown of herbs Mother and Father gave her before they left. It was in her jerkin now, and she removed it slowly as she lay sideways on the ground. The crown was frayed and dry, thinned of most of its material, but she could still see the artistry of the elf weaving in it. She smiled, held it close to her chest, and closed her eyes.

* * * * *

"*Druai*."

"I'm busy, Scion. I can't see you now."

"Listen, this is serious. The queen wishes to speak with you. She's displeased with your experiments in spellcraft.

What the—what in blazes are you doing?"

"Tell her I'm coming. I'll just be a moment."

"No, you'll come with me now! Don't you know how much trouble you've already brought yourself? And now you're attempting another spell?"

"I've realized something. I've gone about it all wrong. You see, my spells can redirect the energy of a world, twist it around or cover it with glamers, but I can't cause it to be at odds with its purpose. I've been trying to reverse the essence of the world, force it to contradict its soul. I've been doomed to fail from the start."

"Enough. You've been doomed to fail, because you've defied the will of Oona. Please come with me."

"No, not because of Oona! I failed because this world's purpose is to hold darkness. I can't bend the rules to stop that from happening, any more than I can stop the march of night following night. If you cause a world to violate its own purpose, you . . ."

"*Druai*, I've been sent here to bring you to the queen, and I'm permitted to use force. I don't want to, but I will."

". . . you destroy it. I see that now. The world's very nature resists that kind of spellcraft. But there's something one can do. The only thing one can do, the only thing my magic is worthy of accomplishing. That is to ease the suffering of those who must live among this world's sorrow."

"*Druai*, stop, now."

"Just one last spell, Scion, to right a wrong I caused. He's suffered enough. I owe it to him."

"No. I'm sorry, *Druai*. You've forced me to do this."

"Stop! Just a moment—what are you—?"

"You won't finish that spell."

"I will! I—"

* * * * *

The banshee's scream trailed off.

Yasgo's mind rang with the sound. He stood, unmoving, sword in hand, waiting for it to subside. The banshee's veil of mist was parting, but he didn't look for the elf's broken form. He knew she was gone. Like Joffin and Furto.

The banshee approached him, her tattered gown drifting just above the ground. The face underneath the veil was clear, the expression placid. The spectral glow made the banshee look almost beautiful. "You've done well, boggart," she said.

Yasgo grimaced. "I done nothing."

"You brought to me a powerful force, an elf capable of transforming the darkness in which I tread into light. You led her to me, and for that I thank you."

"You tricked me."

But he knew it was true. He could have led Valya away. He knew the elf couldn't stand up to the grim power of the banshee, harbinger of death, but he chose to encourage her vendetta anyway. He had pretended it was some lighthearted romp through the forest with his elf friend, pretended their adventure wouldn't end in disaster. Through his self-deception he had delivered her directly into the hands of the fiend who slew his warren mates.

"Now I have other errands for you," she said.

"No!" spat Yasgo. "You monster. Nothing else for you. Can't kill you, so I leave you. Back home. You never see me again."

"On the contrary. You'll continue to be my servant, as you have been ever since you died," said the banshee.

"No. Good-bye." Yasgo stopped, and his mouth hung open for a long moment. "Since I . . . what?"

* * * * *

Valya didn't expect to open her eyes. If she was being honest, she didn't anticipate that the afterlife would involve eyelids at all. She didn't expect it to involve the throbbing pain of a crushed ankle, either. It took her several eye blinks to realize that she must be, in fact, still alive.

She was still lying on the dirt of the banshee's mound. All around her was a blasted halo of death—insects and weeds that had been killed by the banshee's scream—with her at the center, inexplicably conscious.

In front of her was a little pile of dried herbs. The herb crown—suddenly she knew that it had somehow saved her. She had worn it as a memento, but it must have been a charm, enchanted with the protective magic of her parents, and the safety of her home. Thank you, Mother and Father. Thank you for giving me this chance.

The banshee was still there, but her back was turned. She was talking to someone—the boggart. As she looked around for her sword—there, stuck into the ground a body's length away—she realized that the air didn't feel thick anymore. She could move with her normal grace, except for the ragged pain of the ankle. She dragged herself toward her blade, and took it by the hilt. Biting her lip against a wave of nausea, she staggered to her feet. She took a breath and squeezed the flax woven over the handle of her sword. The crown of herbs had saved her from death once, but the banshee's wail had spent its magic. She was only going to get one shot at this.

* * * * *

"Yes, you are dead, little boggart spirit," the banshee was saying. "Some nights ago, I felt the night moving upward like a geyser—a faerie's spell of twisting darkness. It arced up into the sky and fell back to earth again. I followed it to your warren, where I came upon your body. The spell of darkness had struck your body dead, but your soul didn't pass on. You awoke as a *tacharan,* a restless spirit, unaware that you were not still a living, breathing boggart."

Yasgo looked at his hand. Now that he took a moment, he was shocked to see that the ground showed dimly through his palm. His body was slightly translucent.

"And so I took you as my own—I bound your spirit to me. Then as your master, I charged you with a task—to bring to me any bringers of light, any being who might challenge the tide of darkness of this world. At first you brought two useless boggarts to me. But I am pleased with your latest gift, your elf, a defender of beauty from a storied safehold. And now, you will go out and bring me more such victims."

"No, he won't," said Valya, who rammed her sword into the back of the banshee's neck, shoving the point all the way through so that it blossomed out of her throat.

The banshee tried to scream, but only managed a rasping hiss. She staggered around to Valya, the sword still plunged through her neck, her eyes wide white orbs. She flailed, mist pouring out of the wound. In an instant the mist became a dense cloud around her.

Valya and Yasgo stood back. As they watched, the banshee became a swirling sphere of night, and then she quickly dwindled to nothing, taking Valya's sword along with her. The hissing sound of her throat wound faded away. Crickets chirped.

Yasgo looked morose. Valya watched his ghostly features for a long moment as she performed a mending spell on her ankle.

"The banshee's gone," she said finally. "You're free now, it seems. So why the long face?"

"Free. But not alive. Ghost."

"Yes, but that hasn't stood in your way, has it?"

Yasgo considered this.

"Listen, I must get back to the safehold. I trust you'll be all right?"

Yasgo scratched behind his ear. It was odd knowing it was just a ghost's ear. It was odd that he felt hungry—he still hadn't eaten since his raid—but then, he had been dead since sometime before that. The hunger was comforting, somehow—easy to understand and familiar.

"Yes, fine. Thank you, elf."

He watched Valya turn and leave, and listened to frogs down in the bog sing a droning lullaby. He sat in the dirt and pawed at clods of soil, carving out little holes in the ground.

He wondered if it had hurt, when he died. Yasgo tried to imagine the geyser of dark energy the banshee had described, to see if it triggered a memory of it coming down on him. It didn't. He remembered nothing of that moment. Merciful, perhaps. He dug in the dirt until his ghostly claws were covered in muck, creating a deeper and deeper hole. It was as if the answers were below him somewhere, down in the heart of this knoll the banshee had haunted. He listened to the frogs as he dug, and gradually the task in front of him became vague and distant. Dirt rolled down the sides toward him, but he dug steadily, imagining how nice it would be to have a meal. Perhaps cervin flesh.

His fingers faded, and became only the motion of digging. Then the motion faded, and the dirt collapsed where Yasgo had been.

* * * * *

"Yes, Queen. The *druai's* behavior has been—curbed, as you commanded. The dream pollen we took from him after his death has been added to your stores. All is now as it should be! No, he never got his spell to succeed the way he wanted, although he certainly seemed to feel he was close to something important. His words indicated madness to me, but you know better than I, of course. His attempts did cause a nasty stir among the boggarts, and the spell attracted the banshee, but that was taken care of when—Yes, we will name a new *druai* soon, as you wish, but I don't think anyone will come as close as he did to affecting your plans. Of course, if I knew *why* we were doing this, we could—no. Of course. As you wish."

* * * * *

Valya's empty scabbard bumped against her hip as she made her way back through the leafless woods. Thanks to her efforts, these woods were one iota safer now. She had avenged her parents. She had released a ghost from its shackles. Yet she wasn't sure she could ever cherish her memories of these events, or retell them with pride. Simply being done with them, she decided, would have to be enough. She took a full breath, and hoped Grandmother would have tea ready when she returned.

Matt Cavotta

In a small one-room home, the kithkin family Cobbik went about their morning business. It was a stout dwelling, just under five feet at its highest vaulted beam, squat and sturdily built with thick stone blocks and broad timbers. A warm amber light shone from the open hearth, playing softly upon the room's rough stone and knotty wood. At one end Wyb was rooting around in an open cabinet. A series of heavy locks clanked as they dangled open from a steel clasp on the oaken door. Near the hearth wall, his wife Betrys turned an iron crank that was bolted to the side of the stone hearth. As she muscled the crank around, a blackened iron door lowered like a portcullis over the open hearth. The hearth door grated shut and a small sphere of light illuminated just above it, casting a magical glow similar to that of the hearth fire. "Morning bread will be ready shortly," she announced. "And no peeking, Gwyb. It'll spoil the rise."

Gwyb, the Cobbik's only child, sat upon the hearth seat, knocking his heels against the warm stone. He turned his wide eyes from his mum to his pop, though his nose kept its attention on the baking breakfast. He watched as his father squeezed on a smallhelm and double-buckled its leather chinstrap. Gwyb stifled a chuckle. He respected his father greatly, but could not help but think the little helmet looked comical upon his pop's round head.

"You find this funny, eh Gwyb?" said his father, having

waited just long enough for Gwyb to believe he had not noticed. Wyb raised a bushy eyebrow over a wide glassy eye and waited. Gwyb's face flushed pink. Gwyb did not have to say anything. Wyb felt his son's regret, the same way he had felt his son's suppressed amusement. Wyb and his son were linked, as all kithkin were, by the mindweft. It is through the mindweft that kithkin communicate thoughts and impulses. They use it to punctuate their words with emotion and to convey secret thoughts. But most often, they use it to alarm their neighbors.

Many young kithkin, like Gwyb, did not yet have the ability to decipher the tangle of alien thoughts and feelings that buzzed on the periphery of their minds. They had not yet reached their "age of weaving." But young kithkin did, without realizing it, broadcast their own feelings for others to perceive.

"You cannot sneak a dream past a waking kithkin," said Wyb with a hint of a smile.

"Yeah, I know," replied Gwyb glumly. He had heard that line many times, but always seemed to forget. "Sorry, Pop."

"Don't be sorry . . . be wise," said Wyb. "This helm may look funny, but its purpose is gravely serious. Here, let me show you." Wyb unbuckled the strap and wrestled his head out of the oil-hardened leather helmet. He pointed to the high curves at the brow and sides. "See here. These broad openings leave plenty of room for the eyes and ears. One cannot afford to obstruct his hearing or peripheral vision. These helmets are for expeditions to the outside, Son, and the outside is where nasty boggarts and dripping merrows prowl.

"Your great-uncle Kypper had a neighbor 'cross the way and one down who was from Ballynock. Like the other

'Nockers, he fancied big, deep hoods. Here in Greymeadow we know that keeping eyes and ears open is more important than fashion, or protection from wind or rain. Kypper's neighbor was eaten by the Tattermunge—chomped down, cowl and all. Ballynockers—something's just not right about 'em." Wyb sat a moment with a wrinkled brow, and then his face lit up. "Ah, yes. This funny looking hat," he said, patting it like a trusted friend, "helps keep us out of the jaws of hungry boggarts."

Gwyb juggled his thoughts for a moment. On the one hand, his pop had a good point. He had heard about Uncle Kyp and the grisly attack. But on the other, there was the little hat squeezed over a plump kithkin head. He looked at the helm again, but his eyes wandered to the other equipment that his father had not yet readied. Ropes. Belts. Armor. Shield. His eyes settled on a short blade in its scabbard. It seemed to solidify his wavering thoughts, and cut a wry little smile across his face.

"It is a good helmet," said Gwyb, "for other kithkin."

"Other kithkin?" asked Wyb in the softened tone a father uses when baiting a child into a lesson.

"Yes," announced Gwyb, lifting his chin and puffing his chest, "the other kithkin who are afraid of the merrows and boggarts. If I have my shield and short blade, I won't need the funny helmet." Gwyb had risen from the hearth seat and was striking battle poses with his imaginary sword.

"So, you're a brave one, eh?" Wyb asked. Gwyb nodded, crossing his arms. "You're not afraid?" Gwyb shook his head emphatically. "Impossible," said his father.

"I am not afraid," insisted Gwyb.

"No. No you're not," replied Wyb, disappointed. He shuffled forward and put his hands firmly, but gently on Gwyb's shoulders. He leaned in, looking directly into his son's round, yellow eyes. "Son, to be brave is to take action in spite of fear. It is impossible to be brave without first being afraid. To take action without fear is not brave, it is foolish."

Gwyb brandished his imaginary sword. Wyb's brow wrinkled once again.

"Gwyb, my son, I am going out on expedition today, as I have done many times before. Each time I have returned it has been because of fear—fear of boggarts and merrows and of more things than I have names for." Wyb paused to try and find the right things to say. He wished the mindweft could help him convey the gravity of his words. He was frustrated. He wanted Wyb to feel his father's fear as his own. He looked at his son and saw a blank stare. He would have to go about it the long way.

"I have seen merrows in my work. I have seen them dart through the water, skid upon the banks, then shuffle into the brush on their slimy little fins. I have heard them creeping—with their quick, wet steps and labored, gurgling breaths. I live to tell you about their under-bitten maws and empty eyes because I fear them . . . and because of what that fear has wrought."

"Can I go with you?" blurted Gwyb excitedly. Wyb's brow furled deeper. He put down the helmet, pushed aside an armored shirt and his sword, and picked up his shield. He held it up for Gwyb to see. It was a broad, circular shield of peened metal with a simple, unembellished face.

"Long ago," began Wyb, "before the walls, there was a kithnapping here. Merrows slinked in under cover of night and storm to steal sleepers from their beds. The 'weft did not alert others until the abducted were awakened by the awkward skittering of their fleeing captors. Some kithkin gave chase, but merrows are not the witless carp they look like. They are well aware of their shortcomings on land and make sure to arm themselves with deadly arrows and other jagged missiles that would keep quicker enemies away. One of the pursuers was killed." Wyb paused for a moment to let the last word sink in. "See, Gwyb, those kithkin saw the merrows. They watched them shoot deadly arrows and drag friends into the cold deep." Wyb set the shield upon his lap and turned it around so Gwyb could see the inside. "They *knew* to fear, and fear inspired this." He ran his fingers around the two-inch rim of tiny mechanisms— metal springs, rods, and hinges that neatly encircled the outer edge of the shield's arm side.

"Yes, it is nifty, isn't it," said Wyb, feeling the curiosity spill over from his son's mind into his own.

"What does it do?" asked Gwyb with wide eyes and anxiously dancing fingers.

"It protects us, like all great kithkin engineering. See, it works like a regular shield . . . like this," Wyb snapped the heavy snaps on the leather arm straps, then slipped his arm through and hoisted the shield. "We can now protect ourselves from their arrows. But while we huddle behind the shield, avoiding jagged blades with inky poisons from the sea, they shuffle away to the safety of the waters."

"They do?" moaned Gwyb.

"They would, if we couldn't do this. . . ." Wyb stood up, wielding the shield in front of him in mock combat. He barked out, *"Warchod!"* In a whirr of clicks and twangs, the shield's arm straps unsnapped, it popped off of Wyb's arm, and a segmented tripod snapped out from the rim of the shield and held it in place a few inches from the floor. Wyb continued his charade, pretending to use a crossbow, firing at imaginary foes from behind his self-propped shield. Gwyb's body recoiled, startled by the sudden noise, but his eyes were fixed in amazement upon the shield.

"Fear, my son," said Wyb slowly and methodically, "breeds invention."

"That was amazing!" cried Gwyb. "It popped out so fast. *Thwack!*—and then you start shooting!" Gwyb stood and pretended to engage in battle with a shield of his own. "You'll not slither away this time, merrow!" he proclaimed boldly, fixing his glare on a butter churn. Not taking his eyes off his foe, he asked, "Pop, what was that word, the one that makes it work?"

"Warchod. It is a magic word."

"All right you two," Betrys interjected. "I have a magic word for the both of you: breakfast."

"But Mum," whined Gwyb, "we're fighting the merrows! Look at this shield!"

"Yes Gwyb, it's a very good shield," said Betrys. "But your pop needs to eat if he's to have the wits to use it today."

"That's right, Son. Like all the Greymeadow mums say, 'eat your grits to keep your wits.' " Wyb motioned for his son to follow. The two moved to the heavy wooden table in the center of the room. Betrys had already cut the loaf into pieces and set them out. Gwyb looked back at the shield a number of times before settling in at his plate.

"The mechanics are all functional," Wyb explained through a mouthful of bread. "But there are a lot of them— snaps to be unsnapped and catches to be tripped—too many to operate by hand. So the mages put a spell on our shields, a spell that instantly sets all the mechanisms into motion when you speak the word. Come, eat quick. I still have much to do, much to show you."

Even as he took his seat at the table, Gwyb continued

to stare back at his father's shield. "You know," said Wyb, leaning toward his son, "our armor uses a magic word too. If you hop to it and eat your breakfast, perhaps there will be time to see that as well."

Gwyb moved to pick up his bread, but started rubbing his eyes instead.

"You've been staring too long," chided his mother. "Mind your eyes, Gwyb. Blink." She gave her son a mother's look of disapproval, with a few exaggerated blinks.

"Yes, yes. 'Tis important that you do not stare too long at any one thing," instructed Wyb. "Not only will your eyes dry and get blurry, but staring at one thing keeps you from looking 'round at everything else that might be creeping up on you. Remember, 'Dry eyes, a kithkin's demise.' "

"But only blink when it's safe!" added Betrys quickly. "Only when it's safe."

"Your mum makes a good point." said Wyb. "You can't just stroll around blinking willy-nilly. There are sneaky-quick nasties out in the world that can get you in the blink of an eye."

Gwyb was confused. "Is it safe now?" he asked as he rubbed and blinked the dry out of his eyes.

"Yes, son. It is safe here in our home," replied Wyb, giving in to habit and stealing a few glances this way and that. He saw Betrys doing the same. "But on the outside," he continued, "it is a different story." Wyb finished up the last crumbs of his breakfast and got up from the table. As he made his way back to his equipment cabinet, he began speaking again.

"There is no need to worry, Son. I will be able to blink safely, even on the outside." Wyb sat in front of the cabinet and picked up the shield. "I will be traveling in a kith-compass." He began skillfully folding up the tripod and repacking it into the rim of the shield. "You remember what I've told you about the compass, eh, Son?"

Gwyb's attention was again fixed on his father's shield. He watched intently, slowly chewing his bread as his father's fingers nimbly manipulated the shield's tiny workings.

"Son?"

Wyb stopped working, folded his hands together, and waited for his son to reply. Gwyb snapped out of his reverie, made an effort to blink a few times, and then took a big bite of his breakfast. Wyb huffed.

"One day, my boy. One day you will appreciate the precision and intricacy of the kith-compass too. When it gets going, it's really a thing to see. Like silent, revolving clockwork."

"Words, Wyb," said Betrys, "just words. You cannot expect the boy to be as interested in your rambling as he is in what he can see right there in your hands."

Wyb was struck by his wife's wisdom. He thought for a moment. He could feel her presence in his mind. How could he expect Gwyb to comprehend the artistry of the compass without seeing it? More importantly, how could he expect his son to appreciate the *need* for the compass without showing it to him outside of the protective embrace of the home? They looked to each other in concurrence.

"Gwyb," announced Wyb, "you are coming with me today."

"I am?" replied Gwyb, muffled by a mouthful of bread. He chewed and swallowed as fast as he could. "I am? I am coming with you in your"—Gwyb searched for the word—"compass?"

"Yes."

Gwyb stood up, hardly able to contain himself. "Do I get

a sword?" he asked excitedly. "And a magic shield?"

"Slow down, Son."

"Beware, nasties!" barked the boy, pointing an imaginary sword. "Gwyb watches the north, and you can't hurt him!"

"Son!" snapped Wyb. "Do not get carried away." He paused, and continued with a soft, but stern tone. "You will not be part of the compass, and this"—he motioned toward the boy in his imaginary battle—"is exactly why. What have I been saying? Something—who knows what it is—but something can *always* hurt you." Gwyb deflated. His parents could feel his confusion.

"You will come with me to First Gate, to meet the others in my compass. You will watch from the First Gate tower while we head on to the outside."

Wyb resumed his preparations in silence. He finished resetting the shield. As he put on his armor, carefully attending to all the clasps and cinches, Wyb considered his decision to allow his son to see the outside. He had long waited to feel a change in Gwyb's mind, perhaps a small spark of unease, anything that he might be able to fan into the illuminating flames of fear. Perhaps Gwyb's eyes would teach him what his father's words could not. It was time to stop shielding the boy, and to let him learn to shield himself. With renewed vigor, Wyb made final checks of his safety gear—armor, shield, sword, and helm.

"Put on your boots," Wyb said to his son. "We are just about ready to go." Wyb crossed the small room and put his hands on Betrys's shoulders. Betrys stopped working on the rope net she was knotting. They shared a thought and each glanced at their son. Wyb leaned over and touched his forehead to hers. The two exchanged a lengthy wordless farewell. After a long silence, Wyb spoke.

"Come, Son." He turned and strode toward the door.

"Have you checked everything?" asked Betrys. "Have you all your gear?"

"I have," Wyb replied, rapping his shield arm twice against his armored chest. "I will be safe."

Betrys shot Wyb a thought, like a mental nudge with the elbow. She glanced down at the net she was working on.

"Oh, of course." Wyb hustled back to his equipment cabinet and grabbed two tightly bound, knotted silk nets. He lashed them to his belt. "Now we are ready," he said to Gwyb, shepherding him to the door.

"Eswyn says saltwort is on the wester!" Betrys called after them. "Take extra care!"

"Of course." Wyb nodded in agreement but found himself thinking an odd thought. He actually hoped, if only for a second, that this dark omen of the west wind would come to pass. He thought, if Gwyb were only to *see*. . . . Wyb dashed the crazy notion from his mind, shook his head, and opened the door. He bent forward slowly and took a furtive look in each direction. Then he scurried off with Gwyb in tow, out into the haze of morning.

The sky hung low, an ochre stain in the air just above the doun. The dampness darkened the cobbled streets and stone homes, speckling them with reflections of the brownish sky. All around them kithkin hastened down cobbled lanes and between squat homes. They scuttled like rodents, stopping to listen, spinning 'round to take looks in all directions. Bug-eyed faces peered around corners. Doors thumped shut, latches and locks clicking behind them. Window shutters clacked open and closed as housemaids and homebodies took leery peeks at the outside world. As Wyb hustled with his son through the morn, he was glad to feel reassurance through the mindweft, a shared thought from those he passed that all was safe and sound.

A short way down the lane Wyb stopped. Other folk scurried around them. Wyb's eyebrows perked, then he turned and led the boy back the way they had come. After a brisk walk down the lane and around a corner they came to a house much like their own. Wyb stopped at the door and knocked the Moonday morning knock, rapping thrice with his knuckles and adding two thuds with his booted toe. The sound of sliding metal and clicking latches followed. The door opened just enough for one bulging kithkin eye to peer out and squint, then it opened all the way to reveal Dagub, a wiry, white-bearded kithkin with a long scar between his one missing eye and what was left of his right ear. Dagub quickly stepped aside and let them into his home. He shut the door and locked all of the locks.

"We were to meet at the gate," he said, his one eye wide with worry.

"Yes, Dagub," said Wyb, with calm reassurance through the mindweft. "Just a minor change in plans." Dagub narrowed his eye and tightened his lips. Wyb could feel Dagub's wariness. "I would not have come, were it not important," said Wyb, indicating to Dagub with his eyes and his mind that Gwyb was the reason for the altered plan.

"Ah." Dagub nodded. "It looks to me like there is one Cobbik more than I was expecting this morn," he said, turning his blue, moonlike eye and wide smile toward the boy. "Are you to be the fifth in our compass today?"

"Fit me with armor and sword!" exclaimed Gwyb, forgetting what his father had told him earlier.

"No, no," said Wyb, putting a steady hand on Gwyb's shoulder. He looked to Dagub with a thought and an expression far more serious than his tone. "Gwyb is not ready for expeditions just yet. He is in need of more than just armor and sword."

"Oh, 'tis a shame," played Dagub, "he looks to be a hearty warrior, this one."

"I am," pleaded Gwyb, assuming a battle stance with his imaginary sword. "I will slay every nasty I see!"

"I believe you would," said Dagub, turning to Wyb with a nod of understanding. "But, young kithkin, you do not necessarily *see* every nasty." Dagub was already in his armor and had laid out the rest of his equipment on the long table. He brushed some aside to make elbow room for his guests. "Come, Cobbiks, sit a spell. I will tell you a story while we wait for Cefin and the Kennies to arrive." He sat on the hearth seat and spoke, making frequent eye contact with the boy. Gwyb could not help but stare, following the purple-red line from darkened crinkle to half-ear and back again.

"I remember, a long time ago, some lads and I were out along the merrow lanes, returning from an expedition to Barenton. We were lost." Dagub's eye opened wide and round. "The rivers move, you know. Dirty merrows." He sneered, furrowing his brow and squeezing his eye to an icy blue sliver. "They use foul magic to reroute the rivers to trap us. We tried to find our way for hours, but to no avail. Then we came upon a fortuitous little island, a hill popping out of the water, a lucky bit of elevation that could give us a dandy view of our location, and of any 'nasties,' as you call them.

"But in a twist likely twirled by Oona herself, our lucky lookout spot turned out to be a nasty of its own. As we clambered to the top of the craggy hill, it started rising up from the riverbank. There was a rumbling groan from beneath us. 'We've awoken a giant!' we howled to each other. But we had no such luck. The hill lurched suddenly and I tumbled off its side, landing in the muck at the edge of the water. What I saw then was a horror beyond horrors. The underside of the hill broke open into a great roaring maw. Out sprung a tangle of long flailing tentacles!" Dagub wiggled his fingers in front of his scowling face then stopped abruptly, pointing one finger toward his eye. "And that was the last thing I saw. One of those scaly tentacles must have whipped across my face," he said, raking his finger from eye to ear, "dashing out my eye and slicing off my ear. I was stunned. I lay there in blind silence, half-submerged, my good eye and ear buried in the cold muck.

"But I still felt the horror in the 'weft. Flashes of fear, of awe, and of hopelessness. Then, one by one, those flashes were snuffed. I knew what was happening, but I could do nothing. I was glad to be knocked out in the mud, blind and deaf to the grisly demise of my friends, each one of them gulped down by the Isleback. That's what they call it now. The Isleback Spawn. The worst thing this one eye has ever seen."

Dagub and Wyb watched the boy intently. Gwyb did not move. He was running through the scene in his mind, glancing through wincing eyes at Dagub's scarred face.

"What happened to it?" stammered Gwyb. "Where is it now?"

"Lucky for me, it did not look farther than its own back for a meal. I don't know for sure what happened next, but I know it wasn't there when I came to. It is still out there, under the murk of the rivers."

There it was! They felt it, but just for a moment. Gwyb was confounded by the unknown, and a tiny candle of fear flickered within him. But then it was gone, snuffed out by the whirl of a youthful mind. Without words, both men acknowledged a minor victory.

There was a familiar series of raps at the door. Wyb started toward the door.

"Wait!" urged Dagub in a hushed voice. "I've heard tell of wily noggles duping knocks and eating folk in their very own homes!" He turned and barked toward the door, "Give me the midday knock or be gone with you!" A new series of knocks and thuds followed. Wyb, being fully armored, positioned himself at the doorway. He worked the locks and opened it just a crack.

"Ah," said Wyb, shooting a quick nod to Dagub. "It's the Kennies. And Cefin." Wyb stood aside and twin kithkin entered, one male and one female. Each was clad in full armor. They were whispering to each other and shuffled into the room without acknowledging Wyb or Dagub. Cefin entered slowly, cautiously backing in, keeping his eyes on the street. After they had all cleared the entryway, Dagub locked the door. Once the last lock clicked, the mindful quiet was broken.

"A black bird perches on the priory spire," said Cefin gravely.

Wyb, Dagub, and the Kennies exchanged concerned looks and, without a word, set about readying and rechecking their equipment. Dagub shuffled around the Cobbiks and made his way to the far end of the cluttered table. There he picked up a container made of two small turtle shells wrapped in rope.

"A black bird?" asked Gwyb, following his father through the anxious bustle of the others. "What does it mean?" Wyb could feel his son's concern.

"I cannot be sure. The omens do not tell, only warn."

"Must you go today, when there is danger about?"

Wyb stopped. His inclination was to comfort Gwyb, but that was not the purpose of the day. He looked down at his boy and said, "There is danger every day."

Wyb turned back to the others. There the five kithkin knelt, each rolling down the cuff of their left boot. Dagub was pulling thick, black worms out of the turtle shell container, handing one to each kithkin. Each dropped the worm into a small silk pocket sewn to the inside of their boot.

Next, they unraveled their slings and ensured that a sling bullet was wrapped within and ready. While checking their gear they repeated sequences of code words and signal whistles. When they finished going over all the signals, they set the starting order of their kith-compass. Standard security measures were completed. But, given the omens of the day, they agreed to add any other safety equipment that was on hand. From Dagub's own stockpile, the Kennies each took a crossbow. To each in the compass Dagub passed a fog pot, a sealed clay sphere filled with dust enchanted with a pyromancer's glamer.

"We are set. Let us make haste to First Gate," said Wyb. As the compass began filing toward the door, Wyb stopped Dagub. "Fetch an extra bait sack too, the omens are many, and the razormouth are wily."

The six kithkin made their way from house of Dagub into the heart of Greymeadow. They strode purposefully down narrow lanes that cut a labyrinthine path through the glut of small, squat structures. They wove through the town toward the high tower that was easily seen over the low, thatched rooftops. They were again treated to the sounds of a Greymeadow day—the clatter of shutters, doors, and latching locks, the foot-patter of the crowds that had come out into the center yard. There was very little talking but for a terse warning or hushed relay of an omen. The six cut through the center yard market, where vendors cautiously watched over the stacks of crates that held their wares. They wrapped around a clutch of shops and came to the base of the tower, First Gate.

The First Gate watchtower was, like all Greymeadow structures, constructed of large stone block, thick wood, and iron reinforcements. Its base was built out from the ten foot high stone wall that encircled the heart of the town. The tower was square and wide at the bottom, and housed the doors of First Gate. Unlike other Greymeadow structures, it was tall and imposing, standing three stories higher than the wall. Jutting out from its corners, like the arms of a towering kithkin guardian, were massive wooden levers. From the end of each lever hung a heavy chain that connected to a huge round boulder resting upon the ground.

Gwyb had seen the tower before. To him, the tower's stalwart pose had always threatened, "Keep Out!" But on this day, the towering guardian, with its arms outstretched and flails in hand, seemed to warn, "Keep In!" The great doors it straddled were shut, and Gwyb wanted them to stay that way.

The group approached the tower. Wyb led the others around one of the massive boulders and off to the right of the tower doors. Wyb stopped the group and approached the guard stationed there. The two greeted each other warmly then talked, occasionally glancing back at Gwyb. The guard looked up toward the tower and barked the gate call. Faces popped out of windows all around the height of the tower, peering out over the town and its surroundings. These watchers signalled back and forth to each other and to the gate guards on the ground. The guard patted Wyb on the shoulder. Wyb motioned for Gwyb to join him.

"I will be going through the gate soon, with the others," said Wyb to his son. "You will wait for us in the tower. Potrig will be there with you."

"Will I be safe?"

"Worrying about safety is the first step to being safe," replied Wyb, patting the boy proudly.

Potrig pulled his gray tunic over his head. He knelt in front of Gwyb and draped it over his head and shoulders.

"Ah!" chirped Potrig, moving to stand beside Gwyb. "Official Grays become you. First Gate is now one kithkin closer to safe." A noise from within the tower interrupted the farewell. "The gate, it opens."

Wyb thanked Potrig and gave his son a hearty hug. "If you go high enough," he said to Gwyb, "You will still be able to see us." He rose quickly and marched toward his compass mates. "We go."

The lever on the right rose, its chain went taut, and the weight at its end was hefted from the ground. As it rose, the great wooden doors creaked open. The doors swung slowly, opening up to a tunnel that ran beneath the tower to another set of outer doors. The left lever engaged and the outer doors began opening to the second yard. The tower strained and groaned, echoing with gear-churning, timber-bending protest. It stood with its arms aloft, bearing the great weight of open doors, just long enough for the compass to pass beneath it. No sooner had the five passed into second yard when both weights dropped, releasing the tower works and slamming the tower doors shut with a commanding boom.

Gwyb shifted uneasily. The tower now stood between him and his father, and between his father and safety. Potrig put a reassuring hand on Gwyb's shoulder. "Come," he said, leading Gwyb in a small door around the side of the tower. They climbed all the way up a stone staircase, passing doors at each landing. When they came to the very last one, they entered. Potrig took a position at a window and invited Gwyb to come and look. He raced over and peered out. Just outside the tower was the wide open expanse of the second yard. The dusty open yard was abuzz with military activity, marching drills, and target practice. Gwyb could see his father's group cutting a path through the activity toward the Second Gate tower. It was much shorter than First Gate tower, rising just a few feet higher than the stone wall into which it was built. Just beyond that was the Outer Gate and outer wall, wrapping all the way around just a stone's throw from the second wall. Gwyb watched as his father passed through Second Gate, but he was not high enough to see them come out into the outer yard. From what he had heard, outer yard was always empty anyway. He let his attention stray back to second yard. He crossed his arms on the windowsill, plopped his head on top of them, and watched some crossbow archers firing at straw dummies.

Gwyb looked out beyond the Outer Gate. He caught sight of his father and his mates swirling out through the meadow. They were on the outside. The waters of the Meander wound a few hundred paces from the outer wall. The group moved in a straight line toward the river, but four of them always orbited the fifth, revolving around him in a tight circle, peering out in every direction. Every twenty paces or so, without breaking the fluid motion, the center kithkin switched position with one of the outer four. As the compass grew closer to the river, the center kithkin sheathed his sword and produced a round object from his pack. The others continued circling and watching. As long as the four keep watch, thought Gwyb, the one in the middle is able to. . . . Gwyb blinked his dry eyes hard, and quickly caught sight of the compass again.

"That's right," said Potrig. He tugged lightly at Gwyb's gray tunic. "Kithkin of the watch always mind their eyes."

Kithkin of the watch, Gwyb thought proudly to himself. He looked down at the official Greymeadow seal on his chest, then back out the window. Gwyb kept his eyes peeled, scanning the far reaches that kithkin on the ground would not be able to see.

Nearly an hour passed and Gwyb spotted no signs of danger. The scene out the window of the tower was warm, slow-moving, and silent. Sounds echoed through the halls of the tower, and from the bustle of the second yard, but the skies, waters, and meadows were quiet. Still, Gwyb watched vigilantly. Occasionally, he stole looks back at his father, surrounded by his compass, casting a fishing net into the water. After each toss of the net, his father would pull it in, rotate out of the center position, and cycle through the compass. Each time the net was empty. Each time Gwyb wished his father would pack up and return to the doun.

The skies grew darker, the mid-morn ochre giving way to russet and then deep red. Gwyb's mood darkened as well. He scanned the distances in every direction. Back at the riverbank his father was scattering bait from a large sack into the water. The red of the sky reflected upon the river's rippling surface. It looked like a wound across the face of the meadow. Gwyb felt a hand on his shoulder.

"Let your worry keep you sharp," said Potrig.

Gwyb strained to open his eyes wider and wider, his gaze darting faster and faster. As the day reddened and his anxiety mounted, Gwyb strained to see what might be hidden in the shadows growing long over heath and water. Shadows. They seemed to creep toward him on the ground and over top of him in the sky. And still his father remained out there. Gwyb clutched the windowsill. He craned his neck out the window to see more, but darkness was thwarting him.

Then he saw it. A shadow in the water. A shape beneath the surface. It was a blackened mass with swirls and trails slowly twisting in and out of sight. It was huge, and it was moving. It headed, in ominous silence, straight for his father. Gwyb's stomach wrenched with fear.

The silence broke. There was a rush of noise from all around. Gwyb spun around to see what the commotion was, but the room was still. Potrig was calmly gazing out the window. Gwyb heard a voice through the noise. He knew the voice to be Potrig's, though his mouth did not move to form words.

"All is well," said Potrig, turning to Gwyb with a reassuring wink. Gwyb was confused. Gwyb heard the words, but could not concentrate enough to process their meaning. He could not understand the strange echo he had just experienced. Potrig continued to talk, but Gwyb could hear nothing over the whorl of thoughts in his head. His mind was abuzz with ideas and feelings he could not grasp. He felt bombarded with anxieties, humor, memories, and impulses. He reached out, sifting through a chaos of fragile notions until he finally gripped something solid, something familiar—his fear.

". . . watch always minds his post," Gwyb heard. He felt Potrig's hands, one patting his back, the other firmly upon his shoulder. Gwyb looked down at his own hands, sweating and clutching on to the windowsill. He looked again out the window. It was still out there, still moving closer. Gwyb wanted to shout, to warn his pop. Instinctively he called out, but the room remained quiet. He called out with the only words he could find in the loudest thoughts he could muster, *Flee! The river!* Potrig was startled. He looked down, wide-eyed, at Gwyb, and then at the river. The compass stopped moving. They held their formation, though their focus seemed to be on the waters in front of them. Potrig leaned forward out the window and squinted his eyes. He called out. Voices from outside answered.

They see it! thought Gwyb. *It is there!* The noise in Gwyb's mind began to take on a rhythm, like the din at a tavern becoming a priory chant. The skein of differing impulses began to straighten out, to become uniform, and to darken. More and more he encountered alarm, alarm that was not his own. Gwyb's head began to ache. He felt a heaving and pulling sensation. Panic was pulsing through his mind, beating an ever-quickening cadence. He could feel foreign thoughts coming into step with the panic. But there were others, strong feelings that seemed to fight against the wave of chaos.

More voices called out from the tower and from the guards below. A trumpet rang out.

Potrig grasped Gwyb firmly and turned him, fixing a calm, stern stare upon him. "Keep your focus," he said. Gwyb's quivering mind felt a moment of stillness, of support, like hands cradling a shivering bird. Gwyb took a deep breath. Potrig turned back to the window and Gwyb did the same. Off in the distance, the compass had retreated from the water, stopping to maintain position about twenty paces from the river. But there, out in the water, the shadow quickly approached the bank.

"Get back!" shrieked Gwyb, falling immediately back

into the cold, empty hall of echoing panic.

"What is it, boy?" cried Potrig, "What do you see?"

Gwyb felt the rhythm of fear in his mind growing stronger. Potrig spoke, but Gwyb could hardly make sense of it. Thoughts were grasping for purchase outside of the rhythm, but those feelings were washed away by the chorus of minds now singing in hysteria.

"What did you see?" Gwyb could not gather his thoughts to answer. What is it? Danger. Is it? Lurking. Could it be? Gwyb's young mind wandered. The tide of panic swept him toward one thought, and then made the terrible thought known to all—*Isleback*.

The word was sent skipping across the mindweft like sparks popping across a drought crop. With each exchange and each new mind considering the dreaded word, the fire of fear grew brighter. Gwyb fought through the noise in his mind to try and keep his focus on his father. The compass was in disarray. One kithkin broke formation to flee. He dropped his shield, then barked a word and shed his armor. He was at a dead sprint before it hit the ground. The other four seemed to freeze for a moment. In swift succession, each sprung his shield onto its stand. Ducking behind their shields, they drew weapons. Two hurled fog pots while the others trained sling and crossbow on the waters before them. The riverbank was soon shrouded in a thick, billowing haze.

Out on the meadow, in the doun yards, and up in the tower, courageous minds still fought against the accumulating fear. But the courage of the few broke down under the fear of the many. The mindweft coalesced. The pattern of panic, fear, and thoughts of a fabled beast became one continuous note of white terror.

Gwyb was petrified. Watchers howled out. Wall guards

loosed arrows into the mist. The compass panicked, hurl-ing fog pots and firing their weapons at anything and everything. They fled at top speed, ditching their armor and weapons as they tore through the brush toward the Outer Gate and into the swirling white brume they had created.

The east end of the doun buzzed like an agitated ant hill. Kithkin scattered this way and that. Others sought comfort of snug hiding places. Few were those who thought against the current of the mindweft. Elders and sages made their way from center yard to the east, providing solidity and strength to the brittle consciousness. Atop the outer wall, the cenn and doun elders watched the breeze slowly sweep away the fog, revealing a meadow riddled with arrows and a river free of the giant beast. There, on that wall, they agreed that it would be wise to build a fourth wall, a new Outer Wall to protect them from the monster that still lurked out there, under the cover of the deep.

* * * * *

Just below the surface of the river, the stragglers of a massive school of razormouth scrounged for remnants of the kithkin's bait worms. Finding nothing, they break back to rejoin the inky mass of black-scaled river fish. The school swims slowly, having gorged on two full sacks of blood and grubs.

JOHN DELANEY

The forest didn't begin at the prairie's edge. Rather, it encroached on it. As the luxurious beds of golden grass and nettlewheat grew shorter and less dense, the first scrawny, gnarled trunks poked through. Other, stouter trees ventured out behind them in ones and twos as the last diminutive blades of grass gave way to cracked, dry earth and twisted undergrowth. A careless traveller could find himself well within the forest's domain before realising he had ever left the plains.

As far as Virkole knew or cared, this forest had no name. From his vantage point on the last high ridge before the forest began its invasion, the cinder could see only sparse details beyond where the grass truly ended. The twisting and curling of the trees themselves conspired to block his view more than the shadows and the perpetual dusk. The dark air above the forest was calm and unmoving, no warmer or colder than the air above the grassland. The forest itself showed none of the natural heat that a typical woodland might display. To Virkole's eyes it was simply a massive, cool blank. There was no sound from within the dark mass. For all intents and purposes, the forest was a dead place.

It was precisely as Lishe had described it.

Virkole nodded to himself and hopped down off his low ridge, skittering down the slight incline and into the dense field of nettlewheat once again. The nettlewheat responded immediately, every barbed blade nearby leaning gently toward him as he waded past. The long trek from Ashenmoor had taken Virkole through many miles of open wheat country, and he had soon grown to despise the stuff. It did him no harm, of course. Fleshier races avoided these fields as much as possible. Those who didn't would emerge covered in scratches and scrapes that glowed bright red and took agonizing weeks to heal. Virkole's hard, stony body was immune to that pesky irritation, but that fact only accentuated the other irritant, the sound. The constant grinding rustle of the nettlewheat as he moved through it had driven him to distraction almost the entire length of the journey. Virkole mentally added the end of the grass to his list of rewards that the forest held.

Far ahead, the forest almost seemed as though it were awaiting his arrival. Its grim, unchanging silence taunted him, beckoned him onward. It felt deep, ancient, cold, and hateful.

Precisely as Lishe had described.

* * * * *

"Not long now, no, no. Not now, not now. Ehehehe!"

Virkole didn't look up. He kept his gaze fixed on the small pile of kindling he had built and continued to heap the dry moss around its edges. Mitemoss smoked without flame, but at least it kept the heat going. The ragged voice on the opposite side of it didn't seem to notice Virkole's deliberate lack of interest, however. "Ehehehe! No fire. Not long now, though, no, not long now!"

He finally tossed the remainder of his foraging onto the pile of twigs and glared up at the cinder across from him. "You have wood?" Virkole demanded.

The old cinder stared back, a wide grin splitting his cracked face. The stranger had approached Virkole's little tinder pile a short time ago and hadn't seemed inclined to move on. Clearly the old coal's many years had not been kind to him, either physically or mentally. Many cinders had at least some small spots of flame in their bodies. More were like Virkole, mere embers, living skeletons of blackened charcoal that smoked and glowed red from within but could not sustain even a spark of essential fire. This figure, however, did not have even that red gleam. His stony torso and wide, chipped face were a dull black, the eyes merely white holes. A thin haze of smoke floated up from within him, but otherwise, if he but laid still, Virkole would have mistaken him for dead.

He did not lie still. Virkole doubted he even had the ability. As well as the constant chuckling and rambling, the old cinder rocked gently back and forth on his haunches as he watched Virkole's attempts to build the fire. Flakes of soot and cracked stone would occasionally dislodge and tumble down through his exposed form, adding a disconcerting clink to his already unsettling demeanor. Rather than silence him, Virkole's question only seemed to delight him.

"Wood? Yes! Ehehehe! Wood and fire, wood and fire! Yes! Not long now, fire, fire, yes!" He cackled again, swaying back and forth, then suddenly stopped. He fixed a vacant smile on Virkole.

"I have no wood."

Virkole shook his head and went back to tending his fire. All he could do was ignore him. He couldn't move on himself. The three small, charred sticks at the core of his fire had been a lucky find, and he wouldn't abandon them because of this nuisance. This part of the landscape was probably once a rolling hillside covered in trees, but that was long before Virkole's time. Now it was a scorched wasteland, its blackened rock and miserable charcoal stumps stretching away to merge, horizonless, with the endless black of the night sky. It was part of Ashenmoor now. Given that his kind had ruled it for so long, finding those sticks had been nothing short of miraculous.

"I have no fire either. Eheheh! No fire! Extinguisher took it!"

The crazed old cinder resumed his rocking back and forth. Virkole carefully coaxed his pitiful little mound of charred sticks and mitemoss. At last, a spark took hold, and in another moment a small, blue flame licked along one of his sticks. Virkole carefully rearranged the moss and leaned back. It might last about twenty minutes, and he was determined to enjoy it.

"Ah! Happy with your fire? Good, good! Not long now, no! Twigs, good, yes, wood and fire! Eheheh! Wood and fire!"

The old smoke leaned over the fire to Virkole and fixed him with a smile.

"Wood and fire."

He gave a quick nod and sat back, apparently satisfied that he was making perfect sense. Virkole just stared. If he was going to be forced to share the fire with this strange old coal, so be it. The fire had caught hold now, in a way, and small tongues of pale yellow flame licked the edges of the moss bowl Virkole had constructed. The faint heat rising lazily from it soothed Virkole's eyes. It had been days since he had seen any real heat, or felt its soft rippling upon his face.

His visitor, meanwhile, stared directly into the glowing heart of the fire, his grin unmoving. Finally he looked up and met Virkole's gaze.

"Fire, good. Extinguisher is very miserly. Very miserly! Extinguisher doesn't share fire with anybody. I know why. Eheheh! You know why! Yes, fire! Fire is *good!* Hah! Not long now. No! You know Extinguisher?"

Virkole just nodded dismissively. He was no longer in the mood to be irritated. He didn't bother looking away from the old drifter. There wasn't anything else worth looking at for miles around. Ignoring him hadn't worked. Feigning attention probably wouldn't either, but it was easier.

"Eheh. Yes, yes, Extinguisher wants all the fire. Very miserly, yes, yes! Eheheh! Took all the fire, hides it!"

Virkole nodded again. The sky was black because a great cinder had tried to burn it for warmth. Boggarts ate everything they saw because a young boggart had once eaten a faerie's bluebell pie and the faerie had cast a spell on them all as punishment. And cinders had no flame because a wicked cinder, called the Extinguisher, had stolen it all for herself. It had been many years since Virkole had been lulled to sleep by such tales, but now, in the scant but welcome warmth of his pathetic little campfire, it seemed that it may happen one more time.

"But where? Eheheh! All that fire. Very bright! Can't hide bright fire in the dark! No! Cinders would see it, see it, take it back! Not long now, not long. No! Yes! Where? Eheheh! Where is the fire?"

Virkole shrugged and idly gestured the sky.

The old cinder's grin never changed, but nonetheless became the grin of one who knew more than he was saying.

"Ah. Young firemaker doesn't know. No."

He leaned again over the fire and locked his gaze with Virkole's.

"Lishe knows."

* * * * *

Finally, the nettlewheat began to recede, giving away to
smooth blades of golden grass that glinted an eerie white
in the twilight. With the grating reeds behind him, the full
force of the forest's silence hit Virkole like a physical blow.
This close to the forest, right on its threshold, the cinder
was under no doubt that the silence was a real thing, not
merely the absence of noise.

Virkole was among the first pathetic trees now, stunted
specimens that burst out of the grass and stretched up a few
feet before withering away. They were a sickly brown color.
He laid a hand on one bole, and it came away covered in
the fine, gray dust of rotten wood. The tree was alive, but
only grudgingly so.

He moved on into the forest proper. The grass dwindled away to nothing, and his feet now crunched through
crumbling clay and dry twigs. A few days ago he would
have given anything for such a haul, but now he didn't
even look down. The trees around him twisted in bizarre
loops, their branches knotting overhead to block out the
sky. There was no natural path to follow. Virkole picked
his way around trees and through thorny, splintering
undergrowth, clambering over rocks and exposed roots.
Less than a minute after leaving the grass he lost sight of
it entirely. He had passed other forests on his way here. He
had passed many types of terrain, but none felt as closed
and alien as this place.

A treefolk stood in his way.

Virkole stopped. He almost hadn't noticed it was a creature at all. It was taller than him and looked just like the
gnarled trunks all around—a warped and tortured array of
jagged branches. This one had a face, though, a flattened

patch of bark seemingly hung onto its frontmost limbs. Its features were blank yet incredibly sad, two dark holes for eyes and a dreary, stretched crack for its mouth. The face cocked to one side and spoke.

"What a strange thing you are."

Its slow, measured speech was like the cracking of dead wood. Virkole had never seen a treefolk before, let alone heard one speak. The mouth moved with the words, but the voice seemed to churn up from within the thing itself.

"Strange to find you here. Very strange indeed."

Lishe had told him that treefolk lived in this forest. He had not encountered any in the forests on the way here, so he took this creature's presence as a good sign. It didn't look like budging, so Virkole stepped back around the withered trunk to his side.

The treefolk blocked his way there, too.

Virkole stopped again. He hadn't heard it move. A thing like that—its bark cracked and flaking, its branches seemingly ready to splinter in a sudden breeze—should surely have woken the dead with every step. It simply stood there again, and cocked its face quizzically.

"Strange. You don't wish to speak?"

Virkole pointed past the treefolk and said, "I wish to pass."

The treefolk cocked its face again and considered this for a moment, then shook its head of branches slowly. And silently, Virkole noted.

"No. This is no place for one such as you. You are a cinder, yes? A coalling. You cannot be here. You are a danger to us. What if you were to stumble over a root and fall on the dry ground?"

The treefolk raised its three longest limbs high and spread them in a slow, dramatic arc, all the while exhaling a low, whooshing breath from within. The noise gave way to a throaty, coughing sound. Virkole realized that the treefolk was laughing at its own little joke.

Virkole shot forward, covering the short distance between them in a single bound, and slammed into the creature's trunk, plunging both hands into its dense network of branches. The wafer-dry shoots snapped and broke off like scorched grass. His right hand found no purchase, but he felt solid hardwood with his left and grabbed it tight. Using that arm as leverage, he swung his right fist back and rammed it into the treefolk's face. An ominous *crack* sounded, one Virkole felt in the creature's hardwood spine.

He had trekked for days. He was actually inside the forest now. He was in no mood for delays.

The onslaught was so fast that the treefolk never had a chance to react. Despite its crumbling appearance and small stature, however—Lishe had described treefolk that towered many feet above him—it did not fall down or even step back. That had been the plan Virkole had formulated in the split second after his lunge, but even though he hadn't managed to knock it down and carry on past it, he was in a good position to press his attack. He drew his right arm back and slammed the treefolk's face again.

The wooden creature shrieked—a wrenching, hollow moan that echoed up through its leafless limbs—and thrashed, trying to shrug the cinder off. Virkole had latched onto it just below what would have been its right shoulder, so it swung at him with its leftmost bough. Caught mid-punch, Virkole was knocked loose and landed several feet away against a thick root.

The treefolk continued to moan, and scrabbled at its bristle of branches as though trying to reach some deep pain. Its face had slipped, and now hung at an angle. Virkole scrambled to his feet and launched himself at it again before it had time to turn on him.

This time, he lashed out with both knees and struck the creature firmly in the trunk. Virkole's stone knees smashed clear through two inches of rotten bark before impacting on solid wood. The outer layers flaked off in a shower of white dust.

The treefolk moaned again and keeled back. Virkole planted his shoulder beneath its faceplate and shoved, sending the heavy creature crashing back onto the ground. It flailed its arms as it fell, and landed hard on its right bough. With an earsplitting crack, and a howl of agony from the beast, it splintered off at the elbow.

Virkole stood over the treefolk's writhing form, carefully out of the way of its still-working other arms, and stared down at it until its cries quieted to whimpers. When it turned its face to him, he pointed down at it and said, "You have the Fire?"

Still moaning, the treefolk merely cocked its head in confusion. With a roar, Virkole bent and drove his fingers up into the soft wood behind that dreary, expressionless faceplate and wrenched it off in a spray of rotten bark. A small swarm of black-shelled insects immediately spilled out through the horrible gap where its face had been. As the torso's struggles died away, more beetles emerged from the fetid deadwood through any gap they could find and dispersed through the twigs and undergrowth all around. Virkole remained absolutely still until the last insect had vanished and the forest was once again silent and dark.

He stood upright and examined the dead faceplate in his hands. Its forlorn expression still hadn't changed. An image crossed his mind, an image of Lishe and the horrible things he had carried with him.

* * * * *

Skulls. They were three dry, black skulls.

Lishe sat and gently rocked back and forth, occasionally muttering "not long now" to himself as Virkole examined the skulls. Lishe had carried them inside his soot-caked leather garments, strung from hooks sewn inside his belt. Virkole couldn't guess how old they'd been when they died. All three cinder faceplates were badly damaged, riddled with cracks and notches. Most of the lower half of one was missing. He turned that one over in his hands.

"Eheheh. Grimfa, that one. Poor Grimfa. Close. Close! Yes! Not long now, no! Poor Grimfa."

Virkole looked up at the manic old stranger. Sootstoke. That's what Lishe had turned out to be. Virkole knew the word, but had never met a sootstoke in the stone. That was understandable. Virkole had never left Ashenmoor, and sootstokes by their nature rarely returned to it. Instead, they wandered far and wide, searching for a way to reignite the cinder fire and return life and dignity to a race that had never deserved it. Right-minded cinders dismissed sootstokes as misled dements who, in the absence of true hope, created false hope for themselves to fill the void. Sootstokes were generally left alone to their deluded misery. The absence of hope was a cinder's unavoidable fate.

"Grimfa. Yes." Lishe stopped rocking for a moment, then raised one arm and brought his fist down to the ground.

"Smashed. Close. Very close. We could *feel* it. Yes! We could feel it! Not long now! Then, smashed."

Virkole leaned over the fire and handed the skull back to the old smoke. He didn't notice how low his little mossy fire had burned. Lishe had been recounting, in his halting, shattered manner, his own quest for the Rekindling, and Virkole had found himself listening more and more intently.

Lishe rolled the black faceplate from hand to hand and gazed into the distance.

"Friends. Yes! Allies. Yes! Yes, believers, yes, yes! So close. Yes! Not long now! No. Close. The fire, the wood, the wood and the fire. In the wood! The fire! Eheheh, yes, yes! Not long now."

Virkole took in every word, but in order to make sense of the old coal's ramblings he had to filter out and ignore nine out of every ten. Lishe tossed the skull to the ground and spread his arms wide.

"Yes! Close! Yes! Not long now, not long!" He leaned in toward Virkole. *"Fire."*

He leaned back, and Virkole nodded.

Lishe believed he had found the Fire. The true flame, the primeval fire of the cinders. Virkole had always known it didn't really exist. Every sane cinder knew that there was no true flame, and that cinders were now as they always had been, the spite-born afterthoughts of a bitter, uncaring world.

But what if there *was* a true flame?

Lishe was clearly not among the sane, but at the same time, there was too much in what he said that made sense. Virkole couldn't imagine that everything he had listened to was purely the product of a severely addled mind. A lunatic's ravings, no matter how clouded by broken language and nonsensical meanderings, could not have told these stories.

From what Virkole had heard, Lishe had found where

the Fire was. He and three other cinders had set out to retrieve it and restore it to their kind. Clearly, Grimfa and the other two had met unfortunate ends, and Lishe had escaped with his life, if not his sanity. Beaten, old, and weak, Lishe had returned to Ashenmoor empty-handed, save for the death masks of his fallen comrades.

But returned from *where?*

The vehemence of the thought surprised Virkole. He raised a hand and pointed at Lishe.

"Where is the Fire?"

Lishe's grin widened. He reached down into the feeble little hearth and, careful not to knock the baked moss wall down, extracted one of Virkole's three precious sticks. The flames had long since died off, and the ingot was little more than a sooty, blackened rod that crawled with tiny red embers. Lishe tapped it with a finger, and a small flame briefly flickered out from beneath the blackened exterior before dying away again.

"In the wood."

* * * * *

Specifically, this wood.

Virkole stepped carefully between massive, towering boles that twisted and blended into an unseen, leafless canopy far overhead. These were old trees, deep in the center of the forest, that had long since established their dominance over any other forms of plant life. Whereas the edge of the forest had featured knots and tangles of twisted bark and undergrowth, each shrub and tree yet fighting its own corner, in here, Virkole stepped unimpeded over ancient, knurled roots and beds of rotted, discarded sticks.

The crunch of sticks had been the only sounds he had heard since he felled the treefolk, and the trees rising like wraiths out of the solid darkness, the only sights.

After seeing the extent of the rot in his fallen opponent's corpse, Virkole tested other, actual trees. Their bark cleaved off as easily as the treefolk's, revealing damp, turgid layers of rot infested with insects. These old, strong trees were no different. Their bark was covered in ugly, black growth, and their roots were riddled with fungal beds. The entire forest was in an advanced state of decay.

The ground began to dip now, and the spaces between the trees widened. Through the dusk, Virkole began to perceive a huge shape ahead, and quickened his pace.

It was an oak, perched atop a steep mound.

The tree was majestic by the standards of those around it, but it was also much shorter, and didn't join the canopy of knitted branches far overhead. Its two main branches curled and twisted out from the central trunk, with countless smaller, dry shoots coiling and intertwining around each other with what seemed an almost easy meticulousness. Its bark shared the black splotchy growths and chalky texture of every other tree he had seen so far.

The oak itself was about three times as tall as Virkole. What had given the shape that extra massiveness as it grew out of the gloom was the huge embankment it stood on, easily twice the cinder's height. The hillock rose steeply out of the blanket of dead twigs covering the ground. Virkole noticed that the land all around the mound's base seemed to slant gently down toward it, as though the mound and the tree themselves were responsible for the shallow depression.

Virkole regarded the tree for a long moment, then raised his arm and pointed.

"You have the Fire."

His voice echoed dimly through the surrounding trees, and then perfect silence descended in around him. This was absolute quiet. The crunch of wood beneath his feet had kept it at bay until now, but here it was almost smothering. The sudden, utter lack of noise almost made him dizzy.

A long time passed with Virkole standing isolated in the inky blackness, surrounded by the ghosts of tall trees and pointing up to the solemn, crumbling oak. He felt as though he were frozen in place by the sheer, deep shadow. His challenge seemed to provoke no response. He wasn't even certain that he had expected one. He had called out to the towering oak, but only because he saw it as an avatar of the entire forest. He hadn't thought this far ahead when he had set out from Ashenmoor. Lishe had said that the Fire was in these woods, but his directions were no more specific than that. However, standing there calling those words seemed right.

Virkole lowered his arm. The soft grinding of his elbow and shoulder as he did so seemed loud compared to what he had just endured.

The best place to hide something is not the place where it cannot be found, but that place where no one would think to look. It took a cinder as mad as Lishe to look in this cold, dark, unwelcoming void.

From the very corner of his eye, Virkole caught the briefest glimpse of a stir in the darkness above him, and hurled himself to the side. Immediately, the ground where he had been standing erupted in an explosion of dirt, rock, and twigs. He quickly scrambled onto his elbows and looked back up at the oak tree.

This was no oak tree. It was leaning forward now, twisted around and arched over the edge of the mound.

One massive, twisted limb extended down to the soil where Virkole had stood moments ago. In its new shape, the gnarls and furrows in the wood caught the shadows differently. There, two dark pinholes Virkole had noticed before became the pits of eyes which now glinted with disdain. Its second limb shuddered, and Virkole quickly clambered back as that arm, too, bore down on him. It shattered the ground before him.

Virkole pulled himself to his feet and hopped back, just out of range of any follow-up strike. A low, hollow moan rippled through the oak treefolk, shaking dust and debris from its mane of branches. It pulled its arms back and straightened. Virkole could now make out the thing's mouth, lost in the centuries of warped and cankerous bark.

"Fire." It hissed the word with perfect contempt, and twisted again to regard the cinder. "You were most unwise to come here, coalling. Most foolish."

The mound shook. As Virkole watched, a huge, thick root burst out the side. As the dirt around it collapsed, another root burst out from the opposite side, and the rest of the clay slipped away in a cloud of dust. The mound had only covered the creature's legs. How long must it have stood there, motionless, for such a mound to form around it?

The towering oak strode out from the cloud, raised its two thick arms above its branches, and balled the ends into a single fist. Virkole darted to one side again as the treefolk brought its arms down and slammed them into the soil, and backed up against a nearby tree. The gritty bark flaked away as he pulled himself around to the other side. His hands felt scuttling bugs.

It crossed his mind that the oak may be reluctant to attack him if it might harm a tree.

No such luck. The rampaging treefolk swept its arms across the forest floor and smashed right through the brittle base of the trunk. Virkole caught the full force of the treefolk's massive fists in his back. Screaming white stars blinded him as he was sent flying.

Crashing into the ground, he came to rest in an awkward, agonizing heap. The pain was almost uniform throughout his body. He couldn't tell where he was hurt worst or which of his limbs might be missing, so he willed himself to move regardless.

He hadn't been flung as far as he had thought. The oak seemed to have lost sight of him in the darkness, but once it found him, three or four strides would have it towering above him again. The tree that had provided him such poor cover was still upright, despite the fact that an entire length of its trunk was missing. Its branches, knotted into the canopy above, seemed to be holding the remaining bole's weight.

A series of pops and groans from high above signaled that this was about to end. The trunk suddenly shunted straight down, its jagged end splintering against what had been its own roots moments before. It stopped, teetered for a moment, and then tilted toward Virkole.

Virkole shook his head to clear the dizziness and scrambled back. The trunk hit the ground with a ferocious crash beside him. Weakened by whatever desiccating disease riddled its wood, it collapsed with the impact, shedding layers of bark and sending up a cloud of dry, wooden dust.

The oak spied Virkole as the tree fell and clumped purposefully toward him. The effort to stand almost made Virkole black out, but he managed to pull himself up and hobbled in against the fallen tree trunk. The pain was beginning to recede a little, but in places it simply localized into specific excruciating hotspots. His left leg could barely support him. He glanced down and noticed a new crack running up the stone of his calf.

The oak roared, and the tree trunk beside Virkole suddenly lurched upward. It rained down flakes of bark as the huge creature hefted it up and glared down at him.

Virkole turned and ran as fast as his battered body would allow toward the nearest upright tree. The last one had provided little cover but it was the best available. The oak roared again and tossed the fallen trunk aside.

Virkole rounded the tree and kept going. The treefolk simply ploughed through it, showering the cinder with an explosion of rotten wood. Its momentum dragged the severed trunk forward with it. This tree clearly was not as tightly knit into the canopy as the last, and the trunk immediately shifted down, ramming into the matted branches covering the oak treefolk's head. The weight drove the oak face first into the soil. The rest of the trunk fell back along the downed treefolk, fracturing into two long segments before finally coming to rest.

The thunder of the tree's fall eventually dissipated into the surrounding blackness. The dark was lessened by the absence of two trees from the canopy, creating an eerie, moon-tinted glade. The soft rain of broken branches from the cover above died out. The oak didn't move.

Slowly, careful not to put too much weight on his bad leg, Virkole approached the creature. As he drew near, he could make out a low, pathetic keening. The monster was whimpering.

Its face was at an awkward angle to the rest of its body, turned sideways and pressed into the ground. Through its branches, Virkole could make out some of the massive damage the rogue trunk had done to the back of its neck, ripping away the bark and pulverizing the heartwood. One of its eyes was shattered. The other regarded Virkole with palpable hatred. The creature drew a labored, ragged breath.

"Coalling," it spat.

Virkole tapped his chest.

"Cinder," he corrected.

"Why . . . did you come here?"

Virkole felt his shoulders tense. It was lying here in the dirt, its body destroyed, death surely only moments away, and still it held out? He pointed one hand toward the treefolk's working eye.

"You have the Fire."

The treefolk wheezed.

"Fire. You speak in . . . riddles, little coalling. What is it . . . that you want?"

Virkole balled his hand into a fist and rammed it deep into the creature's good eye.

The treefolk screamed in agony. Virkole wrenched his arm in deeper, up to his elbow.

"Show it to me."

The treefolk continued to scream. Virkole twisted his arm in even deeper, ramming it through until his entire arm had disappeared into the treefolk's eye socket. Curse them all, how many treefolk would he have to murder in this forest before one of them told him where the Fire was?

It *was* here. It *had* to be. Lishe had been absolutely mad, but on this point, Virkole knew—he simply knew—that the old smoke had been correct. The Fire was in these woods.

An image of Lishe came to him, the old cinder drawing one of the charred sticks out of Virkole's fire. The old cinder's manic, knowing grin as he coaxed the tiny lick of flame from it. There had been no fire on it when he had plucked it out. It had been in the wood.

In the *wood*.

Virkole rammed his other fist into the dying creature's forehead. It smashed through several layers of rotten bark before stopping against solid hardwood at wrist depth.

"Show me the Fire!"

The Fire was all around him. He could feel it now, he knew he could. This was what Lishe must have felt like, surrounded by the Fire but unable to see it or sense its warmth, its heat, because these abominable wooden creatures hid it, hid it out of pure spite, hid it because they were cold, rotten, and dying and wanted to drag the cinders with them out of pure *spite*.

The treefolk ceased its wailing and started to shudder. This one was the worst of them. Virkole loathed this one now, could almost feel his fury flowing through his arms and into its worthless, diseased corpse. This one had tried to kill him for merely coming *close*. Virkole would see this one *burn*.

What was left of the back of the treefolk's head erupted in a gush of heat and light. Flame exploded up through the creature, raw fire shooting out of every crack in the thing's ruined crown. The bark crinkled and blackened before catching fire from within. In seconds, the entire upper trunk was a ball of fire that quickly began to spread over the rest of the body and across the forest floor.

Virkole stared. Was this it? The heat at his fists was intense, and he gingerly withdrew them. They were blasted black. Was this the Fire?

He rested one hand carefully on the treefolk's burning hide. The warmth in his palm was exhilarating. Never in his life had he experienced such heat. The treefolk's head collapsed in on itself, leaving a pile of roasting embers and a mass of roaring flame.

This *was* the Fire. Virkole had found it.

He realized that he was not alone.

The blaze spread easily through the dry forest debris on the ground. The darkness thinned as the flames advanced, revealing not just the trees, but also several other hulking shapes. Treefolk. They were all around. Several closely resembled the one he had slain at the forest's edge.

He remembered how silently that treefolk had moved to block his path. How long had they been there? Had they been following him the whole time? What had they been planning?

The sudden release of the Fire had obviously startled them. Virkole was no expert at reading emotions, and certainly not those of trees, but they seemed to be confused now, uncertain of how to react to this change of circumstance.

They're no longer in control. Not now that the Fire has been returned to the cinders.

Virkole picked out the nearest one, a melancholy bramble like the first, and pointed. The flames between him and his target swirled in the air and then blew outward on some unseen gust, licking the thing gently in the face. It reared back, its face covered in tiny tongues of flame. Not enough to burn, it was more than enough to cause panic. The treefolk toppled backward, clutching its face. Its hands caught fire, and within moments this treefolk, too, was ablaze.

Virkole darted out and leaped up on top of the struggling creature. Like he had done before, he rammed his fists through its thin bark and thought of fire. Immediately, a ball of flame erupted from inside it.

By now, the other treefolk had stirred from their shock

and were advancing gingerly around the flames in the center of the new clearing. The nearest was only feet away. Virkole pointed, and to his delight a stream of flame shot from his hand and enveloped the creature's raised arm. The flames caught, but the treefolk ignored them, swinging its burning fist and catching Virkole with a hard backhand. The cinder was knocked off the tree corpse onto his back.

The creature would have been on him immediately, but the flames had become too much to ignore. Virkole was still impressed by how it still struggled forward, glaring at him through the pain. Now its flame joined with the flame on the other treefolk corpse and it finally toppled over.

Virkole got to his feet and glared at the other approaching treefolk. How had creatures like these ever held the Fire captive? Breaking them and taking it was proving to be so easy.

The huge bonfires were attracting more of them out of the dark now. Two squat, smooth-branched treefolk rumbled down the incline toward him. He raised his hand and another jet of white flame erupted, catching both of them across their midsections. One went down immediately, but the other continued its charge and swung a gnarled branch. Virkole stepped back and around it then planted his hand against its face and blasted the back of its trunk out. A third charged from the side. Virkole ducked its swing and rammed his fist into its bark, incinerating it with a thought.

Still they came. Virkole started to head back toward the relative safety of the largest fire behind him, but had to torch two more of the beasts on the way. Could they not understand how simple it was to defeat them? Did they not see that every corpse Virkole made only added to the blaze?

Virkole clambered up onto the remains of the oak's torso, the highest point in the inferno. The flames had spread wide now, and were climbing the trunks of at least six of the nearby trees. From up here, Virkole could feel the raw heat of the Fire churning up through the wood, a heat more intense and terrible than he had ever thought possible.

It was all Virkole's. Every shred of it.

With this heat running through him, it was a simple task to wave his hand in a slow arc and incinerate two treefolk trying to fight through the flame toward him. A flick of the wrist, and another was immolated where it stood. Still they came. Virkole lowered his arms and concentrated hard on that core of heat beneath him, then mentally wrenched that heat up. The entire blaze flared, catching another half a dozen treefolk who all went down screaming. Virkole roared in triumph as their carcasses added themselves to his fire.

The darkness roared back. Virkole looked around.

Two large treefolk stomped out of the dark and into the burning glade, stopping just short of the flames. These were slightly taller than the oak had been, but were bent almost double. Their multiple root-legs were thick and sturdy. Their branches were thin and wiry and jutted out in seemingly random clusters from their bodies. Each had a large triangular head defined by a long, drooping nose and wide sneer. They examined the scene before them for a moment, and then ploughed straight into the flame.

Their bark ignited at once, the smaller twigs burning away to nothing. Both grimaced but kept coming. Virkole raised his fist and sent a blast of fire at one but it simply barged through it, its face now a mess of heat cracks and flame.

Virkole leaped backward off his post as the other smashed a fist down, cleaving right through the oak embers.

The other leaped over it and landed beside Virkole. It batted a hand down through the flames. Virkole dodged it easily and commanded the flames to wrap around its head. The fire complied, and the treefolk roared and backed away.

The first giant treefolk kicked its way through the oak's remains and approached the cinder. Its bark was scorched black now, most of its smaller branches crumbling away to ash. The flames rippling around its face gave its sneer an even more sinister aspect. Virkole sent more flames surging toward it and circled quickly around its feet while it flailed blindly. He clambered back up onto the oak's embers.

There was a sudden loud, rolling creak. One of the trees, now wreathed in fire almost to the canopy, collapsed at the base and crashed down, joining Virkole's pyre. It flattened the other monstrous treefolk and sent up a cloud of burning ash, which spread over a group of smaller treefolk that had been trying to stamp his fire out at the edges.

Virkole leaped from his perch and landed on the back of the treefolk he had just blinded. As he hit its hide he heard a crack before a rush of pain clouded his vision. It was his leg, the one the oak had injured earlier. He shook his head and glanced down at the crack. It now ran the entire length of his calf.

The treefolk reared up, trying to knock him loose, but its own gnarled, twisted hide provided ample bracing for his arms and one good leg. He grimaced and pulled his free leg over one of the creature's branches, then rammed the bark with his fist. It didn't give. This treefolk's wood, though rotten and black with disease, was solid as rock. That was how they were able to survive inside the fire.

Virkole scowled to himself. The fire that these creatures kept must be great indeed. He tried a blast of flame but only managed to crack the wood.

He looked up along the treefolk's body toward a cluster of jagged branches behind its face. Perhaps there.

Before he could move, he was swept up in a huge wooden hand as long as Virkole was tall. The grip was vicelike. One of Virkole's arms was free, but the other was wrenched painfully by his side. The hand brought him around to face a third treefolk, just like the other two. This one must have entered the inferno from another direction. Its face was also baked black from the flames, and its tight grimace showed that these creatures were in considerable pain despite their endurance. Virkole brought around his free hand and sent a stream of those flames into his captor's face. It squealed and released him.

Virkole dropped to the ground and folded in a heap as his broken leg gave beneath him, sending jolts of agony through his body. Every scratch and bruise he had received so far seemed magnified by the wave of pain. The only thought that filled his mind was to get to safety. He willed himself to get to his feet and make for the oak carcass.

One of the two enormous treefolk grabbed his arm and wrenched it clean off.

This time, the pain was smothered by a sudden, pure rage. Virkole whirled to face his attacker and screamed in fury. The treefolk disintegrated in a spray of crimson ash, not an inch of its tough hide remaining intact. Virkole heard his severed arm land with a soft thud nearby. He would have to leave it. He could collect it when the entire forest was as black as Ashenmoor.

First, though, he had to find cover. White stars danced around his vision, and he gritted his jaw against the pain in his shoulder and leg. The final giant treefolk was searching around in the flames for him. Even with these creatures' stony bark, it couldn't ignore the pain and damage forever.

Moving as fast as his shattered leg would allow, he made for the oak. He would simply wait for this marauder to either succumb to the flames or flee.

The cinder limped carefully around to the other side of the oak. It was barely recognizable now. The majority of its trunk was gone, leaving only the hard interior. Every step of the way was sheer agony. Virkole finally reached the far side and made his way toward the chunk of fallen tree that had killed the mighty oak. Even less of this remained, but what did remain was propped against the oak's spine. He could rest underneath it and wait for the fire itself to avenge him.

As he drew near, another treefolk appeared above the flames. This was not one of the massive, fire-resistant ones. This one was smaller, its yellow eyes and lumpy nose nestled inside a thick briar of netted sticks and twigs. It didn't see Virkole, as it seemed intent on batting the flames out with its multiple thick limbs. A sense of horror began to rise through the pain, rage, and exhaustion. He peered out through the flames and glimpsed dozens of treefolk out there, all shapes, all along the edge of the inferno, stamping and smothering and hurling great boughfuls of clay onto the fire. They were very near now. They were succeeding.

They were driving the fire back.

The huge treefolk in the flames behind him roared—he had been spotted. He turned and looked up at it as the treefolk stepped around the oak and stalked toward him.

He had nothing left. He had lost an arm. His leg was shattered. He couldn't even flee. His body was wracked with exhausting injuries. Where was the Fire? The birthright of the cinders? It was all around him. It was being trampled underfoot by a horde of trees. How could it be so weak? It had burned so *bright*. He stood, slumped to one side, clutching his ragged shoulder with his remaining hand, in the greatest, most glorious conflagration he or any other cinder had ever known. Yet, it was dying.

The treefolk paused as it approached, perhaps expecting a trick or another blast of heat. Some small part of Virkole willed himself to summon that heat, to bend what remained of this holy fire and tear that wooden monstrosity from the face of Shadowmoor. The rest of Virkole, by far the majority, was tired. Somehow, even while being bathed by this glorious heat, Virkole was more tired than he could remember ever being.

Apparently deciding that Virkole had no tricks left, the massive treefolk stepped closer, right up to the cinder. It glared down for a moment, then grinned savagely and raised its foot. Virkole looked down to the ground, scorched black and glowing red through the flames. He closed his eyes and sighed in defeat.

"Lishe, I'm sorry."

* * * * *

The glade was quiet again. The hole ripped in the canopy by the death of three trees meant that the darkness was not so strong there, but the meager light that fell from the black sky above barely illuminated the thick layer of ash and soot that covered the ground. Charred corpses of fallen trees and treefolk littered the space. The center of the ash heap was dominated by the remains of several large treefolk, but at least two dozen others lay scattered around it. Nothing moved in this dead place.

A low, gentle cackling broke the silence, intermixed with quiet mutterings. It grew louder, and soon a stooped figure stepped out of the darkness between scorched black trees. Lishe surveyed the scene before him.

"Yes! Eheheh. Fire, yes, yes! Very good. Very good, eheheh! Yes. Not long now, no! Not long now!"

He moved out toward the center of the clearing, examining the ground and muttering and cackling all the while. Finally, he spied what he was looking for and reached down into the ash.

Lishe plucked Virkole's cold, blackened skull from the dirt and held it up to the light. Cinder skulls did not break easily, and this one was still largely intact, despite the savage battering it had clearly received. Lishe studied it for another moment and then grinned.

"Extinguisher burnt cinders, not trees! Eheheheh!"

He lifted the folds of his clothing to reveal the three cinder skulls already hanging from his belt, and clicked his new trophy into place alongside them. He then turned and headed back toward the glade's edge, chuckling and cackling to himself.

Just at the edge of the darkness, he paused and looked down at the corpse of a treefolk lying at his feet. He gave its trunk a sharp kick, then reached down and plucked three charred sticks from its shoulders. With a chuckle, he slipped these up one sleeve, glanced back across the ash one last time, and disappeared into the shadows.

JENNA HELLAND

Dying was more peaceful than he expected. The wakeripper had sliced open his belly and swam away empty handed, leaving the young elf on his hands and knees watching his blood seep into the ground. He was still in the shadow of the wall, and for a moment he had enough strength to call to one of the guards. But in that instant he realized he didn't love the desperate, clawing existence that had become his life. So he dragged himself under a nearby tree, where he could watch the weak morning light spread across the sky through the silhouette of the branches. Above him was a spiderweb covered in dew, and in his last moment, he saw more colors in a single droplet than he had ever before.

When the guards brought in the body, Ehroe covered it with a linen sheet as was expected of the leader of the Dusklight Safehold. No one knew why the young warrior had ventured outside the fortress alone without cover from archers on the wall or how he was attacked on the western—on ground once believed safe from the merrows. The wakerippers' methods were becoming more deadly, and ground that appeared solid hid a waterway perfect for a merrow to stalk a landwalker. And so they had lost another one. Ehroe had lost another one.

The merrows who lived in the marshy land east of the safehold were responsible for most of the deaths these days, though boggarts had slaughtered a hunting party a few weeks before. And elf children kept falling ill, probably from the stagnant water that now surrounded the fortress on three sides. It was a swamp too young to have a name, and merrow raiders were moving in faster than the spike grass and black needlerush could grow. Soon, the merrows would triumph over the elves of Dusklight simply by attrition, one elf sliced to death where he stood, another dragged and held under the murky water until she drowned. As their leader, Ehroe knew he was failing. Failing in the duty passed to him by his wife, Reika, on the night she died. And by failing to protect the dwindling population, he was betraying her.

Hours later, Ehroe stopped his warriors at the edge of the forest. He was still thinking about the young warrior—one of his own gutted within a stone's throw of the fortress. Below them in the valley lay the kithkin village of Ballygol. There were a dozen neat white cottages—each with a tidy kitchen garden and springjack pen—inside a rectangle of high wooden walls. Peat smoke was rising from the chimneys and most families would be sitting down for their nighttime meal. If not for the guards, the spikes on top of the walls, and the reinforced gate, it would have been a pleasant scene of domestic life.

While the kithkin weren't allied with the elves, they weren't enemies either. Ehroe had been inside the walls several times to exchange information with Cenn Tyack or trade for some item. The kithkin were never hospitable, but they had always been honest in their dealings. As always, he wondered how Reika would have handled this task. Before her death, Reika had been the leader of these elite warriors known as the safewrights. Ehroe had followed her into the wilds as they searched for hallowhelds.

Ehroe's mount stamped its hooves and twitched its

long ears impatiently. Ehroe stroked the russet hair on the back of the cervin's slender neck. Like him, the animal was happy to be beyond the confines of the black, tangled trees and eager to be in the open country of the valley. Still, Ehroe hesitated. Beside him, Cavan looked at Ehroe expectantly.

"Why do you wait?" Cavan asked, his violet eyes scanning the horizon. Cavan was the finest warrior among the Dusklight elves and had been Ehroe's closest friend since childhood. "Is something amiss?"

Cavan required no explanation. He would follow Ehroe without question, just the way he followed Reika when she had been alive. It was the other warriors that concerned Ehroe. There was a tense, weary mood among the riders every time they rode into the wild. There was little to eat in the safehold, each of them was grieving someone, and now the merrows could kill them on solid ground and vanish like mist. As the noose tightened around the elves, venturing outside the walls held less appeal. They wanted to hide in their fortress like foxes in their dens and keep back the night as best they could. Ehroe understood, but he couldn't let it happen.

"Circle around," Ehroe said gruffly. "The seer knows of the Wellspring Lyre. The kithkin recovered it when they killed the boggarts in the scrublands. Cenn Tyack has agreed to the exchange. But the seer . . ."

Ehroe trailed off. He had a hard time referring to Eily as the seer. She was a freckle-faced youth who had lost both her parents at the same time he'd lost his wife. Reika had been particularly fond of Eily and believed there was something special about her. A few months after Reika died, Eily stumbled into the courtyard where Cavan and Ehroe were finishing their dinner of barely palatable tubers mixed with equally unappealing crawroot. She mumbled something about a blackthorn staff in a cave on the ridge. Then she fainted, although the quick-footed Cavan caught her before she fell to the ground. Cavan insisted they ride out that very day, and when he and Ehroe found the staff in the cave, Eily's status as a visionary was sealed.

"The kithkin may have recovered something else," Ehroe said.

Cavan looked sharply in his direction, but Ehroe didn't meet his eyes. The other safewrights exchanged glances.

"We haven't had word of the cloudbreaker in ages. But it is possible. The boggarts were of the same band that seized the beacon-stone before."

All hallowhelds were sacred, and the lyre was known as an object of renowned beauty. But the cloudbreaker was greater than all else. It was legend. They had heard the story since they were infants. The cloudbreaker was the hope of the elves, a beacon that held the power to call forth the Ally to destroy their enemies. At their time of greatest need, the elves would smash the stone and release the breath of the Ally that had been captured inside the translucent rock. The Ally would leave its home in the realm of the sky, part the clouds and secure the elves' victory over brutality and darkness.

"We will make the trade for the lyre," Ehroe said. "Then we will request the cloudbreaker. It is of no use to the kithkin and rightfully belongs to the elves."

Ehroe carefully searched the faces of each of the safewrights. Having once been one of them, he knew their combat styles but not the contours of their thoughts. Reika had understood them in a way he never would. She made no lofty speeches or empty promises, but all the warriors followed willingly in her wake, searching for a single stone in world of endless shadows. As the waters rose threatening to choke the life out of the safehold, every thought in her clever head focused on finding the cloudbreaker. And when she died, there was nothing to show for it. If it were possible, Ehroe would have destroyed all knowledge of the beacon—the thing that consumed his wife and left them with nothing but a devastated community on the brink of despair. But if he'd learned anything in his short time as leader, it was that the legend of the cloudbreaker would not die.

"I have word that the kithkin are in league with the merrows. If Cenn Tyack denies the existence of the beaconstone, it means he has plans to trade it to them. We cannot let the cloudbreaker fall into the hands of the merrows."

He had the safewrights' full attention now. It was infuriating to think of the muck-dwelling merrows secreting the cloudbreaker in the depths of some river, just to keep it out of the hands of its rightful owners.

"Hope when all hope is lost . . ." Ehroe began.

" 'Hope when all hope is lost . . .' " the elves chorused and followed him down the muddy hill to the village.

The guard on the wall saw them coming and gave the order to open the gate. They were expected, but as usual, not welcomed. Cenn Tyack had been at his dinner, and his napkin was still tucked in his collar. The stocky kithkin trotted into the courtyard without his usual entourage of guards. He stared up at Ehroe with blank yellow eyes that never seemed to blink or betray emotion of any kind.

"All right, elf," he said, unceremoniously tossing a large velvet bag up to Ehroe. "Here is your token. Now, where are my seeds?"

Ehroe nodded to Cavan, who pulled two bags from his pack and dropped them to the ground. "A mixture of winter wheat and barley from our stores. I can promise you the supply is pure."

Like the elves, the kithkin were living on tubers, winter squash, and not much else. Without new harvests, seeds were scarce. The cenn grunted in satisfaction.

"A fair trade," Ehroe agreed. "But I wish to call your attention to the third sack of seeds I have brought with me."

Already hurrying back toward his cottage, the cenn called over his shoulder, "I have no more tokens for you. If I come across them, I will send a runner."

"You have the cloudbreaker."

Cenn Tyack stopped in his tracks. Like most inhabitants of the realm, he was familiar with the legend. No one else gave it any credence, particularly since it seemed to only benefit the elves. Cenn Tyack had never understood the elves' fondness for things such as the lyre, which they died to obtain and then simply deposited in the mud chamber under their safehold. He'd always believed if they were foolish enough to trade good foodstuffs for them, he was happy to oblige them. He was not, however, pleased with the elf's accusation. Tyack would no more bring the so-called cloudbreaker into his home than he would a wounded wolf cub.

"Be gone. I'll have none of your mumblings here."

"You've no use for the beacon-stone. We will give you these seeds for a trade, or not. But we will take the cloudbreaker regardless."

Tyack did not like the turn of the conversation. He pulled the napkin out of his shirt collar and turned to motion the guard down from the wall. But before he could raise the alarm, Ehroe sent an arrow flying dangerously close to the kithkin's ear.

"That was a warning, Tyack," he said. "It doesn't have to be this way."

"And what way is that, elf?" the cenn growled. "Since when did you become our enemies?"

"We aren't your enemies," Ehroe said. "But you don't know what we're up against there on the edge of the swamp."

"Your trials are no more than ours," Tyack replied.

"I have little ones to protect, just like you," Ehroe said, his voice pleading. "Give me the cloudbreaker, and we'll leave you in peace."

The kithkin gave a barking laugh. "There is no *peace*. You know it as well as I."

Tyack sprinted to the gatehouse, but Ehroe's arrow felled him before he crossed the muddy yard.

"Take out the guards," Ehroe urged Cavan. "On the wall! Do it now!"

Clenching his jaw, Cavan slowly raised his bow. Hearing the raised voices, the guards turned toward the courtyard, where Tyack lay bleeding on the ground.

"He's keeping the cloudbreaker for himself," Ehroe shouted as the guards raised their bows. "We have no allies but ourselves."

Cavan shot the nearest guard before the kithkin could notch his arrow. As soon as Cavan fired, the other safewrights followed his example, and the guards fell before they ever fired a shot. Drawn by the commotion, the villagers emerged from their cottages and stared in confusion at the elves on their high mounts with their weapons in hand.

Ehroe looked pained as he turned to his safewrights. "Search everywhere. Burn it down."

* * * * *

From the treetop platform high above the fortress walls, Eily saw the safewrights leave the forest and make their way toward the safehold. Below her, the archers were poised on the wall in case the merrows attempted another attack. With all the murderous creatures lurking in the world, the ground outside their own walls had become the most treacherous of all.

It made her too anxious to watch Ehroe until he cleared the walls, so Eily knelt down in front of her low worktable where she mixed poultices and tinctures from the rare plants she had a talent for growing. From across the swamp, she could hear Callem the Builder shouting at the clouds, but until the wind shifted she wouldn't be able to make out his words. Sometimes it was nonsense anyway, just a lone giant raging into the wind.

She surveyed the neat rows of seedlings, her tools and her chests of books with satisfaction. She was privileged to have this garden, which was built in the top branches of the towering pillar oak that grew at the center of the safehold. Eily spent her time cultivating healing flowers while the other rootkeeps toiled in the waterlogged fields that only produced sickly, wilted crops. So far, she managed to grow enough dawnglove to keep the safehold supplied with dawnglow, a healing potion essential to the elves.

Eily stood up and crossed to the eastern railing, where she had the best view of Callem and his latest tower. The lean, shaggy giant had settled onto the rocky shoreline on the other side of the swamp around the same time Eily had transformed the platform into a garden. Most of the elves ignored the existence of the twelve-foot creature sharing the swamp with them, but Eily had been curious about him from the beginning. At first she assumed he was like many other bleary-minded giants of the realm who seemed to care about nothing but the repetition of some task that was often as destructive as it was meaningless.

For Callem it was building towers—haphazard constructions that were basically boulders tossed on top of one another. He would spend days in a building frenzy and then smash them in a fit of anger. He would sleep for weeks, and then begin yet another tower that was doomed to be a failure, all the while screaming at the sky as if he expected it to answer back. After months of watching him, Eily began to recognize words and phrases in Callem's rantings. And one day, she realized that the giant was watching her as much as she was watching him.

Today, Callem was trying to roll a rock up the trunk of a tree that was propped against the base of the tower. The boulder was larger than anything she had seen him try to move before—it looked as if he'd torn off the top of a cliff. After a few attempts, he let the rock drop onto the ground. He turned toward the swamp, and despite the distance, Eily could tell he was looking in her direction.

"Water-wards depths dwellers," he called. "Charged moat shore."

"Water-wards" was his name for merrows, and Eily looked down at the swamp to see what he was talking about. She could see shadows darting under the surface, but the aerial view revealed little about the merrows' activities under the murky water. Back when the safehold had been surrounded by a meadow, the platform was a useful lookout against boggart marauders hiding in the dark-blue grasses and shrubby trees. In those days, the meadow was cut by a swift-flowing river, just one of the many tributaries of the Lanes. But a year ago, the floods came and changed the shape of the land. It rained for a hundred days without ceasing and the river spilled out of the banks and spread day by day until it lapped at the walls of the safehold.

Only magic kept the hallowheld chamber beneath the

fortress from filling with the murky, fetid water. Slugs, bogles, and even creatures like the lank-haired mud selkies tried to scale the walls of the fortress to take refuge from the relentless water. There was no color during those days, nor warmth or rest. It was a time of relentless rain and bodies stacked in the muddy courtyard. The ground was too wet to bury them so they lay in the open air under a rain-swollen sky that would not permit a pyre.

Eily loved Ehroe even before the floods, back when his wife had been the vigilant of the safehold, and all eyes turned to her to save them. In desperation, Reika sent the safewrights farther and farther a field searching for the cloudbreaker. Near death, one of the warriors had crawled back infected with a coughing sickness that killed half the population, including Eily's parents and eventually Reika herself. She died believing that the cloudbreaker was the only thing that would save them from a death that seemed inevitable.

"Eily."

Eily turned to look at Ehroe, who was standing at the edge of the platform. He'd removed his silver helm but still wore a muddy cloak.

"Safe home, Ehroe," she said quietly.

"I've found something for you," he said.

That was unexpected. He reached inside his cloak and pulled out a pig's bladder wrapped tight with a leather cord and stained with some thick black substance.

"I see you've found the cloudbreaker at last," she said sarcastically.

Ehroe frowned. "Don't jest. The cloudbreaker is a thing of beauty."

"And you are holding a boar's innards. Where is the beauty in that?"

"Eily," he said, with a hint of warning in his voice.

Dutifully, she opened the bag. At first she saw nothing but dirt, but then there was the telltale glow of pale seeds.

"Dawnglove?" she breathed in amazement. Her supplies of the flower were dwindling and without dawnglow they wouldn't be able to ward off the wasting sickness that was afflicting the youngest elves.

Ehroe grinned at her. "Indeed. If anyone can make them show themselves, it will be you."

Eily flushed at his compliment, but she refused to smile back.

"I heard what you did," she said. "The scout arrived this morning with the news."

"At Ballygol? We recovered the lyre."

"You burned out the kithkin," she said angrily.

"It was necessary."

"You had the lyre. Why was it necessary?"

"The cloudbreaker—"

"The cloudbreaker was never in that village. You know that as well as I do!"

Ehroe came and stood in front of her, placing his hands securely on her shoulders, but she refused to look him in the eye.

"Look at me."

But Eily wouldn't. "You shouldn't have destroyed Ballygol."

"You're not angry at me because of that," he said, taking a shuddering breath. "Reika's been gone for less than a year."

"Reika wasn't gone when it happened! How has she become your excuse?"

It had been the last clear day before the rains came, but of course, none of them knew it at the time. Reika was in the wilds with the safewrights, but Ehroe volunteered for nightwatch and remained home. At eveningtide, he'd sought out Eily on some pretense he couldn't even remember. She was striking, with reddish hair against tawny skin the color of a fawn, and he'd seen her eyes darting away when he caught her looking at him. She was pleasant but young, and had taken the encounter more to heart than he expected.

"The cloudbreaker is with the merrows of the lake," Eily said, her eyes bright with tears. "I told you that two months ago. You asked me to keep quiet, and I have. But. . . ."

"You have to trust me, Eily," Ehroe said.

"More of us are dying every day!"

"We will bring the beacon-stone home soon," Ehroe said. "And we will call the Ally. But the time has to be right."

Eily twisted away from him. "Why do you get to decide when the time is *right?*"

"You tell me where there is beauty, and I seek it out. You may be the knowledge, but I am the sword. Remember, without me, your words mean nothing."

As he climbed down the ladder, she returned to her worktable and lifted each seed out of the bag with wooden tongs before gently placing it into seedling pots. There were fifteen seeds in all. Even if only five sprouted, that would be enough to make a good supply of dawnglow. She'd tied a golden ribbon to the railing to remind her of wind shifts. Seeing it dance on the currents, she grabbed her book and pen and perched on the edge of the railing. Her bare feet dangled in the air as she watched Callem struggle with the boulder and heard his low voice rumble across the expanse.

"The sky king realm of darkness. Fleet of tattered wing. The shadow fall and treasure of black ire . . .

At the word treasure, Eily began to write.

* * * * *

Five days later, the first bloom appeared. Eily pushed a wind-whipped strand of hair out of her eyes and stared at the flower, which was not white at all, but a startling crimson with veins of black running through the petals. This was not dawnglove. This was something she'd never seen before.

In a realm of perpetual dusk, colors are as scarce as sunlight. A deep purple stone or a blue shell is precious simply because of the hue. Eily had always considered red, however, to be the color of pain and death. The blood-soaked garments of a wounded elf. The crusty red skin of boggart marauders. The red-tinged eyes of an elf grieving yet another lost loved one. She had never seen a red so beautiful that it took her breath away.

"Cramoisy," Ehroe said, appearing over her shoulder.

"What?"

"It's cramoisy. The killing flower. No one's seen it in the wild for ages. I can't image where the kithkin found it."

"A pity it's not dawnglove."

"Perhaps." Ehroe looked thoughtful. "If it's mixed in the same way as dawnglow, it creates a poison strong enough to fell a giant."

"I'll make it for you," Eily said automatically.

Ehroe looked unsure. "Wear leather gloves. Make sure none is spilled on your skin—it will kill you in seconds. Perhaps one of the older rootkeeps . . ."

Eily scowled. "You don't think I'm capable."

"I can't bear another dead elf," he said.

"Then bring home the cloudbreaker," she said urgently. "I've been thinking about this every moment. I can't wait until . . ."

"Eily, please. . . ." Ehroe interrupted.

"If you don't tell them where the cloudbreaker is, I will," Eily finished forcefully.

Ehroe said nothing, but there was a tightening in the muscles around his lips and his eyes darkened. "I think that would be mistake."

"Ballygol was a mistake," she said. "I can't imagine why you leave the beacon-stone in the hands of the merrows."

"Because having it would be worse than not having it."

"That doesn't make sense!" Eily shouted.

"Stop using your heart instead of your head. What do you think will happen when we get the cloudbreaker?"

"We'll summon the Ally. He'll part the clouds and kill our enemies."

"So say the stories. But what if the stories aren't true, Eily? Have you ever thought of that?"

"How can you say that?"

"One elf tells another and another, and so everyone believes. But where did the story first come from? And what if there is no Ally at all?"

"But what if there is?" Eily cried. "Reika believed it! She died for it!"

"I loved my wife," Ehroe said softly, placing his hand against Eily's cheek. "But that doesn't mean she was perfect."

"We know where the stone is," Eily said. She was weeping now. He reached out to her, but she took a step away from him. "Bring it home, and you can stop all the death and pain."

"Or destroy the greatest source of hope we have."

"The Ally is real. You can't keep it from the safehold any longer."

"If you do this, every elf that dies from here until the

end will be on your shoulders," he said harshly. "And there will be nothing you can do to make it better."

Eily hurried down the ladder and away from the garden. Still unsure of whether to cross Ehroe, she decided to find Cavan and seek his counsel. She knew where he should be—resting in his bed. He had suffered what appeared to be a minor head wound during the raid on Ballygol. But a few days later, dark red streaks appeared around the injury. When Eily carried a bowl of dawnglow to Cavan's quarters in the guard tower, she was not surprised to see him dressing for the night watch.

"You're supposed to be resting," she said.

Cavan raised his eyebrows. "What are you going to do about it, Healer?"

Eily gently pushed him onto the bed. "Sit and rest, or I won't waste any of this on your worthless head."

"Ouch," Cavan complained as she spread the gunky mixture against his skin. "You have the touch of a boggart."

"Why didn't you stop him in Ballygol?" Eily asked after a moment.

"The safewrights are losing faith. Ehroe did what he needed to do." Cavan rested his hand against Eily's hip. "You're not losing faith, too, are you, Seer?"

"That's Healer to you," Eily said. She brushed her fingertips against his hand before she pushed him away. "I need to talk to you."

"Of course," he said, losing his playful demeanor instantly. He moved over so she could sit on the cot beside him. She hesitated.

"I can't . . ."

Cavan feigned exasperation. "Just talk! I'll keep my wandering hands to myself."

Eily stared at the bowl in her hands as if noticing it for

the first time. She walked across the room and set it on the chest in the corner.

"There isn't much air in here, is there? You should think about moving into one of the rooms near the armory. There's a nice breeze in the morning."

Cavan groaned. "Quit prattling and say it, Eily. And then you'll be free of it."

"I made a mistake. I thought I was doing the right thing, but it's become . . . different than I intended."

He stared at her with such intensity that she wanted to melt into the wall. Sometimes it was hard to even look at Cavan. She didn't know if he knew about her and Ehroe or what he thought about her if he did. When he didn't say anything, she continued, staring at her hands instead of his lean face and curious eyes.

"I made everyone believe I am something I'm not," she said, sitting on the cot beside him.

"I see Eily. What are you besides that?"

"The only thing special about me is that I've lived when so many others have died."

Cavan put his arm around her shoulders. "Everyone who's safe within these walls tonight can say the same thing. That is why we must protect every elf, as if each were a beloved child. As if their lives are the only the reason we still draw breath."

Eily relaxed against his chest. "I'm not a seer," she whispered. Cavan leaned forward to hear what she was saying. "It's all a lie."

"But you've sent us into the wilds many times," Cavan protested. "And we've always come back with a hallow-held. How is that possible?"

"It's the giant, Cavan. He's the visionary. I just learned how to listen."

Cavan's grip tightened on her shoulders. "Does Ehroe know?"

"No!" Eily drew her knees up to her chest and buried her face in her hands.

"What else is troubling you?" Cavan asked quietly. "You can't live a lie, Eily. It will kill you in the end."

Eily took a deep breath. Ehroe might hate her, but he had given her no choice. "I know where the cloudbreaker is."

"Where?"

"With the merrows of the lake."

"Have you told Ehroe?"

Eily hesitated. There was no reason for Cavan to know how long Ehroe had kept the secret from the rest of the safehold. "He does now."

Cavan embraced Eily. "This is a time to rejoice. Whether it's from your head or the giant's doesn't matter now. Let me go talk to Ehroe, and we'll organize a search party immediately."

"Thank you," she said.

He tipped his head thoughtfully. "Now that I think about it, it makes sense that you aren't a real seer."

"Why?"

"Because you can't even see what's right in front of you," he said, giving her a crooked smile.

She remained alone in his quarters for a moment, trying to understand what he meant. When she heard the excited voices of the elves in the courtyard, she made herself stand up. She would mix the poison for Ehroe and bring it to him. It would give her a reason to say good-bye before he left.

* * * * *

Just hours after the warriors left, the merrows arrived. They slunk out of the swamp and surrounded the walls as if waiting for someone to throw them food. The lead guard that night was an elf named Ramsey, who had been a fine warrior in his younger years, but now his hands shook against the hilt of his sword. He sent a runner to fetch Cavan, the only safewright remaining in the walls. Cavan might be injured, but he was still the best archer they had.

"Climb the corner tower and cover the gate," he told Cavan when he arrived. "I've never seen anything like it before."

As Ramsey pondered the nature of the merrows' passive assault, a dark shape shot over the wall. It was definitely an animal of some kind, Ramsey realized as it passed by him on its trajectory into the courtyard. In the second before he screamed and his heart stopped, Ramsey realized what the merrows had brought upon his kin.

Eily awoke to Ramsey's shuddering wail and then abrupt silence. The air around her pulsed with energy. It seemed like world had drawn in a breath and then frozen, unable to release it. Trembling, Eily stumbled out of bed and threw open the door where she saw the safehold in chaos.

Above her on the wall, an elf fell to his knees clawing at his face while another ran frantically along the balcony before hurling himself over the outer wall. Eily heard the thud as he hit the ground and the hissing sound of merrows as they set upon his body. Again, there was a distortion in the air and the landscape stuttered and then blinked back in a different location. Eily spun in a circle, watching elves locked in the grip of something terrifying, but without a focus for their horror and no assailant she could see. Unless it was invisible or spirits, Eily thought, feeling the dread well up inside her.

As she neared the armory, the skin on her face and arms felt prickly and hot. She saw a young elf named Aine cowering behind a stack of rain barrels. Aine's mouth was locked in a silent scream, and there was blood around her lips as if she had been chewing on something not quite dead. Eily ducked behind the barrels and tried to pull her out, but she realized that Aine was not alone in the dark corner.

Eily saw its shadow first, a hulking mass with spiky bristles along its spine. She raised her eyes and caught the black-eyed gaze of a fear elemental. Crackling with pulses of heat, the fear elemental would ruin the mind of anyone who lingered near it too long. When her gaze locked with the creature's, Eily's thoughts dissolved like sand. Putting as much distance between her and the monstrosity was the only thing that mattered. She dropped Aine and ran.

But the map of the world had changed. The safehold blinked away, and she found herself halfway up Callem's tower. Except it wasn't a teetering stack of boulders, it was a pyramid constructed of seemingly endless layers, each no taller than her hand. Her hands gripped a roughly hewn ladder, but mist obscured the sky, and she couldn't see how far she was from the top of the structure. A figure climbed the ladder above her, and she knew instinctively that it was Ehroe. She hurried to close the distance between them.

"Ehroe, wait!" she pleaded.

"Hurry, love," he called down. "We have to get to the top."

"What's at the top?" she cried, her breath like a dagger against her ribs.

"You'll see," he called. His voice sounded happy, as if he hadn't a care in the world. Eily's hands were bleeding, and she could barely keep her fingers on the rungs. Below her, the ground churned with black, twisted creatures that gaped up with hungry, pitiless eyes. But Ehroe beckoned to her. He reached down and took her hand, pulling her onto an empty plane of white stone. But the air was so thick and heavy that Eily couldn't see Ehroe clearly.

"What is it?" she asked. "What must I see?"

"Watch," he whispered, his lips against her ear. He put his arms around her and pulled her close to his chest. "The clouds will break, and then you'll see."

As if he had willed it, the mist rolled away and the dark clouds parted. No elf had ever glimpsed what lay above the sky's perpetual clouds, but it was known as the home of the Ally and many had imagined a green, verdant country waiting in the dome of the heavens. But as the dark clouds parted, Eily saw no tapestry of colors or realm of beauty. Her heart fell at the sight of a black void, empty and infinite. It wasn't beautiful. There was no potential. It was oblivion, and it was worse than death.

"What is it?" she gasped.

"Nothing," he smiled. "The journey itself was hope of the elves, just like I told you."

He placed his hand against his chest. When he pulled it away, blood streamed from his fingertips and ran in rivulets along the white stone.

"I told you so," he said again. "Yet you killed me anyway."

"No!"

Grinning, he turned away and strolled off the edge of the stone as if there was something waiting to stop his fall. She tried to follow him, but her body had lost all memory of motion, and she couldn't wade across the rivers of blood . . .

"Eily!"

Her head jerked back, the muscles in her neck stretching painfully. Wasn't she alone here, where the world exhausted itself?

"Eily! Stop!"

Her own name cut into her ears—sharp enough to scrape the skin from her bones. It wasn't Ehroe calling. He was gone. If not him, then who?

"Eily! Look at me!"

Suddenly, a cool breeze blew across her face, clearing her vision and thoughts. Like someone had torn a blindfold off her eyes, the landscape slid into focus. Under the influence of the elemental, she had unwittingly scaled to the upper branches of the pillar oak and was just a few feet under her treetop garden. If she took another step, she would plummet to the ground, where she could see elves still twisted in pain and delusion. The elemental moved aimlessly among them—there was no one on the ground that could threaten it anymore.

"What's happening?" Cavan shouted from the corner tower, where he crouched with his bow. His eyes darted from her to the gate and the merrows waiting patiently outside the walls. Only she and Cavan were high enough to escape the creature's influence.

"It's a fear elemental," she screamed.

"Where! Where!"

"See the shadow, there by the armory door!"

Instantly, Cavan rotated his body, scoped the target, and rapidly emptied his quiver into the creature. Ten arrows in all, and not one missed its mark. There was a hissing sound, a small crackle, and a ripple of wind moved across the ground. Eily saw the beast topple and lay still. Within seconds, the elves farthest from the creature recovered their senses while those who had been closest remained twitching on the ground. As soon as the merrows saw the elves retake their positions on the wall, they slunk into the darkness, sliding into the water without a sound.

* * * * *

While the elves of Dusklight tended to the wounded and prepared the dead for burial, Cavan rode through the Wilt-Leaf Forest to carry the news of the raid. He arrived at dawn just as Ehroe and the warriors were breaking camp. When Ehroe saw his friend ride into the clearing, he immediately thought of the night Reika died. He'd been on watch, having left her bedside just an hour before with reassurances from the healers that his wife was doing better. It was Cavan who brought the news that night, walking across the courtyard with the same purposeful gait and grim face. Unexpectedly, Ehroe's thoughts turned to Eily. He rose to his feet with a sick feeling in his chest.

"What news?" he asked.

"A fear elemental," Cavan told him. "Courtesy of the muck-dwellers."

"How many lost?"

"Twelve. Six guards. Five holdkeeps. One child."

"Who?"

Cavan shook his head. "There will be time for mourning later, but Eily is not among the dead."

"Any lasting damage . . . marred minds?"

"It's too soon to tell."

"What about defense . . ."

"The merrows retreated once the elemental was killed. There are able warriors watching the wall now."

"How could they have captured a fear elemental without destroying their own?"

"Help from a shaman? A protection spell? There are many ways, Ehroe."

That the merrows launched their most treacherous attack ever against the safehold on the same night the safewrights began their last journey toward the cloudbreaker was no coincidence. Ehroe knew there were many things in the world he would never understand. Why creatures existed for the sole purpose of destroying anything precious and beautiful, for example. Or why the elves must suffer to protect things that should be sacred to everyone. It was as if there were thin strands connecting infinite points. If only the veil could be lifted and the hidden things of the world could be revealed. How was he to know what sequence of events he set forth, just by setting his foot outside the safehold? Or what Eily created simply by burying a seed in the earth.

"What do you suggest?" Cavan asked quietly, not wanting to disturb Ehroe's thoughts, but there were many who needed them back home.

"Send the others to the safehold," Ehroe replied. "This is something you and I can do alone."

Cavan gave his friend a half smile. "I doubt that. Do you remember our first hunting trip? You were foiled by a bogle. A baby bogle, if I recall."

Ehroe shook his head in mock shame. "I was very young. And it was an injured baby bogle. It had strength beyond reckoning."

"If believing that helps you live with the memory, then so be it."

When the rest of the safewrights had ridden away, Ehroe and Cavan left their cervins in a clearing and headed down a rocky embankment toward a spring of water that welled out of the rocks and ran down the ridge into the flat country. Cavan had been to this spring many times, and it always amazed him that a trickle of water could transform into an extensive river system—the highway by which the merrows traveled the world.

Ehroe reached inside his cloak and took out the vial of cramoisy that Eily had prepared. When he saw the distinctive crimson color, Cavan's eyes widened.

"You are my oldest friend," Ehroe said quietly. "No one could make me hesitate but you."

Cavan had no love for the merrows. Last night's attack was another link in a long line of atrocities that the merrows had committed against the elves. He would never forget the sounds as they devoured the guards who had leaped blindly into their midst.

"I held Aine's ruined body," Cavan said. "The merrows were waiting for the elemental to do its work. Then they would have killed us all and taken the hallowhelds."

"And yet you pause."

Cavan sighed. "Perhaps the time for hesitation is over. It's just . . . don't you remember what it was like before the floods? We sought beauty wherever it hid with no one to guide us. We simply searched the world."

"There were many times we came back empty-handed," Ehroe reminded him. "Eily gave us purpose. Focused our efforts."

"I know," Cavan said gravely. "And it was Eily who saved us last night. I didn't know the source of the outrage until she showed me where the beast lurked."

Ehroe crouched beside the spring and held the vial up against the dark sky. "They are killing us faster than we kill them. We're losing, Cavan."

"You have the burden of leadership, and I don't envy you. But I've always been stronger at war than wisdom. I can't find words to stop you."

Ehroe removed the cork from the vial and tipped the contents into the water. They watched the red stain spread out to fill the narrow banks of the stream. The elves headed down the ridge along the river and an ever-expanding trail of corpses. Some of the larger creatures managed to drag themselves onto the banks, but most of the fish and smaller beasts died in the water and floated to the surface.

At the bottom of the ridge, Cavan saw the first merrow body. It was a red and black female, and she had crawled onto the shore before she died. Most of the merrows of the realm had piscine features, but this one's face looked almost like an elf's. The poison had wrought no damage on her, she was simply curled on her side and curved into a half-circle—the red of her scales dramatic against the dark soil. Cavan wondered what she had been thinking when she died. Everything that she had been, whether it was good or bad, was lost.

Ehroe saw his friend looking at the body.

"She could have been one of the attackers at the safe-hold," Ehroe reminded him, nudging the merrows's body with his boot. "Have you forgotten so quickly?"

"I have forgotten nothing."

"The currents might dilute the poison before it reaches the settlement. We may still have work to do."

But when they reached the lake, the wide expanse of the river was filled with floating corpses. There was no sign of life, only the slow movement of the bodies bumping against one another as they moved downstream with the current. Beside him, Cavan stumbled, and Ehroe caught his arm.

"Hope when all hope is lost."

Cavan didn't reply.

The two elves waited on the bank until the merrow bodies had washed downstream. Ehroe picked one of the weedy flowers that grew by the river and dipped it into the water.

"You severed it from its roots. What's that going to tell you?"

"That the water is safe," Ehroe said, pulling off his cloak and boots.

The cold water was a shock against their skin. But it wasn't deep, and with the dim light filtering down from the surface, they could see the submerged structures that had once been a kithkin village—another casualty of last year's flooding. According to Eily, the chest was in the communal lodge at the center of the village. They located the building and swam back to the surface for air.

"We'd better hurry," Cavan said nodding at the towering figure that was loping across the valley toward them. Ehroe recognized the long, lean form of Callem. The giant moved quickly and gracefully, quite unlike most of his lumbering, clumsy kin. His arrival was a concern, but Ehroe didn't have time to ponder why Callem had left his swamp-side dwelling and sought them out. He couldn't imagine how word of the poisoned river spread so quickly that it reached the ears of a nonsensical giant on the other side of the forest.

He and Cavan swam down to the rotting building and through the gaping hole in the roof. Despite the shallowness, Ehroe's head felt as if it were pounding with pressure. The wooden chest was not large, but it took both Cavan and Ehroe to pull it to the surface. Callem waited for them on the bank, shouting incomprehensibly and tossing rocks ineffectually in their direction. Ehroe and Cavan swam to the far shore and lugged the heavy chest onto the bank. The giant was already wading into the water, his shouts rumbling across the water like thunder. He would be across the lake in no time.

"Go for the cervins," Ehroe said. "We'll meet near the mouth of the spring."

"You'll never outrun him with the chest," Cavan protested.

"If he wants the chest, let him have it," Ehroe knelt down and snapped the metal braces open. Inside was a width of unblemished yellow silk wrapped around something weighty. He thrust the cloth into Cavan's hand.

"You take it," Cavan insisted. "I'll distract him."

Ehroe shook his head. "It's in your care now. Go!"

Cavan sprinted down the bank, leaping over corpses as he ran. The giant cast an eye at the fleeing elf but continued toward the chest, which Ehroe had closed and was attempting to drag up the hill. With two massive strides, Callem closed the distance between him and Ehroe, who saw no point in trying to outrun the sinewy giant.

"Where is red-haired elflet?" the giant bellowed, reaching down and snatching the chest off the ground. "Rotting corpse bringer. River choked with filth. Death bringer."

Ehroe backed away slowly while Callem tried to pull off the lid. There were intricate carvings on the front of the chest—a sun and a winged creature of some kind. By itself, the box was beautiful enough for the hallowheld chamber.

"Tower to quiet place," the giant shouted. "Cloudwalk for elflet."

Callem crushed the chest with his fist. When he saw it was empty, he began to howl, throwing the shattered pieces on the ground and pawing through them. With the giant distracted, Ehroe sprinted for the ridge. Callem halfheartedly followed him. He could have easily over taken Ehroe, but instead he stopped and stared out at the lake and the river beyond, which was still choked with the bloated creatures. As if he felt Ehroe watching him, he turned and looked up at the elf, his eyes mournful and very much aware.

"Tower to quiet place," he said. "The dark things of the world come."

Ehroe turned and ran up the steep path to the spring where Cavan had just arrived with the cervins. Cavan dismounted when he saw Ehroe and handed him the length of silk. Unwinding the cloth, Ehroe uncovered a translucent stone about the size of his fist. Trapped inside was swirling gray mist—the breath of the Ally, captured and waiting to be released.

"The stories were right," Ehroe said in awe. "This really is the cloudbreaker."

"How long have you known it was in the lake?" Cavan asked gravely.

"Did Eily tell you that I knew?"

Cavan shook his head. "She did not."

Ehroe looked puzzled. "Then how did you . . . ?"

"How long have you known?" Cavan repeated.

"I've known for several months, but I had reason. Remember how we felt when we'd ride out each time? The possibility of finding the cloudbreaker was foremost in our minds. It kept us going back into the wilds, time and time again. You know that as well as I do."

"Don't you believe in the Ally?"

"It was possible, of course it was possible," Ehroe whispered. "But I couldn't take it on faith the way you seemed to, Cavan. You had no more proof than I, yet your life has been dictated by belief of its existence. I always envied you for that."

Hands shaking, he cupped the cloudbreaker, feeling its unnaturally heavy weight. There was a low pulsing coming from the stone, almost as if it had a heartbeat of its own.

"I thought nothing would ever replace that hope, but now holding this . . ." Ehroe trailed off. "Maybe I was wrong."

"Either way, you went too far," Cavan said, coming up behind him and looping a strap of leather around his neck. Ehroe struggled, but Cavan was stronger. He always had been, ever since they were children. In minutes, Ehroe was still.

"I'll tell them a good story," Cavan said, picking up the cloudbreaker from where it had dropped onto the mud. "It is important they believe you died with your sword in your hand, fighting for them until the last."

* * * * *

When the dawnglow ran out, Eily left the safehold. She couldn't save anyone else, and her head was ringing from the night before. Ehroe's death was as real as a memory. She was afraid that it wasn't just a creation of her mind, but a true vision. Callem was the seer, and he was the only who might be able to help her.

Because she was careful to test every footfall, it took several hours to cross the swamp to the jagged outcropping of land where Callem lived. She brought her sword expecting to meet merrows, but the waters were unusually silent and empty. Another hour to climb the cliff face, and she found herself at the foot of his tower on ground littered with the bones and decaying meat of dead animals. There were no vestiges from her vision—no intricate pyramid, no horde of creatures waiting below. It was still a teetering stack of boulders that tilted dangerously toward the swamp while a flock of carrion birds rested near the top. Callem was nowhere to be seen.

Something was happening across the swamp, however. Eily could see a steady stream of dark treefolk, scath, and spriggan emerging from the Wilt-Leaf and heading for the safehold, which glowed vainly in the distance. Eily couldn't imagine what had sparked the interest of such an unusual group of creatures and had brought their collective ire upon the elves. Behind her, the sound of hoof beats distracted her from the onslaught of attackers. It was Cavan, who reined his cervin to a halt and leaped off. She could tell from his face that all was not well.

"Cavan!" Eily cried running toward him. "What's happening?"

Cavan took her hand and hurried to the edge of the cliff. The safehold would soon be surrounded.

"I didn't expect them to come so quickly."

"Where is Ehroe?"

Cavan pulled the cloudbreaker from inside his cloak.

"You found it? Cavan! Call the Ally! We still have time before the safehold is overrun."

Cavan pressed the cloudbreaker into Eily's hand. She tried to push it away.

"What are you doing? Smash it!"

"We can't use it."

"What? We have to. Everyone will die if we don't."

"We don't deserve to use it."

"Cavan, there are fires outside the wall. We can't wait."

"We have become desperate, ugly. We have become everything we hate."

"No! We protected beauty."

Cavan shook his head. "We used to be apart from the

world. It besieged us, but we were separate, above it somehow. But with Ehroe as our leader . . . the things he did made us a part of the world. We are tarnished, Eily."

"The things he did? What do you mean?"

"Once he knew where the hallowhelds were, he was willing to take any means to get them. He burned the kithkin village. Today he used the cramoisy in the Lanes. He killed scores of merrows. Scores. I hope to never see such a sight again in all my life."

"It is my fault, then," Eily said. "I told him where the hallowhelds were. We can talk to him, Cavan. He'll understand."

"Ehroe's dead."

"What?" Eily gasped. "How?"

"He died saving me."

"Then he sacrificed himself so you could bring the cloudbreaker home!"

Cavan stepped forward and embraced Eily. "When I saw you last night, walking blindly toward the edge, I wanted to die myself. I've never felt so helpless."

"But I didn't die," Eily cried. "And you didn't either. And for the first time in so long there truly is something to live for. I am holding it in my hands."

"I wish I had the chance to prove myself to you," he said, pulling her closer, his face against the curve of her neck. "I loved you for so long, and you never saw it."

"Cavan."

"We can't use the beacon. We are not worthy of that power."

"What do we do then?" Eily asked. "Cast it into the water and pretend to search for it? Isn't that what Ehroe believed? That as long as we search for it, it gives us hope to continue? People think that I am the seer, and they expect to find the cloudbreaker. As long as I am here, they'll demand it."

"You're right, they will," Cavan said. He brushed back the hair from her face. As he kissed her, he pulled his dagger from his belt and plunged it into her belly.

Cavan helped Eily fall to the ground. Then he took the cloudbreaker from her bloody fingers and laid it at the foot of Callem's tower. Across the swamp, the safehold was burning. He mounted his cervin and rode toward the swamp to where the dark things of the world waited for him. It took a while for Eily to bleed to death, so she had time to watch the silhouettes of the birds against the sky. Dying was more peaceful than she expected.

About the Authors

Doug Beyer went from being a MAGIC: THE GATHERING® fan to web developer for magicthegathering.com, then prolific flavor text writer, and eventually, the coordinator for MAGIC™ creative text. His background is in philosophy, software design, and amateur ghost hunting.

Matt Cavotta's body lives in Ohio with his wife, Kylie, and daughters, Grace and Greta. It is frequently seen with a paintbrush, writing quill, or football in hand. Matt's mind lives . . . elsewhere.

John Delaney lives in the west of Ireland. He spends most of his time playing MAGIC: THE GATHERING, debating with his pet budgie Bismarck, or trying in vain to pacify irate message-boards members. His story in this book is, like the FUTURE SIGHT novel, the first thing he has written for Wizards of the Coast.

Denise R. Graham is the author of two books in the KNIGHTS OF THE SILVER DRAGON® series and a number of shorter works. She lurks in her supervillain secret lair deep in the heart of darkest mid-America with her co-supervillain, the inimitable Ron Morris, and their henchmen, er . . . henchdemons, Kafka and Morrigan.

Jenna Helland is a writer and editor for Wizards of the Coast in Renton, Washington. Before moving to the Northwest, she was a journalist in Missouri, Virginia, and California. She has a history degree from Trinity College in Dublin, Ireland, and a journalism degree from the Missouri School of Journalism in Columbia, Missouri. She enjoys playing MAGIC: THE GATHERING, reading books with pictures, and running.

By night, **Cory J. Herndon** is the author of a half-dozen MAGIC: THE GATHERING novels; by day he's a writer and world designer for the online roleplaying game *Pirates of the Burning Sea*. His nonfiction work has appeared in such magazines as *Amazing Stories*, *TopDeck*, *Dragon*, *Star Wars Insider* and *3-2-1 Contact*. Cory lives in Seattle with two cats, several plants, and the charming Miss S.P. Miskowski.

Once, long ago, **Jess Lebow** was the MAGIC: THE GATHERING line editor. Now he's the Content Director for Flying Lab Software on the hit MMO *Pirates of the Burning Sea*.

Will McDermott has written in the worlds of MAGIC: THE GATHERING, WARHAMMER 40K, and Monte Cook's LANDS OF THE DIAMOND THRONE. He has also published mainstream SF outside the gaming industry. During the day, Will writes for the *Guild Wars* online role-playing game. He lives in Bothell, Washington with his game-designing wife, three energetic kids, and an insane, orange dog.

Scott McGough lives in Seattle with a pair of cats and an Australian Cattle Dog. He has written or co-written over a dozen novels and short stories for MAGIC: THE GATHERING; he also provided random pirate voices for an upcoming computer game and portrayed a shambling, gut-munching zombie extra in a local low-budget film. Based on his acting performances so far, everyone agrees he should keep writing.

Ken Troop is a game designer and writer currently living in Seattle, WA.

TRACY HICKMAN

PRESENTS

THE ANVIL OF TIME

With the power of the Anvil of Time, the Journeyman can travel
the river of time as simply as walking upstream, visiting the
ancient past of Krynn with ease.

VOLUME ONE
THE SELLSWORD
Cam Banks

Vanderjack, a mercenary with a price on his head, agrees out of
desperation to retrieve a priceless treasure for a displaced noble. The
treasure is deep within enemy territory, and he must survive an army of
old foes, a chorus of unhappy ghosts, and the questionable assistance of
a mad gnome to find it.

April 2008

VOLUME TWO
THE SURVIVORS
Dan Willis

A goodhearted dwarf is warned of an apocalyptic flood by the god
Reorx, and he and his motley followers must decide whether the
warning is real—and then survive the disaster that sweeps
through their part of Krynn.

November 2008

RICHARD A. KNAAK

THE OGRE TITANS

The Grand Lord Golgren has been savagely crushing
all opposition to his control of the harsh ogre lands of
Kern and Blöde, first sweeping away rival chieftains, then
rebuilding the capital in his image. For this he has had to
deal with the ogre titans, dark, sorcerous giants who have
contempt for his leadership.

VOLUME ONE
THE BLACK TALON

Among the ogres, where every ritual demands blood and every ally can
become a deadly foe, Golgren seeks whatever advantage he can obtain,
even if it means a possible alliance with the Knights of Solamnia, a
questionable pact with a mysterious wizard, and trusting an elven slave
who might wish him dead.

VOLUME TWO
THE FIRE ROSE

Attacked by enemies on all sides, Golgren must abandon his throne
to undertake the quest for the Fire Rose before Safrag, master
of the Ogre Titans can locate it and claim supremacy
over all ogres—and perhaps all of Krynn.

December 2008

VOLUME THREE
THE GARGOYLE KING

Forced from the throne he has so long coveted, Golgren makes a final
stand for control of the ogre lands against the Titans . . . against an
enemy as ancient and powerful as a god.

December 2009

FORGOTTEN REALMS

They were built to display might.
They were built to hold secrets.
They will still stand while their builders fall.

THE CITADELS

NEVERSFALL
ED GENTRY

It was supposed to be Estagund's stronghold in monster-ridden Veldorn, an unassailable citadel to protect the southern lands ... until the regiment holding Neversfall disappeared, leaving no hint of what took them.

OBSIDIAN RIDGE
JESS LEBOW

Looming like a storm cloud, the Obsidian Ridge appears silently and without warning over the kingdom of Erlkazar, prepared to destroy everything in its reach, unless its master gets what he wants.

April 2008

THE SHIELD OF WEEPING GHOSTS
JAMES P. DAVIS

Frozen Shandaular fell to invaders over two thousand years ago, its ruins protected by the ghosts and undead that haunt the ancient citadel. But to anyone who can evade the weeping dead, the northwest tower holds a deadly secret.

May 2008

SENTINELSPIRE
MARK SEHESTEDT

The ancient fortress of Sentinelspire draws strength from the portals that feed its fires and pools, as well as the assassins that call it home. Both promise great power to those dangerous enough to seize them.

July 2008

Stand-alone novels that can be read in any order!

EBERRON

In the shadow of the Last War, the heroes aren't all shining knights.

PARKER DeWOLF

The Lanternlight Files

Ulther Whitsun is a fixer. When you've got a problem, if you can't find someone to take care of it, he's your man—as long as you can pay the price. If you can't, or you won't . . . gods have mercy on your soul.

Book 1
The Left Hand of Death

Ulther finds himself in possession of a strange relic. His enemies want it, he wants its owner, and the City Watch wants him locked away for good. When a job turns this dangerous, winning or losing are no longer an option. It may be all one man can do just to stay alive.

Book 2
When Night Falls

Ulther teams up with a young and ambitious chronicler to stop a revolution. But treachery may kill him, and salvation comes from unexpected places.

July 2008

Book 3
Death Comes Easy

Gangs in lower Sharn are at each other's throats. And they don't care who gets killed in the battle. But now Ulther had been hired to put an end to the violence. And he doesn't care who he steps on to do his job.

December 2008